The Collected Stories of
Robert Silverberg

VOLUME SEVEN

We Are for the Dark
1987-90

The Collected Stories of
Robert Silverberg

VOLUME SEVEN

We Are for the Dark
1987-90

ROBERT SILVERBERG

SUBTERRANEAN PRESS 2012

First Edition

ISBN
978-1-59606-501-7

Subterranean Press
PO Box 190106
Burton, MI 48519

www.subterraneanpress.com

COPYRIGHT ACKNOWLEDGMENTS:

"The Dead Man's Eyes" and "A Sleep and a Forgetting" first appeared in *Playboy*.

"To the Promised Land" first appeared in *Omni*.

"Enter a Soldier. Later: Enter Another," "Chip Runner," "In Another Country," and "We Are for the Dark" first appeared in *Isaac Asimov's Science Fiction Magazine*.

"The Asenion Solution" first appeared in *Foundation's Friends*.

"Lion Time in Timbuctoo" was first published by Axolotl Press.

"A Tip on a Turtle" first appeared in *Amazing Stories*.

For Alice K. Turner
Gardner Dozois
Ellen Datlow
Byron Preiss
Martin H. Greenberg
Kristine Kathryn Rusch
Kim Mohan

TABLE OF CONTENTS

INTRODUCTION

A couple of working definitions:

    1) A short story is a piece of prose fiction in which just one significant thing happens.

    2) A science-fiction short story is a piece of prose fiction in which just one *extraordinary* thing happens.

These are not definitions of my devising, nor are they especially recent. The first was formulated by Edgar Allan Poe more than a century and a half ago, and the second by H.G. Wells about fifty years after that. Neither one is an absolute commandment: it's quite possible to violate one or both of these definitions and still produce a story that will fascinate its readers. But they're good working rules, and I've tried to keep them in mind throughout my writing career.

What Poe spoke of, actually, was the "single effect" that every story should create. Each word in the story, he said, should work towards that effect. That might be interpreted to be as much a stylistic rule as a structural one: the "effect" could be construed as eldritch horror, farce, philosophical contemplation, whatever. But in fact Poe, both in theory and in practice, understood virtually in the hour of the birth of the short story that it must be constructed around one central point and only one. Like a painting, it must be capable of being taken in at a single glance, although close inspection or repeated viewings would reveal complexities and subtleties not immediately perceptible.

Thus Poe, in "The Fall of the House of Usher," say, builds his story around the strange bond linking Roderick Usher and his sister, Lady Madeline. The baroque details of the story, rich and vivid, serve entirely to tell us that *the Ushers are very odd people and something extremely peculiar has been going on in their house*, and ultimately the truth is revealed. There are no subplots, but if there had been (Roderick Usher's dispute with the local vicar, or Lady Madeline's affair with the gardener, or the narrator's anxiety over a stock-market maneuver), they would have had to be integrated with the main theme or the story's power would have been diluted.

Similarly, in Guy de Maupassant's classic "The Piece of String," one significant thing happens: Maitre Hauchecorne sees a piece of string on the ground, picks it up, and puts it in his pocket. As a result he is suspected of having found and kept a lost wallet full of cash, and he is driven to madness and an early death by the scorn of his fellow villagers. A simple enough situation, with no side-paths, but Maupassant manages, within a few thousand words that concentrate entirely on M. Hauchecorne's unfortunate entanglement, to tell us a great many things about French village life, peasant thrift, the ferocity of bourgeois morality, and the ironies of life in general. A long disquisition about M. Hauchecorne's unhappy early marriage or the unexpected death of his neighbor's grandchild would probably have added nothing and subtracted much from the impact of the story.

H. G. Wells, who towards the end of the nineteenth century employed the medium of the short story to deal with the thematic matter of what we now call science fiction—and did it so well that his stories still can hold their own with the best s-f of later generations—refined Poe's "single effect" concept with special application to the fantastic:

The thing that makes such imaginations [i.e., s-f themes] interesting is their translation into commonplace terms and a rigid exclusion of other marvels from the story. Then it becomes human. "How would you feel and what might not happen to you?" is the typical question, if for instance pigs could fly and one came rocketing over a bridge at you. How would you feel and what might not happen to you if suddenly you were changed into an ass and couldn't tell anyone about it? Or if you suddenly became invisible? But no one would think twice about the answer if hedges and houses also began to fly, or if people changed into lions, tigers, cats, and dogs left and right, or if anyone could vanish anyhow. Nothing remains interesting where anything may happen.

Right on the mark. *Nothing remains interesting where anything may happen.* The science-fiction story is at its best when it deals with the consequences, however ramifying and multifarious, of a single fantastic assumption. What will happen the first time our spaceships meet those of another intelligent species? Suppose there were so many suns in the sky that the stars were visible only one night every two thousand years: what would that night be like? What if a twentieth-century doctor suddenly found himself in possession of a medical kit of the far future? What about *toys* from the far future falling into the hands of a couple of twentieth-century kids? One single wild assumption; one significant thing has happened, and it's a very strange one. And from each hypothesis has come great science fiction: each of these four is a one-sentence summary of a story included in the definitive 1970 anthology of classics of our field, *The Science Fiction Hall of Fame*.

I think it's an effective way to construct a story, though not necessarily the only effective way, and in general I've kept the one-thing-happens precept in mind through more than fifty years of writing them. The stories collected here, written between August of 1987 and May of 1990, demonstrate that I still believe in the classical unities. Of course, what seems to us a unity now might not have appeared that way when H.G. Wells was writing his wonderful stories in the nineteenth century. Wells might have argued that my "To the Promised Land" is built around *two* speculative fantastic assumptions, one that the Biblical Exodus from Egypt never happened, the other that it is possible to send rocketships to other worlds. But in fact we've sent plenty of rocketships to other worlds by now, so only my story's alternative-world speculation remains fantasy today. Technically speaking the space-travel element of the plot has become part of the given; it's the other big assumption that forms the central matter of the story.

Three of the stories in this book, "In Another Country," "We Are for the Dark," and "Lion Time in Timbuctoo," are actually not short stories at all, but novellas—a considerably different form, running three to five times as long as the traditional short story. The novella form is one of which I'm particularly fond, and one that I think lends itself particularly well to science-fiction use. But it too is bound by the single-effect/single-assumption Poe/Wells prescriptions. A novel may sprawl; it may jump freely from character to character, from subplot to subplot, even from theme to countertheme. A short story, as I've already shown, is best held under rigid technical discipline. But the novella is an intermediate form, partaking of some of the discursiveness of the novel yet benefiting from the discipline of the short story. A single startling assumption; the rigorous exploration of the consequences of that assumption; a resolution, eventually, of the problems that those consequences have engendered: the schema works as well for a novella as it does for a short story. The difference lies in texture, in detail, in breadth. In a novella the writer is free to construct a richly imagined background and to develop extensive insight into character as it manifests itself within a complex plot. In a short story those things, however virtuous, may blur and even ruin the effect the story strives to attain.

One story in this collection is neither fish nor fowl, and I point that out for whatever light it may cast on these problems of definition. "Enter a Soldier. Later: Enter Another" may be considered either a very short novella or a very long short story, but in my mind it verges on being a novella without quite attaining a novella's full complexity, while at the same time being too intricate to be considered a short story. Its primary structure is that of a short science-fiction story: one speculation is put forth. ("What if computers were capable of creating artificial-intelligence replications of famous figures of history?") But because Pizarro and Socrates are such powerful characters, they launch into an extensive dialog that carries the story far beyond the conventional limits of short fiction—without, however, leading it into the complexities of plot that a novella might develop.

And yet I think the story, whatever it may be, is a success—an opinion backed by the readers who voted it a Hugo for best novelette the year after it was published. The credit, I think, should go to Socrates and Pizarro, who carry it all along. As a rule, I think it's ordinarily better to stick to the rules as I understand them. But, as this story shows, there are occasions when they can safely be abandoned.

Writing novels is an exhausting proposition: months and months of living with the same group of characters, the same background situation, the same narrative voice, trying to keep everything consistent day after day until the distant finish line is reached. When writing a novel, I always yearned for the brevity and simplicity of short-story writing. But then I would find myself writing a short story, and I felt myself in the iron clamp of the disciplines that govern that remorseless form, and longed for the range and expansiveness of novel-writing. I have spent many decades now moving from one extreme of feeling to the other, and the only conclusion I can draw from it is that writing is tough work.

So is reading, sometimes. But we go on doing it. Herewith are ten stories long and short that illustrate some of my notions of what science fiction ought to have been attempting in the later years of the twentieth century. Whether they'll last as long as those of Poe and Wells is a question I'd just as soon not spend much time contemplating; but I can say quite certainly that they would not have been constructed as they were but for the work of those two early masters. Even in a field as supposedly revolutionary as science fiction, the hand of tradition still governs what we do.

—Robert Silverberg

THE DEAD MAN'S EYES

A crime story, one of the few I've ever written. Crime fiction has never interested me as a reader, let alone as a writer. I've read the Sherlock Holmes stories with pleasure, yes, and some Simenons, and in 1985 I suddenly read seven or eight Elmore Leonard books in one unceasing burst. But such acknowledged masters of the genre as P.D. James or John D. MacDonald inspire only yawns in me, which is not to say that they aren't masters, only that the thing they do so well is a thing that basically does not speak to any of my concerns. Doubtless a lot of mystery writers feel the same way about even the best science fiction. "The Dead Man's Eyes" isn't a detective story, but it is crime fiction, to the extent that it seems actually to have been in the running for the Edgar award given out by the Mystery Writers of America. It's also science fiction, though, built as it is around a concept of detection that exists today only as the wildest speculation.

I wrote it in a moment of agreeable ease and fluency in the summer of 1987, and Alice Turner of Playboy *bought it in an equally uncomplicated way and published it in her August, 1988 issue. I'm never enthusiastic about complications, but the summer is a time when I particularly like everything to go smoothly. This one did.*

On a crisp afternoon of high winds late in the summer of 2017 Frazier murdered his wife's lover, a foolish deed that he immediately regretted. To murder anyone was stupid, when there were so many more effective alternatives available; but even so, if murder was what he had to do, why murder the *lover?* Two levels of guilt attached there: not only the taking of a life, but the taking of an irrelevant life. If you had to kill someone, he told himself immediately afterward, then you should have killed *her.* She was the one who had committed the crime against the marriage, after all. Poor Hurwitt had been only a means, a tool, virtually an innocent bystander. Yes, kill *her*, not him. Kill yourself, even. But Hurwitt was the one he had killed, a dumb thing to do and done in a dumb manner besides.

It had all happened very quickly, without premeditation. Frazier was attending a meeting of the Museum trustees, to discuss expanding the Hall of Mammals. There was a recess; and because the day was so cool, the air so crystalline and bracing, he stepped out on the balcony that connected the old building with the Pilgersen Extension for a quick breather. Then the sleek bronze door of the Pilgersen opened far down the way and a dark-haired man in a grubby blue-gray lab coat appeared. Frazier saw at once, by the rigid set of his high shoulders and the way his long hair fluttered in the wind, that it was Hurwitt.

He wants to see me, Frazier thought. He knows I'm attending the meeting today and he's come out here to stage the confrontation at last, to tell me that he loves my famous and beautiful wife, to ask me bluntly to clear off and let him have her all to himself.

Frazier's pulse began to rise, his face grew hot. Even while he was thinking that it was oddly old-fashioned to talk of *letting* Hurwitt have Marianne, that in fact Hurwitt had probably already had Marianne in every conceivable way and vice versa but that if now he had some idea of setting up housekeeping with her—unbelievable, unthinkable!—this was hardly the appropriate place to discuss it with him, another and more primordial area of his brain was calling forth torrents of adrenaline and preparing him for mortal combat.

But no: Hurwitt didn't seem to have ventured onto the balcony for any man-to-man conference with his lover's husband. Evidently he was simply taking the short-cut from his lab in the Pilgersen to the fourth-floor cafeteria in the old building. He walked with his head down, his brows knitted, as though pondering some abstruse detail of trilobite anatomy, and he took no notice of Frazier at all.

"Hurwitt?" Frazier said finally, when the other man was virtually abreast of him.

Caught by surprise, Hurwitt looked up, blinking. He appeared not to recognize Frazier for a moment. For that moment he was frozen in mid-blink, his unkempt hair a dark halo about him, his awkward rangy body off balance between strides, his peculiar glinting eyes flashing like yellow beacons. In fury Frazier imagined this man's bony nakedness, pale and gaunt, probably with sparse ropy strands of black hair sprouting on a white chest, imagined those long arms wrapped around Marianne, imagined those huge knobby fingers cupping her breasts, imagined that thin-lipped wide mouth covering hers. Imagined the grubby lab coat lying crumpled at the foot of the bed, and her silken orange wrap beside it. That was what sent Frazier over the brink, not the infidelities themselves, not the thought of the sweaty embraces—there was plenty of that in each of her films, and it had never meant a thing to him, for he knew it was only well-paid make-believe—and not the rawboned look of the man or his uncouth stride or even the manic glint of those strange off-color eyes, those eerie topaz eyes, but the lab coat, stained and worn with a button missing and a pocket-flap dangling, lying beside Marianne's discarded silk. For her to take such a lover, a pathetic dreary poker of fossils, a hollow-chested laboratory drudge—no, no, no—

"Hello, Loren," Hurwitt said. He smiled amiably, he offered his hand. His eyes, though, narrowed and seemed almost to glow. It must be those weird eyes, Frazier thought, that Marianne has fallen in love with. "What a surprise, running into you out here."

And stood there smiling, and stood there holding out his hand, and stood there with his frayed lab coat flapping in the breeze.

Suddenly Frazier was unable to bear the thought of sharing the world with this man an instant longer. He watched himself as though from a point just behind his own right ear as he went rushing forward, seized not Hurwitt's hand but his wrist, and pushed rather than pulled, guiding him swiftly backward toward the parapet and tipping him up and over. It took perhaps a quarter of a second. Hurwitt, gaping, astonished, rose as though floating, hovered for an instant, began to descend. Frazier had one last look at Hurwitt's eyes, bright as glass, staring straight into his own, photographing his assailant's face; and then Hurwitt went plummeting downward.

My God, Frazier thought, peering over the edge. Hurwitt lay face down in the courtyard five stories below, arms and legs splayed, lab coat billowing about him.

✦

He was at the airport an hour later, with a light suitcase that carried no more than a day's change of clothing and a few cosmetic items. He flew first to Dallas, endured a 90-minute layover, went on to San Francisco, doubled back to Calgary as darkness descended, and caught a midnight special to Mexico City, where he checked into a hotel using the legal commercial alias that he employed when doing business in Macao, Singapore, and Hong Kong.

Standing on the terrace of a tower thirty stories above the Zona Rosa, he inhaled musky smog, listened to the squeals of traffic and the faint sounds of far-off drums, watched flares of green lightning in the choking sky above Popocatepetl, and wondered whether he should jump. Ultimately he decided against it. He wanted to share nothing whatever with Hurwitt, not even the manner of his death. And suicide would be an overreaction anyway. First he had to find out how much trouble he was really in.

The hotel had InfoLog. He dialed in and was told that queries were billed at five million pesos an hour, pro rated. Vaguely he wondered whether that was as expensive as it sounded. The peso was practically worthless, wasn't it? What could that be in dollars, a hundred bucks, five hundred, maybe? Nothing.

"I want Harvard Legal," he told the screen. "Criminology. Forensics. Technical. Evidence technology." Grimly he menued down and down until he was near what he wanted. "Eyeflash," he said. "Theory, techniques. Methods of detail recovery. Acceptance as evidence. Reliability of record. Frequency of reversal on appeal. Supreme Court rulings, if any."

Back to him, in surreal fragments which, at an extra charge of three million pesos per hour, pro rated, he had printed out for him, came blurts of information:

Perceptual pathways in outer brain layers...broad-scale optical architecture...images imprinted on striate cortex, or primary visual cortex... inferior temporal neurons...cf. McDermott and Brunetti, 2007, utilization of lateral geniculate body as storage for visual data...inferior temporal cortex...uptake of radioactive glucose...downloading...degrading of signal... degeneration period...Pilsudski signal-enhancement filter...Nevada vs. Bensen, 2011...hippocampus simulation...amygdala...acetylcholine...U.S. Supreme Court, 23 March 2012...cf Gross and Bernstein, 13 Aug 2003... Mishkin...Appenzeller...

Enough. He shuffled the printouts in a kind of hard-edged stupor until dawn; and then, after a hazy calculation of time-zone differentials, he called his lawyer in New York. It took four bounces, but the telephone tracked him down in the commute, driving in from Connecticut.

Frazier keyed in the privacy filter. All the lawyer would know was that some client was calling; the screen image would be a blur, the voice would be rendered universal, generalized, unidentifiable. It was more for the lawyer's protection than Frazier's: there had been nasty twists in jurisprudence lately, and lawyers were less and less willing to run the risk of being named accomplices after the fact. Immediately came a query about the billing. Bill to my hotel room, Frazier replied, and the screen gave him a go-ahead.

"Let's say I'm responsible for causing a fatal injury and the victim had a good opportunity to see me as the act was occurring. What are the chances that they can recover eyeflash pictures?"

"Depends on how much damage was received in the process of the death. How did it happen?"

"Privileged communication?"

"Sorry. No."

"Even under filter?"

"Even. If the mode of death was unique or even highly distinctive and unusual, how can I help but draw the right conclusion? And then I'll know more than I want to know."

"It wasn't unique," Frazier said. "Or distinctive, or unusual. But I still won't go into details. I can tell you that the injury wasn't the sort that would cause specific brain trauma. I mean, nothing like a bullet between the eyes, or falling into a vat of acid, or—"

"All right. I follow. This take place in a major city?"

"Major, yes."

"In Missouri, Alabama, or Kentucky?"

"None of those," said Frazier. "It took place in a state where eyeflash recovery is legal. No question of that."

"And the body? How long after death do you estimate it would have been found?"

"Within minutes, I'd say."

"And when was that?"

Frazier hesitated. "Within the past twenty-four hours."

"Then there's almost total likelihood that there's a readily recoverable photograph in your victim's brain of whatever he saw at the moment of death. Beyond much doubt it's already been recovered. Are you sure he was looking at you as he died?"

"Straight at me."

"My guess is there's probably a warrant out for you already. If you want me to represent you, kill the privacy filter so I can confirm who you are, and we'll discuss our options."

"Later," Frazier said. "I think I'd rather try to make a run for it."

"But the chances of your getting away with—"

"This is something I need to do," said Frazier. "I'll talk to you some other time."

He was almost certainly cooked. He knew that. He had wasted critical time running frantically back and forth across the continent yesterday, when he should have been transferring funds, setting up secure refuges, and such. The only question now was whether they were already looking for him, in which case there'd be blocks on his accounts everywhere, a passport screen at every airport, worldwide interdicts of all sorts. But if that was so they'd already have traced him to this hotel. Evidently they hadn't, which meant that they hadn't yet uncovered the Southeast Asian trading alias and put interdicts on that. Well, it was just a lousy manslaughter case, or maybe second-degree at worst: they had more serious things to worry about, he supposed.

Checking out of the hotel without bothering about breakfast, he headed for the airport and used his corporate credit card to buy himself a flight to Belize. There he bought a ticket to Surinam, and just before his plane was due to leave he tried his personal card in the cash disburser and was pleasantly surprised to find that it hadn't yet been yanked. He withdrew the maximum. Of course now there was evidence that Loren Frazier had been in Belize this day, but he wasn't traveling as Frazier, and he'd be in Surinam before long, and by the time they traced him there, assuming that they could, he'd be somewhere else, under some other name entirely. Maybe if he kept dodging for six or eight months he'd scramble his trail so thoroughly that they'd never be able to find him. Did they pursue you forever, he wondered? A time must come when they file and forget. Of course, he might not want to keep running forever, either. Already he missed Marianne. Despite what she had done.

He spent three days in Surinam at a little pastel-green Dutch hotel at the edge of Paramaribo, eating spicy noodle dishes and waiting to be arrested. Nobody bothered him. He used a cash machine again, keying up one of his corporate accounts and transferring a bundle of money into the account of Andreas Schmidt of Zurich, which was a name he had used seven years ago for some exportimport maneuvers involving Zimbabwe and somehow, he knew not why, had kept alive for eventualities unknown. This was an eventuality, now. When he checked the Schmidt account he found that there was money in it already, significant money, and that his Swiss passport had not yet expired. The Swiss charge-d'affaires in Guyana was requested to prepare a duplicate for him. A quick boat trip up the Marowijne River took him to St. Laurent on the French Guiana side of the river, where he was able to hire a driver to take him to Cayenne, and from there he flew to Georgetown in Guyana. A smiling proxy lawyer named Chatterji obligingly picked up his passport for him from the Swiss, and under the name of Schmidt he went on to Buenos Aires. There he destroyed all his Frazier documentation. He resisted the temptation to find out whether there was a Frazier interdict out yet. No sense handing them a trail extending down to Buenos Aires just to gratify his curiosity. If they weren't yet looking for him because he had murdered Hurwitt, they'd be looking for him on a simple missing-persons hook by this time. One way or another, it was best to forget about his previous identity and operate as Schmidt from here on.

This is almost fun, he thought.

But he missed his wife terribly.

While sitting in sidewalk cafes on the broad Avenida de 9 Julio, feasting on huge parrilladas sluiced down by carafe after carafe of red wine, he brooded obsessively on Marianne's affair. It made no sense. The world-famous actress and the awkward rawboned paleontologist: why? How was it possible? She had been making a commercial at the museum—Frazier, in fact, had helped to set the business up in his capacity as member of the board of trustees—and Hurwitt, who was the head of the department of invertebrate paleontology, or some such thing, had volunteered to serve as the technical consultant. Very kind of him, everyone said. Taking time away from his scientific work. He seemed so bland, so juiceless: who could suspect him of harboring lust for the glamorous film personality? Nobody would have imagined it. But things must have started almost at once. Some chemistry between them, beyond all understanding. People began to notice, and then to give Frazier strange little knowing looks. Eventually even he caught on. A truly loving husband is generally just about the last one to know, because he will always put the best possible interpretation on the data. But after a time the accumulation of data becomes impossible to overlook or deny or reason away. There are always small changes when something like that has begun: they start to read books of a kind they've never read before, they talk of different things, they may even show some new moves in bed. Then comes the real carelessness, the seemingly unconscious slips that scream the actual nature of the situation. Frazier was forced finally to an acceptance of the truth. It tore at his heart. There was no room in their marriage for such stuff. Despite his money, despite his power, he had never gone in for the casual morality of the intercontinental set, and neither, so he thought, had Marianne. This was the second marriage for each: the one that was supposed to carry them happily on to the finish. And now look.

"Senor? Another carafe?"

"No," he said. "Yes. Yes." He stared at his plate. It was full of sausages, sweetbreads, grilled steak. Where had all that come from? He was sure he had eaten everything. It must have grown back. Moodily he stabbed a plump blood sausage and ate without noticing. Took a drink. They mixed the wine with seltzer water here, half and half. Maybe it helped you put away those tons of meat more easily.

Afterward, strolling along the narrow, glittering Calle Florida with the stylish evening promenade flowing past him on both sides, he caught sight of Marianne coming out of a jeweler's shop. She wore gaucho leathers, emerald earrings, skin-tight trousers of gold brocade. He grunted as though he had been struck and pressed his elbows against his sides as one might do if expecting a second blow. Then an elegant young Argentinian uncoiled himself from a curbside table and trotted quickly toward her, and they laughed and embraced and ran off arm in arm, sweeping right past without even a glance. He remembered, now: women all over the world were wearing Marianne's face this season. This one, in fact, was too tall by half a head. But he would have to be prepared for such incidents wherever he went. Mariannes everywhere, bludgeoning him with their beauty and never even knowing what they had done. He found himself wishing that the one who had been sleeping with that museum man was just another Marianne clone, that the real one was at home alone now, waiting for him, wondering, wondering.

●

In Montreal six weeks later, using a privacy filter and one of his corporate cards, he risked putting through a call to his apartment and discovered that there was an interdict on his line. When he tried the office number an android mask appeared on the screen and he was blandly told that Mr. Frazier was unavailable. The android didn't know when Mr. Frazier would be available. Frazier asked for Markman, his executive assistant, and a moment later a bleak, harried, barely recognizable face looked out at him. Frazier explained that he was a representative of the Bucharest account, calling about a highly sensitive matter. "Don't you know?" Markman said. "Mr. Frazier's disappeared. The police are looking for him." Frazier asked why, and Markman's face dissolved in an agony of shame, bewilderment, protective zeal. "There's a criminal charge against him," Markman whispered, nearly in tears.

He called his lawyer next and said, "I'm calling about the Frazier case. I don't want to kill the filter but I imagine you won't have much trouble figuring out who I am."

"I imagine I won't. Just don't tell me where you are, okay?"

The situation was about as he expected. They had recovered the murder prints from the dead man's eyes: a nice shot, embedded deep in the cortical tissue, Frazier looming up against Hurwitt, nose to nose, a quick cut to the hand reaching for Hurwitt's arm, a wild free-form pan to the sky as Frazier lifted Hurwitt up and over the parapet. "Pardon me for saying this, but you looked absolutely deranged," the lawyer told him. "The prints were on all the networks the next day. Your eyes—it was really scary. I'm absolutely sure we could get impairment of faculties, maybe even crime of passion. Suspended sentence, but of course there'd be rehabilitation. I don't see any way around that, and it could last a year or two, and you might not be as effective in your profession afterward, but considering the circumstances—"

"How's my wife?" Frazier said. "Do you know anything about what she's been doing?"

"Well, of course I don't represent her, you realize. But she does get in the news. She's said to be traveling."

"Where?"

"I couldn't say. Look, I can try to find out, if you'd like to call back this time tomorrow. Only I suggest that for your own good you call me at a different number, which is—"

"For my good or for yours?" Frazier said.

"I'm trying to help," said the lawyer, sounding annoyed.

He took refresher courses in French, Italian, and German to give himself a little extra plausibility in the Andreas Schmidt identity, and cultivated a mild Teutonic accent. So long as he didn't run up against any real Swiss who wanted to gabble with him in Romansch or Schwyzerdeutsch he suspected he'd make out all right. He kept on moving, Strasbourg, Athens, Haifa, Tunis. Even though he knew that no further fund transfers were possible, there was enough money stashed under the Schmidt accounts to keep him going nicely for ten or fifteen years, and by then he hoped to have this thing figured out.

He saw Mariannes in Tel Aviv, in Heraklion on Crete, and in Sidi bou Said, just outside Tunis. They were all clones, of course. He recognized that after just a quick queasy instant. Still, seeing that delicate high-bridged nose once again, those splendid amethyst eyes, those tight auburn ringlets, it was all he could do to keep himself from going up to them and throwing his arms around them, and he had to force himself each time to turn away, biting down hard on his lip.

In London, outside the Connaught, he saw the real thing. The Connaught was where they had spent their wedding trip back in '07, and he winced at the sight of its familiar grand facade, and winced even more when Marianne came out, young and radiant, wearing a shimmering silver cloud. Dazzling light streamed from her. He had no doubt that this was no trendy clone but the true Marianne: she moved in that easy confident way, with that regal joy in her own beauty, that no cosmetic surgeon could ever impart even to the most intent imitator. The pavement itself seemed to do her homage. But then Frazier saw that the man on whose arm she walked was himself, young and radiant too, the Loren Frazier of that honeymoon journey of seven years back, his hair dark and thick, his love of life and success and his magnificent new wife cloaking him like an imperial mantle; and Frazier realized that he must merely be hallucinating, that the breakdown had moved on to a new and more serious stage. He stood gaping while Mr. and Mrs. Frazier swept through him like the phantoms they were and away in the direction of Grosvenor Square, and then he staggered and nearly fell. To the Connaught doorman he admitted that he was unwell, and because he was well dressed and spoke with the hint of an accent and was able to find a twenty-sovereign piece in the nick of time the doorman helped him into a cab and expressed his deepest concern. Back at his own hotel, ten minutes over on the other side of Mayfair, he had three quick gins in a row and sat shivering for an hour before the image faded from his mind.

"I advise you to give yourself up," the lawyer said, when Frazier called him from Nairobi. "Of course you can keep on running as long as you like. But you're wearing yourself out, and sooner or later someone will spot you, so why keep on delaying the inevitable?"

"Have you spoken to Marianne lately?"

"She wishes you'd come back. She wants to write to you, or call you, or even come and see you, wherever you are. But I've told her you refuse to provide me with any information about your location. Is that still your position?"

"I don't want to see her or hear from her."

"She loves you."

"I'm a homicidal maniac. I might do the same thing to her that I did to Hurwitt."

"Surely you don't really believe—"

"No," Frazier said. "Not really."

"Then let me give her an address for you, at least, and she can write to you."

"It could be a trap, couldn't it?"

"Surely you can't possibly believe—"

"Who knows? Anything's possible."

"A postal box in Caracas, say," the lawyer suggested, "and let's say that you're in Rio, for the sake of the discussion, and I arrange an inter-mediary to pick up the letter and forward it care of American Express in Lima, and then on some day of your own choosing, known to nobody else, you make a quick trip in and out of Peru and—"

"And they grab me the moment I collect the letter," Frazier said. "How stupid do you think I am? You could set up forty intermediaries and I'd still have to create a trail leading to myself if I want to get the letter. Besides, I'm not in South America any more. That was months ago."

"It was only for the sake of the dis—" the lawyer said, but Frazier was gone already.

He decided to change his face and settle down somewhere. The lawyer was right: all this compulsive traveling was wearing him down. But by staying in one place longer than a week or two he was multiplying the chances of being detected, so long as he went on looking like himself. He had always wanted a longer nose anyway, and not quite so obtrusive a chin, and thicker eyebrows. He fancied that he looked too Slavic, though he had no Eastern European ancestry at all. All one long rainy evening at the mellow old Addis Ababa Hilton he sketched a face for himself that he thought looked properly Swiss: rugged, passionate, with the right mix of French elegance, German stolidity, Italian passion. Then he went downstairs and showed the printout to the bartender, a supple little Portuguese.

"Where would you say this man comes from?" Frazier asked.

"Lisbon," the bartender replied at once. "That long jaw, those lips—unmistakably Lisbon, though perhaps his grandmother on his mother's side is of the Algarve. A man of considerable distinction, I would say. But I do not know him, Senhor Schmidt. He is no one I know. You would like your dry martini, as usual?"

"Make it a double," Frazier said.

He had the work done in Vienna. Everyone agreed that the best people for that sort of surgery were in Geneva, but Switzerland was the one country in the world he dared not enter, so he used his Zurich banking connections to get him the name of the second-best people, who were said to be almost as good, remarkably good, he was told. That seemed high praise indeed, Frazier thought, considering it was a Swiss talking about Austrians. The head surgeon at the Vienna clinic, though, turned out to be Swiss himself, which provided Frazier with a moment of complete terror, pretending as he was to be a native of Zurich. But the surgeon had been at his trade long enough to know that a man who wants his perfectly good face transformed into something entirely different does not wish to talk about his personal affairs. He was a big, cheerful extravert named Randegger with a distinct limp. Skiing accident, the surgeon explained. Surely getting your leg fixed must be easier than getting your face changed, Frazier thought, but he decided that Randegger was simply waiting for the off season to undergo repair. "This will be no problem at all," Randegger told him, studying Frazier's printout. "I have just a few small suggestions." He went deftly to work with a lightpen, broadening the cheekbones, moving the ears downward and forward. Frazier shrugged. Whatever you want, Dr. Randegger, he thought. Whatever you want. I'm putty in your hands.

It took six weeks from first cut to final healing. The results seemed fine to him—suave, convincing, an authoritative face—though at the beginning he was afraid it would all come apart if he smiled, and it was hard to get used to looking in a mirror and seeing someone else. He stayed at the clinic the whole six weeks. One of the nurses wore the Marianne face, but the body was all wrong, wide hips, startling steatopygous rump, short muscular legs. Near the end of his stay she lured him into bed. He was sure he'd be impotent with her, but he was wrong. There was only one really bad moment, when she reared above him and he couldn't see her body at all, only her beautiful, passionate, familiar face.

Even now, he couldn't stop running. Belgrade, Sydney, Rabat, Barcelona, Milan: they went by in a blur of identical airports, interchangeable hotels, baffling shifts of climate. Almost everywhere he went he saw Mariannes, and sometimes was puzzled that they never recognized him, until he remembered that he had altered his face: why should they know him now, even after the seven years of their marriage? As he traveled he began to see another ubiquitous face, dark and Latin and pixyish, and realized that Marianne's vogue must be beginning to wane. He hoped that some of the Mariannes would soon be converting themselves to this newer look. He had never really felt at ease with all these simulacra of his wife, whom he still loved beyond all measure.

That love, though, had become inextricably mixed with anger. He could not even now stop thinking about her incomprehensible, infuriating violation of the sanctity of their covenant. It had been the best of marriages, amiable, passionate, close, a true union on every level. He had never even thought of wanting another woman. She was everything he wanted; and he had every reason to think that his feelings were reciprocated. That was the worst of it, not the furtive little couplings she and Hurwitt must have enjoyed, but the deeper treason, the betrayal of their seeming harmony, her seemingly whimsical destruction of the hermetic seal that enclosed their perfect world.

He had overreacted, he knew. He wished he could call back the one absurd impulsive act that had thrust him from his smooth and agreeable existence into this frantic wearisome fugitive life. And he felt sorry for Hurwitt, who probably had been caught up in emotions beyond his depth, swept away by the astonishment of finding himself in Marianne's arms. How could he have stopped to worry, at such a time, about what he might be doing to someone else's marriage? How ridiculous it had been to kill him! And to stare right into Hurwitt's eyes, incontrovertibly incriminating himself, while he did! If he needed any proof of his temporary insanity, the utter foolishness of the murder would supply it.

But there was no calling any of it back. Hurwitt was dead; he had lived on the run for—what, two years, three?—and Marianne was altogether lost to him. So much destruction achieved in a single crazy moment. He wondered what he would do if he ever saw Marianne again. Nothing violent, no, certainly not. He had a sudden image of himself in tears, hugging her knees, begging her forgiveness. For what? For killing her lover? For bringing all sorts of nasty mess and the wrong kind of publicity into her life? For disrupting the easy rhythms of their happy marriage? No, he thought, astonished, aghast. What do I have to be forgiven for? From her, nothing. She's the one who should go down on her knees before me. I wasn't the one who was fooling around. And then he thought, No, no, we must forgive each other. And after that he thought, Best of all, I must take care never to have anything to do with her for the rest of my life. And that thought cut through him like a blade, like Dr. Randegger's fiery scalpel.

✺

Six months later he was walking through the cavernous, ornate lobby of the Hotel de Paris in Monte Carlo when he saw a Marianne standing in front of a huge stack of suitcases against a marble pillar no more than twenty feet from him. He was inured to Mariannes by this time and at first the sight of her had no impact; but then he noticed the familiar monogram on the luggage, and recognized the intricate little bows of red plush cord with which the baggage tags were tied on, and he realized that this was the true Marianne at last. Nor was this any hallucination like the Connaught one. She was visibly older, with a vertical line in her left cheek that he had never seen before. Her hair was a darker shade and somehow more ordinary in its cut, and she was dressed simply, no radiance at all. Even so, people were staring at her and whispering. Frazier swayed, gripped a nearby pillar with his suddenly clammy hand, fought back the impulse to run. He took a deep breath and went toward her, walking slowly, impressively, his carefully cultivated distinguished-looking-Swiss-businessman walk.

"Marianne?" he said.

She turned her head slightly and stared at him without any show of recognition.

"I do look different, yes," he said, smiling. "I'm sorry, but I don't—"

A slender, agile-looking man five or six years younger than she, wearing sunglasses, appeared from somewhere as though conjured out of the floor. Smoothly he interpolated himself between Frazier and Marianne. A lover? A bodyguard? Simply part of her entourage? Pleasantly but forcefully he presented himself to Frazier as though saying, Let's not have any trouble now, shall we?

"Listen to my voice," Frazier said. "You haven't forgotten my voice. Only the face is different."

Sunglasses came a little closer. Looked a little less pleasant.

Marianne stared.

"You haven't forgotten, have you, Marianne?" Frazier said.

Sunglasses began to look definitely menacing.

"Wait a minute," Marianne said, as he glided into a nose-to-nose with Frazier. "Step back, Aurelio." She peered through the shadows. "Loren?" she said.

Frazier nodded. He went toward her. At a gesture from Marianne, Sunglasses faded away like a genie going back into the bottle. Frazier felt strangely calm now. He could see Marianne's upper lip trembling, her nostrils flickering a little. "I thought I never wanted to see you again," he said. "But I was wrong about that. The moment I saw you and knew it was really you, I realized that I had never stopped thinking about you, never stopped wanting you. Wanting to put it all back together."

Her eyes widened. "And you think you can?"

"Maybe."

"What a damned fool you are," she said, gently, almost lovingly, after a long moment.

"I know. I really messed myself up, doing what I did."

"I don't mean that," she said. "You messed us both up with that. Not to mention him, the poor bastard. But that can't be undone, can it? If you only knew how often I prayed to have it not have happened." She shook her head. "It was nothing, what he and I were doing. Nothing. Just a silly fling, for Christ's sake. How could you possibly have cared so much?"

"What?"

"To *kill* a man, for something like that? To wreck three lives in half a second? For *that*?"

"What?" he said again. "What are you telling me?"

Sunglasses suddenly was in the picture again. "We're going to miss the car to the airport, Marianne."

"Yes. Yes. All right, let's go."

Frazier watched, numb, immobile. Sunglasses beckoned and a swarm of porters materialized to carry the luggage outside. As she reached the vast doorway Marianne turned abruptly and looked back, and in the dimness of the great lobby her eyes suddenly seemed to shift in color, to take on the same strange topaz glint that he had imagined he had seen in Hurwitt's. Then she swung around and was gone.

An hour later he went down to the Consulate to turn himself in. They had a little trouble locating him in the list of wanted fugitives, but he told them to keep looking, going back a few years, and finally they came upon his entry. He was allowed half a day to clear up his business affairs, but he said he had none to clear up, so they set about the procedure of arranging his passage to the States, while he watched like a tourist who is trying to replace a lost passport.

Coming home was like returning to a foreign country that he had visited a long time before. Everything was familiar, but in an unfamiliar way. There were endless hearings, conferences, psychological examinations. His lawyers were excessively polite, as if they feared that one wrong word would cause him to detonate, but behind their silkiness he saw the contempt that the orderly have for the self-destructive. Still, they did their job well. Eventually he drew a suspended sentence and two years of rehabilitation, after which, they told him, he'd need to move to some other city, find some appropriate line of work, and establish a stable new existence for himself. The rehabilitation people would help him. There would be a probation period of five years when he'd have to report for progress conferences every week.

At the very end one of the rehab officers came to him and told him that his lawyers had filed a petition asking the court to let him have his original face back. That startled him. For a moment Frazier felt like a fugitive again, wearily stumbling from airport to airport, from hotel to hotel.

"No," he said. "I don't think that's a good idea at all. The man who had that face, he's somebody else. I think I'm better off keeping this one. What do you say?"

"I think so too," said the rehab man.

ENTER A SOLDIER. LATER: ENTER ANOTHER (1987)

A curious phenomenon of American science-fiction publishing in the late 1980s, one which will probably not be dealt with in a kindly way by future historians of the field, was the "shared world" anthology. I use the past tense for it because the notion of assembling a group of writers to produce stories set in a common background defined by someone else has largely gone out of fashion today. But for a time in 1987 and thereabouts it began to seem as though everything in science fiction was becoming part of some shared-world project.

I will concede that some excellent fiction came out of the various shared-world enterprises, though mainly they produced a mountain of junk. The idea itself was far from new in the 1980s; it goes back at least to 1952 and The Petrified Planet, *a book in which the scientist John D. Clark devised specifications for an unusual planet and the writers Fletcher Pratt, H. Beam Piper, and Judith Merril wrote superb novellas set on that world. Several similar books followed in the next few years.*

In the late 1960s I revived the idea with a book called Three For Tomorrow—*fiction by James Blish, Roger Zelazny, and myself, based on a theme proposed by Arthur C. Clarke—and I did three or four similar collections later on. In 1975 came Harlan Ellison's* Medea, *an elaborate and brilliantly conceived colossus of a book that made use of the talents of Frank Herbert, Theodore Sturgeon, Frederik Pohl, and a whole galaxy of other writers of that stature. But the real deluge of shared-world projects* began a few years afterward, in the wake of the vast commercial success of Robert Asprin's fantasy series, Thieves' World. Suddenly, every publisher in the business wanted to duplicate the Thieves' World bonanza, and from all sides appeared platoons of hastily conceived imitators.

I dabbled in a couple of these books myself—a story that I wrote for one of them won a Hugo, in fact—but my enthusiasm for the shared-world whirl cooled quickly once I perceived how shapeless and incoherent most of the anthologies were. The writers tended not to pay much attention to the specifications, and simply went off in their own directions; the editors, generally, were too lazy or too cynical or simply too incompetent to do anything about it; and the books became formless jumbles of incompatible work.

Before I became fully aware of that, though, I let myself be seduced into editing one shared-world series myself. The initiator of this was Jim Baen, the publisher of Baen Books, whose idea centered around pitting computer-generated simulacra of historical figures against each other in intellectual conflict. That appealed to me considerably, and I agreed to work out the concept in detail and serve as the series' general editor.

I produced an elaborate prospectus outlining the historical background of the near-future world in which these simulacra would hold forth; I rounded up a group of capable writers; and to ensure that the book would unfold with consistency to my underlying vision, I wrote the first story myself in October of 1987, a 15,000-word opus for which I chose Socrates and Francisco Pizarro as my protagonists and which I called "Enter a Soldier. Later: Enter Another."

The whole thing was, I have to admit, a matter of commerce rather than art: just a job of work, to fill somebody's current publishing need. But a writer's intention and the ultimate result of his work don't bear any necessary relationship. In this case I was surprised and delighted to find the story taking on unanticipated life as I wrote, and what might have been a routine job of word-spinning turned out, unexpectedly, to be rather more than that when I was done with it.

Gardner Dozois published it in the June, 1989 issue of Isaac Asimov's Science Fiction Magazine, and then I used it as the lead story in the shared-world anthology, Time Gate. Dozois picked it for his 1989 Year's Best Science Fiction Collection, and in 1990 it was a finalist on both the Nebula and Hugo ballots—one of my most widely liked stories in a long time. The Nebula eluded me, but at the World Science Fiction Convention in Holland in August, 1990, "Enter a Soldier" brought me a Hugo award, my fourth, as the year's best novelette.

Even so, I decided soon after to avoid further involvement in the shared-world milieu, and have done no work of that sort in many years. Perhaps it was always unrealistic to think that any team of gifted, independent-minded writers could produce what is in essence a successful collaborative novel that has been designed by someone else. But my brief sojourn as editor of Time Gate *did, at least, produce a story that I now see was one of the major achievements of my career.*

It might be heaven. Certainly it wasn't Spain and he doubted it could be Peru. He seemed to be floating, suspended midway between nothing and nothing. There was a shimmering golden sky far above him and a misty, turbulent sea of white clouds boiling far below. When he looked down he saw his legs and his feet dangling like child's toys above an unfathomable abyss, and the sight of it made him want to puke, but there was nothing in him for the puking. He was hollow. He was made of air. Even the old ache in his knee was gone, and so was the everlasting dull burning in the fleshy part of his arm where the Indian's little arrow had taken him, long ago on the shore of that island of pearls, up by Panama.

It was as if he had been born again, sixty years old but freed of all the harm that his body had experienced and all its myriad accumulated injuries: freed, one might almost say, of his body itself.

"Gonzalo?" he called. "Hernando?"

Blurred dreamy echoes answered him. And then silence.

"Mother of God, am I dead?"

No. No. He had never been able to imagine death. An end to all striving? A place where nothing moved? A great emptiness, a pit without a bottom? Was this place the place of death, then? He had no way of knowing. He needed to ask the holy fathers about this.

"Boy, where are my priests? Boy?"

He looked about for his page. But all he saw was blinding whorls of light coiling off to infinity on all sides. The sight was beautiful but troublesome. It was hard for him to deny that he had died, seeing himself afloat like this in a realm of air and light. Died and gone to heaven. This is heaven, yes, surely, surely. What else could it be?

So it was true, that if you took the Mass and took the Christ faithfully into yourself and served Him well you would be saved from your sins, you would be forgiven, you would be cleansed. He had wondered about that. But he wasn't ready yet to be dead, all the same. The thought of it was sickening and infuriating. There was so much yet to be done. And he had no memory even of being ill. He searched his body for wounds. No, no wounds. Not anywhere. Strange. Again he looked around. He was alone here. No one to be seen, not his page, nor his brother, nor De Soto, nor the priests, nor anyone. "Fray Marcos! Fray Vicente! Can't you hear me? Damn you, where are you? Mother of God! Holy Mother, blessed among women! Damn you, Fray Vicente, tell me—tell me—"

His voice sounded all wrong: too thick, too deep, a stranger's voice. The words fought with his tongue and came from his lips malformed and lame, not the good crisp Spanish of Estremadura but something shameful and odd. What he heard was like the spluttering foppishness of Madrid or even the furry babble that they spoke in Barcelona; why, he might almost be a Portuguese, so coarse and clownish was his way of shaping his speech.

He said carefully and slowly, "I am the Governor and Captain-General of New Castile."

That came out no better, a laughable noise.

"Adelantado—Alguacil Mayor—Marques de la Conquista—"

The strangeness of his new way of speech made insults of his own titles. It was like being tongue-tied. He felt streams of hot sweat breaking out on his skin from the effort of trying to frame his words properly; but when he put his hand to his forehead to brush the sweat away before it could run into his eyes he seemed dry to the touch, and he was not entirely sure he could feel himself at all.

He took a deep breath. "I am Francisco Pizarro!" he roared, letting the name burst desperately from him like water breaching a rotten dam.

The echo came back, deep, rumbling, mocking. *Frantheethco. Peetharro.*

That too. Even his own name, idiotically garbled.

"O great God!" he cried. "Saints and angels!"

More garbled noises. Nothing would come out as it should. He had never known the arts of reading or writing; now it seemed that true speech itself was being taken from him. He began to wonder whether he had been right about this being heaven, supernal radiance or no. There was a curse on his tongue; a demon, perhaps, held it pinched in his claws. Was this hell, then? A very beautiful place, but hell nevertheless?

He shrugged. Heaven or hell, it made no difference. He was beginning to grow more calm, beginning to accept and take stock. He knew—had learned, long ago—that there was nothing to gain from raging against that which could not be helped, even less from panic in the face of the unknown. He was here, that was all there was to it—wherever *here* was—and he must find a place for himself, and not this place, floating here between nothing and nothing. He had been in hells before, small hells, hells on Earth. That barren isle called Gallo, where the sun cooked you in your own skin and there was nothing to eat but crabs that had the taste of dog-dung. And that dismal swamp at the mouth of the Rio Biru, where the rain fell in rivers and the trees reached down to cut you like swords. And the mountains he had crossed with his army, where the snow was so cold that it burned, and the air went into your throat like a dagger at every breath. He had come forth from those, and they had been worse than this. Here there was no pain and no danger; here there was only soothing light and a strange absence of all discomfort. He began to move forward. He was walking on air. Look, look, he thought, I am walking on air! Then he said it out loud. "I am walking on air," he announced, and laughed at the way the words emerged from him. "Santiago! Walking on air! But why not? I am Pizarro!" He shouted it with all his might, "Pizarro! Pizarro!" and waited for it to come back to him.

Peetharro. Peetharro.

He laughed. He kept on walking.

Tanner sat hunched forward in the vast sparkling sphere that was the ninth-floor imaging lab, watching the little figure at the distant center of the holotank strut and preen. Lew Richardson, crouching beside him with both hands thrust into the data gloves so that he could feed instructions to the permutation network, seemed almost not to be breathing—seemed to be just one more part of the network, in fact.

But that was Richardson's way, Tanner thought: total absorption in the task at hand. Tanner envied him that. They were very different sorts of men. Richardson lived for his programming and nothing but his programming. It was his grand passion. Tanner had never quite been able to understand people who were driven by grand passions. Richardson was like some throwback to an earlier age, an age when things had really mattered, an age when you were able to have some faith in the significance of your own endeavors.

"How do you like the armor?" Richardson asked. "The armor's very fine, I think. We got it from old engravings. It has real flair."

"Just the thing for tropical climates," said Tanner. "A nice tin suit with matching helmet."

He coughed and shifted about irritably in his seat. The demonstration had been going on for half an hour without anything that seemed to be of any importance happening—just the minuscule image of the bearded man in Spanish armor tramping back and forth across the glowing field—and he was beginning to get impatient.

Richardson didn't seem to notice the harshness in Tanner's voice or the restlessness of his movements. He went on making small adjustments. He was a small man himself, neat and precise in dress and appearance, with faded blond hair and pale blue eyes and a thin, straight mouth. Tanner felt huge and shambling beside him. In theory Tanner had authority over Richardson's research projects, but in fact he always had simply permitted Richardson to do as he pleased. This time, though, it might be necessary finally to rein him in a little.

This was the twelfth or thirteenth demonstration that Richardson had subjected him to since he had begun fooling around with this historical-simulation business. The others all had been disasters of one kind or another, and Tanner expected that this one would finish the same way. And basically Tanner was growing uneasy about the project that he once had given his stamp of approval to, so long ago. It was getting harder and harder to go on believing that all this work served any useful purpose. Why had it been allowed to absorb so much of Richardson's group's time and so much of the lab's research budget for so many months? What possible value was it going to have for anybody? What possible use?

It's just a game, Tanner thought. One more desperate meaningless technological stunt, one more pointless pirouette in a meaningless ballet. The expenditure of vast resources on a display of ingenuity for ingenuity's sake and nothing else: now *there's* decadence for you.

The tiny image in the holotank suddenly began to lose color and definition.

"Uh-oh," Tanner said. "There it goes. Like all the others."

But Richardson shook his head. "This time it's different, Harry."

"You think?"

"We aren't losing him. He's simply moving around in there of his own volition, getting beyond our tracking parameters. Which means that we've achieved the high level of autonomy that we were shooting for."

"Volition, Lew? Autonomy?"

"You know that those are our goals."

"Yes, I know what our goals are supposed to be," said Tanner, with some annoyance. "I'm simply not convinced that a loss of focus is a proof that you've got volition."

"Here," Richardson said. "I'll cut in the stochastic tracking program. He moves freely, we freely follow him." Into the computer ear in his lapel he said, "Give me a gain boost, will you?" He made a quick flicking gesture with his left middle finger to indicate the quantitative level.

The little figure in ornate armor and pointed boots grew sharp again. Tanner could see fine details on the armor, the plumed helmet, the tapering shoulder-pieces, the joints at the elbows, the intricate pommel of his sword. He was marching from left to right in a steady hip-rolling way, like a man who was climbing the tallest mountain in the world and didn't mean to break his stride until he was across the summit. The fact that he was walking in what appeared to be mid-air seemed not to trouble him at all.

"There he is," Richardson said grandly. "We've got him back, all right? The conqueror of Peru, before your very eyes, in the flesh. So to speak."

Tanner nodded. Pizarro, yes, before his very eyes. And he had to admit that what he saw was impressive and even, somehow, moving. Something about the dogged way with which that small armored figure was moving across the gleaming pearly field of the holotank aroused a kind of sympathy in him. That little man was entirely imaginary, but *he* didn't seem to know that, or if he did he wasn't letting it stop him for a moment: he went plugging on, and on and on, as if he intended actually to get somewhere. Watching that, Tanner was oddly captivated by it, and found himself surprised suddenly to discover that his interest in the entire project was beginning to rekindle.

"Can you make him any bigger?" he asked. "I want to see his face."

"I can make him big as life," Richardson said. "Bigger. Any size you like. Here."

He flicked a finger and the hologram of Pizarro expanded instantaneously to a height of about two meters. The Spaniard halted in mid-stride as though he might actually be aware of the imaging change.

That can't be possible, Tanner thought. That isn't a living consciousness out there. Or is it?

Pizarro stood poised easily in mid-air, glowering, shading his eyes as if staring into a dazzling glow. There were brilliant streaks of color in the air all around him, like an aurora. He was a tall, lean man in late middle age with a grizzled beard and a hard, angular face. His lips were thin, his nose was sharp, his eyes were cold, shrewd, keen. It seemed to Tanner that those eyes had come to rest on him, and he felt a chill.

My God, Tanner thought, he's *real*.

It had been a French program to begin with, something developed at the Centre Mondiale de la Computation in Lyons about the year 2119. The French had some truly splendid minds working in software in those days. They worked up astounding programs, and then nobody did anything with them. That was *their* version of Century Twenty-Two Malaise.

The French programmers' idea was to use holograms of actual historical personages to dress up the *son et lumiere* tourist events at the great monuments of their national history. Not just preprogrammed robot mockups of the old Disneyland kind, which would stand around in front of Notre Dame or the Arc de Triomphe or the Eiffel Tower and deliver canned spiels, but apparent reincarnations of the genuine great ones, who could freely walk and talk and answer questions and make little quips. Imagine Louis XIV demonstrating the fountains of Versailles, they said, or Picasso leading a tour of Paris museums, or Sartre sitting in his Left Bank café exchanging existential *bons mots* with passersby! Napoleon! Joan of Arc! Alexandre Dumas! Perhaps the simulations could do even more than that: perhaps they could be designed so well that they would be able to extend and embellish the achievements of their original lifetimes with new accomplishments, a fresh spate of paintings and novels and works of philosophy and great architectural visions by vanished masters.

The concept was simple enough in essence. Write an intelligencing program that could absorb data, digest it, correlate it, and generate further programs based on what you had given it. No real difficulty there. Then start feeding your program with the collected written works—if any—of the person to be simulated: that would provide not only a general sense of his ideas and positions but also of his underlying pattern of approach to situations, his style of thinking—for *le style*, after all, *est l'homme meme*. If no collected works happened to be available, why, find works *about* the subject by his contemporaries, and use those. Next, toss in the totality of the historical record of the subject's deeds, including all significant subsequent scholarly analyses, making appropriate allowances for conflicts in interpretation—indeed, taking advantages of such conflicts to generate a richer portrait, full of the ambiguities and contradictions that are the inescapable hallmarks of any human being. Now build in substrata of general cultural data of the proper period so that the subject has a loam of references and vocabulary out of which to create thoughts that are appropriate to his place in time and space. Stir. *Et voila!* Apply a little sophisticated imaging technology and you had a simulation capable of thinking and conversing and behaving as though it is the actual self after which it was patterned.

Of course, this would require a significant chunk of computer power. But that was no problem, in a world where 150-gigaflops networks were standard laboratory items and ten-year-olds carried pencil-sized computers with capacities far beyond the ponderous mainframes of their great-great-grandparents' day. No, there was no theoretical reason why the French project could not have succeeded. Once the Lyons programmers had worked out the basic intelligencing scheme that was needed to write the rest of the programs, it all should have followed smoothly enough.

Two things went wrong: one rooted in an excess of ambition that may have been a product of the peculiarly French personalities of the original programmers, and the other having to do with an abhorrence of failure typical of the major nations of the midtwenty-second century, of which France was one.

The first was a fatal change of direction that the project underwent in its early phases. The King of Spain was coming to Paris on a visit of state; and the programmers decided that in his honor they would synthesize Don Quixote for him as their initial project. Though the intelligencing program had been designed to simulate only individuals who had actually existed, there seemed no inherent reason why a fictional character as well documented as Don Quixote could not be produced instead. There was Cervantes' lengthy novel; there was ample background data available on the milieu in which Don Quixote supposedly had lived; there was a vast library of critical analysis of the book and of the Don's distinctive and flamboyant personality. Why should bringing Don Quixote to life out of a computer be any different from simulating Louis XIV, say, or Moliere, or Cardinal Richelieu? True, they had all existed once, and the knight of

La Mancha was a mere figment; but had Cervantes not provided far more detail about Don Quixote's mind and soul than was known of Richelieu, or Moliere, or Louis XIV?

Indeed he had. The Don—like Oedipus, like Odysseus, like Othello, like David Copperfield—had come to have a reality far more profound and tangible than that of most people who had indeed actually lived. Such characters as those had transcended their fictional origins. But not so far as the computer was concerned. It was able to produce a convincing fabrication of Don Quixote, all right—a gaunt bizarre holographic figure that had all the right mannerisms, that ranted and raved in the expectable way, that referred knowledgeably to Dulcinea and Rosinante and Mambrino's helmet. The Spanish king was amused and impressed. But to the French the experiment was a failure. They had produced a Don Quixote who was hopelessly locked to the Spain of the late sixteenth century and to the book from which he had sprung. He had no capacity for independent life and thought—no way to perceive the world that had brought him into being, or to comment on it, or to interact with it. There was nothing new or interesting about that. Any actor could dress up in armor and put on a scraggly beard and recite snatches of Cervantes. What had come forth from the computer, after three years of work, was no more than a predictable reprocessing of what had gone into it, sterile, stale.

Which led the Centre Mondial de la Computation to its next fatal step: abandoning the whole thing. *Zut!* and the project was cancelled without any further attempts. No simulated Picassos, no simulated Napoleons, no Joans of Arc. The Quixote event had soured everyone and no one had the heart to proceed with the work from there. Suddenly it had the taint of failure about it, and France—like Germany, like Australia, like the Han Commercial Sphere, like Brazil, like any of the dynamic centers of the modern world, had a horror of failure. Failure was something to be left to the backward nations or the decadent ones—to the Islamic Socialist Union, say, or the Soviet People's Republic, or to that slumbering giant, the United States of America. So the historic-personage simulation scheme was put aside.

The French thought so little of it, as a matter of fact, that after letting it lie fallow for a few years they licensed it to a bunch of Americans, who had heard about it somehow and felt it might be amusing to play with.

✸

"You may really have done it this time," Tanner said.

"Yes. I think we have. After all those false starts."

Tanner nodded. How often had he come into this room with hopes high, only to see some botch, some inanity, some depressing bungle? Richardson had always had an explanation. Sherlock Holmes hadn't worked because he was fictional: that was a necessary recheck of the French Quixote project, demonstrating that fictional characters didn't have the right sort of reality texture to take proper advantage of the program, not enough ambiguity, not enough contradiction. King Arthur had failed for the same reason. Julius Caesar? Too far in the past, maybe: unreliable data, bordering on fiction. Moses? Ditto. Einstein? Too complex, perhaps, for the project in its present level of development: they needed more experience first. Queen Elizabeth I? George Washington? Mozart? We're learning more each time, Richardson insisted after each failure. This isn't black magic we're doing, you know. We aren't necromancers, we're programmers, and we have to figure out how to give the program what it needs.

And now Pizarro?

"Why do you want to work with *him*?" Tanner had asked, five or six months earlier. "A ruthless medieval Spanish imperialist, is what I remember from school. A bloodthirsty despoiler of a great culture. A man without morals, honor, faith—"

"You may be doing him an injustice," said Richardson. "He's had a bad press for centuries. And there are things about him that fascinate me."

"Such as?"

"His drive. His courage. His absolute confidence. The other side of ruthlessness, the good side of it, is a total concentration on your task, an utter unwillingness to be stopped by any obstacle. Whether or not you approve of the things he accomplished, you have to admire a man who—"

"All right," Tanner said, abruptly growing weary of the whole enterprise. "Do Pizarro. Whatever you want."

The months had passed. Richardson gave him vague progress reports, nothing to arouse much hope. But now Tanner stared at the tiny strutting figure in the holotank and the conviction began to grow in him that Richardson finally had figured out how to use the simulation program as it was meant to be used.

"So you've actually recreated him, you think? Someone who lived—what, five hundred years ago?"

"He died in 1541," said Richardson.

"Almost six hundred, then."

"And he's not like the others—not simply a recreation of a great figure out of the past who can run through a set of pre-programmed speeches. What we've got here, if I'm right, is an artificially generated intelligence which can think for itself in modes other than the ones its programmers think in. Which has more information available to itself, in other words, than we've provided it with. That would be the real accomplishment. That's the fundamental philosophical leap that we were going for when we first got involved with this project. To use the program to give us new programs that are capable of true autonomous thought—a program that can think like Pizarro, instead of like Lew Richardson's idea of some historian's idea of how Pizarro might have thought."

"Yes," Tanner said.

"Which means we won't just get back the expectable, the predictable. There'll be surprises. There's no way to learn anything, you know, except through surprises. The sudden combination of known components into something brand new. And that's what I think we've managed to bring off here, at long last. Harry, it may be the biggest artificial-intelligence breakthrough ever achieved."

Tanner pondered that. Was it so? Had they truly done it?

And if they had—

Something new and troubling was beginning to occur to him, much later in the game than it should have. Tanner stared at the holographic figure floating in the center of the tank, that fierce old man with the harsh face and the cold, cruel eyes. He thought about what sort of man he must have been—the man after whom this image had been modeled. A man who was willing to land in South America at age fifty or sixty or whatever he had been, an ignorant illiterate Spanish peasant wearing a suit of ill-fitting armor and waving a rusty sword, and set out to conquer a great empire of millions of people spreading over thousands of miles. Tanner wondered what sort of man would be capable of carrying out a thing like that. Now that man's eyes were staring into his own and it was a struggle to meet so implacable a gaze.

After a moment he looked away. His left leg began to quiver. He glanced uneasily at Richardson.

"Look at those eyes, Lew. Christ, they're scary!"

"I know. I designed them myself, from the old prints."

"Do you think he's seeing us right now? Can he do that?"

"All he is is software, Harry."

"He seemed to know it when you expanded the image."

Richardson shrugged. "He's very good software. I tell you, he's got autonomy, he's got volition. He's got an electronic *mind*, is what I'm saying. He may have perceived a transient voltage kick. But there are limits to his perceptions, all the same. I don't think there's any way that he can see anything that's outside the holotank unless it's fed to him in the form of data he can process, which hasn't been done."

"You don't *think*? You aren't sure?"

"Harry. Please."

"This man conquered the entire enormous Incan empire with fifty soldiers, didn't he?"

"In fact I believe it was more like a hundred and fifty."

"Fifty, a hundred fifty, what's the difference? Who knows what you've actually got here? What if you did an even better job than you suspect?"

"What are you saying?"

"What I'm saying is, I'm uneasy all of a sudden. For a long time I didn't think this project was going to produce anything at all. Suddenly I'm starting to think that maybe it's going to produce more than we can handle. I don't want any of your goddamned simulations walking out of the tank and conquering *us*."

Richardson turned to him. His face was flushed, but he was grinning. "Harry, Harry! For God's sake! Five minutes ago you didn't think we had anything at all here except a tiny picture that wasn't even in focus. Now you've gone so far the other way that you're imagining the worst kind of—"

"I see his eyes, Lew. I'm worried that his eyes see me."

"Those aren't real eyes you're looking at. What you see is nothing but a graphics program projected into a holotank. There's no visual capacity there as you understand the concept. His eyes will see you only if I want them to. Right now they don't."

"But you can make them see me?"

"I can make them see anything I want them to see. I created him, Harry."

"With volition. With autonomy."

"After all this time you start worrying *now* about these things?"

"It's my neck on the line if something that you guys on the technical side make runs amok. This autonomy thing suddenly troubles me."

"I'm still the one with the data gloves," Richardson said. "I twitch my fingers and he dances. That's not really Pizarro down there, remember. And that's no Frankenstein monster either. It's just a simulation. It's just so much data, just a bunch of electromagnetic impulses that I can shut off with one movement of my pinkie."

"Do it, then."

"Shut him off? But I haven't begun to show you—"

"Shut him off, and then turn him on," Tanner said.

Richardson looked bothered. "If you say so, Harry."

He moved a finger. The image of Pizarro vanished from the holotank. Swirling gray mists moved in it for a moment, and then all was white wool. Tanner felt a quick jolt of guilt, as though he had just ordered the execution of the man in the medieval armor. Richardson gestured again, and color flashed across the tank, and then Pizarro reappeared.

"I just wanted to see how much autonomy your little guy really has," said Tanner. "Whether he was quick enough to head you off and escape into some other channel before you could cut his power."

"You really don't understand how this works at all, do you, Harry?"

"I just wanted to see," said Tanner again, sullenly. After a moment's silence he said, "Do you ever feel like God?"

"Like God?"

"You breathed life in. Life of a sort, anyway. But you breathed free will in, too. That's what this experiment is all about, isn't it? All your talk about volition and autonomy? You're trying to recreate a human mind—which means to create it all over again—a mind that can think in its own special way, and come up with its own unique responses to situations, which will not necessarily be the responses that its programmers might anticipate, in fact almost certainly will not be, and which not might be all that desirable or beneficial, either, and you simply have to allow for that risk, just as God, once he gave free will to mankind, knew that He was likely to see all manner of evil deeds being performed by His creations as they exercised that free will—"

"Please, Harry—"

"Listen, is it possible for me to talk with your Pizarro?"

"Why?"

"By way of finding out what you've got there. To get some first-hand knowledge of what the project has accomplished. Or you could say I just want to test the quality of the simulation. Whatever. I'd feel more a part of this thing, more aware of what it's all about in here, if I could have some direct contact with him. Would it be all right if I did that?"

"Yes. Of course."

"Do I have to talk to him in Spanish?"

"In any language you like. There's an interface, after all. He'll think it's his own language coming in, no matter what, sixteenth-century Spanish. And he'll answer you in what seems like Spanish to him, but you'll hear it in English."

"Are you sure?"

"Of course."

"And you don't mind if I make contact with him?"

"Whatever you like."

"It won't upset his calibration, or anything?"

"It won't do any harm at all, Harry."

"Fine. Let me talk to him, then."

There was a disturbance in the air ahead, a shifting, a swirling, like a little whirlwind. Pizarro halted and watched it for a moment, wondering what was coming next. A demon arriving to torment him, maybe. Or an angel. Whatever it was, he was ready for it.

Then a voice out of the whirlwind said, in that same comically exaggerated Castilian Spanish that Pizarro himself had found himself speaking a little while before, "Can you hear me?"

"I hear you, yes. I don't see you. Where are you?"

"Right in front of you. Wait a second. I'll show you." Out of the whirlwind came a strange face that hovered in the middle of nowhere, a face without a body, a lean face, close-shaven, no beard at all, no mustache, the hair cut very short, dark eyes set close together. He had never seen a face like that before.

"What are you?" Pizarro asked. "A demon or an angel?"

"Neither one." Indeed he didn't sound very demonic. "A man, just like you."

"Not much like me, I think. Is a face all there is to you, or do you have a body too?"

"All you see of me is a face?"

"Yes."

"Wait a second."

"I will wait as long as I have to. I have plenty of time."

The face disappeared. Then it returned, attached to the body of a big, wide-shouldered man who was wearing a long loose gray robe, something like a priest's cassock, but much more ornate, with points of glowing light gleaming on it everywhere. Then the body vanished and Pizarro could see only the face again. He could make no sense out of any of this. He began to understand how the Indians must have felt when the first Spaniards came over the horizon, riding horses, carrying guns, wearing armor.

"You are very strange. Are you an Englishman, maybe?"

"American."

"Ah," Pizarro said, as though that made things better. "An American. And what is that?"

The face wavered and blurred for a moment. There was mysterious new agitation in the thick white clouds surrounding it. Then the face grew steady and said, "America is a country north of Peru. A very large country, where many people live."

"You mean New Spain, which was Mexico, where my kinsman Cortes is Captain-General?"

"North of Mexico. Far to the north of it."

Pizarro shrugged. "I know nothing of those places. Or not very much. There is an island called Florida, yes? And stories of cities of gold, but I think they are only stories. I found the gold, in Peru. Enough to choke on, I found. Tell me this, am I in heaven now?"

"No."

"Then this is hell?"

"Not that, either. Where you are—it's very difficult to explain, actually—"

"I am in America."

"Yes. In America, yes."

"And am I dead?"

There was silence for a moment.

"No, not dead," the voice said uneasily.

"You are lying to me, I think."

"How could we be speaking with each other, if you were dead?"

Pizarro laughed hoarsely. "Are you asking *me*? I understand nothing of what is happening to me in this place. Where are my priests?

50

Where is my page? Send me my brother!" He glared. "Well? Why don't you get them for me?"

"They aren't here. You're here all by yourself, Don Francisco."

"In America. All by myself in your America. Show me your America, then. Is there such a place? Is America all clouds and whorls of light? Where is America? Let me see America. Prove to me that I am in America."

There was another silence, longer than the last. Then the face disappeared and the wall of white cloud began to boil and churn more fiercely than before. Pizarro stared into the midst of it, feeling a mingled sense of curiosity and annoyance. The face did not reappear. He saw nothing at all. He was being toyed with. He was a prisoner in some strange place and they were treating him like a child, like a dog, like— like an Indian. Perhaps this was the retribution for what he had done to King Atahuallpa, then, that fine noble foolish man who had given himself up to him in all innocence, and whom he had put to death so that he might have the gold of Atahuallpa's kingdom.

Well, so be it, Pizarro thought. Atahuallpa accepted all that befell him without complaint and without fear, and so will I. Christ will be my guardian, and if there is no Christ, well, then I will have no guardian, and so be it. So be it.

The voice out of the whirlwind said suddenly, "Look, Don Francisco. This is America."

A picture appeared on the wall of cloud. It was a kind of picture Pizarro had never before encountered or even imagined, one that seemed to open before him like a gate and sweep him in and carry him along through a vista of changing scenes depicted in brilliant, vivid bursts of color. It was like flying high above the land, looking down on an infinite scroll of miracles. He saw vast cities without walls, roadways that unrolled like endless skeins of white ribbon, huge lakes, mighty rivers, gigantic mountains, everything speeding past him so swiftly that he could scarcely absorb any of it. In moments it all became chaotic in his mind: the buildings taller than the highest cathedral spire, the swarming masses of people, the shining metal chariots without beasts to draw them, the stupendous landscapes, the close-packed complexity of it all. Watching all this, he felt the fine old hunger taking possession of him again: he wanted to grasp this strange vast place, and seize it, and clutch it close, and ransack it for all it was worth. But the thought of that was overwhelming. His eyes grew glassy and his heart began to pound so terrifyingly that he supposed he would be able to feel it thumping if he put his hand to the front of his armor. He turned away, muttering, "Enough. Enough."

The terrifying picture vanished. Gradually the clamor of his heart subsided.

Then he began to laugh.

"Peru!" he cried. "Peru was nothing, next to your America! Peru was a hole! Peru was mud! How ignorant I was! I went to Peru, when there was America, ten thousand times as grand! I wonder what I could find, in America." He smacked his lips and winked. Then, chuckling, he said, "But don't be afraid. I won't try to conquer your America. I'm too old for that now. And perhaps America would have been too much for me, even before. Perhaps." He grinned savagely at the troubled staring face of the short-haired beardless man, the American. "I really am dead, is this not so? I feel no hunger, I feel no pain, no thirst, when I put my hand to my body I do not feel even my body. I am like one who lies dreaming. But this is no dream. Am I a ghost?"

"Not—exactly."

"Not exactly a ghost! Not exactly! No one with half the brains of a pig would talk like that. What is that supposed to mean?"

"It's not easy explaining it in words you would understand, Don Francisco."

"No, of course not. I am very stupid, as everyone knows, and that is why I conquered Peru, because I was so very stupid. But let it pass. I am not exactly a ghost, but I am dead all the same, right?"

"Well—"

"I am dead, yes. But somehow I have not gone to hell or even to purgatory but I am still in the world, only it is much later now. I have slept as the dead sleep, and now I have awakened in some year that is far beyond my time, and it is the time of America. Is this not so? Who is king now? Who is pope? What year is this? 1750? 1800?"

"The year 2130," the face said, after some hesitation.

"Ah." Pizarro tugged thoughtfully at his lower lip. "And the king? Who is king?"

A long pause. "Alfonso is his name," said the face.

"Alfonso? The kings of Aragon were called Alfonso. The father of Ferdinand, he was Alfonso. Alfonso V, he was."

"Alfonso XIX is King of Spain now."

"Ah. Ah. And the pope? Who is pope?"

52

A pause again. Not to know the name of the pope, immediately upon being asked? How strange. Demon or no, this was a fool.

"Pius," said the voice, when some time had passed. "Pius XVI."

"The sixteenth Pius," said Pizarro somberly. "Jesus and Mary, the sixteenth Pius! What has become of me? Long dead, is what I am. Still unwashed of all my sins. I can feel them clinging to my skin like mud, still. And you are a sorcerer, you American, and you have brought me to life again. Eh? Eh? Is that not so?"

"It is something like that, Don Francisco," the face admitted.

"So you speak your Spanish strangely because you no longer understand the right way of speaking it. Eh? Even I speak Spanish in a strange way, and I speak it in a voice that does not sound like my own. No one speaks Spanish any more, eh? Eh? Only American, they speak. Eh? But you try to speak Spanish, only it comes out stupidly. And you have caused me to speak the same way, thinking it is the way I spoke, though you are wrong. Well, you can do miracles, but I suppose you can't do everything perfectly, even in this land of miracles of the year 2130. Eh? Eh?" Pizarro leaned forward intently. "What do you say? You thought I was a fool, because I don't have reading and writing? I am not so ignorant, eh? I understand things quickly."

"You understand very quickly indeed."

"But you have knowledge of many things that are unknown to me. You must know the manner of my death, for example. How strange that is, talking to you of the manner of my death, but you must know it, eh? When did it come to me? And how? Did it come in my sleep? No, no, how could that be? They die in their sleep in Spain, but not in Peru. How was it, then? I was set upon by cowards, was I? Some brother of Atahuallpa, falling upon me as I stepped out of my house? A slave sent by the Inca Manco, or one of those others? No. No. The Indians would not harm me, for all that I did to them. It was the young Almagro who took me down, was it not, in vengeance for his father, or Juan de Herrada, eh? or perhaps even Picado, my own secretary—no, not Picado, he was my man, always—but maybe Alvarado, the young one, Diego—well, one of those, and it would have been sudden, very sudden or I would have been able to stop them—am I right, am I speaking the truth? Tell me. You know these things. Tell me of the manner of my dying." There was no answer. Pizarro shaded his eyes and peered into the dazzling pearly whiteness. He was no longer able to see the face of the American. "Are you there?" Pizarro said. "Where have you gone? Were you only a dream? American! American! Where have you gone?"

✸

The break in contact was jolting. Tanner sat rigid, hands trembling, lips tightly clamped. Pizarro, in the holotank, was no more than a distant little streak of color now, no larger than his thumb, gesticulating amid the swirling clouds. The vitality of him, the arrogance, the fierce probing curiosity, the powerful hatreds and jealousies, the strength that had come from vast ventures recklessly conceived and desperately seen through to triumph, all the things that were Francisco Pizarro, all that Tanner had felt an instant before—all that had vanished at the flick of a finger.

After a moment or two Tanner felt the shock beginning to ease. He turned toward Richardson.

"What happened?"

"I had to pull you out of there. I didn't want you telling him anything about how he died."

"I don't know how he died."

"Well, neither does he, and I didn't want to chance it that you did. There's no predicting what sort of psychological impact that kind of knowledge might have on him."

"You talk about him as though he's alive."

"Isn't he?" Richardson said.

"If I said a thing like that, you'd tell me that I was being ignorant and unscientific."

Richardson smiled faintly. "You're right. But somehow I trust myself to know what I'm saying when I say that he's alive. I know I don't mean it literally and I'm not sure about you. What did you think of him, anyway?"

"He's amazing," Tanner said. "Really amazing. The strength of him—I could feel it pouring out at me in waves. And his mind! So quick, the way he picked up on everything. Guessing that he must be in the future. Wanting to know what number pope was in office. Wanting to see what America looked like. And the cockiness of him! Telling me that he's not up to the conquest of America, that he might have tried for it instead of Peru a few years earlier, but not now, now he's a little too old for that. Incredible! Nothing could faze him for long, even when he realized that he must have been dead for a long time. Wanting to know how he died, even!" Tanner frowned. "What age did you make him, anyway, when you put this program together?"

"About sixty. Five or six years after the conquest, and a year or two before he died. At the height of his power, that is."

"I suppose you couldn't have let him have any knowledge of his actual death. That way he'd be too much like some kind of a ghost."

"That's what we thought. We set the cutoff at a time when he had done everything that he had set out to do, when he was the complete Pizarro. But before the end. He didn't need to know about that. Nobody does. That's why I had to yank you, you see? In case you knew. And started to tell him."

Tanner shook his head. "If I ever knew, I've forgotten it. How did it happen?"

"Exactly as he guessed: at the hands of his own comrades."

"So he saw it coming."

"At the age we made him, he already knew that a civil war had started in South America, that the conquistadores were quarreling over the division of the spoils. We built that much into him. He knows that his partner Almagro has turned against him and been beaten in battle, and that they've executed him. What he doesn't know, but obviously can expect, is that Almagro's friends are going to break into his house and try to kill him. He's got it all figured out pretty much as it's going to happen. As it *did* happen, I should say."

"Incredible. To be that shrewd."

"He was a son of a bitch, yes. But he was a genius too."

"Was he, really? Or is it that you made him one when you set up the program for him?"

"All we put in were the objective details of his life, patterns of event and response. Plus an overlay of commentary by others, his contemporaries and later historians familiar with the record, providing an extra dimension of character density. Put in enough of that kind of stuff and apparently they add up to the whole personality. It isn't *my* personality or that of anybody else who worked on this project, Harry. When you put in Pizarro's set of events and responses you wind up getting Pizarro. You get the ruthlessness and you get the brilliance. Put in a different set, you get someone else. And what we've finally seen, this time, is that when we do our work right we get something out of the computer that's bigger than the sum of what we put in."

"Are you sure?"

Richardson said, "Did you notice that he complained about the Spanish that he thought you were speaking?"

"Yes. He said that it sounded strange, that nobody seemed to know how to speak proper Spanish any more. I didn't quite follow that. Does the interface you built speak lousy Spanish?"

"Evidently it speaks lousy sixteenth-century Spanish," Richardson said. "Nobody knows what sixteenth-century Spanish actually sounded like. We can only guess. Apparently we didn't guess very well."

"But how would *he* know? You synthesized him in the first place! If you don't know how Spanish sounded in his time, how would he? All he should know about Spanish, or about anything, is what you put into him."

"Exactly," Richardson said.

"But that doesn't make any sense, Lew!"

"He also said that the Spanish he heard himself speaking was no good, and that his own voice didn't sound right to him either. That we had *caused* him to speak this way, thinking that was how he actually spoke, but we were wrong."

"How could he possibly know what his voice really sounded like, if all he is is a simulation put together by people who don't have the slightest notion of what his voice really—"

"I don't have any idea," said Richardson quietly. "But he *does* know."

"Does he? Or is this just some diabolical Pizarro-like game that he's playing to unsettle us, because *that's* in his character as you devised it?"

"I think he does know," Richardson said.

"Where's he finding it out, then?"

"It's there. We don't know where, but he does. It's somewhere in the data that we put through the permutation network, even if we don't know it and even though we couldn't find it now if we set out to look for it. He can find it. He can't manufacture that kind of knowledge by magic, but he can assemble what look to us like seemingly irrelevant bits and come up with new information leading to a conclusion which is meaningful to him. That's what we mean by artificial intelligence, Harry. We've finally got a program that works something like the human brain: by leaps of intuition so sudden and broad that they seem inexplicable and non-quantifiable, even if they really aren't. We've fed in enough stuff so that he can assimilate a whole stew of ostensibly unrelated data and come up with new information. We don't just have a ventriloquist's dummy in that tank. We've got something that thinks it's Pizarro and thinks like Pizarro and knows things that Pizarro knew and we don't. Which means we've accomplished the qualitative jump in artificial intelligence capacity that we set out to achieve with this project. It's awesome. I get shivers down my back when I think about it."

"I do too," Tanner said. "But not so much from awe as fear."

"Fear?"

"Knowing now that he has capabilities beyond those he was programmed for, how can you be so absolutely certain that he can't commandeer your network somehow and get himself loose?"

"It's technically impossible. All he is is electromagnetic impulses. I can pull the plug on him any time I like. There's nothing to panic over here. Believe me, Harry."

"I'm trying to."

"I can show you the schematics. We've got a phenomenal simulation in that computer, yes. But it's still only a simulation. It isn't a vampire, it isn't a werewolf, it isn't anything supernatural. It's just the best damned computer simulation anyone's ever made."

"It makes me uneasy. *He* makes me uneasy."

"He should. The power of the man, the indomitable nature of him— why do you think I summoned him up, Harry? He's got something that we don't understand in this country any more. I want us to study him. I want us to try to learn what that kind of drive and determination is really like. Now that you've talked to him, now that you've touched his spirit, of course you're shaken up by him. He radiates tremendous confidence. He radiates fantastic faith in himself. That kind of man can achieve anything he wants—even conquer the whole Inca empire with a hundred fifty men, or however many it was. But I'm not frightened of what we've put together here. And you shouldn't be either. We should all be damned proud of it. You as well as the people on the technical side. And you will be, too."

"I hope you're right," Tanner said.

"You'll see."

For a long moment Tanner stared in silence at the holotank, where the image of Pizarro had been.

"Okay," said Tanner finally. "Maybe I'm overreacting. Maybe I'm sounding like the ignoramus layman that I am. I'll take it on faith that you'll be able to keep your phantoms in their boxes."

"We will," Richardson said.

"Let's hope so. All right," said Tanner. "So what's your next move?"

Richardson looked puzzled. "My next move?"

"With this project? Where does it go from here?"

Hesitantly Richardson said, "There's no formal proposal yet. We thought we'd wait until we had approval from you on the initial phase of the work, and then—"

"How does this sound?" Tanner asked. "I'd like to see you start in on another simulation right away."

"Well—yes, yes, of course—"

"And when you've got him worked up, Lew, would it be feasible for you to put him right there in the tank with Pizarro?"

Richardson looked startled. "To have a sort of dialog with him, you mean?"

"Yes."

"I suppose we could do that," Richardson said cautiously. "*Should* do that. Yes. Yes. A very interesting suggestion, as a matter of fact." He ventured an uneasy smile. Up till now Tanner had kept in the background of this project, a mere management functionary, an observer, virtually an outsider. This was something new, his interjecting himself into the planning process, and plainly Richardson didn't know what to make of it. Tanner watched him fidget. After a little pause Richardson said, "Was there anyone in particular you had in mind for us to try next?"

"Is that new parallax thing of yours ready to try?" Tanner asked. "The one that's supposed to compensate for time distortion and myth contamination?"

"Just about. But we haven't tested—"

"Good," Tanner said. "Here's your chance. What about trying for Socrates?"

There was billowing whiteness below him, and on every side, as though all the world were made of fleece. He wondered if it might be snow. That was not something he was really familiar with. It snowed once in a great while in Athens, yes, but usually only a light dusting that melted in the morning sun. Of course he had seen snow aplenty when he had been up north in the war, at Potidaea, in the time of Pericles. But that had been long ago; and that stuff, as best he remembered it, had not been much like this. There was no quality of coldness about the whiteness that surrounded him now. It could just as readily be great banks of clouds.

But what would clouds be doing *below* him? Clouds, he thought, are mere vapor, air and water, no substance to them at all. Their natural place was overhead. Clouds that gathered at one's feet had no true quality of cloudness about them.

Snow that had no coldness? Clouds that had no buoyancy? Nothing in this place seemed to possess any quality that was proper to itself in this place, including himself. He seemed to be walking, but his feet touched nothing at all. It was more like moving through air. But how could one move in the air? Aristophanes, in that mercilessly mocking play of his, had sent him floating through the clouds suspended in a basket, and made him say things like, "I am traversing the air and contemplating the sun." That was Aristophanes' way of playing with him, and he had not been seriously upset, though his friends had been very hurt on his behalf. Still, that was only a play.

This felt real, insofar as it felt like anything at all.

Perhaps he was dreaming, and the nature of his dream was that he thought he was really doing the things he had done in Aristophanes' play. What was that lovely line? "I have to suspend my brain and mingle the subtle essence of my mind with this air, which is of the same nature, in order clearly to penetrate the things of heaven." Good old Aristophanes! Nothing was sacred to him! Except, of course, those things that were truly sacred, such as wisdom, truth, virtue. "I would have discovered nothing if I had remained on the ground and pondered from below the things that are above: for the earth by its force attracts the sap of the mind to itself. It's the same way with watercress." And Socrates began to laugh.

He held his hands before him and studied them, the short sturdy fingers, the thick powerful wrists. His hands, yes. His old plain hands that had stood him in good stead all his life, when he had worked as a stonemason as his father had, when he had fought in his city's wars, when he had trained at the gymnasium. But now when he touched them to his face he felt nothing. There should be a chin here, a forehead, yes, a blunt stubby nose, thick lips; but there was nothing. He was touching air. He could put his hand right through the place where his face should be. He could put one hand against the other, and press with all his might, and feel nothing.

This is a very strange place indeed, he thought.

Perhaps it is that place of pure forms that young Plato liked to speculate about, where everything is perfect and nothing is quite real. Those are ideal clouds all around me, not real ones. This is ideal air upon which I walk. I myself am the ideal Socrates, liberated from my coarse ordinary body. Could it be? Well, maybe so. He stood for a while, considering that possibility. The thought came to him that this might be the life after life, in which case he might meet some of the gods, if there were any gods in the first place, and if he could manage to find them. I would like that, he thought. Perhaps they would be willing to speak with me. Athena would discourse with me on wisdom, or Hermes on speed, or Ares on the nature of courage, or Zeus on—well, whatever Zeus cared to speak on. Of course I would seem to be the merest fool to them, but that would be all right: anyone who expects to hold discourse with the gods as though he were their equal *is* a fool. I have no such illusion. If there are gods at all, surely they are far superior to me in all respects, for otherwise why would men regard them as gods?

Of course he had serious doubts that the gods existed at all. But if they did, it was reasonable to think that they might be found in a place such as this.

He looked up. The sky was radiant with brilliant golden light. He took a deep breath and smiled and set out across the fleecy nothingness of this airy world to see if he could find the gods.

Tanner said, "What do you think now? Still so pessimistic?"

"It's too early to say," said Richardson, looking glum.

"He *looks* like Socrates, doesn't he?"

"That was the easy part. We've got plenty of descriptions of Socrates that came down from people who knew him, the flat wide nose, the bald head, the thick lips, the short neck. A standard Socrates face that everybody recognizes, just as they do Sherlock Holmes, or Don Quixote. So that's how we made him look. It doesn't signify anything important. It's what's going on inside his head that'll determine whether we really have Socrates."

"He seems calm and good-humored as he wanders around in there. The way a philosopher should."

"Pizarro seemed just as much of a philosopher when we turned him loose in the tank."

"Pizarro may *be* just as much of a philosopher," Tanner said. "Neither man's the sort who'd be likely to panic if he found himself in some mysterious place." Richardson's negativism was beginning to bother him. It was as if the two men had exchanged places: Richardson now uncertain of the range and power of his own program, Tanner pushing the way on and on toward bigger and better things.

Bleakly Richardson said, "I'm still pretty skeptical. We've tried the new parallax filters, yes. But I'm afraid we're going to run into the same problem the French did with Don Quixote, and that we did with Holmes and Moses and Caesar. There's too much contamination of the data by myth and fantasy. The Socrates who has come down to us is as much fictional as real, or maybe *all* fictional. For all we know, Plato made up everything we think we know about him, the same way Conan Doyle made up Holmes. And what we're going to get, I'm afraid, will be something second-hand, something lifeless, something lacking in the spark of self-directed intelligence that we're after."

"But the new filters—"

"Perhaps. Perhaps."

Tanner shook his head stubbornly. "Holmes and Don Quixote are fiction through and through. They exist in only one dimension, constructed for us by their authors. You cut through the distortions and fantasies of later readers and commentators and all you find underneath is a made-up character. A lot of Socrates may have been invented by Plato for his own purposes, but a lot wasn't. He really existed. He took an actual part in civic activities in fifth-century Athens. He figures in books by a lot of other contemporaries of his besides Plato's dialogues. That gives us the parallax you're looking for, doesn't it—the view of him from more than one viewpoint?"

"Maybe it does. Maybe not. We got nowhere with Moses. Was *he* fictional?"

"Who can say? All you had to go by was the Bible. And a ton of Biblical commentary, for whatever that was worth. Not much, apparently."

"And Caesar? You're not going to tell me that Caesar wasn't real," said Richardson. "But what we have of him is evidently contaminated with myth. When we synthesized him we got nothing but a caricature, and I don't have to remind you how fast even that broke down into sheer gibberish."

"Not relevant," Tanner said. "Caesar was early in the project. You know much more about what you're doing now. I think this is going to work."

Richardson's dogged pessimism, Tanner decided, must be a defense mechanism, designed to insulate himself against the possibility of a new failure. Socrates, after all, hadn't been Richardson's own choice. And this was the first time he had used these new enhancement methods, the parallax program that was the latest refinement of the process.

Tanner looked at him. Richardson remained silent.

"Go on," Tanner said. "Bring up Pizarro and let the two of them talk to each other. Then we'll find out what sort of Socrates you've conjured up here."

Once again there was a disturbance in the distance, a little dark blur on the pearly horizon, a blotch, a flaw in the gleaming whiteness. Another demon is arriving, Pizarro thought. Or perhaps it is the same one as before, the American, the one who liked to show himself only as a face, with short hair and no beard.

But as this one drew closer Pizarro saw that he was different from the last, short and stocky, with broad shoulders and a deep chest. He was nearly bald and his thick beard was coarse and unkempt. He looked old, at least sixty, maybe sixty-five. He looked very ugly, too, with bulging eyes and a flat nose that had wide, flaring nostrils, and a neck so short that his oversized head seemed to sprout straight from his trunk. All he wore was a thin, ragged brown robe. His feet were bare.

"You, there," Pizarro called out. "You! Demon! Are you also an American, demon?"

"Your pardon. An Athenian, did you say?"

"*American* is what I said. That's what the last one was. Is that where you come from too, demon? America?"

A shrug. "No, I think not. I am of Athens." There was a curious mocking twinkle in the demon's eyes.

"A Greek? This demon is a Greek?"

"I am of Athens," the ugly one said again. "My name is Socrates, the son of Sophroniscus. I could not tell you what a Greek is, so perhaps I may be one, but I think not, unless a Greek is what you call a man of Athens." He spoke in a slow, plodding way, like one who was exceedingly stupid. Pizarro had sometimes met men like this before, and in his experience they were generally not as stupid as they wanted to be taken for. He felt caution rising in him. "And I am no demon, but just a plain man: very plain, as you can easily see."

Pizarro snorted. "You like to chop words, do you?"

"It is not the worst of amusements, my friend," said the other, and put his hands together behind his back in the most casual way, and stood there calmly, smiling, looking off into the distance, rocking back and forth on the balls of his feet.

"Well?" Tanner said. "Do we have Socrates or not? I say that's the genuine article there."

Richardson looked up and nodded. He seemed relieved and quizzical both at once. "So far so good, I have to say. He's coming through real and true."

"Yes."

"We may actually have worked past the problem of information contamination that ruined some of the earlier simulations. We're not getting any of the signal degradation we encountered then."

"He's some character, isn't he?" Tanner said. "I liked the way he just walked right up to Pizarro without the slightest sign of uneasiness. He's not at all afraid of him."

"Why should he be?" Richardson asked.

"Wouldn't you? If you were walking along through God knows what kind of unearthly place, not knowing where you were or how you got there, and suddenly you saw a ferocious-looking bastard like Pizarro standing in front of you wearing full armor and carrying a sword—" Tanner shook his head. "Well, maybe not. He's Socrates, after all, and Socrates wasn't afraid of anything except boredom."

"And Pizarro's just a simulation. Nothing but software."

"So you've been telling me all along. But Socrates doesn't know that."

"True," Richardson said. He seemed lost in thought a moment. "Perhaps there *is* some risk."

"Huh?"

"If our Socrates is anything like the one in Plato, and he surely ought to be, then he's capable of making a considerable pest of himself. Pizarro may not care for Socrates' little verbal games. If he doesn't feel like playing, I suppose there's a theoretical possibility that he'll engage in some sort of aggressive response."

That took Tanner by surprise. He swung around and said, "Are you telling me that there's some way he can *harm* Socrates?"

"Who knows?" said Richardson. "In the real world one program can certainly crash another one. Maybe one simulation can be dangerous to another one. This is all new territory for all of us, Harry. Including the people in the tank."

The tall grizzled-looking man said, scowling, "You tell me you're an Athenian, but not a Greek. What sense am I supposed to make of that? I could ask Pedro de Candia, I guess, who is a Greek but not an Athenian. But he's not here. Perhaps you're just a fool, eh? Or you think I am."

"I have no idea what you are. Could it be that you are a god?"

"A *god?*"

"Yes," Socrates said. He studied the other impassively. His face was harsh, his gaze was cold. "Perhaps you are Ares. You have a fierce warlike look about you, and you wear armor, but not such armor as I have ever seen. This place is so strange that it might well be the abode of the gods, and that could be a god's armor you wear, I suppose. If you are Ares, then I salute you with the respect that is due you. I am Socrates of Athens, the stonemason's son."

"You talk a lot of nonsense. I don't know your Ares."

"Why, the god of war, of course! Everyone knows that. Except barbarians, that is. Are you a barbarian, then? You sound like one, I must say—but then, I seem to sound like a barbarian myself, and I've spoken the tongue of Hellas all my life. There are many mysteries here, indeed."

"Your language problem again," Tanner said. "Couldn't you even get classical Greek to come out right? Or are they both speaking Spanish to each other?"

"Pizarro thinks they're speaking Spanish. Socrates thinks they're speaking Greek. And of course the Greek is off. We don't know how *anything* that was spoken before the age of recordings sounded. All we can do is guess."

"But can't you—"

"Shhh," Richardson said.

Pizarro said, "I may be a bastard, but I'm no barbarian, fellow, so curb your tongue. And let's have no more blasphemy out of you either."

"If I blaspheme, forgive me. It is in innocence. Tell me where I trespass, and I will not do it again."

"This crazy talk of gods. Of my being a god. I'd expect a heathen to talk like that, but not a Greek. But maybe you're a heathen kind of Greek, and not to be blamed. It's heathens who see gods everywhere. Do I look like a god to you? I am Francisco Pizarro, of Trujillo in Estremadura, the son of the famous soldier Gonzalo Pizarro, colonel of infantry, who served in the wars of Gonzalo de Cordova whom men call the Great Captain. I have fought some wars myself."

"Then you are not a god but simply a soldier? Good. I too have been a soldier. I am more at ease with soldiers than with gods, as most people are, I would think."

"A soldier? You?" Pizarro smiled. This shabby ordinary little man, more bedraggled-looking than any self-respecting groom would be, a soldier? "In which wars?"

"The wars of Athens. I fought at Potidaea, where the Corinthians were making trouble, and withholding the tribute that was due us. It was very cold there, and the siege was long and bleak, but we did our duty. I fought again some years later at Delium against the Boeotians. Laches was our general then, but it went badly for us, and we did our best fighting in retreat. And then," Socrates said, "when Brasidas was in Amphipolis, and they sent Cleon to drive him out, I—"

"Enough," said Pizarro with an impatient wave of his hand. "These wars are unknown to me." A private soldier, a man of the ranks, no doubt. "Well, then this is the place where they send dead soldiers, I suppose."

"Are we dead, then?"

"Long ago. There's an Alfonso who's king, and a Pius who's pope, and you wouldn't believe their numbers. Pius the Sixteenth, I think the demon said. And the American said also that it is the year 2130. The last year that I can remember was 1539. What about you?"

The one who called himself Socrates shrugged again. "In Athens we use a different reckoning. But let us say, for argument's sake, that we are dead. I think that is very likely, considering what sort of place this seems to be, and how airy I find my body to be. So we have died, and this is the life after life. I wonder: is this a place where virtuous men are sent, or those who were not virtuous? Or do all men go to the same place after death, whether they were virtuous or not? What would you say?"

"I haven't figured that out yet," said Pizarro.

"Well, were you virtuous in your life, or not?"

"Did I sin, you mean?"

"Yes, we could use that word."

"Did I sin, he wants to know," said Pizarro, amazed. "He asks, Was I a sinner? Did I live a virtuous life? What business is that of his?"

"Humor me," said Socrates. "For the sake of the argument, if you will, allow me a few small questions—"

"So it's starting," Tanner said. "You see? You really *did* do it! Socrates is drawing him into a dialog!"

Richardson's eyes were glowing. "He is, yes. How marvelous this is, Harry!"

"Socrates is going to talk rings around him."

"I'm not so sure of that," Richardson said.

"I gave as good as I got," said Pizarro. "If I was injured, I gave injury back. There's no sin in that. It's only common sense. A man does what is necessary to survive and to protect his place in the world. Sometimes I might forget a fast day, yes, or use the Lord's name in vain—those are sins, I suppose, Fray Vicente was always after me for things like that— but does that make me a sinner? I did my penances as soon as I could find time for them. It's a sinful world and I'm no different from anyone else, so why be harsh on me? Eh? God made me as I am. I'm done in His image. And I have faith in His Son."

"So you are a virtuous man, then?"

"I'm not a sinner, at any rate. As I told you, if ever I sinned I did my contrition, which made it the same as if the sin hadn't ever happened."

"Indeed," said Socrates. "Then you are a virtuous man and I have come to a good place. But I want to be absolutely sure. Tell me again: is your conscience completely clear?"

"What are you, a confessor?"

"Only an ignorant man seeking understanding. Which you can provide, by taking part with me in the exploration. If I have come to the place of virtuous men, then I must have been virtuous myself when I lived. Ease my mind, therefore, and let me know whether there is anything on your soul that you regret having done."

Pizarro stirred uneasily. "Well," he said, "I killed a king."

"A wicked one? An enemy of your city?"

"No. He was wise and kind."

"Then you have reason for regret indeed. For surely that is a sin, to kill a wise king."

"But he was a heathen."

"A what?"

"He denied God."

"He denied his own god?" said Socrates. "Then perhaps it was not so wrong to kill him."

"No. He denied mine. He *preferred* his own. And so he was a heathen. And all his people were heathens, since they followed his way. That could not be. They were at risk of eternal damnation because they followed him. I killed him for the sake of his people's souls. I killed him out of the love of God."

"But would you not say that all gods are the reflection of the one God?"

Pizarro considered that. "In a way, that's true, I suppose."

"And is the service of God not itself godly?"

"How could it be anything but godly, Socrates?"

"And you would say that one who serves his god faithfully according to the teachings of his god is behaving in a godly way?"

Frowning, Pizarro said, "Well—if you look at it that way, yes—"

"Then I think the king you killed was a godly man, and by killing him you sinned against God."

"Wait a minute!"

"But think of it: by serving his god he must also have served yours, for any servant of a god is a servant of the true God who encompasses all our imagined gods."

"No," said Pizarro sullenly. "How could he have been a servant of God? He knew nothing of Jesus. He had no understanding of the Trinity. When the priest offered him the Bible, he threw it to the ground in scorn. He was a heathen, Socrates. And so are you. You don't know anything of these matters at all, if you think that Atahuallpa was godly. Or if you think you're going to get me to think so."

"Indeed I have very little knowledge of anything. But you say he was a wise man, and kind?"

"In his heathen way."

"And a good king to his people?"

"So it seemed. They were a thriving people when I found them."

"Yet he was not godly."

"I told you. He had never had the sacraments, and in fact he spurned them right up until the moment of his death, when he accepted baptism. *Then* he came to be godly. But by then the sentence of death was upon him and it was too late for anything to save him."

"Baptism? Tell me what that is, Pizarro."

"A sacrament."

"And that is?"

"A holy rite. Done with holy water, by a priest. It admits one to Holy Mother Church, and brings forgiveness from sin both original and actual, and gives the gift of the Holy Spirit."

"You must tell me more about these things another time. So you made this good king godly by this baptism? And then you killed him?"

"Yes."

"But he was godly when you killed him. Surely, then, to kill him was a sin."

"He had to die, Socrates!"

"And why was that?" asked the Athenian.

* * *

"Socrates is closing in for the kill," Tanner said. "Watch this!"

"I'm watching. But there isn't going to be any kill," said Richardson. "Their basic assumptions are too far apart."

"You'll see."

"Will I?"

* * *

68

Pizarro said, "I've already told you why he had to die. It was because his people followed him in all things. And so they worshipped the sun, because he said the sun was God. Their souls would have gone to hell if we had allowed them to continue that way."

"But if they followed him in all things," said Socrates, "then surely they would have followed him into baptism, and become godly, and thus done that which was pleasing to you and to your god! Is that not so?"

"No," said Pizarro, twisting his fingers in his beard.

"Why do you think that?"

"Because the king agreed to be baptized only after we had sentenced him to death. He was in the way, don't you see? He was an obstacle to our power! So we had to get rid of him. He would never have led his people to the truth of his own free will. That was why we had to kill him. But we didn't want to kill his soul as well as his body, so we said to him, Look, Atahuallpa, we're going to put you to death, but if you let us baptize you we'll strangle you quickly, and if you don't we'll burn you alive and it'll be very slow. So of course he agreed to be baptized, and we strangled him. What choice was there for anybody? He had to die. He still didn't believe the true faith, as we all well knew. Inside his head he was as big a heathen as ever. But he died a Christian all the same."

"A what?"

"A Christian! A Christian! One who believes in Jesus Christ the Son of God!"

"The *son* of God," Socrates said, sounding puzzled. "And do Christians believe in God too, or only his son?"

"What a fool you are!"

"I would not deny that."

"There is God the Father, and God the Son, and then there is the Holy Spirit."

"Ah," said Socrates. "And which one did your Atahuallpa believe in, then, when the strangler came for him?"

"None of them."

"And yet he died a Christian? Without believing in any of your three gods? How is that?"

"Because of the baptism," said Pizarro in rising annoyance. "What does it matter what he believed? The priest sprinkled the water on him! The priest said the words! If the rite is properly performed, the soul is saved regardless of what the man understands or believes! How else

69

could you baptize an infant? An infant understands nothing and believes nothing—but he becomes a Christian when the water touches him!"

"Much of this is mysterious to me," said Socrates. "But I see that you regard the king you killed as godly as well as wise, because he was washed by the water your gods require, and so you killed a good king who now lived in the embrace of your gods because of the baptism. Which seems wicked to me; and so this cannot be the place where the virtuous are sent after death, so it must be that I too was not virtuous, or else that I have misunderstood everything about this place and why we are in it."

"Damn you, are you trying to drive me crazy?" Pizarro roared, fumbling at the hilt of his sword. He drew it and waved it around in fury. "If you don't shut your mouth I'll cut you in thirds!"

"Uh-oh," Tanner said. "So much for the dialectical method."

Socrates said mildly, "It isn't my intention to cause you any annoyance, my friend. I'm only trying to learn a few things."

"You are a fool!"

"That is certainly true, as I have already acknowledged several times. Well, if you mean to strike me with your sword, go ahead. But I don't think it'll accomplish very much."

"Damn you," Pizarro muttered. He stared at his sword and shook his head. "No. No, it won't do any good, will it? It would go through you like air. But you'd just stand there and let me try to cut you down, and not even blink, right? Right?" He shook his head. "And yet you aren't stupid. You argue like the shrewdest priest I've ever known."

"In truth I am stupid," said Socrates. "I know very little at all. But I strive constantly to attain some understanding of the world, or at least to understand something of myself."

Pizarro glared at him. "No," he said. "I won't buy this false pride of yours. I have a little understanding of people myself, old man. I'm on to your game."

"What game is that, Pizarro?"

"I can see your arrogance. I see that you believe you're the wisest man in the world, and that it's your mission to go around educating poor sword-waving fools like me. And you pose as a fool to disarm your adversaries before you humiliate them."

"Score one for Pizarro," Richardson said. "He's wise to Socrates' little tricks, all right."

"Maybe he's read some Plato," Tanner suggested.

"He was illiterate."

"That was then. This is now."

"Not guilty," said Richardson. "He's operating on peasant shrewdness alone, and you damned well know it."

"I wasn't being serious," Tanner said. He leaned forward, peering toward the holotank. "God, what an astonishing thing this is, listening to them going at it. They seem absolutely real."

"They are," said Richardson.

"No, Pizarro, I am not wise at all," Socrates said. "But, stupid as I am, it may be that I am not the least wise man who ever lived."

"You think you're wiser than I am, don't you?"

"How can I say? First tell me how wise you are."

"Wise enough to begin my life as a bastard tending pigs and finish it as Captain-General of Peru."

"Ah, then you must be very wise."

"I think so, yes."

"Yet you killed a wise king because he wasn't wise enough to worship God the way you wished him to. Was that so wise of you, Pizarro? How did his people take it, when they found out that their king had been killed?"

"They rose in rebellion against us. They destroyed their own temples and palaces, and hid their gold and silver from us, and burned their bridges, and fought us bitterly."

"Perhaps you could have made some better use of him by *not* killing him, do you think?"

"In the long run we conquered them and made them Christians. It was what we intended to accomplish."

"But the same thing might have been accomplished in a wiser way?"

"Perhaps," said Pizarro grudgingly. "Still, we accomplished it. That's the main thing, isn't it? We did what we set out to do. If there was a better way, so be it. Angels do things perfectly. We were no angels, but we achieved what we came for, and so be it, Socrates. So be it."

"I'd call that one a draw," said Tanner.
"Agreed."
"It's a terrific game they're playing."
"I wonder who we can use to play it next," said Richardson.
"I wonder what we can do with this besides using it to play games," said Tanner.

"Let me tell you a story," said Socrates. "The oracle at Delphi once said to a friend of mine, 'There is no man wiser than Socrates,' but I doubted that very much, and it troubled me to hear the oracle saying something that I knew was so far from the truth. So I decided to look for a man who was obviously wiser than I was. There was a politician in Athens who was famous for his wisdom, and I went to him and questioned him about many things. After I had listened to him for a time, I came to see that though many people, and most of all he himself, thought that he was wise, yet he was not wise. He only imagined that he was wise. So I realized that I must be wiser than he. Neither of us knew anything that was really worthwhile, but he knew nothing and thought that he knew, whereas I neither knew anything nor thought that I did. At least on one point, then, I was wiser than he: I didn't think that I knew what I didn't know."

"Is this intended to mock me, Socrates?"

"I feel only the deepest respect for you, friend Pizarro. But let me continue. I went to other wise men, and they too, though sure of their wisdom, could never give me a clear answer to anything. Those whose reputations for wisdom were the highest seemed to have the least of it. I went to the great poets and playwrights. There was wisdom in their works, for the gods had inspired them, but that did not make *them* wise, though they thought that it had. I went to the stonemasons and potters and other craftsmen. They were wise in their own skills, but most of them seemed to think that that made them wise in everything, which did not appear to be the case. And so it went. I was unable to find anyone who showed true wisdom. So perhaps the oracle was right: that although I am an ignorant man, there is no man wiser than I am. But oracles often are right without their being much value in it, for I think that all she was saying was that no man is wise at all, that wisdom is reserved for the gods. What do you say, Pizarro?"

"I say that you are a great fool, and very ugly besides."

"You speak the truth. So, then, you are wise after all. And honest."

"Honest, you say? I won't lay claim to that. Honesty's a game for fools. I lied whenever I needed to. I cheated. I went back on my word. I'm not proud of that, mind you. It's simply what you have to do to get on in the world. You think I wanted to tend pigs all my life? I wanted gold, Socrates! I wanted power over men! I wanted fame!"

"And did you get those things?"

"I got them all."

"And were they gratifying, Pizarro?"

Pizarro gave Socrates a long look. Then he pursed his lips and spat.

"They were worthless."

"Were they, do you think?"

"Worthless, yes. I have no illusions about that. But still it was better to have had them than not. In the long run nothing has any meaning, old man. In the long run we're all dead, the honest man and the villain, the king and the fool. Life's a cheat. They tell us to strive, to conquer, to gain—and for what? What? For a few years of strutting around. Then it's taken away, as if it had never been. A cheat, I say." Pizarro paused. He stared at his hands as though he had never seen them before. "Did I say all that just now? Did I mean it?" He laughed. "Well, I suppose I did. Still, life is all there is, so you want as much of it as you can. Which means getting gold, and power, and fame."

"Which you had. And apparently have no longer. Friend Pizarro, where are we now?"

"I wish I knew."

"So do I," said Socrates soberly.

"He's real," Richardson said. "They both are. The bugs are out of the system and we've got something spectacular here. Not only is this going to be of value to scholars, I think it's also going to be a tremendous entertainment gimmick, Harry."

"It's going to be much more than that," said Tanner in a strange voice.

"What do you mean by that?"

"I'm not sure yet," Tanner said. "But I'm definitely on to something big. It just began to hit me a couple of minutes ago, and it hasn't really taken shape yet. But it's something that might change the whole goddamned world."

Richardson looked amazed and bewildered.

"What the hell are you talking about, Harry?"

Tanner said, "A new way of settling political disputes, maybe. What would you say to a kind of combat-at-arms between one nation and another? Like a medieval tournament, so to speak. With each side using champions that we simulate for them—the greatest minds of all the past, brought back and placed in competition—" He shook his head. "Something like that. It needs a lot of working out, I know. But it's got possibilities."

"A medieval tournament—combat-at-arms, using simulations? Is that what you're saying?"

"Verbal combat. Not actual jousts, for Christ's sake."

"I don't see how—" Richardson began.

"Neither do I, not yet. I wish I hadn't even spoken of it."

"But—"

"Later, Lew. Later. Let me think about it a little while more."

"You don't have any idea what this place is?" Pizarro said.

"Not at all. But I certainly think this is no longer the world where we once dwelled. Are we dead, then? How can we say? You look alive to me."

"And you to me."

"Yet I think we are living some other kind of life. Here, give me your hand. Can you feel mine against yours?"

"No. I can't feel anything."

"Nor I. Yet I see two hands clasping. Two old men standing on a cloud, clasping hands." Socrates laughed. "What a great rogue you are, Pizarro!"

"Yes, of course. But do you know something, Socrates? You are too. A windy old rogue. I like you. There were moments when you were driving me crazy with all your chatter, but you amused me too. Were you really a soldier?"

"When my city asked me, yes."

"For a soldier, you're damned innocent about the way the world works, I have to say. But I guess I can teach you a thing or too."

"Will you?"

"Gladly," said Pizarro.

"I would be in your debt," Socrates said.

"Take Atahuallpa," Pizarro said. "How can I make you understand why I had to kill him? There weren't even two hundred of us, and twenty-four millions of them, and his word was law, and once he was gone they'd have no one to command them. So of *course* we had to get rid of him if we wanted to conquer them. And so we did, and then they fell."

"How simple you make it seem."

"Simple is what it was. Listen, old man, he would have died sooner or later anyway, wouldn't he? This way I made his death useful: to God, to the Church, to Spain. And to Francisco Pizarro. Can you understand that?"

"I think so," said Socrates. "But do you think King Atahuallpa did?"

"Any king would understand such things."

"Then he should have killed you the moment you set foot in his land."

"Unless God meant us to conquer him, and allowed him to understand that. Yes. Yes, that must have been what happened."

"Perhaps he is in this place too, and we could ask him," said Socrates.

Pizarro's eyes brightened. "Mother of God, yes! A good idea! And if he didn't understand, why, I'll try to explain it to him. Maybe you'll help me. You know how to talk, how to move words around and around. What do you say? Would you help me?"

"If we meet him, I would like to talk with him," Socrates said. "I would indeed like to know if he agrees with you on the subject of the usefulness of his being killed by you."

Grinning, Pizarro said, "Slippery, you are! But I like you. I like you very much. Come. Let's go look for Atahuallpa."

TO THE PROMISED LAND

As is true of many of my stories in the past couple of decades, this one was initiated by a request from outside. Gregory Benford and Martin H. Greenberg were editing an anthology of parallel-world stories called What Might Have Been, *and invited me to contribute. Each story was supposed to deal with the consequences of altering one major event of world history.*

I worked backwards to generate my story idea, first imagining a variant world, then trying to explain what alteration of history had summoned it into being. It was the autumn of 1987. I had been reading in the history of Imperial Rome—no particular reason, just recreational reading. So Rome was on my mind when the request for a story arrived. What if the Roman Empire hadn't fallen to the barbarians in the fifth century A.D., I asked myself, but had survived and endured into our own era?

All right. A good starting point. But to what cause was I going to attribute the fall of Rome?

To the rise of Christianity, I told myself. Edward Gibbon had made a convincing case for that in The Decline and Fall of the Roman Empire— *convincing to me, at any rate. One could put forth all sorts of other reasons for Rome's fall, such as the tendency to hire mercenary soldiers of barbarian ancestry for the army; but for the sake of the speculation I stuck with the classic Gibbon theory that the socialist practices of early Christianity, spreading upward until they reached the highest levels of the Empire, had so sapped the Imperial virtues of the Romans that they were easy prey to their enemies.*

How, in my story, was I going to prevent Christianity from developing and taking over Rome, then?

Well, I could have had Jesus die of measles at the age of five. But that was too obvious and too trivial. Besides, how would I ever communicate that to the reader without simply dragging it in by brute force, heedless of the irrelevance of the death of one small boy to the context of the times? ("Meanwhile, in Nazareth, the carpenter Joseph and his wife Mary were mourning the death of their little boy Jesus...")

No. Even if Jesus had died in childhood, some other prophet might well have arisen in Palestine and filled his historical niche. I had to take the problem back a stage. If the monotheistic Jews had never reached Palestine in the first place, there'd have been no Jesus or Jesus-surrogate figure in the Middle East to give rise to the troublesome and ultimately destructive new religion. Well, then, should I suppose the Jews had gone somewhere else when they made their Exodus from Egypt? Have them build their Holy Land down in the Congo, say, safely beyond contact with Imperial Rome? Have them sail off to China? Settle in Australia? No, too far-fetched, all of them. The best idea was simply to leave them in Egypt, a backwater province of the Roman Empire. The Exodus must have miscarried, somehow. Pharaoh's soldiers had caught up with Moses and his people before they reached the Red Sea. So the Philistines had remained in possession of the land that would otherwise have become the Kingdom of Israel, and the Jews would have continued to be an unimportant sect in Egypt, serving as scribes and such.

There it was. No Exodus, no Jewish population in Palestine, no Jesus, no Christianity in Europe. Now come up to the alternative-world equivalent of our twentieth century. The scene is Egypt; the narrator is a Jewish historian; a new Moses has arisen, planning a very modern kind of Exodus. Everything was in place and I had my story. I wrote it in November, 1987 and, since I was allowed to place the story in a magazine before it appeared in the Benford-Greenberg anthology, I sent it to Ellen Datlow, who bought it for Omni for her issue of May, 1989.

But, as I sometimes tend to do, I had got a little carried away doing the background details, and Ellen asked for four or five pages of cuts. I would sooner sell my cats into slavery than let anybody else cut my work without my seeing the result, but I'm perfectly willing to listen to an editor's suggestions. Ellen, during the course of a very long phone call, pointed out all sorts of places where the story would benefit from a little trimming. Here and there I stuck to my text, but mainly I found myself in agreement with her, and slashed away. I'm glad I did. Eventually, working backward piece by piece from this story over the next fourteen years, I told the entire story of my alternative Roman Empire in my book Roma Eterna, *which was published in 2003.*

When "To the Promised Land" appeared later in the What Might Have Been *anthology, it was illustrated on the book's cover by a moody, brooding painting of the twentieth-century Memphis that I had created. The artist's vision was of something a little like the world of the film* Blade Runner, *plus sphinxes, Egyptian temples, and a giant pyramid-shaped hotel next to the downtown freeway. A man named Paul Swendsen painted it. I think it's a marvel.*

They came for me at high noon, the hour of Apollo, when only a crazy man would want to go out into the desert. I was hard at work and in no mood to be kidnapped. But to get them to listen to reason was like trying to get the Nile to flow south. They weren't reasonable men. Their eyes had a wild metallic sheen and they held their jaws and mouths clamped in that special constipated way that fanatics like to affect. As they swaggered about in my little cluttered study, poking at the tottering stacks of books and pawing through the manuscript of my nearly finished history of the collapse of the Empire, they were like two immense irresistible forces, as remote and terrifying as gods of old Aiguptos come to life. I felt helpless before them.

The older and taller one called himself Eleazar. To me he was Horus, because of his great hawk nose. He looked like an Aiguptian and he was wearing the white linen robe of an Aiguptian. The other, squat and heavily muscled, with a baboon face worthy of Thoth, told me he was Leonardo di Filippo, which is of course a Roman name, and he had an oily Roman look about him. But I knew he was no more Roman than I am. Nor the other, Aiguptian. Both of them spoke in Hebrew, and with an ease that no outsider could ever attain. These were two Israelites, men of my own obscure tribe. Perhaps di Filippo had been born to a father not of the faith, or perhaps he simply liked to pretend that he was one of the world's masters and not one of God's forgotten people. I will never know.

Eleazar stared at me, at the photograph of me on the jacket of my account of the Wars of the Reunification, and at me again, as though trying to satisfy himself that I really was Nathan ben-Simeon. The picture was fifteen years old. My beard had been black then. He tapped the book and pointed questioningly to me and I nodded. "Good," he said. He told me to pack a suitcase, fast, as though I were going down to Alexandria for a weekend holiday. "Moshe sent us to get you," he said. "Moshe wants you. Moshe needs you. He has important work for you."

"Moshe?"

"The Leader," Eleazar said, in tones that you would ordinarily reserve for Pharaoh, or perhaps the First Consul. "You don't know anything about him yet, but you will. All of Aiguptos will know him soon. The whole world."

"What does your Moshe want with me?"

"You're going to write an account of the Exodus for him," said di Filippo.

"Ancient history isn't my field," I told him.

"We're not talking about ancient history."

"The Exodus was three thousand years ago, and what can you say about it at this late date except that it's a damned shame that it didn't work out?"

Di Filippo looked blank for a moment. Then he said, "We're not talking about that one. The Exodus is now. It's about to happen, the new one, the real one. That other one long ago was a mistake, a false try."

"And this new Moshe of yours wants to do it all over again? Why? Can't he be satisfied with the first fiasco? Do we need another? Where could we possibly go that would be any better than Aiguptos?"

"You'll see. What Moshe is doing will be the biggest news since the burning bush."

"Enough," Eleazar said. "We ought to be hitting the road. Get your things together, Dr. Ben-Simeon."

So they really meant to take me away. I felt fear and disbelief. Was this actually happening? Could I resist them? I would not let it happen. Time for some show of firmness, I thought. The scholar standing on his authority. Surely they wouldn't attempt force. Whatever else they might be, they were Hebrews. They would respect a scholar. Brusque, crisp, fatherly, the *melamed*, the man of learning. I shook my head. "I'm afraid not. It's simply not possible."

Eleazar made a small gesture with one hand. Di Filippo moved ominously close to me and his stocky body seemed to expand in a frightening way. "Come on," he said quietly. "We've got a car waiting right outside. It's a four-hour drive, and Moshe said to get you there before sundown."

My sense of helplessness came sweeping back. "Please. I have work to do, and—"

"Screw your work, professor. Start packing, or we'll take you just as you are."

The street was silent and empty, with that forlorn midday look that makes Menfe seem like an abandoned city when the sun is at its height. I walked between them, a prisoner, trying to remain calm. When I glanced back at the battered old gray facades of the Hebrew Quarter where I had lived all my life, I wondered if I would ever see them again, what would happen to my books, who would preserve my papers. It was like a dream.

A sharp dusty wind was blowing out of the west, reddening the sky so that it seemed that the whole Delta must be aflame, and the noontime heat was enough to kosher a pig. The air smelled of cooking oil, of orange blossoms, of camel dung, of smoke. They had parked on the far side of Amenhotep Plaza just behind the vast ruined statue of Pharaoh, probably in hope of catching the shadows, but at this hour there were no shadows and the car was like an oven. Di Filippo drove, Eleazar sat in back with me. I kept myself completely still, hardly even breathing, as though I could construct a sphere of invulnerability around me by remaining motionless. But when Eleazar offered me a cigarette I snatched it from him with such sudden ferocity that he looked at me in amazement.

We circled the Hippodrome and the Great Basilica where the judges of the Republic hold court, and joined the sparse flow of traffic that was entering the Sacred Way. So our route lay eastward out of the city, across the river and into the desert. I asked no questions. I was frightened, numbed, angry, and—I suppose—to some degree curious. It was a paralyzing combination of emotions. So I sat quietly, praying only that these men and their Leader would be done with me in short order and return me to my home and my studies.

"This filthy city," Eleazar muttered. "How I despise it!"

In fact it had always seemed grand and beautiful to me: a measure of my assimilation, some might say, though inwardly I feel very much the Israelite, not in the least Aiguptian. Even a Hebrew must concede that Menfe is one of the world's great cities. It is the most majestic city this side of Roma, so everyone says, and so I am willing to believe, though I have never been beyond the borders of the province of Aiguptos in my life.

The splendid old temples of the Sacred Way went by on both sides, the Temple of Isis and the Temple of Sarapis and the Temple of Jupiter Ammon and all the rest, fifty or a hundred of them on that great boulevard whose pavements are lined with sphinxes and bulls: Dagon's temple, Mithra's and Cybele's, Baal's, Marduk's, Zarathustra's, a temple for every god and goddess anyone had ever imagined, except, of course, the One True God, whom we few Hebrews prefer to worship in our private way behind the walls of our own Quarter. The gods of all the Earth have washed up here in Menfe like so much Nile mud. Of course hardly anyone takes them very seriously these days, even the supposed faithful. It would be folly to pretend that this is a religious age. Mithra's shrine still gets some worshippers, and of course that of Jupiter Ammon. People go to those to do business, to see their friends, maybe to ask favors on high. The rest of the temples might as well be museums. No one goes into them except Roman and Japanese tourists. Yet here they still stand, many of them thousands of years old. Nothing is ever thrown away in the land of Misr.

"Look at them," Eleazar said scornfully, as we passed the huge half-ruined Sarapion. "I hate the sight of them. The foolishness! The waste! And all of them built with our forefathers' sweat."

In fact there was little truth in that. Perhaps in the time of the first Moshe we did indeed labor to build the Great Pyramids for Pharaoh, as it says in Scripture. But there could never have been enough of us to add up to much of a work force. Even now, after a sojourn along the Nile that has lasted some four thousand years, there are only about twenty thousand of us. Lost in a sea of ten million Aiguptians, we are, and the Aiguptians themselves are lost in an ocean of Romans and imitation Romans, so we are a minority within a minority, an ethnographic curiosity, a drop in the vast ocean of humanity, an odd and trivial sect, insignificant except to ourselves.

The temple district dropped away behind us and we moved out across the long slim shining arch of the Caesar Augustus Bridge, and into the teeming suburb of Hikuptah on the eastern bank of the river, with its leather and gold bazaars, its myriad coffeehouses, its tangle of medieval alleys. Then Hikuptah dissolved into a wilderness of fig trees and canebrake, and we entered a transitional zone of olive orchards and date palms; and then abruptly we came to the place where the land changes from black to red and nothing grows. At once the awful barrenness and solitude of the place struck me like a tangible force. It was a fearful land, stark and empty, a dead place full of terrible ghosts. The sun was a scourge above us. I thought we would bake; and when the car's engine once or twice began to cough and sputter, I knew from the grim look on Eleazar's face that we would surely perish if we suffered a breakdown. Di Filippo drove in a hunched, intense way, saying nothing, gripping the steering stick with an unbending rigidity that spoke of great uneasiness. Eleazar too was quiet. Neither of them had said much since our departure from Menfe, nor I, but now in that hot harsh land they fell utterly silent, and the three of us neither spoke nor moved, as though the car had become our tomb. We labored onward, slowly, uncertain of engine, with windborne sand whistling all about us out of the west. In the great heat every breath was a struggle. My clothing clung to my skin. The road was fine for a while, broad and straight and well paved, but then it narrowed, and finally it was nothing more than a potholed white ribbon half covered with drifts. They were better at highway maintenance in the days of Imperial Roma. But that was long ago. This is the era of the Consuls, and things go to hell in the hinterlands and no one cares.

"Do you know what route we're taking, doctor?" Eleazar asked, breaking the taut silence at last when we were an hour or so into that bleak and miserable desert.

My throat was dry as strips of leather that have been hanging in the sun a thousand years, and I had trouble getting words out. "I think we're heading east," I said finally.

"East, yes. It happens that we're traveling the same route that the first Moshe took when he tried to lead our people out of bondage. Toward the Bitter Lakes, and the Reed Sea. Where Pharaoh's army caught up with us and ten thousand innocent people drowned."

There was crackling fury in his voice, as though that were something that had happened just the other day, as though he had learned of it not from the Book of Aaron but from this morning's newspaper. And he gave me a fiery glance, as if I had had some complicity in our people's long captivity among the Aiguptians and some responsibility for the ghastly failure of that ancient attempt to escape. I flinched before that fierce gaze of his and looked away.

"Do you care, Dr. Ben-Simeon? That they followed us and drove us into the sea? That half our nation, or more, perished in a single day in horrible fear and panic? That young mothers with babies in their arms were crushed beneath the wheels of Pharaoh's chariots?"

"It was all so long ago," I said lamely.

As the words left my lips I knew how foolish they were. It had not been my intent to minimize the debacle of the Exodus. I had meant only that the great disaster to our people was sealed over by thousands of years of healing, that although crushed and dispirited and horribly reduced in numbers we had somehow gone on from that point, we had survived, we had endured, the survivors of the catastrophe had made new lives for themselves along the Nile under the rule of Pharaoh and under the Greeks who had conquered Pharaoh and the Romans who had conquered the Greeks. We still survived, did we not, here in the long sleepy decadence of the Imperium, the Pax Romana, when even the everlasting Empire had crumbled and the absurd and pathetic Second Republic ruled the world?

But to Eleazar it was as if I had spat upon the scrolls of the Law. "*It was all so long ago,*" he repeated, savagely mocking me. "And therefore we should forget? Shall we forget the Patriarchs too? Shall we forget the Covenant? Is Aiguptos the land that the Lord meant us to inhabit? Were we chosen by Him to be set above all the peoples of the Earth, or were we meant to be the slaves of Pharaoh forever?"

"I was trying only to say—"

What I had been trying to say didn't interest him. His eyes were shining, his face was flushed, a vein stood out astonishingly on his broad forehead. "We were meant for greatness. The Lord God gave His blessing to Abraham, and said that He would multiply Abraham's seed as the stars of the heaven, and as the sand which is upon the seashore. And the seed of Abraham shall possess the gate of his enemies. And in his seed shall all the nations of the earth be blessed. Have you ever heard those words before, Dr. Ben-Simeon? And do you think they signified anything, or were they only the boasting of noisy little desert chieftains? No, I tell you we were meant for greatness, we were meant to shake the world: and we have been too long in recovering from the catastrophe at the Reed Sea. An hour, two hours later and all of history would have been different. We would have crossed into Sinai and the fertile lands beyond; we would have built our kingdom there as the Covenant decreed; we would have made the world listen to the thunder of our God's voice; and today the entire world would look up to us as it has looked to the Romans these past twenty centuries. But it is not too late, even now. A new Moshe is in the land and he will succeed where the first one failed. And we *will* come forth from Aiguptos, Dr. Ben-Simeon, and we *will* have what is rightfully ours. At last, Dr. Ben-Simeon. At long last."

He sat back, sweating, trembling, ashen, seemingly exhausted by his own eloquence. I didn't attempt to reply. Against such force of conviction there is no victory; and what could I possibly have gained, in any case, by contesting his vision of Israel triumphant? Let him have his faith; let him have his new Moshe; let him have his dream of Israel triumphant. I myself had a different vision, less romantic, more cynical. I could easily imagine, yes, the children of Israel escaping from their bondage under Pharaoh long ago and crossing into Sinai, and going on beyond it into sweet and fertile Palestina. But what then? Global dominion? What was there in our history, in our character, our national temperament, that would lead us on to that? Preaching Jehovah to the Gentiles? Yes, but would they listen, would they understand? No. No. We would always have been a special people, I suspected, a small and stubborn tribe, clinging to our knowledge of the One God amidst the hordes who needed to believe in many. We might have conquered Palestina, we might have taken Syria too, even spread out a little further around the perimeter of the Great Sea; but still there would have been the Assyrians to contend with, and the Babylonians, and the Persians, and Alexander's Greeks, and the Romans, especially the stolid dull invincible Romans, whose destiny it was to engulf every corner of the planet and carve it into Roman provinces full of Roman highways and Roman bridges and Roman whorehouses. Instead of living in Aiguptos under the modern Pharaoh, who is the puppet of the First Consul who has replaced the Emperor of Roma, we would be living in Palestina under the rule of some minor procurator or proconsul or prefect, and we would speak some sort of Greek or Latin to our masters instead of Aiguptian, and everything else would be the same. But I said none of this to Eleazar. He and I were different sorts of men. His soul and his vision were greater and grander than mine. Also his strength was superior and his temper was shorter. I might take issue with his theories of history, and he might hit me in his rage; and which of us then would be the wiser?

The sun slipped away behind us and the wind shifted, hurling sand now against our front windows instead of the rear. I saw the dark shadows of mountains to the south and ahead of us, far across the strait that separates Aiguptos from the Sinai wilderness. It was late afternoon, almost evening. Suddenly there was a village ahead of us, springing up out of nowhere in the nothingness.

It was more a camp, really, than a village. I saw a few dozen lopsided tin huts and some buildings that were even more modest, strung together of reed latticework. Carbide lamps glowed here and there. There were three or four dilapidated trucks and a handful of battered old cars scattered haphazardly about. A well had been driven in the center of things and a crazy network of aboveground conduits ran off in all directions. In back of the central area I saw one building much larger than the others, a big tinroofed shed or lean-to with other trucks parked in front of it.

I had arrived at the secret headquarters of some underground movement, yet no attempt had been made to disguise or defend it. Situating it in this forlorn zone was defense enough: no one in his right mind would come out here without good reason. The patrols of the Pharaonic police did not extend beyond the cities, and the civic officers of the Republic certainly had no cause to go sniffing around in these remote and distasteful parts. We live in a decadent era but a placid and trusting one.

Eleazar, jumping out of the car, beckoned to me, and I hobbled after him. After hours without a break in the close quarters of the car I was creaky and wilted and the reek of gasoline fumes had left me nauseated. My clothes were acrid and stiff from my own dried sweat. The evening coolness had not yet descended on the desert and the air was hot and close. To my nostrils it had a strange vacant quality, the myriad stinks of the city being absent. There was something almost frightening about that. It was like the sort of air the Moon might have, if the Moon had air.

"This place is called Beth Israel," Eleazar said. "It is the capital of our nation."

Not only was I among fanatics; I had fallen in with madmen who suffered the delusion of grandeur. Or does one quality go automatically with the other?

A woman wearing man's clothing came trotting up to us. She was young and very tall, with broad shoulders and a great mass of dark thick hair tumbling to her shoulders and eyes as bright as Eleazar's.

She had Eleazar's hawk's nose, too, but somehow it made her look all the more striking. "My sister Miriam," he said. "She'll see that you get settled. In the morning I'll show you around and explain your duties to you."

And he walked away, leaving me with her.

She was formidable. I would have carried my bag, but she insisted, and set out at such a brisk pace toward the perimeter of the settlement that I was hard put to keep up with her. A hut all my own was ready for me, somewhat apart from everything else. It had a cot, a desk and type-writer, a washbasin, and a single dangling lamp. There was a cupboard for my things. Miriam unpacked for me, setting my little stock of fresh clothing on the shelves and putting the few books I had brought with me beside the cot.

Then she filled the basin with water and told me to get undressed. I stared at her, astounded. "You can't wear what you've got on now," she said. "While you're having a bath I'll take your things to be washed." She might have waited outside, but no. She stood there, arms folded, looking impatient. I shrugged and gave her my shirt, but she wanted everything else, too. This was new to me, her straightforwardness, her absolute indifference to modesty. There have been few women in my life and none since the death of my wife; how could I strip myself before this one, who was young enough to be my daughter? But she insisted. In the end I gave her every stitch—my nakedness did not seem to matter to her at all—and while she was gone I sponged myself clean and hastily put on fresh clothing, so she would not see me naked again. But she was gone a long time. When she returned, she brought with her a tray, my dinner, a bowl of porridge, some stewed lamb, a little flask of pale red wine. Then I was left alone. Night had fallen now, desert night, awesomely black with the stars burning like beacons. When I had eaten I stepped outside my hut and stood in the darkness. It scarcely seemed real to me, that I had been snatched away like this, that I was in this alien place rather than in my familiar cluttered little flat in the Hebrew Quarter of Menfe. But it was peaceful here. Lights glimmered in the distance. I heard laughter, the pleasant sound of a kithara, someone singing an old Hebrew song in a deep, rich voice. Even in my bewildering captivity I felt a strange tranquility descending on me. I knew that I was in the presence of a true community, albeit one dedicated to some bizarre goal beyond my comprehension. If I had dared, I would have gone out among them and made myself known to them; but I was a stranger, and afraid. For a long while I stood in the darkness, listening, wondering. When the night grew cold I went inside. I lay awake until dawn, or so it seemed, gripped by that icy clarity that will not admit sleep; and yet I must have slept at least a little while, for there were fragments of dreams drifting in my mind in the morning, images of horsemen and chariots, of men with spears, of a great black-bearded angry Moshe holding aloft the tablets of the Law.

A small girl shyly brought me breakfast. Afterwards Eleazar came to me. In the confusion of yesterday I had not taken note of how overwhelming his physical presence was: he had seemed merely big, but now I realized that he was a giant, taller than I by a span or more, and probably sixty minas heavier. His features were ruddy and a vast tangle of dark thick curls spilled down to his shoulders. He had put aside his Aiguptian robes this morning and was dressed Roman style, an open-throated white shirt, a pair of khaki trousers.

"You know," he said, "we don't have any doubt at all that you're the right man for this job. Moshe and I have discussed your books many times. We agree that no one has a firmer grasp of the logic of history, of the inevitability of the processes that flow from the nature of human beings."

To this I offered no response.

"I know how annoyed you must be at being grabbed like this. But you are essential to us; and we knew you'd never have come of your own free will."

"Essential?"

"Great movements need great chroniclers."

"And the nature of your movement—"

"Come," he said.

He led me through the village. But it was a remarkably uninformative walk. His manner was mechanical and aloof, as if he were following a pre-programmed route, and whenever I asked a direct question he was vague or even evasive. The big tin-roofed building in the center of things was the factory where the work of the Exodus was being carried out, he said, but my request for further explanation went unanswered. He showed me the house of Moshe, a crude shack like all the others. Of Moshe himself, though, I saw nothing. "You will meet him at a later time," Eleazar said. He pointed out another shack that was the synagogue, another that was the library, another that housed the electrical generator. When I asked to visit the library he merely shrugged and kept walking. On the far side of it I saw a second group of crude houses on the lower slope of a fair-sized hill that I had not noticed the night before. "We have a population of five hundred," Eleazar told me.

More than I had imagined.

"All Hebrews?" I asked.

"What do you think?"

It surprised me that so many of us could have migrated to this desert settlement without my hearing about it. Of course, I have led a secluded scholarly life, but still, five hundred Israelites is one out of every forty of us. That is a major movement of population, for us. And not one of them someone of my acquaintance, or even a friend of a friend? Apparently not. Well, perhaps most of the settlers of Beth Israel had come from the Hebrew community in Alexandria, which has relatively little contact with those of us who live in Menfe. Certainly I recognized no one as I walked through the village.

From time to time Eleazar made veiled references to the Exodus that was soon to come, but there was no real information in anything he said; it was as if the Exodus were merely some bright toy that he enjoyed cupping in his hands, and I was allowed from time to time to see its gleam but not its form. There was no use in questioning him. He simply walked along, looming high above me, telling me only what he wished to tell. There was an unstated grandiosity to the whole mysterious project that puzzled and irritated me. If they wanted to leave Aiguptos, why not simply leave? The borders weren't guarded. We had ceased to be the slaves of Pharaoh two thousand years ago. Eleazar and his friends could settle in Palestina or Syria or anyplace else they liked, even Gallia, even Hispania, even Nuova Roma far across the ocean, where they could try to convert the redskinned men to Israel. The Republic wouldn't care where a few wild-eyed Hebrews chose to go. So why all this pomp and mystery, why such an air of conspiratorial secrecy? Were these people up to something truly extraordinary? Or, I wondered, were they simply crazy?

That afternoon Miriam brought back my clothes, washed and ironed, and offered to introduce me to some of her friends. We went down into the village, which was quiet. Almost everyone is at work, Miriam explained. But there were a few young men and women on the porch of one of the buildings: this is Deborah, she said, and this is Ruth, and Reuben, and Isaac, and Joseph, and Saul. They greeted me with great respect, even reverence, but almost immediately went back to their animated conversation as if they had forgotten I was there. Joseph, who was dark and sleek and slim, treated Miriam with an ease bordering on intimacy, finishing her sentences for her, once or twice touching her lightly on the arm to underscore some point he was making. I found that unexpectedly disturbing. Was he her husband? Her lover? Why did it matter to me? They were both young enough to be my children. Great God, why did it matter?

Unexpectedly and with amazing swiftness my attitude toward my captors began to change. Certainly I had had a troublesome introduction to them—the lofty pomposity of Eleazar, the brutal directness of di Filippo, the ruthless way I had been seized and taken to this place—but as I met others I found them generally charming, graceful, courteous, appealing. Prisoner though I might be, I felt myself quickly being drawn into sympathy with them.

In the first two days I was allowed to discover nothing except that these were busy, determined folk, most of them young and evidently all of them intelligent, working with tremendous zeal on some colossal undertaking that they were convinced would shake the world. They were passionate in the way that I imagined the Hebrews of that first and ill-starred Exodus had been: contemptuous of the sterile and alien society within which they were confined, striving toward freedom and the light, struggling to bring a new world into being. But how? By what means? I was sure that they would tell me more in their own good time; and I knew also that that time had not yet come. They were watching me, testing me, making certain I could be trusted with their secret.

Whatever it was, that immense surprise which they meant to spring upon the Republic, I hoped there was substance to it, and I wished them well with it. I am old and perhaps timid but far from conservative: change is the way of growth, and the Empire, with which I include the Republic that ostensibly has replaced it, is the enemy of change. For twenty centuries it had strangled mankind in its benign grip. The civilization that it had constructed was hollow, the life that most of us led was a meaningless trek that had neither values nor purpose. By its shrewd acceptance and absorption of the alien gods and alien ways of the peoples it had conquered, the Empire had flattened every-thing into shapelessness. The grand and useless temples of the Sacred Way, where all gods were equal and equally insignificant, were the best symbol of that. By worshipping everyone indiscriminately, the rulers of the Imperium had turned the sacred into a mere instrument of gover-nance. And ultimately their cynicism had come to pervade everything: the relationship between man and the Divine was destroyed, so that we had nothing left to venerate except the status quo itself, the holy stability of the world government. I had felt for years that the time was long overdue for some great revolution, in which all fixed, fast-frozen relationships, with their train of ancient and venerable prejudices and opinions, would be swept away—a time when all that is solid melts into air, all that is holy is profaned, and man is at last compelled to face with sober senses his real conditions of life. Was that what the Exodus somehow would bring? Profoundly did I hope so. For the Empire was defunct and didn't know it. Like some immense dead beast it lay upon the soul of humanity, smothering it beneath itself: a beast so huge that its limbs hadn't yet heard the news of its own death.

On the third day di Filippo knocked on my door and said, "The Leader will see you now."

The interior of Moshe's dwelling was not very different from mine: a simple cot, one stark lamp, a basin, a cupboard. But he had shelf upon shelf overflowing with books. Moshe himself was smaller than I expected, a short, compact man who nevertheless radiated tremendous, even invincible, force. I hardly needed to be told that he was Eleazar's older brother. He had Eleazar's wild mop of curly hair and his ferocious eyes and his savage beak of a nose; but because he was so much shorter than Eleazar his power was more tightly compressed, and seemed to be in peril of immediate eruption. He seemed poised, controlled, an austere and frightening figure.

But he greeted me warmly and apologized for the rudeness of my capture. Then he indicated a well-worn row of my books on his shelves. "You understand the Republic better than anyone, Dr. Ben-Simeon," he said. "How corrupt and weak it is behind its facade of universal love and brotherhood. How deleterious its influence has been. How feeble its power. The world is waiting now for something completely new: but what will it be? Is that not the question, Dr. Ben-Simeon? *What will it be?*"

It was a pat, obviously preconceived speech, which no doubt he had carefully constructed for the sake of impressing me and enlisting me in his cause, whatever that cause might be. Yet he did impress me with his passion and his conviction. He spoke for some time, rehearsing themes and arguments that were long familiar to me. He saw the Roman Imperium, as I did, as something dead and beyond revival, though still moving with eerie momentum. Call it an Empire, call it a Republic, it was still a world state, and that was an unsustainable concept in the modern era. The revival of local nationalisms that had been thought extinct for thousands of years was impossible to ignore. Roman tolerance for local customs, religions, languages, and rulers had been a shrewd policy for centuries, but it carried with it the seeds of destruction for the Imperium. Too much of the world now had only the barest knowledge of the two official languages of Latin and Greek, and transacted its business in a hodgepodge of other tongues. In the old Imperial heartland itself Latin had been allowed to break down into regional dialects that were in fact separate languages—Gallian, Hispanian, Lusitanian, and all the rest. Even the Romans at Roma no longer spoke true Latin, Moshe pointed out, but rather the simple, melodic, lazy thing called Roman, which might be suitable for singing opera but lacked the precision that was needed for government. As for the religious diversity that the Romans in their easy way had encouraged, it had led not to the perpetuation of faiths but to the erosion of them. Scarcely anyone except the most primitive peoples and a few unimportant encapsulated minorities like us believed anything at all; nearly everyone gave lip-service instead to the local version of the official Roman pantheon and any other gods that struck their fancy, but a society that tolerates all gods really has no faith in any. And a society without faith is one without a rudder: without even a course.

These things Moshe saw, as I did, not as signs of vitality and diversity but as confirmation of the imminence of the end. This time there would be no Reunification. When the Empire had fallen, conservative forces had been able to erect the Republic in its place, but that was a trick that could be managed only once. Now a period of flames unmatched in history was surely coming as the sundered segments of the old Imperium warred against one another.

"And this Exodus of yours?" I said finally, when I dared to break his flow. "What is that, and what does it have to do with what we've been talking about?"

"The end is near," Moshe said. "We must not allow ourselves to be destroyed in the chaos that will follow the fall of the Republic, for we are the instruments of God's great plan, and it is essential that we survive. Come: let me show you something."

We stepped outside. Immediately an antiquated and unreliable-looking car pulled up, with the dark slender boy Joseph at the stick. Moshe indicated that I should get in, and we set out on a rough track that skirted the village and entered the open desert just behind the hill that cut the settlement in half. For perhaps ten minutes we drove north through a district of low rocky dunes. Then we circled another steep hill and on its farther side, where the land flattened out into a broad plain, I was astonished to see a weird tubular thing of gleaming silvery metal rising on half a dozen frail spidery legs to a height of some thirty cubits in the midst of a hubbub of machinery, wires, and busy workers.

My first thought was that it was an idol of some sort, a Moloch, a Baal, and I had a sudden vision of the people of Beth Israel coating their bodies in pigs' grease and dancing naked around it to the sound of drums and tambourines. But that was foolishness.

"What is it?" I asked. "A sculpture of some sort?"

Moshe looked disgusted. "Is that what you think? It is a vessel, a holy ark."

I stared at him.

"It is the prototype for our starship," Moshe said, and his voice took on an intensity that cut me like a blade. "Into the heavens is where we will go, in ships like these—toward God, toward His brightness—and there we will settle, in the new Eden that awaits us on another world, until it is time for us to return to Earth."

"The new Eden—on another world—" My voice was faint with disbelief. A ship to sail between the stars, as the Roman skyships travel between continents? Was such a thing possible? Hadn't the Romans themselves, those most able of engineers, discussed the question of space travel years ago and concluded that there was no practical way of achieving it and nothing to gain from it even if there was? Space was inhospitable and unattainable: everyone knew that. I shook my head. "What other world? Where?"

Grandly he ignored my question. "Our finest minds have been at work for five years on what you see here. Now the time to test it has come. First a short journey, only to the moon and back—and then deeper into the heavens, to the new world that the Lord has pledged to reveal to me, so that the pioneers may plant the settlement. And after that—ship after ship, one shining ark after another, until every Israelite in the land of Aiguptos has crossed over into the promised land—" His eyes were glowing. "Here is our Exodus at last! What do you think, Dr. Ben-Simeon? What do you think?"

I thought it was madness of the most terrifying kind, and Moshe a lunatic who was leading his people—and mine—into cataclysmic disaster. It was a dream, a wild feverish fantasy. I would have preferred it if he had said they were going to worship this thing with incense and cymbals, than that they were going to ride it into the darkness of space. But Moshe stood before me so hot with blazing fervor that to say anything like that to him was unthinkable. He took me by the arm and led me, virtually dragged me, down the slope into the work area. Close up, the starship seemed huge and yet at the same time painfully flimsy. He slapped its flank and I heard a hollow ring. Thick gray cables ran everywhere, and subordinate machines of a nature that I could not even begin to comprehend. Fierce-eyed young men and women raced to and fro, carrying pieces of equipment and shouting instructions to one another as if striving to outdo one another in their dedication to their tasks. Moshe scrambled up a narrow ladder, gesturing for me to follow him. We entered a kind of cabin at the starship's narrow tip; in that cramped and all but airless room I saw screens, dials, more cables, things beyond my understanding. Below the cabin a spiral staircase led to a chamber where the crew could sleep, and below that, said Moshe, were the rockets that would send the ark of the Exodus into the heavens.

"And will it work?" I managed finally to ask.

"There is no doubt of it," Moshe said. "Our finest minds have produced what you see here."

He introduced me to some of them. The oldest appeared to be about twenty-five. Curiously, none of them had Moshe's radiant look of fanatic zeal; they were calm, even businesslike, imbued with a deep and quiet confidence. Three or four of them took turns explaining the theory of the vessel to me, its means of propulsion, its scheme of guidance, its method of escaping the pull of the Earth's inner force. My head began to ache. But yet I was swept under by the power of their conviction. They spoke of "combustion," of "acceleration," of "neutralizing the planet-force." They talked of "mass" and "thrust" and "freedom velocity." I barely understood a tenth of what they were saying, or a hundredth; but I formed the image of a giant bursting his bonds and leaping trium-phantly from the ground to soar joyously into unknown realms. Why not? Why not? All it took was the right fuel and a controlled explosion, they said. Kick the Earth hard enough and you must go upward with equal force. Yes. Why not? Within minutes I began to think that this insane starship might well be able to rise on a burst of flame and fly off into the darkness of the heavens. By the time Moshe ushered me out of the ship, nearly an hour later, I did not question that at all.

Joseph drove me back to the settlement alone. The last I saw of Moshe he was standing at the hatch of his starship, peering impatiently toward the fierce midday sky.

My task, I already knew, but which Eleazar told me again later that dazzling and bewildering day, was to write a chronicle of all that had been accomplished thus far in this hidden outpost of Israel and all that would be achieved in the apocalyptic days to come. I protested mildly that they would be better off finding some journalist, preferably with a background in science; but no, they didn't want a journalist, Eleazar said, they wanted someone with a deep understanding of the long cur-rents of history. What they wanted from me, I realized, was a work that was not merely journalism and not merely history, but one that had the profundity and eternal power of Scripture. What they wanted from me was the Book of the Exodus, that is, the Book of the Second Moshe.

They gave me a little office in their library building and opened their archive to me. I was shown Moshe's early visionary essays, his letters to intimate friends, his sketches and manifestos insisting on the need for an Exodus far more ambitious than anything his ancient namesake could have imagined. I saw how he had assembled—secretly and with some uneasiness, for he knew that what he was doing was profoundly subversive and would bring the fullest wrath of the Republic down on him if he should be discovered—his cadre of young revolutionary scientists. I read furious memoranda from Eleazar, taking issue with his older brother's fantastic scheme; and then I saw Eleazar gradually converting himself to the cause in letter after letter until he became more of a zealot than Moshe himself. I studied technical papers until my eyes grew bleary, not only those of Moshe and his associates but some by Romans nearly a century old, and even one by a Teuton, arguing for the historical necessity of space exploration and for its technical feasibility. I learned something more of the theory of the starship's design and functioning.

My guide to all these documents was Miriam. We worked side by side, together in one small room. Her youth, her beauty, the dark glint of her eyes, made me tremble. Often I longed to reach toward her, to touch her arm, her shoulder, her cheek. But I was too timid. I feared that she would react with laughter, with anger, with disdain, even with revulsion. Certainly it was an aging man's fear of rejection that inspired such caution. But also I reminded myself that she was the sister of those two fiery prophets, and that the blood that flowed in her veins must be as hot as theirs. What I feared was being scalded by her touch.

The day Moshe chose for the starship's flight was the 23rd of Tishri, the joyful holiday of Simchat Torah in the year 5730 by our calendar, that is, 2723 of the Roman reckoning. It was a brilliant early autumn day, very dry, the sky cloudless, the sun still in its fullest blaze of heat. For three days preparations had been going on around the clock at the launch site and it had been closed to all but the inner circle of scientists; but now, at dawn, the whole village went out by truck and car and some even on foot to attend the great event.

The cables and support machinery had been cleared away. The starship stood by itself, solitary and somehow vulnerable-looking, in the center of the sandy clearing, a shining upright needle, slender, fragile. The area was roped off; we would watch from a distance, so that the searing flames of the engines would not harm us.

A crew of three men and two women had been selected: Judith, who was one of the rocket scientists, and Leonardo di Filippo, and Miriam's friend Joseph, and a woman named Sarah whom I had never seen before. The fifth, of course, was Moshe. This was his chariot; this was his adventure, his dream; he must surely be the one to ride at the helm as the *Exodus* made its first leap toward the stars.

One by one they emerged from the blockhouse that was the control center for the flight. Moshe was the last. We watched in total silence, not a murmur, barely daring to draw breath. The five of them wore uniforms of white satin, brilliant in the morning sun, and curious glass helmets like diver's bowls over their faces. They walked toward the ship, mounted the ladder, turned one by one to look back at us, and went up inside. Moshe hesitated for a moment before entering, as if in prayer, or perhaps simply to savor the fullness of his joy.

Then there was a long wait, interminable, unendurable. It might have been twenty minutes; it might have been an hour. No doubt there was some last-minute checking to do, or perhaps even some technical hitch. Still we maintained our silence. We could have been statues. After a time I saw Eleazar turn worriedly toward Miriam, and they conferred in whispers. Then he trotted across to the blockhouse and went inside. Five minutes went by, ten; then he emerged, smiling, nodding, and returned to Miriam's side. Still nothing happened. We continued to wait.

Suddenly there was a sound like a thundercrack and a noise like the roaring of a thousand great bulls, and black smoke billowed from the ground around the ship, and there were flashes of dazzling red flame. The *Exodus* rose a few feet from the ground. There it hovered as though magically suspended, for what seemed to be forever.

And then it rose, jerkily at first, more smoothly then, and soared on a stunningly swift ascent toward the dazzling blue vault of the sky. I gasped; I grunted as though I had been struck; and I began to cheer. Tears of wonder and excitement flowed freely along my cheeks. All about me, people were cheering also, and weeping, and waving their arms, and the rocket, roaring, rose and rose, so high now that we could scarcely see it against the brilliance of the sky.

We were still cheering when a white flare of unbearable light, like a second sun more brilliant than the first, burst into the air high above us and struck us with overmastering force, making us drop to our knees in pain and terror, crying out, covering our faces with our hands.

When I dared look again, finally, that terrible point of ferocious illumination was gone, and in its place was a ghastly streak of black smoke that smeared halfway across the sky, trickling away in a dying trail somewhere to the north. I could not see the rocket. I could not hear the rocket.

"It's gone!" someone cried.

"Moshe! Moshe!"

"It blew up! I saw it!"

"Moshe!"

"Judith—" said a quieter voice behind me.

I was too stunned to cry out. But all around me there was a steadily rising sound of horror and despair, which began as a low choking wail and mounted until it was a shriek of the greatest intensity coming from hundreds of throats at once. There was fearful panic, universal hysteria. People were running about as if they had gone mad. Some were rolling on the ground, some were beating their hands against the sand. "Moshe!" they were screaming. "Moshe! Moshe! Moshe!"

I looked toward Eleazar. He was white-faced and his eyes seemed wild. Yet even as I looked toward him I saw him draw in his breath, raise his hands, step forward to call for attention. Immediately all eyes turned toward him. He swelled until he appeared to be five cubits high.

"Where's the ship?" someone cried. "Where's Moshe?"

And Eleazar said, in a voice like the trumpet of the Lord, "He was the Son of God, and God has called him home."

Screams. Wails. Hysterical shrieks.

"Dead!" came the cry. "Moshe is dead!"

"He will live forever," Eleazar boomed.

"The Son of God!" came the cry, from three voices, five, a dozen. "The Son of God!"

I was aware of Miriam at my side, warm, pressing close, her arm through mine, her soft breast against my ribs, her lips at my ear. "You must write the book," she whispered, and her voice held a terrible urgency. "*His* book, you must write. So that this day will never be forgotten. So that he will live forever."

"Yes," I heard myself saying. "Yes."

In that moment of frenzy and terror I felt myself sway like a tree of the shore that has been assailed by the flooding of the Nile; and I was uprooted and swept away. The fireball of the *Exodus* blazed in my soul like a second sun indeed, with a brightness that could never fade. And I knew that I was engulfed, that I was conquered, that I would remain here to write and preach, that I would forge the gospel of the new Moshe in the smithy of my soul and send the word to all the lands. Out of these five today would come rebirth; and to the peoples of the Republic we would bring the message for which they had waited so long in their barrenness and their confusion, and when it came they would throw off the shackles of their masters; and out of the death of the Imperium would come a new order of things. Were there other worlds, and could we dwell upon them? Who could say? But there was a new truth that we could teach, which was the truth of the second Moshe who had given his life so that we might go to the stars, and I would not let that new truth die. I would write, and others of my people would go forth and carry the word that I had written to all the lands, and the lands would be changed. And some day, who knew how soon, we would build a new ship, and another, and another, and they would carry us from this world of woe. God had sent His Son, and God had called Him home, and one day we would all follow him on wings of flame, up from the land of bondage into the heavens where He dwells eternally.

CHIP RUNNER

In the summer of 1987 the energetic publisher and book packager Byron Preiss, having produced a pair of magnificent illustrated anthologies to which I had been a contributor—The Planets and The Universe—now turned his attention the other way, to the world of the infinitely small. The Microverse was his new project, and Byron asked me to write something for this one too.

The scientific part of the story was easy enough to put together: required by the theme of the book to deal with the universe on the subatomic level, I rummaged about in my file of Scientific American to see what the current state of thinking about electrons and protons and such might be. In the course of my rummaging I stumbled upon something about microchip technology, and that led me to the fictional component of the story. All about me in the San Francisco Bay Area where I live are bright boys and girls with a deep, all-consuming, and spooky passion for computers. I happen to know something, also, about the prevalence of such eating disorders as anorexia and bulimia in Bay Area adolescents—disorders mainly involving girls, but not exclusively so. Everything fit together swiftly: an anorexic computer kid who has conceived the wild idea of entering the subatomic world by starving down to it. The rest was a matter of orchestrating theme and plot and style—of writing the story, that is. Byron had Ralph McQuarrie illustrate it with a fine, terrifying painting when he published it in The Microverse in 1989. Gardner Dozois bought the story also for the November, 1989 issue of Isaac Asimov's Science Fiction Magazine and Donald A. Wollheim selected it for his annual World's Best SF anthology.

He was fifteen, and looked about ninety, and a frail ninety at that. I knew his mother and his father, separately—they were Silicon Valley people, divorced, very important in their respective companies—and separately they had asked me to try to work with him. His skin was blue-gray and tight, drawn cruelly close over the jutting bones of his face. His eyes were gray too, and huge, and they lay deep within their sockets. His arms were like sticks. His thin lips were set in an angry grimace.

The chart before me on my desk told me that he was five feet eight inches tall and weighed 71 pounds. He was in his third year at one of the best private schools in the Palo Alto district. His I.Q. was 161. He crackled with intelligence and intensity. That was a novelty for me right at the outset. Most of my patients are depressed, withdrawn, uncertain of themselves, elusive, shy: virtual zombies. He wasn't anything like that. There would be other surprises ahead.

"So you're planning to go into the hardware end of the computer industry, your parents tell me," I began. The usual let's-build-a-relationship procedure.

He blew it away instantly with a single sour glare. "Is that your standard opening? 'Tell me all about your favorite hobby, my boy'? If you don't mind I'd rather skip all the bullshit, doctor, and then we can both get out of here faster. You're supposed to ask me about my eating habits."

It amazed me to see him taking control of the session this way within the first thirty seconds. I marveled at how different he was from most of the others, the poor sad wispy creatures who force me to fish for every word.

"Actually I do enjoy talking about the latest developments in the world of computers, too," I said, still working hard at being genial.

"But my guess is you don't talk about them very often, or you wouldn't call it 'the hardware end.' Or 'the computer industry.' We don't use mondo phrases like those any more." His high thin voice sizzled with barely suppressed rage. "Come on, doctor. Let's get right down to it. You think I'm anorexic, don't you?"

"Well—"

"I know about anorexia. It's a mental disease of girls, a vanity thing. They starve themselves because they want to look beautiful and they can't bring themselves to realize that they're not too fat. Vanity isn't the issue for me. And I'm not a girl, doctor. Even you ought to be able to see that right away."

"Timothy—"

"I want to let you know right out front that I don't have an eating disorder and I don't belong in a shrink's office. I know exactly what I'm doing all the time. The only reason I came today is to get my mother off my back, because she's taken it into her head that I'm trying to starve myself to death. She said I had to come here and see you. So I'm here. All right?"

"All right," I said, and stood up. I am a tall man, deepchested, very broad through the shoulders. I can loom when necessary. A flicker of fear crossed Timothy's face, which was the effect I wanted to produce. When it's appropriate for the therapist to assert authority, simple-minded methods are often the most effective. "Let's talk about eating, Timothy. What did you have for lunch today?"

He shrugged. "A piece of bread. Some lettuce."

"That's all?"

"A glass of water."

"And for breakfast?"

"I don't eat breakfast."

"But you'll have a substantial dinner, won't you?"

"Maybe some fish. Maybe not. I think food is pretty gross."

I nodded. "Could you operate your computer with the power turned off, Timothy?"

"Isn't that a pretty condescending sort of question, doctor?"

"I suppose it is. Okay, I'll be more direct. Do you think you can run your body without giving it any fuel?"

"My body runs just fine," he said, with a defiant edge.

"Does it? What sports do you play?"

"Sports?" It might have been a Martian word.

"You know, the normal weight for someone of your age and height ought to be—"

"There's nothing normal about me, doctor. Why should my weight be any more normal than the rest of me?"

"It was until last year, apparently. Then you stopped eating. Your family is worried about you, you know."

"I'll be okay," he said sullenly.

"You want to stay healthy, don't you?"

He stared at me for a long chilly moment. There was something close to hatred in his eyes, or so I imagined.

"What I want is to disappear," he said.

That night I dreamed I was disappearing. I stood naked and alone on a slab of gray metal in the middle of a vast empty plain under a sinister coppery sky and I began steadily to shrink. There is often some carryover from the office to a therapist's own unconscious life: we call it counter-transference. I grew smaller and smaller. Pores appeared on the surface of the metal slab and widened into jagged craters, and then into great crevices and gullies. A cloud of luminous dust shimmered about my head. Grains of sand, specks, mere motes, now took on the aspect of immense boulders. Down I drifted, gliding into the darkness of a fathomless chasm. Creatures I had not noticed before hovered about me, astonishing monsters, hairy, many-legged. They made menacing gestures, but I slipped away, downward, downward, and they were gone. The air was alive now with vibrating particles, inanimate, furious, that danced in frantic zigzag patterns, veering wildly past me, now and again crashing into me, knocking my breath from me, sending me ricocheting for what seemed like miles. I was floating, spinning, tumbling with no control. Pulsating waves of blinding light pounded me. I was falling into the infinitely small, and there was no halting my descent. I would shrink and shrink and shrink until I slipped through the realm of matter entirely and was lost. A mob of contemptuous glowing things—electrons and protons, maybe, but how could I tell?—crowded close around me, emitting fizzy sparks that seemed to me like jeers and laughter. They told me to keep moving along, to get myself out of their kingdom, or I would meet a terrible death. "To see a world in a grain of sand," Blake wrote. Yes. And Eliot wrote, "I will show you fear in a handful of dust." I went on downward, and downward still. And then I awoke gasping, drenched in sweat, terrified, alone.

Normally the patient is uncommunicative. You interview parents, siblings, teachers, friends, anyone who might provide a clue or an opening wedge. Anorexia is a life-threatening matter. The patients—girls, almost always, or young women in their twenties—have lost all sense of normal body-image and feel none of the food-deprivation prompts that a normal body gives its owner. Food is the enemy. Food must be resisted. They eat only when forced to, and then as little as possible. They are unaware that they are frighteningly gaunt. Strip them and put them in front of a mirror and they will pinch their sagging empty skin to show you imaginary fatty bulges. Sometimes the process of self-skeletonization is impossible to halt, even by therapy. When it reaches a certain point the degree of organic damage becomes irreversible and the death-spiral begins.

"He was always tremendously bright," Timothy's mother said. She was fifty, a striking woman, trim, elegant, almost radiant, vice president for finance at one of the biggest Valley companies. I knew her in that familiarly involuted California way: her present husband used to be married to my first wife. "A genius, his teachers all said. But strange, you know? Moody. Dreamy. I used to think he was on drugs, though of course none of the kids do that any more." Timothy was her only child by her first marriage. "It scares me to death to watch him wasting away like that. When I see him I want to take him and shake him and force ice cream down his throat, pasta, milkshakes, anything. And then I want to hold him, and I want to cry."

"You'd think he'd be starting to shave by now," his father said. Technical man, working on nanoengineering projects at the Stanford AI lab. We often played racquetball together. "I was. You too, probably. I got a look at him in the shower, three or four months ago. Hasn't even reached puberty yet. Fifteen and not a hair on him. It's the starvation, isn't it? It's retarding his physical development, right?"

"I keep trying to get him to like eat something, anything," his step-brother Mick said. "He lives with us, you know, on the weekends, and most of the time he's downstairs playing with his computers, but sometimes I can get him to go out with us, and we buy like a chili dog for him, or, you know, a burrito, and he goes, Thank you, thank you, and pretends to eat it, but then he throws it away when he thinks we're not looking. He is *so* weird, you know? And scary. You look at him with those ribs and all and he's like something out of a horror movie."

"What I want is to disappear," Timothy said.

He came every Tuesday and Thursday for one-hour sessions. There was at the beginning an undertone of hostility and suspicion to everything he said. I asked him, in my layman way, a few things about the latest developments in computers, and he answered me in monosyllables at first, not at all bothering to hide his disdain for my ignorance and my innocence. But now and again some question of mine would catch his interest and he would forget to be irritated, and reply at length, going on and on into realms I could not even pretend to understand. Trying to find things of that sort to ask him seemed my best avenue of approach. But of course I knew I was unlikely to achieve anything of therapeutic value if we simply talked about computers for the whole hour.

He was very guarded, as was only to be expected, when I would bring the conversation around to the topic of eating. He made it clear that his eating habits were his own business and he would rather not discuss them with me, or anyone. Yet there was an aggressive glow on his face whenever we spoke of the way he ate that called Kafka's hunger artist to my mind: he seemed proud of his achievements in starvation, even eager to be admired for his skill at shunning food.

Too much directness in the early stages of therapy is generally counterproductive where anorexia is the problem. The patient *loves* her syndrome and resists any therapeutic approach that might deprive her of it. Timothy and I talked mainly of his studies, his classmates, his step-brothers. Progress was slow, circuitous, agonizing. What was most agonizing was my realization that I didn't have much time. According to the report from his school physician he was already running at dangerously low levels, bones weakening, muscles degenerating, electrolyte balance cockeyed, hormonal systems in disarray. The necessary treatment before long would be hospitalization, not psychotherapy, and it might almost be too late even for that.

He was aware that he was wasting away and in danger. He didn't seem to care.

I let him see that I wasn't going to force anything on him. So far as I was concerned, I told him, he was basically free to starve himself to death if that was what he was really after. But as a psychologist whose role it is to help people, I said, I had some scientific interest in finding out what made him tick—not particularly for his sake, but for the sake of other patients who might be more interested in being helped. He could relate to that. His facial expressions changed. He became less hostile. It was the fifth session now, and I sensed that his armor might be ready to crack. He was starting to think of me not as a member of the enemy but as a neutral observer, a dispassionate investigator. The next step was to make him see me as an ally. You and me, Timothy, standing together against *them*. I told him a few things about myself, my childhood, my troubled adolescence: little nuggets of confidence, offered by way of trade.

"When you disappear," I said finally, "where is it that you want to go?"

The moment was ripe and the breakthrough went beyond my highest expectations.

"You know what a microchip is?" he asked.

"Sure."

"I go down into them."

Not I *want* to go down into them. But I *do* go down into them.

"Tell me about that," I said.

"The only way you can understand the nature of reality," he said, "is to take a close look at it. To really and truly take a look, you know? Here we have these fantastic chips, a whole processing unit smaller than your little toenail with fifty times the data-handling capacity of the old mainframes. What goes on inside them? I mean, what *really* goes on? I go into them and I look. It's like a trance, you know? You sharpen your concentration and you sharpen it and sharpen it and then you're moving downward, inward, deeper and deeper." He laughed harshly. "You think this is all mystical ka-ka, don't you? Half of you thinks I'm just a crazy kid mouthing off, and the other half thinks here's a kid who's smart as hell, feeding you a line of malarkey to keep you away from the real topic. Right, doctor? Right?"

"I had a dream a couple of weeks ago about shrinking down into the infinitely small," I said. "A nightmare, really. But a fascinating one. Fascinating and frightening both. I went all the way down to the molecular level, past grains of sand, past bacteria, down to electrons and protons, or what I suppose were electrons and protons."

"What was the light like, where you were?"

"Blinding. It came in pulsing waves."

"What color?"

"Every color all at once," I said.

He stared at me. "No shit!"

"Is that the way it looks for you?"

"Yes. No." He shifted uneasily. "How can I tell if you saw what I saw? But it's a stream of colors, yes. Pulsing. And—all the colors at once, yes, that's how you could describe it—"

"Tell me more."

"More what?"

"When you go downward—tell me what it's like, Timothy."

He gave me his lofty look, his pedagogic look. "You know how small a chip is? A MOSFET, say?"

"MOSFET?"

"Metal-oxide-silicon field-effect-transistor," he said. "The newest ones have a minimum feature size of about a micrometer. Ten to the minus sixth meters. That's a millionth of a meter, all right? Small. It isn't down there on the molecular level, no. You could fit 200 amoebas into a MOSFET channel one micrometer long. Okay? Okay? Or a whole army of viruses. But it's still plenty small. That's where I go. And run, down the corridors of the chips, with electrons whizzing by me all the time. Of course I can't see them. Even a lot smaller, you can't see electrons, you can only compute the probabilities of their paths. But you can feel them. I can feel them. And I run among them, everywhere, through the corridors, through the channels, past the gates, past the open spaces in the lattice. Getting to know the territory. Feeling at home in it."

"What's an electron like, when you feel it?"

"You dreamed it, you said. You tell me."

"Sparks," I said. "Something fizzy, going by in a blur."

"You read about that somewhere, in one of your journals?"

"It's what I saw," I said. "What I felt, when I had that dream."

"But that's it! That's it exactly!" He was perspiring. His face was flushed. His hands were trembling. His whole body was ablaze with a metabolic fervor I had not previously seen in him. He looked like a skeleton who had just trotted off a basketball court after a hard game. He leaned toward me and said, looking suddenly vulnerable in a way that he had never allowed himself to seem with me before, "Are you sure it was only a dream? Or do you go there too?"

Kafka had the right idea. What the anorexic wants is to demonstrate a supreme ability. "Look," she says. "I am a special person. I have an extraordinary gift. I am capable of exerting total control over my body. By refusing food I take command of my destiny. I display supreme force of will. Can you achieve that sort of discipline? Can you even begin to understand it? Of course you can't. But I can." The issue isn't really one of worrying about being too fat. That's just a superficial problem. The real issue is one of exhibiting strength of purpose, of proving that you can accomplish something remarkable, of showing the world what a superior person you really are. So what we're dealing with isn't merely a perversely extreme form of dieting. The deeper issue is one of gaining control— over your body, over your life, even over the physical world itself.

He began to look healthier. There was some color in his cheeks now, and he seemed more relaxed, less twitchy. I had the feeling that he was putting on a little weight, although the medical reports I was getting from his school physician didn't confirm that in any significant way—some weeks he'd be up a pound or two, some weeks down, and there was never any net gain. His mother reported that he went through periods when he appeared to be showing a little interest in food, but these were usually followed by periods of rigorous fasting or at best his typical sort of reluctant nibbling. There was nothing in any of this that I could find tremendously encouraging, but I had the definite feeling that I was starting to reach him, that I was beginning to win him back from the brink.

Timothy said, "I have to be weightless in order to get there. I mean, literally weightless. Where I am now, it's only a beginning. I need to lose all the rest."

"Only a beginning," I said, appalled, and jotted a few quick notes.

"I've attained takeoff capability. But I can never get far enough. I run into a barrier on the way down, just as I'm entering the truly structural regions of the chip."

"Yet you do get right into the interior of the chip."

"Into it, yes. But I don't attain the real understanding that I'm after. Perhaps the problem's in the chip itself, not in me. Maybe if I tried a quantum-well chip instead of a MOSFET I'd get where I want to go, but they aren't ready yet, or if they are I don't have any way of getting my hands on one. I want to ride the probability waves, do you see? I want to be small enough to grab hold of an electron and stay with it as it zooms through the lattice." His eyes were blazing. "Try talking about this stuff with my brother. Or anyone. The ones who don't understand think I'm crazy. So do the ones who do."

"You can talk here, Timothy."

"The chip, the integrated circuit—what we're really talking about is transistors, microscopic ones, maybe a billion of them arranged side by side. Silicon or germanium, doped with impurities like boron, arsenic, sometimes other things. On one side are the N-type charge carriers, and the P-type ones are on the other, with an insulating layer between; and when the voltage comes through the gate, the electrons migrate to the P-type side, because it's positively charged, and the holes, the zones of positive charge, go to the N-type side. So your basic logic circuit—" He paused. "You following this?"

"More or less. Tell me about what you feel as you start to go downward into a chip."

It begins, he said, with a rush, an upward surge of almost ecstatic force: he is not descending but floating. The floor falls away beneath him as he dwindles. Then comes the intensifying of perception, dust-motes quivering and twinkling in what had a moment before seemed nothing but empty air, and the light taking on strange new refractions and shimmerings. The solid world begins to alter. Familiar shapes—the table, a chair, the computer before him—vanish as he comes closer to their essence. What he sees now is detailed structure, the intricacy of surfaces: no longer a forest, only trees. Everything is texture and there is no solidity. Wood and metal become strands and webs and mazes. Canyons yawn. Abysses open. He goes inward, drifting, tossed like a feather on the molecular breeze.

It is no simple journey. The world grows grainy. He fights his way through a dust-storm of swirling granules of oxygen and nitrogen, an invisible blizzard battering him at every step. Ahead lies the chip he seeks, a magnificent thing, a gleaming radiant Valhalla. He begins to run toward it, heedless of obstacles. Giant rainbows sweep the sky: dizzying floods of pure color, hammering down with a force capable of deflecting the wandering atoms. And then—then— The chip stands before him like some temple of Zeus rising on the Athenian plain. Giant glowing columns—yawning gateways—dark beckoning corridors—hidden sanctuaries, beyond access, beyond comprehension. It glimmers with light of many colors. A strange swelling music fills the air. He feels like an explorer taking the first stumbling steps into a lost world. And he is still shrinking. The intricacies of the chip swell, surging like metal fungi filling with water after a rain: they spring higher and higher, darkening the sky, concealing it entirely. Another level downward and he is barely large enough to manage the passage across the threshold, but he does, and enters. Here he can move freely.

He is in a strange canyon whose silvery walls, riven with vast fissures, rise farther than he can see. He runs. He runs. He has infinite energy; his legs move like springs. Behind him the gates open, close, open, close. Rivers of torrential current surge through, lifting him, carrying him along. He senses, does not see, the vibrating of the atoms of silicon or boron; he senses, does not see, the electrons and the not-electrons flooding past, streaming toward the sides, positive or negative, to which they are inexorably drawn.

But there is more. He runs on and on and on. There is infinitely more, a world within this world, a world that lies at his feet and mocks him with its inaccessibility. It swirls before him, a whirlpool, a maelstrom. He would throw himself into it if he could, but some invisible barrier keeps him from it. This is as far as he can go. This is as much as he can achieve. He yearns to reach out as an electron goes careening past, and pluck it from its path, and stare into its heart. He wants to step inside the atoms and breathe the mysterious air within their boundaries. He longs to look upon their hidden nuclei. He hungers for the sight of mesons, quarks, neutrinos. There is more, always more, an unending series of worlds within worlds, and he is huge, he is impossibly clumsy, he is a lurching reeling mountainous titan, incapable of penetrating beyond this point—

So far, and no farther— No farther—

He looked up at me from the far side of the desk. Sweat was streaming down his face and his light shirt was clinging to his skin. That

sallow cadaverous look was gone from him entirely. He looked trans-
figured, aflame, throbbing with life: more alive than anyone I had ever
seen, or so it seemed to me in that moment. There was a Faustian fire
in his look, a world-swallowing urgency. Magellan must have looked
that way sometimes, or Newton, or Galileo. And then in a moment
more it was gone, and all I saw before me was a miserable scrawny boy,
shrunken, feeble, pitifully frail.

I went to talk to a physicist I knew, a friend of Timothy's father who
did advanced research at the university. I said nothing about Timothy
to him.

"What's a quantum well?" I asked him.

He looked puzzled. "Where'd you hear of those?"

"Someone I know. But I couldn't follow much of what he was saying."

"Extremely small switching device," he said. "Experimental,
maybe five, ten years away. Less if we're very lucky. The idea is that
you use two different semiconductive materials in a single crystal lattice, a superlattice, something like a three-dimensional checkerboard.
Electrons tunneling between squares could be made to perform digital
operations at tremendous speeds."

"And how small would this thing be, compared with the sort of
transistors they have on chips now?"

"It would be down in the nanometer range," he told me. "That's a bil-
lionth of a meter. Smaller than a virus. Getting right down there close
to the theoretical limits for semiconductivity. Any smaller and you'll be
measuring things in angstroms."

"Angstroms?"

"One ten-billionth of a meter. We measure the diameter of atoms in
angstrom units."

"Ah," I said. "All right. Can I ask you something else?"

He looked amused, patient, tolerant.

"Does anyone know much about what an electron looks like?"

"*Looks* like?"

"Its physical appearance. I mean, has any sort of work been done on
examining them, maybe even photographing them—"

"You know about the Uncertainty Principle?" he asked.

"Well—not much, really—"

"Electrons are very damned tiny. They've got a mass of—ah—about nine times ten to the minus twenty-eighth grams. We need light in order to see, in any sense of the word. We see by receiving light radiated by an object, or by hitting it with light and getting a reflection. The smallest unit of light we can use, which is the photon, has such a long wavelength that it would completely hide an electron from view, so to speak. And we can't use radiation of shorter wavelength—gammas, let's say, or x-rays—for making our measurements, either, because the shorter the wavelength the greater the energy, and so a gamma ray would simply kick any electron we were going to inspect to hell and gone. So we can't "see" electrons. The very act of determining their position imparts new velocity to them, which alters their position. The best we can do by way of examining electrons is make an enlightened guess, a probabilistic determination, of where they are and how fast they're moving. In a very rough way that's what we mean by the Uncertainty Principle."

"You mean, in order to look an electron in the eye, you'd virtually have to be the size of an electron yourself? Or even smaller?"

He gave me a strange look. "I suppose that question makes sense," he said. "And I suppose I could answer yes to it. But what the hell are we talking about, now?"

I dreamed again that night: a feverish, disjointed dream of gigantic grotesque creatures shining with a fluorescent glow against a sky blacker than any night. They had claws, tentacles, eyes by the dozens. Their swollen asymmetrical bodies were bristling with thick red hairs. Some were clad in thick armor, others were equipped with ugly shining spikes that jutted in rows of ten or twenty from their quivering skins. They were pursuing me through the airless void. Wherever I ran there were more of them, crowding close. Behind them I saw the walls of the cosmos beginning to shiver and flow. The sky itself was dancing. Color was breaking through the blackness: eddying bands of every hue at once, interwoven like great chains. I ran, and I ran, and I ran, but there were monsters on every side, and no escape.

Timothy missed an appointment. For some days now he had been growing more distant, often simply sitting silently, staring at me for the whole hour out of some hermetic sphere of unapproachability. That struck me as nothing more than predictable passive-aggressive resistance, but when he failed to show up at all I was startled: such blatant rebellion wasn't his expectable mode. Some new therapeutic strategies seemed in order: more direct intervention, with me playing the role of a gruff, loving older brother, or perhaps family therapy, or some meetings with his teachers and even classmates. Despite his recent aloofness I still felt I could get to him in time. But this business of skipping appointments was unacceptable. I phoned his mother the next day, only to learn that he was in the hospital; and after my last patient of the morning I drove across town to see him. The attending physician, a chunkyfaced resident, turned frosty when I told him that I was Timothy's therapist, that I had been treating him for anorexia. I didn't need to be telepathic to know that he was thinking, *You didn't do much of a job with him, did you?* "His parents are with him now," he told me. "Let me find out if they want you to go in. It looks pretty bad."

Actually they were all there, parents, step-parents, the various children by the various second marriages. Timothy seemed to be no more than a waxen doll. They had brought him books, tapes, even a lap-top computer, but everything was pushed to the corners of the bed. The shrunken figure in the middle barely raised the level of the coverlet a few inches. They had him on an IV unit and a whole webwork of other lines and cables ran to him from the array of medical machines surrounding him. His eyes were open, but he seemed to be staring into some other world, perhaps that same world of rampaging bacteria and quivering molecules that had haunted my sleep a few nights before. He seemed perhaps to be smiling.

"He collapsed at school," his mother whispered.

"In the computer lab, no less," said his father, with a nervous ratcheting laugh. "He was last conscious about two hours ago, but he wasn't talking coherently."

"He wants to go inside his computer," one of the little boys said. "That's crazy, isn't it?" He might have been seven.

"Timothy's going to die, Timothy's going to die," chanted somebody's daughter, about seven.

"Christopher! Bree! Shhh, both of you!" said about three of the various parents, all at once.

I said, "Has he started to respond to the IV?"

"They don't think so. It's not at all good," his mother said. "He's right on the edge. He lost three pounds this week. We thought he was eating, but he must have been sliding the food into his pocket, or something like that." She shook her head. "You can't be a policeman."

Her eyes were cold. So were her husband's, and even those of the step-parents. Telling me, *This is your fault, we counted on you to make him stop starving himself.* What could I say? You can only heal the ones you can reach. Timothy had been determined to keep himself beyond my grasp. Still, I felt the keenness of their reproachful anger, and it hurt.

"I've seen worse cases than this come back under medical treatment," I told them. "They'll build up his strength until he's capable of talking with me again. And then I'm certain I'll be able to lick this thing. I was just beginning to break through his defenses when—when he—"

Sure. It costs no more to give them a little optimism. I gave them what I could: experience with other cases of severe food deprivation, positive results following a severe crisis of this nature, et cetera, et cetera, the man of science dipping into his reservoir of experience. They all began to brighten as I spoke. They even managed to convince themselves that a little color was coming into Timothy's cheeks, that he was stirring, that he might soon be regaining consciousness as the machinery surrounding him pumped the nutrients into him that he had so conscientiously forbidden himself to have.

"Look," this one said, or that one. "Look how he's moving his hands! Look how he's breathing. It's better, isn't it!"

I actually began to believe it myself.

But then I heard his dry thin voice echoing in the caverns of my mind. *I can never get far enough. I have to be weightless in order to get there. Where I am now, it's only a beginning. I need to lose all the rest.*

I want to disappear.

That night, a third dream, vivid, precise, concrete. I was falling and running at the same time, my legs pistoning like those of a marathon runner in the twenty-sixth mile, while simultaneously I dropped in free fall through airless dark toward the silver-black surface of some distant world. And fell and fell and fell, in utter weightlessness, and hit the surface easily and kept on running, moving not forward but downward, the atoms of the ground parting for me as I ran. I became smaller as I descended, and smaller yet, and even smaller, until I was a mere phantom, a running ghost, the bodiless idea of myself. And still I went downward toward the dazzling heart of things, shorn now of all impediments of the flesh.

I phoned the hospital the next morning. Timothy had died a little after dawn.

Did I fail with him? Well, then, I failed. But I think no one could possibly have succeeded. He went where he wanted to go; and so great was the force of his will that any attempts at impeding him must have seemed to him like the mere buzzings of insects, meaningless, insignificant.

So now his purpose is achieved. He has shed his useless husk. He has gone on, floating, running, descending: downward, inward, toward the core, where knowledge is absolute and uncertainty is unknown. He is running among the shining electrons, now. He is down there among the angstrom units at last.

A SLEEP AND A FORGETTING

The Benford and Greenberg alternative-universe anthology for which I wrote "To the Promised Land" was followed by a second volume of similar stories. The first had concentrated on alterations of a single historical event; this one dealt with changes in the lives of great history-making individuals. Again I was invited to contribute; and the individual I chose was Genghis Khan.

His name, of course, has come to be used as an archetype of the monstrous slaughtering-and-plundering barbarian chieftain. Indeed he probably wasn't a nice sort of person, and it's certainly all right with me that the twentieth century, amidst its Hitlers and Stalins and such, didn't have to deal with Genghis Khan as well. But the historical truth is that he was not merely an invincible conqueror but a complex and intelligent leader: an empire-builder who followed a distinctive plan of conquest that not only created a vast realm but also brought governmental order where only anarchy and chaos had been. I'd like to think that he had more in common with Augustus Caesar or Alexander the Great than he did with the classic butchers of history.

But the Mongol Empire's limitations—the limitations inherent in having a family-controlled elite of nomadic horsemen trying to rule vast bureaucratic states—eventually set bounds on the ambitions of Genghis and his descendants. What, I asked myself, would the world have been like if Genghis Khan, that singular man of formidable drive and energy, hadn't been raised as a Mongol nomad at all, but as a civilized city-dweller— as a Byzantine Christian, say? That was the point from which this story emerged. Alice Turner bought it for Playboy, *publishing it in the July, 1989*

117

issue. The following year it appeared in the Benford and Greenberg collection Alternate Heroes, *and Don Wollheim chose it for his best-of-the-year anthology.*

———

C hanneling?" I said. "For Christ's sake, Joe! You brought me all the way down here for dumb bullshit like that?"

"This isn't channeling," Joe said.

"The kid who drove me from the airport said you've got a machine that can talk with dead people."

A slow, angry flush spread across Joe's face. He's a small, compact man with very glossy skin and very sharp features, and when he's annoyed he inflates like a puff-adder.

"He shouldn't have said that."

"Is that what you're doing here?" I asked. "Some sort of channeling experiments?"

"Forget that shithead word, will you, Mike?" Joe sounded impatient and irritable. But there was an odd fluttery look in his eye, conveying— what? Uncertainty? Vulnerability? Those were traits I hadn't ever associated with Joe Hedley, not in the thirty years we'd known each other. "We aren't sure what the fuck we're doing here," he said. "We thought maybe you could tell us."

"Me?"

"You, yes. Here, put the helmet on. Come on, put it on, Mike. Put it on. Please."

I stared. Nothing ever changes. Ever since we were kids Joe's been using me for one cockeyed thing or another, because he knows he can count on me to give him a sober-minded common-sense opinion. Always bouncing this bizarre scheme or that off me, so he can measure the caroms.

The helmet was a golden strip of wire mesh studded with a row of microwave pickups the size of a dime and flanked by a pair of suction electrodes that fit over the temples. It looked like some vagrant piece of death-house equipment.

I ran my fingers over it. "How much current is this thing capable of sending through my head?"

He looked even angrier. "Oh, fuck you, you hypercautious bastard! Would I ever ask you to do anything that could harm you?"

With a patient little sigh I said, "Okay. How do I do this?"

"Ear to ear, over the top of your head. I'll adjust the electrodes for you."

"You won't tell me what any of this is all about?"

"I want an uncontaminated response. That's science talk, Mike. I'm a scientist. You know that, don't you?"

"So that's what you are. I wondered."

Joe bustled about above me, moving the helmet around, pressing the electrodes against my skull.

"How does it fit?"

"Like a glove."

"You always wear your gloves on your head?" he asked.

"You must be goddamn nervous if you think that's funny."

"I am," he said "You must be too, if you take a line like that seriously. But I tell you that you won't get hurt. I promise you that, Mike."

"All right."

"Just sit down here. We need to check the impedances, and then we can get going."

"I wish I understood at least a little bit about—"

"Please," he said. He gestured through a glass partition at a technician in the adjoining room, and she began to do things with dials and switches. This was turning into a movie, a very silly one, full of mad doctors in white jackets and sputtering electrical gadgets. The tinkering went on and on, and I felt myself passing beyond apprehension and annoyance into a kind of gray realm of Zen serenity, the way I sometimes do while sitting in the dentist's chair waiting for the scraping and poking to begin.

On the hillside visible from the laboratory window yellow hibiscus was blooming against a background of billowing scarlet bougainvillea in brilliant California sunshine. It had been cold and raining, this February morning, when I drove to Sea-Tac Airport thirteen hundred miles to the north. Hedley's lab is just outside La Jolla, on a sandy bluff high up over the blue Pacific. When Joe and I were kids growing up in Santa Monica we took this kind of luminous winter day for granted, but I had lived in the Northwest for twenty years now, and I couldn't help thinking I'd gone on a day-trip to Eden. I studied the colors on the hillside until my eyes began to get blurry.

"Here we go, now," Joe said, from a point somewhere far away behind my left shoulder.

It was like stepping into a big cage full of parakeets and mynahs and crazed macaws. I heard scratchy screeching sounds, and a harsh loony almost-laughter that soared through three or four octaves, and a low ominous burbling noise, as if some hydraulic device was about to blow a gasket. I heard weird wire-edged shrieks that went tumbling away as though the sound was falling through an infinite abyss. I heard queeblings. I heard hissings.

Then came a sudden burst of clearly enunciated syllables, floating in isolation above the noise:

—*Onoodor*—

That startled me.

A nonsense word? No, no, a real one, one that had meaning for me, a word in an obscure language that I just happen to understand.

"Today," that's what it means. In Khalkha. My specialty. But it was crazy that this machine would be speaking Khalkha to me. This had to be some sort of coincidence. What I'd heard was a random clumping of sounds that I must automatically have arranged into a meaningful pattern. I was kidding myself. Or else Joe was playing an elaborate practical joke. Only he seemed very serious.

I strained to hear more. But everything was babble again.

Then, out of the chaos:

—*Usan deer*— Khalkha, again: "On the water." It couldn't be a coincidence.

More noise. Skwkaark skreek yubble gobble.

—*Aawa namaig yawuulawa*— "Father sent me."

Skwkaark. Yabble. Eeeeesh.

"Go on," I said. I felt sweat rolling down my back. "Your father sent you where? Where? *Khaana*. Tell me where."

—*Usan deer*—

"On the water, yes."

Yarkhh. Skreek. Tshhhhhhh.

—*Akhanartan*— "To his elder brother. Yes."

I closed my eyes and let my mind rove out into the darkness. It drifted on a sea of scratchy noise. Now and again I caught an actual syllable, half a syllable, a slice of a word, a clipped fragment of meaning. The voice was brusque, forceful, a drill-sergeant voice, carrying an undertone of barely suppressed rage.

Somebody very angry was speaking to me across a great distance, over a channel clotted with interference, in a language that hardly anyone in the United States knew anything about: Khalkha. Spoken a little oddly, with an unfamiliar intonation, but plainly recognizable.

I said, speaking very slowly and carefully and trying to match the odd intonation of the voice at the other end, "I can hear you and I can understand you. But there's a lot of interference. Say everything three times and I'll try to follow."

I waited. But now there was only a roaring silence in my ears. Not even the shrieking, not even the babble.

I looked up at Hedley like someone coming out of a trance.

"It's gone dead."

"You sure?"

"I don't hear anything, Joe."

He snatched the helmet from me and put it on, fiddling with the electrodes in that edgy, compulsively precise way of his. He listened for a moment, scowled, nodded. "The relay satellite must have passed around the far side of the sun. We won't get anything more for hours if it has."

"The relay satellite? Where the hell was that broadcast coming from?"

"In a minute," he said. He reached around and took the helmet off. His eyes had a brassy gleam and his mouth was twisted off to the corner of his face, almost as if he'd had a stroke. "You were actually able to understand what he was saying, weren't you?"

I nodded.

"I knew you would. And was he speaking Mongolian?"

"Khalkha, yes. The main Mongolian dialect."

The tension left his face. He gave me a warm, loving grin. "I was sure you'd know. We had a man in from the university here, the comparative linguistics department—you probably know him, Malmstrom's his name—and he said it sounded to him like an Altaic language, maybe Turkic—is that right, Turkic?—but more likely one of the Mongolian languages, and the moment he said Mongolian I thought, That's it, get Mike down here right away—" He paused. "So it's the language that they speak in Mongolia right this very day, would you say?"

"Not quite. His accent was a little strange. Something stiff about it, almost archaic."

"Archaic."

"It had that feel, yes. I can't tell you why. There's just something formal and old-fashioned about it, something, well—"

"Archaic," Hedley said again. Suddenly there were tears in his eyes. I couldn't remember ever having seen him crying before.

What they have, the kid who picked me up at the airport had said, *is a machine that lets them talk with the dead.*

"Joe?" I said. "Joe, what in God's name is this all about?"

We had dinner that night in a sleek restaurant on a sleek, quiet La Jolla street of elegant shops and glossy-leaved trees, just the two of us, the first time in a long while that we'd gone out alone like that. Lately we tended to see each other once or twice a year at most, and Joe, who is almost always between marriages, would usually bring along his latest squeeze, the one who was finally going to bring order and stability and other such things to his tempestuous private life. And since he always needs to show the new one what a remarkable human being he is, he's forever putting on a performance, for the woman, for me, for the waiters, for the people at the nearby tables. Generally the fun's at my expense, for compared with Hedley I'm very staid and proper and I'm eighteen years into my one and only marriage so far, and Joe often seems to enjoy making me feel that there's something wrong with that. I never see him with the same woman twice, except when he happens to marry one of them. But tonight it was all different. He was alone, and the conversation was subdued and gentle and rueful, mostly about the years we'd had put in knowing each other, the fun we'd had, the regret Joe felt during the occasional long periods when we didn't see much of each other. He did most of the talking. There was nothing new about that. But mostly it was just chatter. We were three quarters of the way down the bottle of silky Cabernet before Joe brought himself around to the topic of the experiment. I hadn't wanted to push.

"It was pure serendipity," he said. "You know, the art of finding what you're not looking for. We were trying to clean up some problems in radio transmission from the Icarus relay station—that's the one that the Japs and the French hung around the sun inside the orbit of Mercury—and we were fiddling with this and fiddling with that, sending out an assortment of test signals at a lot of different frequencies, when out of nowhere we got a voice coming back at us. A man's voice. Speaking a strange language. Which turned out to be Chaucerian English."

"Some kind of academic prank?" I suggested.

He looked annoyed. "I don't think so. But let me tell it, Mike, okay? Okay?" He cracked his knuckles and rearranged the knot of his tie. "We listened to this guy and gradually we figured out a little of what he was saying and we called in a grad student from U.C.S.D. who confirmed it—thirteenth-century English—and it absolutely knocked us on our asses." He tugged at his earlobes and rearranged his tie again. A sort of manic sheen was coming into his eyes. "Before we could even begin to comprehend what we were dealing with, the Englishman was gone and we were picking up some woman making a speech in medieval French. Like we were getting a broadcast from Joan of Arc, do you see? Not that I'm arguing that that's who she was. We had her for half an hour, a minute here and a minute there with a shitload of interference, and then came a solar flare that disrupted communications, and when we had things tuned again we got a quick burst of what turned out to be Arabic, and then someone else talking in Middle English, and then, last week, this absolutely incomprehensible stuff, which Malmstrom guessed was Mongolian and you have now confirmed. The Mongol has stayed on the line longer than all the others put together."

"Give me some more wine," I said.

"I don't blame you. It's made us all crazy too. The best we can explain it to ourselves, it's that our beam passes through the sun, which as I think you know, even though your specialty happens to be Chinese history and not physics, is a place where the extreme concentration of mass creates some unusual stresses on the fabric of the continuum, and some kind of relativistic force warps the hell out of it, so that the solar field sends our signal kinking off into God knows where, and the effect is to give us a telephone line to the Middle Ages. If that sounds like gibberish to you, imagine how it sounds to us." Hedley spoke without raising his head, while moving his silverware around busily from one side of his plate to the other. "You see now about channeling? It's no fucking joke. Shit, we *are* channeling, only looks like it might actually be real, doesn't it?"

"I see," I said. "So at some point you're going to have to call up the Secretary of Defense and say, Guess what, we've been getting telephone calls on the Icarus beam from Joan of Arc. And then they'll shut down your lab here and send you off to get your heads replumbed."

He stared at me. His nostrils flickered contemptuously.

"Wrong. Completely wrong. You never had any notion of flair, did you? The sensational gesture that knocks everybody out? No. Of course not. Not *you*. Look, Mike, if I can go in there and say, We can talk to the dead, and we can *prove* it, they'll kiss our asses for us. Don't you see how fucking sensational it would be, something coming out of these government labs that ordinary people can actually understand and cheer and yell about? Telephone line to the past! George Washington himself, talking to Mr. and Mrs. America! Abe Lincoln! Something straight out of the *National Enquirer*, right, only *real*? We'd all be heroes. But it's got to be real, that's the kicker. We don't need a rational explanation for it, at least not right away. All it has to do is work. Christ, 99% of the people don't even know why electric lights light up when you flip the switch. We have to find out what we really have and get to understand it at least a little and be 200% sure of ourselves. And then we present it to Washington and we say, Here, this is what we did and this is what happens, and don't blame us if it seems crazy. But we have to keep it absolutely to ourselves until we understand enough of what we've stumbled on to be able to explain it to them with confidence. If we do it right we're goddamned kings of the world. A Nobel would be just the beginning. You understand now?"

"Maybe we should get another bottle of wine," I said.

We were back in the lab by midnight. I followed Hedley through a maze of darkened rooms, ominous with mysterious equipment glowing in the night.

A dozen or so staffers were on duty. They smiled wanly at Hedley as if there was nothing unusual about his coming back to work at this hour.

"Doesn't anyone sleep around here?" I asked.

"It's a twenty-four hour information world," Joe said. "We'll be recapturing the Icarus beam in 43 minutes. You want to hear some of the earlier tapes?"

He touched a switch and from an unseen speaker came crackles and bleebles and then a young woman's voice, strong and a little harsh, uttering brief blurts of something that sounded like strange singsong French, to me not at all understandable.

"Her accent's terrible," I said. "What's she saying?"

"It's too fragmentary to add up to anything much. She's praying, mostly. May the king live, may God strengthen his arm, something like that. For all we know it *is* Joan of Arc. We haven't gotten more than a few minutes total coherent verbal output out of any of them, usually a lot less. Except for the Mongol. He goes on and on. It's like he doesn't want to let go of the phone."

"And it really is a phone?" I asked. "What we say here, they can hear there?"

"We don't know that, because we haven't been able to make much sense out of what they say, and by the time we get it deciphered we've lost contact. But it's got to be a two-way contact. They must be getting *something* from us, because we're able to get their attention somehow and they talk back to us."

"They receive your signal without a helmet?"

"The helmet's just for your benefit. The actual Icarus signal comes in digitally. The helmet's the interface between our computer and your ears."

"Medieval people don't have digital computers either, Joe."

A muscle started popping in one of his cheeks. "No, they don't," he said. "It must come like a voice out of the sky. Or right inside their heads. But they hear us."

"How?"

"Do I know? You want this to make sense, Mike? *Nothing* about this makes sense. Let me give you an example. You were talking with that Mongol, weren't you? You asked him something and he answered you?"

"Yes. But—"

"Let me finish. What did you ask him?"

"He said his father sent him somewhere. I asked him where, and he said, On the water. To visit his elder brother."

"He answered you right away?"

"Yes," I said.

"Well, that's actually impossible. The Icarus is 93 million miles from here. There has to be something like an eight-minute time-lag in radio transmission. You follow? You ask him something and it's eight minutes before the beam reaches Icarus, and eight minutes more for his answer to come back. He sure as hell can't hold a real-time conversation with you. But you say he was."

"It may only have seemed that way. It could just have been coincidence that what I asked and what he happened to say next fit together like question and response."

"Maybe. Or maybe whatever kink in time we're operating across eats up the lag for us, too. I tell you, nothing makes sense about this.

But one way or another the beam is reaching them and it carries coherent information. I don't know why that is. It just is. Once you start dealing in impossible stuff, anything might be true. So why can't our voices come out of thin air to them?" Hedley laughed nervously. Or perhaps it was a cough, I thought. "The thing is," he went on, "this Mongol is staying on line longer than any of the others, so with you here we have a chance to have some real communication with him. You speak his language. You can validate this whole goddamn grotesque event for us, do you see? You can have an honest-to-God chat with some guy who lived six hundred years ago, and find out where he really is and what he thinks is going on, and tell us all about it."

I stole a glance at the wall clock. Half past twelve. I couldn't remember the last time I'd been up this late. I lead a nice quiet tenured life, full professor thirteen years now, University of Washington Department of Sinological Studies.

"We're about ready to acquire signal again," Hedley said. "Put the helmet on."

I slipped it into place. I thought about that little communications satellite chugging around the sun, swimming through inconceivable heat and unthinkable waves of hard radiation and somehow surviving, coming around the far side now, beaming electro-magnetic improbabilities out of the distant past at my head.

The squawking and screeching began.

Then, emerging from the noise and murk and sonic darkness, came the Mongol's voice, clear and steady:

"Where are you, you voice, you? Speak to me."

"Here," I said. "Can you hear me?"

Aark. Yaaarp. Tshhhhhhh.

The Mongol said, "Voice, what are you? Are you mortal or are you a prince of the master?"

I wrestled with the puzzling words. I'm fluent enough in Khalkha, though I don't get many opportunities for speaking it. But there was a problem of context here.

"Which master?" I asked finally. "What prince?"

"There is only one Master," said the Mongol. He said this with tremendous force and assurance, putting terrific spin on every syllable, and the capital letter was apparent in his tone. "I am His servant. The *angeloi* are his princes. Are you an *angelos*, voice?"

Angeloi? That was Greek. A Mongol, asking me if I was an angel of God?

"Not an angel, no," I said.

"Then how can you speak to me this way?"

"It's a kind of—" I paused. I couldn't come up with the Khalka for "miracle". After a moment I said, "It's by the grace of heaven on high. I'm speaking to you from far away."

"How far?"

"Tell me where you are."

Skrawwwwk. Tshhhhhh.

"Again. Where are you?"

"Nova Roma. Constantinopolis."

I blinked. "Byzantium?"

"Byzantium, yes."

"I am very far from there."

"*How* far?" the Mongol said fiercely.

"Many many days' ride. Many many." I hesitated. "Tell me what year it is, where you are."

Vzsqkk. Blzzp. Yiiiiiik.

"What's he saying to you?" Hedley asked. I waved at him furiously to be quiet.

"The year," I said again. "Tell me what year it is."

The Mongol said scornfully, "Everyone knows the year, voice."

"Tell me."

"It is the year 1187 of our Savior."

I began to shiver. Our Savior? Weirder and weirder, I thought. A Christian Mongol? Living in Byzantium? Talking to me on the space telephone out of the twelfth century? The room around me took on a smoky, insubstantial look. My elbows were aching, and something was throbbing just above my left cheekbone. This had been a long day for me. I was very tired. I was heading into that sort of weariness where walls melted and bones turned soft. Joe was dancing around in front of me like someone with tertiary St. Vitus'.

"And your name?" I said.

"I am Petros Alexios."

"Why do you speak Khalkha if you are Greek?"

A long silence, unbroken even by the hellish static.

"I am not Greek," came the reply finally. "I am by birth Khalkha Mongol, but raised Christian among the Christians from age eleven, when my father sent me on the water and I was taken. My name was Temujin. Now I am twenty and I know the Savior."

I gasped and put my hand to my throat as though it had been skewered out of the darkness by a spear.

"Temujin," I said, barely getting the word out.

"My father was Yesugei the chieftain."

"Temujin," I said again. "Son of Yesugei." I shook my head.

Aaark. Blzzzp. Tshhhhhh.

Then no static, no voice, only the hushed hiss of silence.

"Are you okay?" Hedley asked.

"We've lost contact, I think."

"Right. It just broke. You look like your brain has shorted out."

I slipped the helmet off. My hands were shaking.

"You know," I said, "maybe that French woman really was Joan of Arc."

"What?"

I shrugged. "She really might have been," I said wearily. "Anything's possible, isn't it?"

"What the hell are you trying to tell me, Mike?"

"Why shouldn't she have been Joan of Arc?" I asked. "Listen, Joe. This is making me just as nutty as you are. You know what I've just been doing? I've been talking to Genghis Khan on this fucking telephone of yours."

I managed to get a few hours of sleep by simply refusing to tell Hedley anything else until I'd had a chance to rest. The way I said it, I left him no options, and he seemed to grasp that right away. At the hotel, I sank from consciousness like a leaden whale, hoping I wouldn't surface again before noon, but old habit seized me and pushed me up out of the tepid depths at seven, irreversibly awake and not a bit less depleted. I put in a quick call to Seattle to tell Elaine that I was going to stay down in La Jolla a little longer than expected. She seemed worried—not that I might be up to any funny business, not me, but only that I sounded so groggy. "You know Joe," I said. "For him it's a twenty-four hour information world." I told her nothing else. When I stepped out on the breakfast patio half an hour later, I could see the lab's blue van already waiting in the hotel lot to pick me up.

Hedley seemed to have slept at the lab. He was rumpled and red-eyed but somehow he was at normal functioning level, scurrying around the place like a yappy little dog. "Here's a printout of last night's contact," he said, the moment I came in. "I'm sorry if the transcript looks cockeyed. The computer doesn't know how to spell in Mongolian." He shoved it into my hands. "Take a squint at it and see if you really heard all the things you thought you heard."

I peered at the single long sheet. It seemed to be full of jabberwocky, but once I figured out the computer's system of phonetic equivalents I could read it readily enough. I looked up after a moment, feeling very badly shaken.

"I was hoping I dreamed all this. I didn't."

"You want to explain it to me?"

"I can't."

Joe scowled. "I'm not asking for fundamental existential analysis. Just give me a goddamned translation, all right?"

"Sure," I said.

He listened with a kind of taut, explosive attention that seemed to me to be masking a mixture of uneasiness and bubbling excitement. When I was done he said, "Okay. What's this Genghis Khan stuff?"

"Temujin was Genghis Khan's real name. He was born around 1167 and his father Yesugei was a minor chief somewhere in northeastern Mongolia. When Temujin was still a boy, his father was poisoned by enemies, and he became a fugitive, but by the time he was fifteen he started putting together a confederacy of Mongol tribes, hundreds of them, and eventually he conquered everything in sight. Genghis Khan means 'Ruler of the Universe.'"

"So? Our Mongol lives in Constantinople, you say. He's a Christian and he uses a Greek name."

"He's Temujin, son of Yesugei. He's twenty years old in the year when Genghis Khan was twenty years old."

Hedley looked belligerent. "Some other Temujin. Some other Yesugei."

"Listen to the way he speaks. He's scary. Even if you can't understand a word of what he's saying, can't you feel the power in him? The coiled-up anger? That's the voice of somebody capable of conquering whole continents."

"Genghis Khan wasn't a Christian. Genghis Khan wasn't kidnapped by strangers and taken to live in Constantinople."

"I know," I said. To my own amazement I added, "But maybe this one was."

"Jesus God Almighty. What's that supposed to mean?"

"I'm not certain."

Hedley's eyes took on a glaze. "I hoped you were going to be part of the solution, Mike. Not part of the problem."

"Just let me think this through," I said, waving my hands above his face as if trying to conjure some patience into him. Joe was peering at me in a stunned, astounded way. My eyeballs throbbed. Things were jangling up and down along my spinal column. Lack of sleep had coated my brain with a hard crust of adrenaline. Bewilderingly strange ideas were rising like sewer gases in my mind and making weird bubbles. "All right, try this," I said at last. "Say that there are all sorts of possible worlds. A world in which you're King of England, a world in which I played third base for the Yankees, a world in which the dinosaurs never died out and Los Angeles gets invaded every summer by hungry tyrannosaurs. And one world where Yesugei's son Temujin wound up in twelfth-century Byzantium as a Christian instead of founding the Mongol Empire. And that's the Temujin I've been talking to. This cockeyed beam of yours not only crosses time-lines, somehow it crosses probability-lines too, and we've fished up some alternative reality that—"

"I don't believe this," Hedley said.

"Neither do I, really. Not seriously. I'm just putting forth one possible hypothesis that might explain—"

"I don't mean your fucking hypothesis. I mean I find it hard to believe that you of all people, my old pal Mike Michaelson, can be standing here running off at the mouth this way, working hard at turning a mystifying event into a goddamned nonsensical one—you, good old sensible steady Mike, telling me some shit about tyrannosaurs amok in Los Angeles—"

"It was only an example of—"

"Oh, fuck your example," Hedley said. His face darkened with exasperation bordering on fury. He looked ready to cry. "Your example is absolute crap. Your example is garbage. You know, man, if I wanted someone to feed me a lot of New Age crap I didn't have to go all the way to Seattle to find one. Alternative realities! Third base for the Yankees!"

A girl in a lab coat appeared out of nowhere and said, "We have signal acquisition, Dr. Hedley."

I said, "I'll catch the next plane north, okay?"

Joe's face was red and starting to do its puff-adder trick and his adam's-apple bobbed as if trying to find the way out.

"I wasn't trying to mess up your head," I said. "I'm sorry if I did. Forget everything I was just saying. I hope I was at least of some help, anyway."

Something softened in Joe's eyes.

"I'm so goddamned tired, Mike."

"I know."

"I didn't mean to yell at you like that."

"No offense taken, Joe."

"But I have trouble with this alternative-reality thing of yours. You think it was easy for me to believe that what we were doing here was talking to people in the past? But I brought myself around to it, weird though it was. Now you give it an even weirder twist, and it's too much. It's too fucking much. It violates my sense of what's right and proper and fitting. You know what Occam's Razor is, Mike? The old medieval axiom, *Never multiply hypotheses needlessly*? Take the simplest one. Here even the simplest one is crazy. You push it too far."

"Listen," I said, "if you'll just have someone drive me over to the hotel—"

"No."

"No?"

"Let me think a minute," he said. "Just because it doesn't make sense doesn't mean that it's impossible, right? And if we get one impossible thing, we can have two, or six, or sixteen. Right? Right?" His eyes were like two black holes with cold stars blazing at their bottoms. "Hell, we aren't at the point where we need to worry about explanations. We have to find out the basic stuff first. Mike, I don't want you to leave. I want you to stay here."

"What?"

"Don't go. Please. I still need somebody to talk to the Mongol for me. Don't go. Please, Mike? Please?"

The times, Temujin said, were very bad. The infidels under Saladin had smashed the Crusader forces in the Holy Land and Jerusalem itself had fallen to the Moslems. Christians everywhere mourn the loss, said Temujin. In Byzantium—where Temujin was captain of the guards in the private army of a prince named Theodore Lascaris—God's grace seemed also to have been withdrawn. The great empire was in heavy weather. Insurrections had brought down two emperors in the past four years and the current man was weak and timid. The provinces of Hungary, Cyprus, Serbia, and Bulgaria were all in revolt. The Normans of Sicily were chopping up Byzantine Greece and on the other side of the empire the Seljuk Turks were chewing their way through Asia Minor. "It is the time of the wolf," said Temujin. "But the sword of the Lord will prevail."

The sheer force of him was astounding. It lay not so much in what he said, although that was sharp and fierce, as in the way he said it. I could feel the strength of the man in the velocity and impact of each syllable. Temujin hurled his words as if from a catapult. They arrived carrying a crackling electrical charge. Talking with him was like holding live cables in my hands.

Hedley, jigging and fidgeting around the lab, paused now and then to stare at me with what looked like awe and wonder in his eyes, as if to say, *You really can make sense of this stuff?* I smiled at him. I felt bizarrely cool and unflustered. Sitting there with some electronic thing on my head, letting that terrific force go hurtling through my brain. Discussing twelfth-century politics with an invisible Byzantine Mongol. Making small talk with Genghis Khan. All right. I could handle it.

I beckoned for notepaper. *Need printout of world historical background late twelfth century,* I scrawled, without interrupting my conversation with Temujin. *Esp. Byzantine history, Crusades, etc.*

The kings of England and France, said Temujin, were talking about launching a new Crusade. But at the moment they happened to be at war with each other, which made cooperation difficult. The powerful Emperor Frederick Barbarossa of Germany was also supposed to be getting up a Crusade, but that, he said, might mean more trouble for Byzantium than for the Saracens, because Frederick was the friend of Byzantium's enemies in the rebellious provinces, and he'd have to march through those provinces on the way to the Holy Land.

"It is a perilous time," I agreed.

Then suddenly I was feeling the strain. Temujin's rapid-fire delivery was exhausting to follow, he spoke Mongolian with what I took to be a Byzantine accent, and he sprinkled his statements with the names of emperors, princes, and even nations that meant nothing to me. Also there was that powerful force of him to contend with—it hit you like an avalanche—and beyond that his anger: the whipcrack inflection that seemed the thinnest of bulwarks against some unstated inner rage, fury, frustration. It's hard to feel at ease with anyone who seethes that way. Suddenly I just wanted to go somewhere and lie down.

But someone put printout sheets in front of me, closely packed columns of stuff from the *Britannica*. Names swam before my eyes: Henry II, Barbarossa, Stephan Nemanya, Isaac II Angelos, Guy of Jerusalem, Richard the Lion-Hearted. Antioch, Tripoli, Thessalonica, Venice. I nodded my thanks and pushed the sheets aside.

Cautiously I asked Temujin about Mongolia. It turned out that he knew almost nothing about Mongolia. He'd had no contact at all with his native land since his abduction at the age of eleven by Byzantine traders who carried him off to Constantinople. His country, his father, his brothers, the girl to whom he had been betrothed when he was still a child—they were all just phantoms to him now, far away, forgotten. But in the privacy of his own soul he still spoke Khalkha. That was all that was left.

By 1187, I knew, the Temujin who would become Genghis Khan had already made himself the ruler of half of Mongolia. His fame would surely have spread to cosmopolitan Byzantium. How could this Temujin be unaware of him? Well, I saw one way. But Joe had already shot it down. And it sounded pretty nutty even to me.

"Do you want a drink?" Hedley asked. "Tranks? Aspirin?"

I shook my head. "I'm okay," I murmured.

To Temujin I said, "Do you have a wife? Children?"

"I have vowed not to marry until Jesus rules again in His own land."

"So you're going to go on the next Crusade?" I asked.

Whatever answer Temujin made was smothered by static.

Awkkk. Skrrkkk. Tsssshhhhhhh.

Then silence, lengthening into endlessness.

"Signal's gone," someone said.

"I could use that drink now," I said. "Scotch."

The lab clock said it was ten in the morning. To me it felt like the middle of the night.

An hour had passed. The signal hadn't returned.

Hedley said, "You really think he's Genghis Khan?"

"I really think he *could* have been."

"In some other probability world."

Carefully I said, "I don't want to get you all upset again, Joe."

"You won't. Why the hell *not* believe we're tuned into an alternative reality? It's no more goofy than any of the rest of this. But tell me this: is what he says consistent with being Genghis Khan?"

"His name's the same. His age. His childhood, up to the point when he wandered into some Byzantine trading caravan and they took him away to Constantinople with them. I can imagine the sort of fight he put up, too. But his life-line must have diverged completely from that point on. A whole new world-line split off from ours. And in that world, instead of turning into Genghis Khan, ruler of all Mongolia, he grew up to be Petros Alexios of Prince Theodore Lascaris' private guards."

"And he has no idea of who he could have been?" Joe asked.

"How could he? It isn't even a dream to him. He was born into another world that wasn't ever destined to have a Genghis Khan. You know the poem:

'Our birth is but a sleep and a forgetting.
The soul that rises with us, our life's star,
Hath had elsewhere its setting,
And cometh from afar.'

"Very pretty. Is that Yeats?" Hedley said.

"Wordsworth," I said. "When's the signal coming back?"

"An hour, two, three. It's hard to say. You want to take a nap, and we'll wake you when we have acquisition?"

"I'm not sleepy."

"You look pretty ragged," Joe said.

I wouldn't give him the satisfaction.

"I'm okay. I'll sleep for a week, later on. What if you can't raise him again?"

"There's always that chance, I suppose. We've already had him on the line five times as long as all the rest put together."

"He's a very determined man," I said.

"He ought to be. He's Genghis fucking Khan."

"Get him back," I said. "I don't want you to lose him. I want to talk to him some more."

Morning ticked on into afternoon. I phoned Elaine twice while we waited, and I stood for a long time at the window watching the shadows of the oncoming winter evening fall across the hibiscus and the bougainvillea, and I hunched my shoulders up and tried to pull in the signal by sheer body english. Contemplating the possibility that they might never pick up Temujin again left me feeling weirdly forlorn. I was beginning to feel that I had a real relationship with that eerie disembodied angry voice coming out of the crackling night. Toward mid-afternoon I thought I was starting to understand what was making Temujin so angry, and I had some things I wanted to say to him about that.

Maybe you ought to get some sleep, I told myself.

At half past four someone came to me and said the Mongol was on the line again.

The static was very bad. But then came the full force of Temujin soaring over it. I heard him saying, "The Holy Land must be redeemed. I cannot sleep so long as the infidels possess it."

I took a deep breath.

In wonder I watched myself set out to do something unlike anything I had ever done before.

"Then you must redeem it yourself," I said firmly.

"I?"

"Listen to me, Temujin. Think of another world far from yours. There is a Temujin in that world too, son of Yesugei, husband to Bortei who is daughter of Dai the Wise."

"Another world? What are you saying?"

"Listen. Listen. He is a great warrior, that other Temujin. No one can withstand him. His own brothers bow before him. All Mongols everywhere bow before him. His sons are like wolves, and they ride into every land and no one can withstand them. This Temujin is master of all Mongolia. He is the Great Khan, the Genghis Khan, the ruler of the universe."

There was silence. Then Temujin said, "What is this to me?"

"He is you, Temujin. You are the Genghis Khan."

Silence again, longer, broken by hideous shrieks of interplanetary noise.

"I have no sons and I have not seen Mongolia in years, or even thought of it. What are you saying?"

"That you can be as great in your world as this other Temujin is in his."

"I am Byzantine. I am Christian. Mongolia is nothing to me. Why would I want to be master in that savage place?"

"I'm not talking about Mongolia. You are Byzantine, yes. You are Christian. But you were born to lead and fight and conquer," I said. "What are you doing as a captain of another man's palace guards? You waste your life that way, and you know it, and it maddens you. You should have armies of your own. You should carry the Cross into Jerusalem."

"The leaders of the new Crusade are quarrelsome fools. It will end in disaster."

"Perhaps not. Frederick Barbarossa's Crusade will be unstoppable."

"Barbarossa will attack Byzantium instead of the Moslems. Everyone knows that."

"No," I said. That inner force of Temujin was rising and rising in intensity, like a gale climbing toward being a hurricane. I was awash in sweat, now, and I was dimly aware of the others staring at me as though I had lost my senses. A strange exhilaration gripped me. I went plunging joyously ahead. "Emperor Isaac Angelos will come to terms with Barbarossa. The Germans will march through Byzantium and go on toward the Holy Land. But there Barbarossa will die and his army will scatter—unless you are there, at his right hand, taking command in his place when he falls, leading them onward to Jerusalem. You, the invincible, the Genghis Khan."

There was silence once more, this time so prolonged that I was afraid the contact had been broken for good.

Then Temujin returned. "Will you send soldiers to fight by my side?" he asked.

"That I cannot do."

"You have the power to send them, I know," said Temujin. "You speak to me out of the air. I know you are an angel, or else you are a demon. If you are a demon, I invoke the name of Christos Pantokrator upon you, and begone. But if you are an angel, you can send me help. Send it, then, and I will lead your troops to victory. I will take the Holy Land from the infidel. I will create the Empire of Jesus in the world and bring all things to fulfillment. Help me. Help me."

"I've done all I can," I said. "The rest is for you to achieve."

There was another spell of silence.

"Yes," Temujin said finally. "I understand. Yes. Yes. The rest is for me."

"Christ, you look peculiar," Joe Hedley said, staring at me almost fearfully. "I've never seen you looking like this before. You look like a wild man."

"Do I?" I said.

"You must be dead tired, Mike. You must be asleep on your feet. Listen, go over to the hotel and get some rest. We'll have a late dinner, okay? You can fill me in then on whatever you've just been jabbering about. But relax now. The Mongol's gone and we may not get him back till tomorrow."

"You won't get him back at all," I said.

"You think?" He peered close. "Hey, are you okay? Your eyes—your face—" Something quivered in his cheek. "If I didn't know better I'd say you were stoned."

"I've been changing the world. It's hard work."

"Changing the world?"

"Not this world. The other one. Look," I said hoarsely, "they never had a Genghis Khan, so they never had a Mongol Empire, and the whole history of China and Russia and the Near East and a lot of other places was very different. But I've got this Temujin all fired up now to be a Christian Genghis Khan. He got so Christian in Byzantium that he forgot what was really inside him, but I've reminded him, I've told him how he can still do the thing that he was designed to do, and he understands. He's found his true self again. He'll go out to fight in the name of Jesus and he'll build an empire that'll eat the Moslem powers for breakfast and then blow away Byzantium and Venice and go on from there to do God knows what. He'll probably conquer all of Europe before he's finished. And I did it. I set it all in motion. He was sending me all this energy, this Genghis Khan zap that he has inside him, and I figured the least I could do for him was turn some of it around and send it back to him, and say, Here, go, be what you were supposed to be."

"Mike—"

I stood close against him, looming over him. He gave me a bewildered look.

"You really didn't think I had it in me, did you?" I said. "You son of a bitch. You've always thought I'm as timid as a turtle. Your good old sober stick-in-the-mud pal Mike. What do you know? What the hell do you know?" Then I laughed. He looked so stunned that I had to soften it for him a little. Gently I touched his shoulder. "I need a shower and a drink. And then let's think about dinner."

Joe gawked at me. "What if it wasn't some other world you changed, though? Suppose it was this one."

"Suppose it was," I said. "Let's worry about that later. I still need that shower."

IN ANOTHER COUNTRY

Writing "In Another Country" was one of the strangest and most challenging things I've ever done in a writing career that now is more than fifty years old.

The impetus to do it came from the anthologist Martin H. Greenberg, who told me one wintry day in 1988 that he was editing a series of books for which contemporary science-fiction writers would be asked to produce companions to classic s-f novellas of the past. The new story and the old one would then be published in the same volume. He invited me to participate; and after hardly a moment's thought I chose C.L. Moore's "Vintage Season" as the story I most wanted to work with.

Now and then I have deliberately chosen to reconstruct some classic work of literature in a science-fictional mode, as a kind of technical exercise. My novel The Man in the Maze of the 1960s is based on the Philoctetes of Sophocles, though you'd have to look hard to find the parallel. Downward to the Earth, from the same era, was written with a nod to Joseph Conrad's Heart of Darkness. My story "To See the Invisible Man" develops an idea that Jorge Luis Borges threw away in a single sentence. In 1989, I reworked Conrad's famous story "The Secret Sharer," translating it completely into an s-f context.

But in all those cases, though I was using the themes and patterns of earlier and greater writers, the stories themselves, and the worlds in which they were set, were entirely invented by me. Essentially I was running my own variations on classic themes, as Beethoven did with the themes of Mozart, or Brahms with Haydn. The task this time was to enter a world already created by a master artist—the world of Moore's classic 1946 story, "Vintage Season"—and work with her material, finding something new to say about a narrative situation that had already been triumphantly, and, one would think, completely, explored in great depth.

The solution was not to write a sequel to Vintage Season—that would have been pointless, a mere time-travelog to some era other than the one visited in the original story—but to produce a work interwoven with Moore's the way the lining of a cape is interwoven with the cape itself. My story is set during the same few weeks as hers, and builds toward the same climax. I used many of her characters, but not as major figures; they move through the background, and the people in the foreground are mine. She told her story from the point of view of a man of the twentieth century who finds himself in the midst of perplexing strangers from the future; I went around to the far side and worked from the point of view of one of the visitors. Where I could, I filled in details of the time-traveling society that Moore had not provided, and clarified aspects of her story that she had chosen to leave undeveloped, thus providing a kind of Silverbergian commentary on her concepts. And though I made no real attempt to write in Moore's style, I adapted my own as well as I could to match the grace and elegance of her tone.

There is perhaps an aspect of real lese-majeste in all of this, or maybe the word I want is hubris. Readers of my autobiographical anthology, Science Fiction 101, will know that C.L. Moore is one of the writers I most revere in our field, that I have studied her work with respect verging on awe. To find myself now going back over the substance of her most accomplished story in the hope of adding something to it of my own was an odd and almost frightening experience. I suspect I would not have dared to do any such thing fifteen or twenty years ago, confident though I was then of my own technical abilities. But now, when my own science-fiction-writing career has extended through a period longer than that of Moore's own, I found myself willing to risk the attempt, if only to see whether I could bring it off.

It was an extraordinary thing for me to enter Moore's world and feel, for the weeks I was at work at it, that I was actually writing, if not Vintage Season itself, then something as close to it as could be imagined. I was there, in that city, at that time, and it all became far more vivid for me than even my many readings of the original story over a 40-year period had been able to achieve. I hope that the result justifies the effort and that I will be forgiven for having dared tinker with a masterpiece this way. And most profoundly do I wish that C.L. Moore could have seen my story and perhaps found a good word or two to say for it.

IN ANOTHER COUNTRY

Gardner Dozois published it in the March, 1989 issue of Asimov's Science Fiction *and Tor brought it out the following year bound with Moore's original story in a double volume.*

The summer had been Capri, at the villa of Augustus, the high summer of the emperor at the peak of his reign, and the autumn had been the pilgrimage to golden Canterbury. Later they would all go to Rome for Christmas, to see the coronation of Charlemagne. But now it was the springtime of their wondrous journey, that glorious May late in the twentieth century that was destined to end in sudden roaring death and a red smoking sky. In wonder and something almost like ecstasy Thimiroi watched the stone walls of Canterbury fade into mist and this newest strange city take on solidity around him. The sight of it woke half-formed poems in his mind. He felt amazingly young, alive, open...vulnerable.

"Thimiroi's in a trance," Denvin said in his light, mocking way, and winked and grinned. He stood leaning casually against the rail of the embankment, a compact, elegant little man, looking back at his two companions.

"Let him alone," said Laliene sharply. In anger she ran her hands over the crimson nimbus of her hair and down the sides of her sleek tanned cheeks. Her gray-violet eyes flashed with annoyance. "Can't you see he's overwhelmed by what he sees out there?"

"By the monstrous ugliness of it?"

"By its beauty," Laliene said, with some ferocity. She touched Thimiroi's elbow. "Are you all right?" she whispered.

Thimiroi nodded.

She gestured toward the city. "How wonderfully discordant it is! How beautifully strident! No two buildings alike. And the surfaces of everything so flat. But colors, shapes, sizes, textures, all different. Not even the trees showing any sort of harmony."

"And the noise," said Denvin. "Don't forget the noise, if you're delighted by discordance. Machinery screeching and clanging and booming, and giving off smelly fumes besides—oh, it's marvelous, Laliene! Those painted things are vehicles, aren't they? Those boxy-looking machines. Honking and bellowing like crazed oxen with wheels. That thing flying around up there, too, the shining thing with wings—listen to it! Just listen!"

"Stop it," Laliene said. "You're going to upset him."

"No," Thimiroi said. "He's not bothering me. But I do think it's very beautiful. Beautiful in its ugliness. Beautiful in its discordance. There's energy here. Whatever else this place may be, it's a place of tremendous energy. And energy is always beautiful." His heart was pounding. It had not pounded like this when they had arrived at any of the other places of their tour through antiquity. But the twentieth century was special: an apocalyptic time, a time of such potent darkness that it cast an eerie black radiance across half a dozen centuries to come. And this was its most poignant moment, when the century was at its highest point, all its earlier turmoil far behind—the moment when splendor and magnificence would be transformed in an instant, by nature's malevolent prank, into stunning catastrophe. "Besides," he said, "not everything here is ugly or discordant anyway. Look at the sky."

"Yes," Laliene said. "That's a sky to remember. It's a sky that absolutely demands a great artist to capture, wouldn't you say? Someone on the order of Nivander, or even Sathimon. Those blues, and the white of the clouds. And then those streaks of gold and purple and red."

"You mean the pollution?" Denvin asked.

She glowered at him. "Don't. Please. If you don't want to be here, tell Kadro when he shows up, and he'll send you home. But don't spoil it for the rest of us."

"Sorry," said Denvin, in a chastened tone. "I do have to admit that that sky is fantastic."

"So intense," Laliene said. "It comes right down and wraps itself around the tops of the buildings like a shimmering blue cloak. And everything so sharp, so vivid, so clear. The sun was brighter back in these days, someone said. That must be why. And the air more transparent, a different mix of elements. Of course, this was an unusual season even for here. That's well known. They say there had never been a month like this one, a magical springtime, everything perfect, almost as if it had been arranged that way for maximum contrast with—with—"

Her voice trailed away.

Thimiroi shook his head. "You both talk too much. Can't you simply stand here and let it all come flooding into your souls? We came here to *experience* this place, not to talk about it. We'll have the rest of our lives to talk about it."

They looked abashed. He grasped their hands in his and laughed—his rich, exuberant, pealing laugh, which some people thought was too much for their delicate sensibilities—to take the sting out of the rebuke. Denvin, after a moment, managed a smile. Laliene gave Thimiroi a curiously impenetrable stare; but then she too smiled, a warmer and more sincere one than Denvin's. Thimiroi nodded and released them, and stepped forward to peer over the edge of the embankment.

They had materialized just a few moments earlier, in what seemed to be a park on the highest slopes of a lush green hillside overlooking a broad, swiftly flowing river. The city was on the far side, stretching out before them in dizzying vastness. Where they stood was in a sort of overlook point, jutting out of the hill, protected by a dark metal railing. Their luggage was beside them. The hour appeared to be midday; the sun was high; the air was mild, and very still and clear. The park was almost empty, though Thimiroi could see a few people strolling on the paths below. Natives of this time and place, he thought. His heart went out to them. He would have run down to them and embraced them, if he could. He longed to know what they were really like, these ancients, these rough earthy primitives, these people of lost antiquity.

Primitives, he thought? Well, yes, what else could they be called? They lived so long ago. But this city is no trifling thing. This is no squalid village of mud-and-wattle huts that lies before us.

In silence Thimiroi stared across the river at the massive blocky gray towers and wide, busy streets of the great metropolis, and at the shimmering silvery bridges to his right and to his left, and at the endless rows of small white and pink houses that rose up and up and up through the green hills on the other side. The weight and size and power of the place were extraordinary. His soul quivered with—what? Joy? Amazement? Fear?—at such immensity. How many people lived here? A million? Five million? He could scarcely conceive of such a number, all packed into a single place. The other ancient cities they had visited on this tour, imperial capitals though they were, were mere citylets—towns, even; piddling little medieval settlements—however grand they might have imagined themselves to be. But the great cities of the twentieth century, he had always been told, marked the high point in human urban concentration: cities of ten million, fifteen million, twenty million people. Unimaginable. This one before him was not even the biggest one, not even close to the biggest. Never before in history had cities grown to this size—and never again, either. Never again. What an extraordinary sight! What an astounding thing to contemplate, this great humming throbbing hive of intense human activity, especially when one knew—when one knew—when one knew the fate that was soon to befall it—

"Thimiroi?" Laliene called. "Kadro's here!"

He turned. The tour leader, a small, fragile-looking man with thick flame-red hair and eerie blue-violet eyes, held out his arms to them. He could only just have arrived himself—they had all been together mere minutes before, in Canterbury—but he was dressed already in twentieth-century costume, curious and quaint and awkward-looking, but oddly elegant on him. Thimiroi had no idea how that trick had been accomplished, but he accepted it untroubledly: The Travel was full of mysteries of all sorts, detours and overlaps and side-jaunts through time. It was Kadro's business to understand such things, not his.

"You'd better change," Kadro said. "There's a transport vehicle on the way up here to take you into town."

He touched something at his hip and a cloud of dark mist sprang up around them. Under its protective cover they opened their suitcases—their twentieth-century clothes were waiting neatly inside, and some of the strange local currency—and set about the task of making themselves look like natives.

"Oh, how wonderful!" Laliene cried, holding a gleaming, iridescent green robe in front of herself and dancing around with it. "How did they think of such things? Look at how it's cut! Look at the way it's fitted together!"

"I've seen you wearing a thousand things more lovely than those," said Denvin sourly.

She made a face at him. Denvin himself had almost finished changing: he was clad now in gray trousers, scarlet shirt open at the throat, charcoal-colored jacket cut with flaring lapels. Like Kadro, he looked splendid in his costume. But Kadro and Denvin looked splendid in anything they wore. The two of them were men of the same sort, Thimiroi thought, both of them dandyish, almost dainty. Perfect men of fashion. He himself, much taller than they and very muscular, almost rawboned, had never quite mastered their knack of seeming at utter ease in all situations. He often felt out of place among such smooth types as they, almost as though he were some sort of throwback, full of hot, primordial passions and drives rarely seen in the refined era into which he had happened to be born. It was, perhaps, his creative intensity, he often thought. His artistic nature. He was too earthy for them, too robust of spirit, too much the primitive. As he slipped into his twentieth-century clothes, the tight yellow pants, the white shirt boldly striped in blue, the jet-black jacket, the tapering black boots, he felt a curious sense of having returned home at last, after a long journey.

"Here comes the car," Kadro said. "Hold out your hands, quickly! I have your implants."

Thimiroi extended his arm. Something silvery-bright, like a tiny gleaming beetle, sparkled between two of Kadro's fingers. He pressed it gently against Thimiroi's skin, just above the long rosy scar of the inoculation, and it made the tiniest of whirring sounds.

"This is their language," said Kadro. He touched it to Denvin's arm also, and to Laliene's. "And this one, the technology and social customs. And this is your medical booster, just in case." Buzz, buzz, buzz. Kadro smiled. He was very efficient. "You're all ready for the twentieth century now. And just in time, too."

A vehicle had pulled up in the roadway behind them, yellow with black markings, and odd projections on its roof. Thimiroi felt a quick faint stab of nausea as a breeze, suddenly stirring out of the quiescent air, swept a whiff of the vehicle's greasy fumes past his face.

The driver hopped out. He was very big, bigger even than Thimiroi, with immense heavy shoulders and a massive column of a neck. His face was unusual, the lips strongly pronounced, the cheekbones broad and jutting like blades. His hair was black and woolly and grew very close to his skull. But the most surprising thing about him was the color of his skin. It was dark brown, almost black: his eyes were bright as beacons against that astonishing chocolate-hued backdrop. Thimiroi had never imagined that anyone might have skin of such a color. Was that what they all were like in the twentieth century? Skin the color of night? No one on Capri had looked like that, or in Canterbury.

"You the people called for a taxi?" the driver asked. "Here—let me put those suitcases in the trunk—"

Perhaps it is a form of ornamentation, Thimiroi thought. They have it artificially done. They think it makes them look more beautiful when they change their skins, when they change their faces, so that they are like this.

And it *was* beautiful. There was a brooding somber power about this black man's face. He was like something carved from a block of some precious and recalcitrant stone.

145

"I'll ride up front," Kadro said. "You three get in back." He turned to the driver. "The Montgomery House is where we are going. You know where that is?"

The driver laughed. "Ain't no one in town who don't know the Montgomery House. But you sure you don't want a hotel that's a little cheaper?"

"The Montgomery House will do," said Kadro.

They had ridden in mule-drawn carts on the narrow winding paths of hilly Capri, and in wagons drawn by oxen on the rutted road to Canterbury. That had been charming and pretty, to ride in such things, to feel the jouncing of the wheels and see the sweat glistening on the backs of the panting animals. There was nothing charming or pretty about traveling in this squat glass-walled wheeled vehicle, this *taxi*. It rumbled and quivered as if it were about to explode. It careered alarmingly around the sharp curves of the road, threatening at any moment to break free of the driver's tenuous control and go spurting over the edge of the embankment in a cataclysmic dive through space. It poured forth all manner of dark noxious gases. It was an altogether terrifying thing.

And yet fascinating and wonderful. Crude and scary though the taxi was, it was not really very different in fundamental concept or design from the silent, flawless vehicles of Thimiroi's world. Contemplating that, Thimiroi had a keen sense of the kinship of this world to his own. We are not that far beyond them in time, he thought. They exist at the edge of the modern era, really. The Capri of the Romans, the Canterbury of the pilgrimage—those are truly alien places, set deep back in the pre-technological past. But there is not the same qualitative difference between our epoch and this twentieth century. The gulf is not so great. The seeds of our world can be found in theirs. Or so it seems to me, Thimiroi told himself, after five minutes' acquaintance with this place.

Kadro said, "Omerie and Kleph and Klia are here already. They've rented a house just down the street from the hotel where you'll be staying."

Laliene smiled. "The Sanciscos! Oh, how I look forward to seeing them again! Omerie is such a clever man. And Kleph and Klia—how beautiful they are, how refreshing to spend time with them!"

"The place they've taken is absolutely perfect for the end of the month," said Kadro. "The view will be supreme. Hollia and Hara wanted to buy it, you know. But Omerie got to it ahead of them."

"Hollia and Hara are going to be here?" Denvin said, sounding surprised.

"*Everyone* will be here. Who would miss it?" Kadro's hands moved in a quick playful gesture of malicious pleasure. "Hollia was beside herself, of course. She couldn't believe that Omerie had beaten her to that house. But, as you say, Laliene, Omerie is such a clever man."

"Hollia is ruthless," said Denvin. "If the place is that good, she'll try to get it away from the Sanciscos. Mark my words, Kadro. She'll try some slippery little trick."

"She may very well. Not that there's any real reason to. I understand that the Sanciscos are planning to invite all of us to watch the show from their front window. Including Hollia and Hara, naturally. So they won't be the worse for it. Except that Hollia would have preferred to be the hostess herself. Cenbe will be coming, you know."

"Cenbe!" Laliene cried.

"Exactly. To finish his symphony. Hollia would have wanted to preside over that. And instead it will be Omerie's party, and Kleph's and Klia's, and she'll just be one of the crowd." Kadro giggled. "Dear Hollia. My heart goes out to her."

"Dear Hollia," Denvin echoed.

"Look there," said Thimiroi, pointing out the side window of the taxi. He spoke brusquely, his voice deliberately rough. All this gossipy chatter bored and maddened him. Who cared whether it was Hollia who gave the party, or the Sanciscos, or the Emperor Augustus himself? What mattered was the event that was coming. The experience. The awesome, wondrous, shattering calamity. "Isn't that Lutheena across the street?" he asked.

They had emerged from the park, had descended to the bank of the river, were passing through a district of venerable-looking three-story wooden houses. One of the bridges was just ahead of them, and the towers of the downtown section rose like huge stone palisades on the other side of the river. Now they were halted at an intersection, waiting for the colored lights that governed the flow of traffic to change; and in the group of pedestrians waiting also to cross was an unmistakably regal figure—yes, it was Lutheena, who else could it be but Lutheena?—who stood among the twentieth-century folk like a goddess among mortals.

The difference was not so much in her clothes, which were scarcely distinguishable from the street clothes of the people around her, nor in her features or her hair, perfect and flawless though they were, as in the way she bore herself: for though she was slender and of a porcelain frailty, and no more than ordinary in height, she held herself with such self-contained majesty, such imperious grace, that she seemed to tower above the others, coarse and clumsy with a thick-ankled peasant cloddishness about them, who waited alongside her.

"I thought she was coming here *after* Charlemagne," Denvin said. "And then going on to Canterbury."

Thimiroi frowned. What was he talking about? Whether she came here first and then went to Canterbury, or journeyed from Canterbury to here as they had done, would they not all be here at the same time? He would never understand these things. This was another of the baffling complexities of The Travel. Surely there was only one May like this one, and one 1347 November, and one 800 December? Though everyone seemed to make the tour in some private order of his own, some going through the four seasons in the natural succession, others hopping about as they pleased, certainly they must all converge on the same point in time at once—was that not so?

"Perhaps it's someone else," he suggested uneasily.

"But of *course* that's Lutheena," said Laliene. "I wonder what she's doing all the way out here by herself."

"Lutheena is like that," Denvin pointed out.

"Yes," Laliene said. "She is, yes." She rapped on the window. Lutheena turned, and stared gravely, and after a moment burst into that incandescent smile of hers, though her luminous eyes remained mysteriously solemn. Then the traffic light changed, the taxi moved forward, Lutheena was lost in the distance. In a few minutes they were on the bridge, and then passing through the heart of the city, alive in all its awesome afternoon clangor, and then upward, up into the hills, up to the lofty street, green with the tender new growth of this heartbreakingly perfect springtime, where they would all wait out that glorious skein of May days that lay between this moment and the terrible hour of doom's arrival.

After the straw-filled mattresses and rank smells of the lodges along the way to Canterbury, and the sweltering musty splendors of their whitewashed villas on the crest of Capri, the Montgomery House was almost palatial.

The rooms had a curious stiffness and angularity about them that Thimiroi was already beginning to associate with twentieth-century architecture in general, and of course there was no sweepdamping, no mood insulation, no gravity gradients, none of the little things that one took for granted when one was in one's own era. All the same, everything seemed comfortable in its way, and with the proper modifications he knew he would have no trouble feeling at home here. The rooms were spacious, the ceilings were high, the windows were clean, no odors invaded from neighboring chambers. There was indoor plumbing: a blessing, after Canterbury. He had a suite of three rooms, furnished in the strange but pleasant late-twentieth-century way that he had seen in museums. There was a box in the main sitting-room that broadcast images in color, flat ones, with no sensory augmentation other than sonics. There were paintings on the wall, maddeningly motionless. The walls themselves were painted—how remarkable!—with some thick substance so porous that he could almost make out its molecular structure if he looked closely.

Laliene's suite was down the hall from his; Denvin was on a different floor. That struck him as odd. He had assumed they were lovers and would be sharing accommodations. But, he reflected, it was always risky to assume things like that.

Thimiroi spent an hour transforming his rooms into a more familiar and congenial environment. From his suitcase he drew carpeting and draperies and coverlets of his own time, all of them supple with life and magic, to replace the harsh, flat, dead ones that they seemed to prefer here. He pulled out the three little tripod tables of fine, intricately worked Sipulva marquetry that went with him everywhere: he would read at the golden one, sip his euphoriac at the copper-hued one, write his poetry at the one that was woven in scarlet and amber. He hung an esthetikon on the wall opposite the window and set it going, filling the room with warm, throbbing color. He sat a music sphere on the dresser. To provide some variation in psychological tonality he activated a little subsonic that he had carried with him, adjusting it to travel through the entire spectrum of positive moods over a twenty-four hour span, from *anticipation* through *excitation* to *culmination* in imperceptible gradations. Then he stood back, surveying the results, and nodded. That would do for now. The room had been made amiable;

the room was *civilized* now. He could bring out other things later. The suitcase was infinitely capacious. All it was, after all, was a pipeline to his own era. At the far end they would put anything in it that he might requisition.

Now at last he could begin to explore the city.

That evening they were supposed to go to a concert. Denvin had arranged it; Denvin was going to take care of all the cultural events. The legendary young violinist Sandra di Santis was playing, in what would turn out to be her final performance, though of course no one of this era could know that yet. But that was hours away. It was still only early afternoon. He would go out—he would savor the sights, the sounds, the smells of this place—

He felt just a moment of hesitation.

But why? Why? He had wandered by himself, unafraid, through the trash-strewn alleys of medieval Canterbury, though he knew that cut-throats and roisterers lurked everywhere. He had scrambled alone across the steep gullied cliffs of Capri, looking down without fear at the blue rock-rimmed Mediterranean, far below, into which a single misstep could plunge him. What was there to be cautious about here? The noisy cars racing so swiftly through the streets, perhaps. But surely a little caution and common sense would keep him from harm. If Lutheena had been out by herself, why not he? But still—still, that nagging uneasiness—

Thimiroi shrugged and left his room, and made his way down the hall to the elevator, and descended to the lobby.

At every stage of his departure wave upon wave of unsettling strangeness assailed him. The simplest act was a challenge. He had to call upon the resources of his technology implant in order to operate the lock of his room door, to summon the elevator, to tell it to take him to the lobby. But he met each of these minor mysteries in turn with a growing sense of accomplishment. By the time he reached the lobby he was moving boldly and confidently, feeling almost at home in this strange land, this unfamiliar country, that was the past.

The lobby, which Thimiroi had seen only briefly when he had arrived, was a somber, cavernous place, intricately divided into any number of smaller open chambers. He studied, as he walked calmly through it toward the brightness at the far end, the paintings, the furnishings, the things on display. Everything had that odd stiffness of form and flatness of texture that seemed to be the rule in this era:

nothing appeared to have any inner life or movement. Was that how they had really liked it to be? Or was this curious deadness merely a function of the limitations of their materials? Probably some of each, Thimiroi decided. These were an artful, sophisticated folk. Of course, he thought, they had not had the advantage of many of our modern materials and devices. All the same, they would not have made everything so drab unless their esthetic saw beauty in the drabness. He would have to examine that possibility more deeply as this month went along, studying everything with an artist's shrewd and sympathetic eye, not interested in finding fault, only in understanding.

People were standing about here and there in the lobby, mainly in twos and threes, talking quietly. They paid no attention to him. Most of them, he noticed, had fair skin much like his own. A few, Thimiroi noticed, were black-skinned like the taxi driver, but others had skin of still another unusual tone, a kind of pale olive or light yellow, and their features too were unusual, very delicate, with an odd tilt to the eyes.

Once again he wondered if this skin-toning might be some sort of cosmetic alteration: but no, no, this time he queried his implant and it told him that in fact in this era there had been several different races of humanity, varying widely in physical appearance.

How lovely, Thimiroi thought. How sad for us that we are all so much alike. Another point for further research: had these black and yellow people, and the other unusual races, been swept away by the great calamity, or was it rather that all mankind had tended toward a uniformity of traits as the centuries went by? Again, perhaps, some of each. Whatever the reason, it was a cause for regret.

He reached the grand doorway that led to the street. A woman said, entering the hotel just as he was leaving it, "How I hate going indoors in weather like this!"

Her companion laughed. "Who doesn't? Can it last much longer, I wonder?"

Thimiroi stepped past them, into the splendor of the soft golden sunlight.

The air was miraculous: amazingly transparent, clear with a limpidity almost beyond belief, despite all the astonishing impurities that Thimiroi knew were routinely poured into it by the unthinking people of this era. It was as though for the long blessed moment of this one last magnificent May all the ordinary rules of nature had been suspended, and the atmosphere had become invulnerable to harm. Beyond that sublime zone of clarity rose the blue shield of the sky, pulsingly brilliant; and from its throne high in the distance the sun sent forth a tranquil, steady radiance that was like no sunlight Thimiroi had ever seen. Small wonder that those who had planned the tour had chosen this time and this place to be the epitome of springtime, he thought. There might never have been such beauty before. There might never be again.

He turned to his left and began to walk, hardly knowing or caring where he might be going.

From all sides came powerful sensory signals: the honking of horns, the sharp spicy scent of something cooking nearby, the subtler fragrance of the light breeze. Great gray buildings soared far into the dazzling sky. Billboards and posters blared their messages in twenty colors. The impact was immediate and profound. Thimiroi beheld everything in wonder and joy.

What richness! What complexity!

And yet there was a paradox here. What he took to be complexity in this street scene was really only a studied lack of harmony. As it had in the hotel lobby, a second glance revealed the true essence of this world's vocabulary of design: a curious rough-hewn plainness, even a severity, that made clear to him how far in the past he actually was. The extraordinary May light seemed to dance along the rooftops, giving the buildings an intricacy of texture they did not in fact possess. These ancient styles were fundamentally simple and harsh, and could all too easily be taken to be primitive and crude. In Thimiroi's own era every surface vibrated in at least half a dozen different ways, throbbing and rippling and pulsating and shimmering and gleaming and quivering. Here everything was flat, stolid, static. The strangeness of that seemed oppressive at first encounter; but now, as he ventured deeper and deeper into this unfamiliar world, Thimiroi came to see the underlying majesty of it. What he had mistaken for deadness was in fact strength. The people of this era were survivors: they had come through monstrous wars, tremendous technological change, immense social upheaval. Those who had outlasted the brutal tests of this taxing century were rugged, hearty, deeply optimistic. Their style of building and decoration showed that plainly. Nothing quivering and shimmery for them—oh, no! Great solid slabs of buildings, constructed out of simple, hard, unadorned materials that looked you straight in the eye—that was the way of things, here in the late twentieth century, in this time of assurance and robust faith in even better things to come.

Of course, Thimiroi thought, there was savage irony in that, considering what actually *was* to come. For a moment he was swept by deep and shattering compassion that brought him almost to tears. But he forced himself to fight the emotion back. Would Denvin weep for these people? Would Omerie, would Cenbe, would Kadro? The past is a sealed book, Thimiroi told himself forcefully. What has happened has happened. The losses are totalled, the debits are irretrievable. We have come here to experience the joys of jarring contrasts, as Denvin might say, not to cry over spilled milk.

He crossed the street. The next block was one of older-looking single-family houses, each set apart in a little garden plot where bright flowers bloomed and the leaves of the trees were just beginning to unfold under springtime's first warmth.

There was music coming from an upstairs window three houses from the corner. He paused to listen.

It was simple straightforward stuff, monochromatic in tone. The instrument, he supposed, was the piano, the one that made its sound by the action of little mallets striking strings stretched across a resonating board. The melodic line was both sinuous and stark, carried in the treble with a little commentary in the bass: music a child could play. Perhaps a child was indeed playing. The simplicity of it made him smile. It was quaint stuff, charming but naive. He began to move onward.

And yet—yet—

Suddenly he felt himself caught and transfixed by a simple, magical turn of phrase that came creeping almost surreptitiously out of the bass line. It held him. Unexpectedly, it touched him.

He remained still, unable to go on, listening while the lovely phrase fled, waiting in hope for its return. Yes, there it was again! And as it came and went, it cast startling illumination over the entire musical pattern. He saw its beauty and its artfully hidden depth now, and he grew angry at himself for having responded at first in that patronizing way, that snide, condescending Denvin-like way. Quaint? Naive? Hardly. Simple, yes: this music achieved its effects with a minimum of means. But what was naive about that? Was a quartet for strings naive, because it did not make use of the resources of a full symphony orchestra? There was something about this music—its directness, its freedom—that the composers of his own time might well want to study, might even look upon with a certain degree of envy. For all their colossal technical resources, could the best of them—yes, even Cenbe—manage to equal the quiet force, Thimiroi wondered, of that easy, graceful little tune?

He stood listening until the music rolled to a gentle climax and a pleasant resolution and came to a halt. Its sudden absence brought him up short. He looked up imploringly at the open window. Play it again, he begged silently. Play it again! But there was no more music.

Impulsively he burst into applause, thinking that that might encourage an encore.

A woman's face appeared at the window. Thimiroi was aware of pale skin, long straight golden hair, warm blue-green eyes. "Very lovely," he called. "Thank you. Thank you very much."

She looked at him in apparent surprise, perhaps frowning a little. Then the frown was replaced for a moment by a quick amiable smile of pleasure; and then, just as quickly, she was gone. Thimiroi remained before her house a while longer, still hoping the music would begin again. But there was no more of it.

He returned to the hotel an hour later, dazzled, awed, weary, his mind full of wonders great and small. Just as he entered his suite, a small machine on the table beside the bed set up a curious insistent tinkling sound: the telephone, it was, so his technology implant informed him. He picked up the receiver.

"This is Thimiroi."

"Back at last." The voice was Laliene's. "Was it an interesting walk?"

"One revelation after another. Certainly this year is going to be the high point of our trip."

Laliene laughed lazily. "Oh, darling Thimiroi, didn't you say the same thing when we came to Canterbury? And when we had the audience with the emperor on Capri?"

He did not reply.

"Anyway," she continued. "We're all going to gather in my suite before we go to the concert. Would you like to come? I've brewed a little tea, of course."

"Of course," he said. "I'll be right there."

She, too, had redone her rooms in the style of their own period. Instead of the ponderous hotel bed she had installed a floater, and in the sitting room now was a set of elegant turquoise slopes mounted around a depth baffle, so that one had the illusion of looking down into a long curving valley of ravishing beauty. Her choice of simso screens was, as usual, superb: wondrous dizzying vistas opened to infinity on every wall. Laliene herself looked sumptuous in a brilliant robe of woven silver mesh and a pair of scarlet gliders.

What surprised him was that no one else was there.

"Oh," she said lightly, "they'll all be coming along soon. We can get a head start."

She selected one of the lovely little cups on the table beside her, and offered it to him. And as he took it from her he felt a sudden transformation of the space between them, an intensification, an amplification. Without warning, Laliene was turning up the psychic voltage.

Her face was flushed, her eyes were glistening. The rich gray of them had deepened almost to purple. There was no mistaking the look. He had seen it many times before: Laliene in her best flirtatious mode, verging on the frankly seductive. Here they were, a man, a woman, well known to one another, together in a hotel room in a strange and distant city, about to enjoy a friendly sip or two of euphoriac tea—well, of course, Laliene could be expected to put on her most inviting manner, if only for the sport of it. But something else was going on here besides mere playful flirtation, Thimiroi realized. There was an odd eagerness to the set of her jaw, a peculiar quirk in the corners of her mouth. As though she *cared*, he thought. As though she were *serious*.

What was this? Was she trying to change the rules of the game?

Deftly she turned a music sphere on without looking away from him. Some barely audible melodikia came stealing like faint azure vapor into the air, and very gradually began to rise and throb. One of Cenbe's songs, he wondered? No. No, too voluptuous for Cenbe: more like Palivandrin's work, or Athaea's. He sipped his euphoriac. The sweet coiling fumes crept sinuously about him. Laliene stood close beside him, making it seem almost as if the music were coming from her and not the sphere. Thimiroi met her languid invitation with a practiced courteous smile, one which acknowledged her beauty, her grace, the intimacy of the moment, the prospect of delights to come, while neither accepting nor rejecting anything that was being proposed.

Of course they could do nothing now. At any moment the others would come trooping in.

But he wondered where this unexpected offer was meant to lead. He could, of course, put down the cup, draw her close: a kiss, a quick caress, an understanding swiftly arrived at, yes. But that did not seem to be quite what she was after, or at least that was not all she was after. And was the offer, he asked himself, all that unexpected? Thimiroi realized abruptly that there was no reason why he should be as surprised by this as he was. As he cast his mind back over the earlier weeks of their journey across time, he came to see that in fact Laliene had been moving steadily toward him since the beginning—in Canterbury, in Capri, a touch of the hand here, a quick private smile there, a quip, a glance. Her defending him so earnestly against Denvin's snobbery and Denvin's sarcasm, just after they had arrived here: what was that, if not the groundwork for some subtle treaty that was to be established subsequently between them? But why? Why? Such romance as could ever have existed for Laliene and him had come and gone long, long ago. Now they were merely friends. Perhaps he was mistaking the nature of this transaction. But no...no. There was no mistake.

Sparring for time, he said, keeping his tone and style carefully neutral, "You should come walking with me tomorrow. I saw marvelous things just a few blocks from here."

"I'd love to, Thimiroi. I want you to show me everything you've discovered."

"Yes. Yes, of course, Laliene."

But as he said it, he felt a deep stab of confusion. Everything? There was the house where that music had been playing. The open window, the simple, haunting melody. And the woman's face, then: the golden hair, the pale skin, the blue-green eyes. Thinking of her, thinking of the music she had played, Thimiroi found himself stirred by powerful and inexplicable forces that made him want to seize Laliene's music sphere and hurl it, and with it the subtle melodikia that it was playing, into the street. How smug that music sounded to him now, how overcivilized, how empty! And Laliene herself, so perfect in her beauty, the crimson hair, the flawless features, the sleek slender body—she was like some finely crafted statue, some life-sized doll: there was no reality to her, no essence of humanity. That woman in the window had shown more vital force in just her quick little half-frown and half-smile than Laliene displayed in all her repertoire of artful movements and expressions.

He stared at her, astounded, shaken.

She seemed shaken too. "Are you all right, Thimiroi?" she whispered.

"A little—tired, perhaps," he said huskily. "Stretched myself farther today than I really knew."

Laliene nodded toward the cup. "The tea will heal you."

"Yes. Yes."

He sipped. There was a knocking at the door. Laliene smiled, excused herself, opened it.

Denvin was there, and others behind him.

"Lutheena—Hollia—Hara—come in, come in, come in all of you! Omerie, how good to see you—Kleph, Klia—dear Klia—come in, everyone! How wonderful, how wonderful! I have the tea all ready and waiting for you!"

The concert that night was an extraordinary experience. Every moment, every note, seemed freighted with unforgettable meaning. Perhaps it was the poignancy of knowing that the beautiful young violinist who played so brilliantly had only a few weeks left to live, and that this grand and sumptuous concert hall itself was soon to be a smoking ruin. Perhaps it was the tiny magical phrase he had heard while listening in the street, which had somehow sensitized him to the fine secret graces of this seemingly simple twentieth-century music. Perhaps it was only the euphoriac they had had in Laliene's room before setting out. Whatever it was, it evoked a mood of unusual, even unique, attentiveness in Thimiroi, and as the minutes went by he knew that this evening at the concert hall would surely resonate joyously in his soul forever after.

That mood was jarred and shaken and irrevocably shattered at intermission, when he was compelled to stand with his stunningly dressed companions in the vestibule and listen to their brittle chirping chatter. How empty they all seemed, how foolish! Omerie stalking around in his most virile and commanding mode, like some sort of peacock, and imperious Lutheena matching him swagger for swagger, and Klia looking on complacently, and Kleph even more complacent, mysteriously lost in mists like some child who has found a packet of narcotic candies. And then of course there was the awesome Miss Hollia, who seemed older than the Pyramids, glowering at Omerie in unconcealed malevolence even while she complimented him on his mastery of twentieth-century costuming, and Hollia's pretty little playmate Hara as usual saying scarcely anything, but lending his support to his owner by glaring at Omerie also—and Denvin, chiming in with his sardonic, too-too-special insights from time to time—

What a wearying crew, Thimiroi thought. These precious connoisseurs of history, these tireless voyagers of the eons. His head began to ache. He stepped away from them and began to walk back toward the auditorium. For the first time he noticed how the other members of the audience were staring at the little group. Wondering what country they came from, no doubt, and how rich they might be. Such perfection of dress, such precision of movement, such elegance of speech—foreign, obviously foreign, but mystifyingly so, for they seemed to belong to no recognizable nationality, and spoke with no recognizable accent. Thimiroi smiled wearily. "Do you want to know the truth about us?" he imagined himself crying. "We are visitors, yes. Tourists from a far country. But where we live is not only beyond your reach, it is beyond even your imaginations. What would you say, if I revealed to you that we are natives of the year—"

"Bored with the concert?" Laliene asked. She had come up quietly beside him, without his noticing it.

"Quite the contrary."

"Bored with us, then." It was not a question.

Thimiroi shrugged. "The intermission's an unfortunate interruption. I wish the music hadn't stopped."

"The music always stops," she said, and laughed her throatiest, smokiest laugh.

He studied her. She was still offering herself to him, with her eyes, her smile, her slightly sidewise stance. Thimiroi felt almost guilty for his wilful failure to accept the gambit. Was he infuriating her? Was he wounding her?

But I do not want her, he told himself.

Once again, as in her room that afternoon while they were sipping euphoriac together, he was struck by the puzzling distaste and even anger that the perfection of her beauty aroused in him. Why this violent reaction? He had always lived in a world of perfect people. He had been accustomed all his life to Laliene's sort of flawlessness. There was no need for anyone to have blemishes of face or form any more. One took that sort of thing for granted; everyone did. Why should it trouble him now? What strange restlessness was this century kindling in his soul?

Thimiroi saw the strain, the tension, the barely suppressed impatience in Laliene's expression, and for a moment he was so abashed by the distress he knew he must be causing her that he came close to inviting her to join him in his suite after the concert. But he could not bring himself to do it. The moment passed; the tension slackened; Laliene made an elegant recovery, smiling and slipping her arm through his to lead him back to their seats, and he moved gratefully into a round of banter with her, and with Kleph, who drifted back up the aisle with them. But the magic and wonder of the concert were forever lost. In the second half he sat in a leaden slump, barely listening, unable to find the patterns that made the music comprehensible.

That night Thimiroi slept alone, and slept badly. After some hours of wakefulness he had to have recourse to one of his drugs. And even that brought him only partial solace, for with sleep came dark dreams of a singularly ominous and disruptive kind, full of hot furious blasts of anguish and panic, and he felt too drained of energy to get up again and rummage through his kit for the drug that banishes dreams. Morning was a long time in coming.

Over the next few days Thimiroi kept mostly to himself. He suspected that his fellow voyagers were talking about him—that they were worried about him—but he shied away from any sort of contact with them. The mere sight of them was something that caused him a perceptible pain, almost like the closing of a clamp about his heart. He longed to recapture that delicious openness to experience, that wonderful vulnerability, that he had felt when he had first arrived here, and he knew that so long as he was with any of them he would never be able to attain it.

By withdrawing from them in this morose way, he realized, he was missing some of the pleasures of the visit. The others were quite serious, as serious as such frivolous people ever could be, about the late twentieth century, and they spent each day moving busily about the city, taking advantage of its wealth of cultural opportunities—many of them obscure even to the natives of the era themselves. Kleph, whose specialty was Golconda studies, put together a small festival of the films of that great actor, and for two days they all, even Hollia, scurried around town seeing him at work in actual original prints. Omerie discovered, and proudly displayed, a first edition of Martin Drexel's *Lyrical Journeys.*

"It cost me next to nothing," Omerie declared in vast satisfaction. "These people don't have the slightest idea of what Drexel achieved." A day or two later, Klia organized a river trip to the birthplace of David Courtney, a short way north of the city. Courtney would not be born, of course, for another seventy years, but his birthplace already existed, and who could resist making the pilgrimage? Thimiroi resisted. "Come with us," Laliene pleaded, with a curious urgency in her voice that he had never heard in it before. "This is one trip you really must not miss." He told her, calmly at first and then more forcefully, as she continued to press the point, that he had no desire to go. She looked at him in a stricken way, as though he had slapped her; but at that point she yielded. The others went on the river journey and he stayed behind, drifting through the streets of the downtown section without purpose, without goal.

Troubled as he was, he found excitement nevertheless in the things he saw on his solitary walks. The vigor and intensity of this era struck resonances in his own unfashionably robust spirit. The noise here, the smells, the colors, the expansive, confident air of the people, who obviously knew that they were living at one of history's great peak periods—everything startled and stimulated him in a way that Roman Capri and Chaucerian Canterbury had not been able to do.

Those older places and times had been too remote in spirit and essence from his native epoch to be truly comprehensible: they were interesting the way a visit to an alien planet can be interesting, but they had not moved him as this era moved him. Possibly the knowledge of impending doom that he had here had something to do with that. But there was something else. Thimiroi sensed, as he had not in any way sensed during the earlier stops, that he might actually be able to *live* in this era, and feel at home in it, and be happy here. For much of his life he had felt somehow out of place in his own world, unable all too often to come to terms with the seamlessness of everything, the impeccability of that immaculate era. Now he thought he understood why. As he wandered the streets of this booming, brawling, far-from-perfect city—taking joy in its curious mixture of earthy marvelous accomplishment and mysterious indifference to its own shortcomings, and finding himself curiously at ease in it—he began to perceive himself as a man of the late twentieth century who by some bewildering prank of the gods

had been born long after his own proper time. And with that perception came a kind of calmness in the face of the storm that was to come.

Toward the end of the first week—it was the day when the others
made their pilgrimage up the river to David Courtney's birthplace—
Thimiroi encountered the golden-haired woman who had been playing the piano in the house down the block from the hotel. He caught
sight of her downtown while he was crossing a plaza paved with pink
cobblestones, which linked twin black towers of almost unthinkable
height and mass near the river embankment.

Though he had only seen her for a moment, that one other time,
and that time only her face and throat at the window, he had no doubt
that it was she. Her blue-green eyes and long straight shining hair were
unmistakable. She was fairly tall and very slender, with a tall woman's
quick way of walking, ankles close together, shoulders slightly hunched
forward. Thimiroi supposed that she was about thirty, or perhaps forty
at most. She was young, at any rate, but not *very* young. He had no
clear idea of how quickly people aged in this era. The first mild signs
of aging seemed visible on her. In his own time that would mean nothing—there, a woman who looked like this might be anywhere between
fifty and a hundred and fifty—but he knew that here they had no significant way of reversing the effects of time, and what she showed was
almost certainly an indication that she had left her girlhood behind by
some years but had not yet gone very far into the middle of the journey.

"Pardon me," he said, a little to his own surprise, as she came
toward him.

She peered blankly at him. "Yes?"

Thimiroi offered her a disarming smile. "I'm a visitor here. Staying
at the Montgomery House."

The mention of the famous hotel—and, perhaps, his gentle manner
and the quality of his clothing—seemed to ease whatever apprehen-
sions she might be feeling. She paused, looking at him questioningly.

He said, "You live near there, don't you? A few days ago, when I was
out for a walk—it was my first day here—I heard you playing the piano.
I'm sure it was you. I applauded when you stopped, and you looked out
the window at me. I think you must have seen me. You frowned, and
then you smiled."

She frowned now, just a quick flicker of confusion; and then again she smiled.

"Just like that, yes," Thimiroi said. "Do you mind if we talk? Are you in a hurry?"

"Not really," she said, and he sensed something troubled behind the words.

"Is there some place near here where we could have a drink? Or lunch, perhaps?" That was what they called the meal they ate at this time of day, he was certain. Lunch. People of this era met often for lunch, as a social thing. He did not think it was too late in the day to be offering her lunch.

"Well, there's the River Cafe," she said. "That's just two or three blocks. I suppose we—" She broke off. "You know, I never ever do anything like this. Let myself get picked up in the street, I mean."

"Picked up? I do not understand."

"What don't you understand?"

"The phrase," Thimiroi said. "Pick up? To lift? Am I lifting you?"

She laughed and said, "Are you foreign?"

"Oh, yes. Very foreign."

"I thought your way of speaking was a little strange. So precise— every syllable perfectly shaped. No one really speaks English that way. Except computers, of course. You aren't a computer, are you?"

"Hardly."

"Good. I would never allow myself to be picked up by a computer in First National Plaza. Or anyplace else, as a matter of fact. Are you still interested in going to the River Cafe?"

"Of course."

She was playful now. "We can't do this anonymously, though. It's too sordid. My name's Christine Rawlins."

"And I am called Thimiroi."

"Timmery?"

"Thimiroi," he said.

"Thim-i-roi," she repeated, imitating his precision. "A very unusual name, I'd say. I've never met anyone named Thimiroi before. What country are you from, may I ask?"

"You would not know it. A very small one, very far away."

"Iran?"

"Farther away than that."

"A lot of people who came here from Iran prefer not to admit that that's where they're from."

"I am not from Iran, I assure you."

"But you won't tell me where?"

"You would not know it," he said again.

Her eyes twinkled. "Oh, you *are* from Iran! You're a spy, aren't you? I see the whole thing: they're getting ready to have a new revolution, there's another Ayatollah on his way from his hiding place in Beirut, and you're here to transfer Iranian assets out of this country before—" She broke off, looking sheepish. "I'm sorry. I'm just being weird. Have I offended you?"

"Not at all."

"You don't have to tell me where you're from if you don't want to."

"I am from Stiinowain," he said, astounded at his own daring in actually uttering the forbidden name.

She tried to repeat the name, but was unable to manage the soft glide of the first syllable.

"You're right," she said. "I don't know anything about it at all. But you'll tell me all about it, won't you?"

"Perhaps," he said.

The River Cafe was a glossy bubble of pink marble and black glass cantilevered out over the embankment, with a semicircular open-air dining area, paved with shining flagstones, that jutted even farther, so that it seemed suspended almost in mid-river. They were lucky enough to find one vacant table that was right at the cafe's outermost edge, looking down on the swift blue riverflow. "Ordinarily the outdoor section doesn't open until the middle of June," Christine told him. "But this year it's been so warm and dry that they opened it a month early. We've been breaking records every day. There's never been a May like this, that's what they're all saying. Just one long run of fabulous weather day after day after day."

"It's been extraordinary, yes."

"What is May like in Stiin—in your country?" she asked.

"Very much like this. As a matter of fact, it is rather like this all the year round."

"Really? How wonderful that must be!"

It must have seemed like boasting to her. He regretted that. "No," he said. "We take our mild climate for granted and the succession of beautiful days means nothing to us. It is better this way, sudden glory rising out of contrast, the darkness of winter giving way to the splendor of spring. The warm sunny days coming upon you like—like the coming of grace, shall I say?—like—" He smiled. "Like that heavenly little theme that came suddenly out of the music you were playing, transforming something simple and ordinary into something unforgettable. Do you know what I mean?"

"Yes," she said. "I think I do."

He began to hum the melody. Her eyes sparkled, and she nodded and grinned warmly, and after a moment or two she started humming along with him. He felt a tightness at his throat, warmth along his back and shoulders, a throbbing in his chest. All the symptoms of a rush of strong emotion. Very strange to him, very primitive, very exciting, very pleasing.

People at other tables turned. They seemed to notice something also. Thimiroi saw them smiling at the two of them with that unmistakable proprietorial smile that strangers will offer to young lovers in the springtime. Christine must have seen those smiles too, for color came to her face, and for a moment she looked away from him as though embarrassed.

"Tell me about yourself," he said.

"We should order first. Are you familiar with our foods? A salad might be nice on a beautiful warm day like this—and then perhaps the cold salmon plate, or—" She stopped abruptly. "Is something wrong?"

Thimiroi struggled to fight back nausea. "Not a salad, no, please. It is—not good for me. And in my country we do not eat fish of any sort, not ever."

"Forgive me."

"But how could you have known?"

"Even so—you looked so distressed—"

"Not really. It was only a moment's uneasiness." He scanned the menu desperately. Nothing on it made sense to him. At home, he would only have to touch the screen beside anything that seemed to be of interest, and he would get a quick flavor-analog appercept to guide his choice. But that was at home. Here he had been taking most of his meals in his room, meals prepared many centuries away by his own autochef and sent to him down the time conduit. On those few occasions when he ate in the hotel dining room with his fellow travelers, he relied on Kadro to choose his food for him. Now, plunging ahead blindly, he selected something called carpaccio for his starter, and vichyssoise to follow.

"Are you sure you don't want anything warm?" Christine asked gently.

"Oh, I think not, not on such a mild day," Thimiroi said casually. He had no idea what he had ordered; but he was determined not to seem utterly ignorant of her era.

The carpaccio, though, turned out to be not merely cold but raw: red raw meat, very thinly sliced, in a light sauce. He stared at it in amazement. His whole body recoiled at the thought of eating raw meat. His bones themselves protested. He saw Christine staring at him, and wondered how much of his horror his expression was revealing to her. But there was no helping it: he slipped his fork under one of the paper-thin slices and conveyed it to his mouth. To his amazement it was delicious. Forgetting all breeding, he ate the rest without pausing once, while she watched in what seemed like a mixture of surprise and amusement.

"You liked that, didn't you?" she said.

"Carpaccio has always been one of my favorites," he told her shamelessly.

Vichyssoise turned out to be a cold dish too, a thick white soup, presumably made from some vegetable. It seemed harmless and proved to be quite tasty. Christine had ordered the salmon, and he tried not to peer at her plate, or to imagine what it must be like to put chunks of sea-creatures in one's mouth, while she ate.

"You promised to tell me something about yourself," he reminded her.

She looked uneasy. "It's not a very interesting story, I'm afraid."

"But you must tell me a little of it. Are you a musician by profession? Surely you are. Do you perform in the concert hall?"

Her look of discomfort deepened. "I know you don't mean to be cruel, but—"

"Cruel? Of course not. But when I was listening there outside the window I could feel the great gift that you have."

"Please."

"I don't understand."

"No, you don't, do you?" she said gently. "You weren't trying to be funny, or to hurt me. But I'm not any sort of gifted pianist, Thimiroi. Believe me. I'm just a reasonably good amateur. Maybe when I was ten years old I dreamed of having a concert career some day, but I came to my senses a long time ago."

"You are too modest."

"No. No. I know what I am. And what the real thing is like. Even *they* don't have an easy time of it. You can't believe how many concert-quality pianists my age there are in this country. With so many genuine geniuses out there, there's no hope at all for a decent third-rater like me."

He shook his head in amazement, remembering the magical sounds that had come from her window. "Third-rater!"

"I don't have any illusions about that," she said. "I'm the sort of pianist who winds up giving piano lessons, not playing in Carnegie Hall. I have a couple of pupils. They come and go. It's not possible to earn a living that way. And the job that I did have, with an export-import firm—well, they say that this is the most prosperous time this country has seen in the past forty years, but somehow I managed to get laid off last week anyway. That's why I'm downtown today—another job interview. You see? Just an ordinary woman, an ordinary life, ordinary problems—"

"There is nothing ordinary about you," said Thimiroi fervently. "Not to me! To me you are altogether extraordinary, Christine!" She seemed almost about to weep as he said that. Compassion and tenderness overwhelmed him, and he reached out to take her hand in his, to comfort her, to reassure her. Her eyes widened and she pulled back instantly, catching her breath sharply, as though he had tried to stab her with his fork.

Thimiroi looked at her sadly. The quickness and vehemence of her reaction mystified him.

"That was wrong?" he said. "To want to touch your hand?"

Awkwardly Christine said, "You surprised me, that's all. I'm sorry. I didn't mean—it was rude of me, actually—oh, Thimiroi, I can't explain—it was just automatic, a kind of dumb reflex—"

Puzzled, he turned his hand over several times, examining it, searching for something about it that might have frightened or repelled her. He saw nothing. It was simply a hand. After a moment she took it lightly with her own, and held it.

He said, "You have a husband? Is that why I should not have done that?"

"I'm not married, no." She glanced away from him, but did not release his hand. "I'm not even—involved. Not currently." Her fingers were lightly stroking his wrist. "I have to confess something," she said, after a moment. "I saw you at Symphony Hall last week. The De Santis concert."

"You did?"

"In the lobby. With your—friends. I watched you all, wondering who you were. There was a kind of glow about the whole group of you. The women were all so beautiful, every one of them. Immaculate. Perfect. Like movie stars, they were."

"They are nothing compared with you."

"Please. Don't say any more things like that. I don't like to be flattered, Thimiroi. Not only does it make me uncomfortable but it simply isn't effective with me. Whatever else I am, I'm a realistic woman. Especially about myself."

"And I am a truthful man. What I tell you is what I feel, Christine." Her hand tightened on his wrist at that. He said, "So you knew who I was, when I approached you in the plaza up above just now."

"Yes," she murmured.

"But pretended you did not."

"I was frightened."

"I am not frightening, Christine."

"Not frightened of you. Of me. When I saw you that first day, standing outside my house—I felt—I don't know, I felt something strange, just looking at you. Felt that I had seen you before somewhere, that I had known you very well in some other life, perhaps, that—oh, Thimiroi, I'm not making any sense, am I? But I knew you had been *important* to me at some other time. Or *would* be important. It's crazy, isn't it? And I don't have any room in my life for craziness. I'm just trying to hold my own, don't you see? Trying to maintain, trying to hang on and not get swept under. In these wonderful prosperous times, I'm all alone, Thimiroi, I'm not sure where I'm heading, what's going to come next for me. Everything seems so uncertain. And so I don't want any extra uncertainties in my life."

"I will not bring you uncertainty," he said.

She stared and said nothing. Her hand still touched his.

"If you are finished with your food," he said, "perhaps you would like to come back to the hotel with me."

There was a long tense silence. After a time she drew her hand away from him and knotted her fingers together, and sat very still, her expression indecipherable.

"You think it was inappropriate of me to have extended such an invitation," he said finally.

"No. Not really."

"I want only to be your friend."

"Yes. I know that."

"And I thought, since you live so close to the hotel, I could offer you some refreshment, and show you some treasures of my own country that I have brought with me. I meant nothing more than that, Christine. Please. Believe me."

She seemed to shed some of her tension. "I'd love to stop off at your hotel with you for a little while," she said.

He had no doubt at all that it was much too soon for them to become lovers. Not only was he completely unskilled in this era's sociosexual rituals and procedures, so that it was probably almost impossible for him to avoid offending or displeasing her by this or that unintentional violation of the accepted courtship customs of her society, but also at this point he was still much too uncertain of the accuracy of his insight into her own nature. Once he knew her better, perhaps he would be less likely to go about things incorrectly, particularly since she already gave him the benefit of many doubts because she knew he came from some distant land.

There was also the not inconsiderable point to consider that it was a profound violation of the rules of The Travel to enter into any kind of emotional or physical involvement with a native of a past era.

That, somehow, seemed secondary to Thimiroi just now. He knew all about the importance of avoiding distortion or contamination of the time-line; they drilled it into you endlessly before you ever started to Travel. But suddenly such issues seemed unreal and abstract to him. What mattered was what he felt: the surge of delight, eagerness, passion, that ran through him when he turned to look at this woman of a far-off time. All his life he had been a stranger among his own people, a prisoner within his own skin; now, here, at last, it seemed to him that he had a chance of breaking through the net of brittle conventions that for so long had bound his spirit, and touching, at last, the soul of another human being. He had read about love, of course—who had not?—but here, he thought, he might actually experience it. Was that a reckless ambition? Well, then, he would be reckless. The alternative was to condemn himself to a lifetime of bitter regret.

Therefore he schooled himself to patience. He dared not be too hasty, for fear of ruining everything.

Christine appeared astounded by what she saw in his rooms. She wandered through them like a child in a wonderland, hardly breathing, pausing here and there to look, to reach out hesitantly, to hold her hand above this or that miraculous object as though afraid actually to touch it but eager to experience its texture.

"You brought all this from your own country?" she asked. "You must have had fifty suitcases!"

"We get homesick very easily. We wish to have our familiar things about us."

"The way a sultan would travel. A pasha." Her eyes were shining with awe. "These little tables—I've never seen anything like them. I try to follow the weave, but the pattern won't stand still. It keeps sliding around its own corners."

"The woodworkers of Sipulva are extremely ingenious," Thimiroi said.

"Sipulva? Is that a city in your country?"

"A place nearby," he said. "You may touch them if you wish."

She caressed the intricately carved surfaces, fingers tracing the weave as it went through its incomprehensible convolutions. Thimiroi, smiling, turned the music sphere on—one of Mirtin's melodikias began to come from it, a shimmering crystalline piece—and set about brewing some tea. Christine drifted onward, examining the draperies, the glistening carpets, the pulsating esthetikon that was sending waves of color through the room, the simso screens with their shifting views of unknown worlds. She was altogether enthralled. It would certainly be easy enough to seduce her now, Thimiroi realized. A little sensuous music, a few sips of euphoriac, perhaps some surreptitious adjustments of the little subsonic so that it sent forth heightened tonalities of *anticipation* and *excitation*—yes, that was all that it would take, he knew. But easy conquest was not what he wanted. He did not intend to pass through her soul like a frivolous tourist drifting through a museum in search of an hour's superficial diversion.

One cup of tea for each of them, then, and no more. Some music, some quick demonstrations of a few of the little wonders that filled his rooms. A light kiss, finally, and then one that was more intense: but a quick restoration, afterward, of the barriers between them. Christine seemed no more willing to breach those barriers today than he was. Thimiroi was relieved at that, and pleased. They seemed to understand each other already.

"I'll walk you home," he said, when they plainly had reached the time when she must either leave or stay much longer.

"You needn't. It's just down the street." Her hand lingered in his. Her touch was warm, her skin faintly moist, pleasantly so. "You'll call me? Here's my number." She gave him a smooth little yellow card. "We could have dinner, perhaps. Or a concert—whatever you'd like to see—"

"Yes. Yes, I'll call you."

"You'll be here at least a few more days, won't you?"

"Until the end of the month."

She nodded. He saw the momentary darkening of her expression, and guessed at the inward calculations: reckoning the number of days remaining to his visit, the possibilities that those days might hold, the rashness of embarking on anything that would surely not extend beyond the last day of May. Thimiroi had already made the same calculations himself, though tempered by information that she could not conceivably have, information which made everything inconceivably more precarious. After the smallest of pauses she said, "That's plenty of time, isn't it? But call me soon, Thimiroi. Will you? Will you?"

A little while later there was a light knocking at the door, and Thimiroi, hoping with a startling rush of eagerness that Christine had found some pretext for returning, opened it to find Laliene. She looked weary. The perfection of her beauty was unmarred, of course, every shining strand of hair in its place, her tanned skin fresh and glistening. But beneath the radiant outer glow there was once again something drawn and tense and ragged about her, a subliminal atmosphere of strain, of fatigue, of devitalization, that was not at all typical of the Laliene he had known. This visit to the late twentieth century did not seem to be agreeing with her.

"May I come in?" she asked. He nodded and beckoned to her. "We've all just returned from the Courtney birthplace," she said. "You really should have gone with us, Thimiroi. You can feel the aura of the man everywhere in the place, even this early, so many years before he even existed." Taking a few steps into the room, Laliene paused, sniffed the air lightly, smiled. "Having a little tea by yourself just now, were you, Thimiroi?"

"Just a cup. It was a long quiet afternoon."

"Poor Thimiroi. Couldn't find anything at all interesting to do? Then you certainly should have come with us." He saw her glance flicking quickly about, and felt pleased and relieved that he had taken the trouble to put the teacups away. It was in fact no business of Laliene's that he had had a guest in here this afternoon, but he did not want her, all the same, to know that he had.

"Can I brew a cup for you?" he asked.

"I think not. I'm so tired after our outing—it'll put me right to sleep, I would say." She turned toward him, giving him a direct inquisitorial stare that he found acutely discomforting. In a straightforward way that verged on bluntness she said, "I'm worried about you, you know, Thimiroi. Keeping off by yourself so much. The others are talking. You really should make an effort to join the group more often."

"Maybe I'm bored with the group, Laliene. With Denvin's snide little remarks, with Hollia's queenly airs, with Hara's mincing inanity, with Omerie's arrogance, with Klia's vacuity—"

"And with my presumptuousness?"

"You said that. Not I."

But it was true, he realized. She was crowding him constantly, forever edging into his psychic space, pressing herself upon him in a strange, almost incomprehensible way. It had been that way since the beginning of the trip: she never seemed to leave him alone. Her approach toward him was an odd mix of seductiveness, protectiveness, and—what?—inquisitiveness? She was like that strangest of antique phenomena, a jealous lover, almost. But jealous of what? Of whom? Surely not Christine. Christine had not so much as existed for him, except as a mysterious briefly-glimpsed face in a window, until this afternoon, and Laliene had been behaving like this for many weeks. It made no sense. Even now, covertly snooping around his suite, all too obviously searching for some trace of the guest who had only a short while before been present here—what was she after?

He took two fresh cups from his cabinet. "If you don't mind, Laliene, I'll put up a little more tea for myself. And it would be no trouble to make some for you."

"I said I didn't want any, Thimiroi. I don't enjoy gulping the stuff down, you know, the way Kleph does."

"Kleph?"

"Certainly you know how heavily she indulges. She's euphoric more often than not these days."

Thimiroi shrugged. "I didn't realize that. I suppose Omerie can get on anyone's nerves. Even Kleph's."

Laliene studied him for a long moment. "You don't know about Kleph, then?" she asked finally. "No, I suppose you don't. Keeping to yourself this way, how would you?"

This was maddening. "What about Kleph?" he said, his voice growing tight.

"Perhaps you should fix some tea for me after all," Laliene said. "It's quite a nasty story. It'll be easier for me with a little euphoriac."

"Very well."

He busied himself over the tiny covered cups. In a short while the fragrant coiling steam began to rise through the fine crescent opening. His hands trembled, and he nearly swept the cups from the tray as he reached for them; but he recovered quickly and brought them to the table. They sipped the drug in silence. Watching her, Thimiroi was struck once more by the inhuman superfluity of Laliene's elegance. Laliene was much too perfect. How different from Christine, whose skin had minute unimportant blemishes here and there, whose teeth were charmingly irregular, whose hair looked like real hair and not like something spun by machines. Christine probably perspired, he thought. She endured the messiness of menstruation. She might even snore. She was wonderfully real, wonderfully human in every regard. Whereas Laliene—Laliene seemed—scarcely real at all—

"What's this about Kleph, now?" Thimiroi said, after a time.

"She's become involved with the man that the Sanciscos are renting their house from."

"Involved?"

"An affair," said Laliene acidly. Her glistening eyes were trained remorselessly on his. "He goes to her room. She gives him too much tea, and has too much herself. She plays music for him, or they watch the simsos. And then—then—"

"How do you know any of this?" Thimiroi asked.

Laliene took a deep draught of the intoxicating tea, and her brow grew less furrowed, her dark rich-hued eyes less troubled. "She told Klia. Klia told me."

"And Omerie? Does he know?"

"Of course. He's furious. Kleph can sleep with anyone she cares to, naturally—but such a violation of the Travel rules, to get involved with one of these ancient people! And so stupid, too—spending so much of the precious time of her visit here letting herself get wrapped up in a useless diversion with some commonplace and extremely uninteresting man. A man who isn't even alive, who's been dead for all these centuries!"

"He doesn't happen to be dead right now," Thimiroi said.

Laliene gave him a look of amazement. "Are you defending her, Thimiroi?"

"I'm trying to comprehend her."

"Yes. Yes, of course. But certainly Kleph must see that although he may be alive at the present moment, technically speaking, the present moment itself isn't really the present moment. Not if you see it from our point of view, and what other point of view is appropriate for us to take? What's past is past, sealed and finished. In absolute reality this person of Kleph's died long ago, at least so far as we're concerned." Laliene shook her head. "No, no, Thimiroi, completely apart from the issue of transgression against the rules of The Travel, it's an unthinkably foolish adventure that Kleph's let herself get into. Unthinkably foolish! It's purely a waste of time. What kind of pleasure can she possibly get from it? She might as well be coupling with—with a donkey!"

"Who is this man?" Thimiroi asked.

"What does that matter? His name is Oliver Wilson. He owns that house where they are, the one that Hollia is trying to buy, and he lives there, too. Omerie neglected to arrange for him to vacate the premises for the month. You may have seen him: a very ordinary-looking pleasant young man with light-colored hair. But he isn't important. What's important is the insane, absurd, destructive thing Kleph is doing. Which particular person of this long-gone era she happens to be doing it with is completely beside the point."

Thimiroi studied her for a time.

"Why are you telling me this, Laliene?"

"Aren't you interested in what your friends are getting themselves mixed up in?"

"Is Kleph my friend?"

"Isn't she?"

"We have come to the same place at the same time, Kleph and I," Thimiroi said. "Does that make us friends? We *know* each other, Kleph and I. Possibly we were even lovers once, possibly not. My relationship with the Sanciscos in general and with Kleph in particular isn't a close one nowadays. So far as this matters to me, Kleph can do what she likes with anyone she pleases."

"She runs the risk of punishment."

"She was aware of that. Presumably she chooses not to be troubled by it."

"She should think of Omerie, then. And Klia. If Kleph is forbidden to Travel again, they will be deprived of her company. They have always Traveled together. They are accustomed to Traveling together. How selfish of her, Thimiroi."

"Presumably she chooses not to be troubled by that, either," said Thimiroi. "In any case, it's no concern of yours or mine." He hesitated. "Do you know what I think *should* trouble her, Laliene? The fact that she's going to pay a very steep emotional price for what she's doing, if indeed she's actually doing it. That part of it ought to be on her mind, at least a little."

"What do you mean?" Laliene asked.

"I mean the effect it will have on her when the meteor comes, and this man is killed by it. Or by what comes after the meteor, and you know what that is. If the meteor doesn't kill him, the Blue Death will take him a week or two later. How will Kleph feel then, Thimiroi? Knowing that the man she loves is dead? And that she has done nothing, nothing at all, to spare him from the fate that she knew was rushing toward him? Poor Kleph! Poor foolish Kleph! What torment it will be for her!"

"The man she loves?"

"Doesn't she?"

Laliene looked astounded. "What ever gave you that idea? It's a game, Thimiroi, only a silly game! She's simply playing with him. And then she'll move along. He won't be killed by the meteor—obviously. He'll be in the same house as all the rest of us when it strikes. And she'll be at Charlemagne's coronation by the time the Blue Death breaks out. She won't even remember his *name*, Thimiroi. How could you possibly have thought that she—she—" Laliene shook her head. "You don't understand a thing, do you?"

"Perhaps I don't." Thimiroi put his cup down and stared at his fingers. They were trembling. "Would you like some more tea, Laliene?"

"No, I—yes. Yes, another, if you will, Thimiroi."

He set about the task of brewing the euphoriac. His head was throbbing. Things were occurring to him that he had not bothered to consider before. While he worked, Laliene rose, roamed the room, toyed with this artifact and that, and drifted out into the hall that led to the bedroom. Did she suspect anything? Was she searching for something, perhaps? He wondered whether Christine had left any trace of her presence behind that Laliene might be able to detect, and decided that probably she had not. Certainly he hoped not. Considering how agitated Laliene seemed to be over Kleph's little fling with her landlord, how would she react if she knew that he, too, was involved with someone of this era?

Involved?

How involved are you, really? he asked himself.

He thought of all that they had said just now about Kleph and her odd little affair with Oliver Wilson. A cold, inescapable anguish began to rise in him. How sorry he had felt for Kleph, a moment ago! The punishment for transgression against the rules, yes—but also the high emotional price that he imagined Kleph would pay for entangling herself with someone who lay under sentence of immediate death—the guilt—the sense of irretrievable loss—

The meteor—the Blue Death—

"The tea is ready," Thimiroi announced, and as he reached for the delicate cups he knocked one into the other, and both of the pretty things went tumbling from the tray, landing at the carpet's edge and cracking like eggshells against the wooden floor. A little rivulet of euphoriac came swirling from them. He gasped, shocked and appalled. Laliene, emerging from one of the far rooms, looked down at the wreckage for a moment, then swiftly knelt and began to sweep the fragments together.

"Oh, Thimiroi," she said, glancing upward at him. "Oh, how sad, Thimiroi, how terribly sad—"

After lunch the next day, he telephoned Christine, certain that she would be out and a little uneasy about that; but she answered on the second ring, and there was an eagerness in her voice that made him think she had been poised beside the phone for some time now, waiting for him to call. Did she happen to be free this afternoon? Yes, yes, she said, she was free. Did she care to—his mind went blank a moment—to go for a walk with him somewhere? Yes, yes, what a lovely idea! She sounded almost jubilant. A perfect day for a walk, yes!

She was waiting outside her house when Thimiroi came down the street. It was a day much like all the other days so far, sharp cloudless sky, brilliant sun, gold blazing against blue. But there was a deeper tinge of warmth in the air, for May was near its end now and spring was relinquishing its hold to the coming summer. Trees which had seemed barely into leaf the week before now unfurled canopies of rich deep green.

"Where shall we go?" she asked him.

"This is your city. I don't know the good places."

"We could walk in Baxter Park, I suppose."

Thimiroi frowned. "Isn't that all the way on the other side of the river?"

"Baxter Park? Oh, no, you must be thinking of Butterfield Gardens. Up on the high ridge, you mean, over there opposite us? The very big park, with the botanical gardens and the zoo and everything? Baxter Park's right near here, just a few blocks up the hill. We could be there in ten minutes."

Actually it was more like fifteen, and no easy walk, but none of that mattered to Thimiroi. Simply being close to Christine awoke unfamiliar sensations of contentment in him. They climbed the steep streets side by side, saying very little as they made the difficult ascent, pausing now and again to catch their breaths. The city was like a giant bowl, cleft by the great river that ran through its middle, and they were nearing its rim.

Baxter Park, like its counterpart across the river that Thimiroi had seen when he first arrived in the twentieth century, occupied a commanding position looking out and down toward the heart of the urban area. But apart from that the two parks were very different, for the other was intricately laid out, with roads and amusement sectors scattered through it, and this one seemed nothing more than a strip of rough, wild semi-forest that had been left undeveloped at the top of the city. Simple paths crudely paved led through its dense groves and tangles of underbrush.

"It isn't much, I know—" Christine said.

"It's beautiful here. So wild, so untamed. And so close to the city. We can look down and see houses and office buildings and bridges, and yet back here it's just as it must have been ten thousand years ago. There is nothing like this where I come from."

"Do you mean that?"

"We took our wilderness away a long time ago. We should have kept a little—just a little, a reminder, the way you have here. But it's too late now. It has been gone so long, so very long." Thimiroi peered into the hazy distance. Shimmering in the midafternoon heat, the city seemed a fairytale place, enchanted, wondrous. Shading his eyes, he peered out and downward, past the residential district to the metropolitan center by the river, and beyond it to the bridges, the suburbs on the far side, the zone of parks and recreational areas barely visible on the opposite slope. How beautiful it all was, how majestic, how grand! The thought that it all must perish in just a matter of days brought the taste of bile to his mouth, and he turned away, coughing, sputtering.

"Is something the matter?" Christine asked.

"Nothing—no—I'll be all right—"

He wondered how far they were right now from the path along which the meteor would travel.

As he understood it, it was going to come in from this side of the city, traveling low across the great urban bowl like a stone that a boy has sent skimming across a stream and striking somewhere midway down the slope, between the zone of older houses just below the Montgomery House hotel and the business district farther on. At the point of impact, of course, everything would be annihilated for blocks around. But the real devastation would come a moment later, so Kadro had explained: when the shock wave struck and radiated outward, flattening whole neighborhoods in a steadily widening circle, as if they had been swatted by a giant's contemptuous hand.

And then the fires, springing up everywhere—

And then, a few days later, when the invading microbes had had a chance to spread through the contaminated water supply of the shattered city, the plague—

"You look so troubled, Thimiroi," Christine said, nestling up beside him, sliding her arm through his.

"Do I?"

"You must miss your homeland very much."

"No. No, that isn't it."

"Why so sad, then?"

"I find it extremely moving," he said, "to look out over your whole city this way. Taking it all in in a single sweep. Seeing it in all its magnificence, all its power."

"But it's not even the most important city in the—"

"I know. But that doesn't matter. The fact that there may be bigger cities takes nothing away from the grandeur of this one. Especially for me. Where I come from, there are no cities of any size at all. Our population is extremely small...*extremely* small."

"But it must be a very wealthy country, all the same."

Thimiroi shrugged. "I suppose it is. But what does that mean? I look at your city here and I think of the transience of all that is splendid and grand. I think of all the great empires of the past, and how they rose, and fell, and were swept away and forgotten. All the empires that ever were, and all those that will ever be."

To his surprise, she laughed. "Oh, how strange you are!"

"Strange?"

"So terribly solemn. So philosophical. Brooding about the rise and fall of empires on a glorious spring day like this. Standing here with the most amazing sunlight pouring down on us and telling me in those elocution-school tones of yours that empires that don't even exist yet are already swept away and forgotten. How can something be forgotten that hasn't yet even happened? And how can you even bother to think about anything morbid in a season like this one?" She moved closer to him, nuzzling against his side almost like a cat. "Do you know what I think, standing here right this minute looking out at the city? I think that the warmth of the sun feels wonderful and that the air is as fresh as new young wine and that the city has never seemed more sparkling or prosperous and that this is the most beautiful spring day in at least half a million years. And the last thing that's going to cross my mind is that the weather may not hold or that the time of prosperity may not last or that great empires always crumble and are forgotten. But perhaps you and I are just different, Thimiroi. Some people are naturally gloomy, and always see the darkest side of everything, and then there are the people who couldn't manage to be moody and broody even if their lives depended on—" She broke off suddenly. "Oh, Thimiroi, I don't mean to offend you. You know that."

"You haven't offended me." He turned to her. "What's an elocution-school voice?"

"A trained one," she said, smiling. "Like the voice of a radio or TV announcer. You have a marvelous voice, you know. You speak right from the center of your diaphragm, and you always pause for breath in the right places, and the tone is so rich, so perfect—a singer's voice, really. You can sing very well, can't you? I know you can. Later, perhaps, I could play for you, and you could sing for me, back at my place, some song of Stiino—of your own country—"

"Yes," he said. "We could try that, yes."

＊

He kissed her, then, and it was a different sort of kiss from either of the two kisses of the day before, very different indeed; and as he held her his hands ran across her back, and over the nape of her neck, and down the sides of her arms, and she pressed herself close against him. Then after a long moment they moved apart again, both of them flushed and excited, and smiled, and looked at each other as though they were seeing each other for the first time.

They walked hand in hand through the park, neither of them saying anything. Small animals were everywhere, birds and odd shiny bright-colored little insects and comical four-legged grayish beasts with big shaggy tails lalloping behind them. Thimiroi was amazed by the richness of all this wildlife, and the shrubs and wildflowers dazzling with early bloom, and the huge thick-boled trees that rose so awesomely above them. What an extraordinary place this century was, he told himself: what a fantastic mixture of the still unspoiled natural world and the world of technology and industry. They had these great cities, these colossal buildings, these immense bridges—and yet, also, they still had saved room for flowers, for beetles and birds, for little furry animals with enormous tails. When the thought of the meteor, and the destruction that it would cause, crept back into his mind, he forced it furiously away. He asked Christine to tell him the names of things: this is a squirrel, she said, and this is a maple tree, and this a grasshopper. She was surprised that he knew so little about them, and asked him what kinds of insects and trees and animals they had in his own country.

"Very few," he told her. "All our wild things went from us long ago."

"Not even squirrels left? Grasshoppers?"

"Nothing like that," he said. "Nothing at all. That is why we travel—to experience life in places such as this. To experience squirrels. To experience grasshoppers."

"Of course. Everyone travels to see things different from what they have at home. But it's hard to believe that there's any country that's done such ecological damage to itself that it doesn't even have—"

"Oh, the problem is not ecological damage," said Thimiroi. "Not as you understand the term. Our country is very beautiful, in its way, and we care for it extremely well. The problem is that it is an extremely civilized place. Too civilized, I think. We have everything under control.

And one thing that we controlled, a very long time ago, is the very thing that this park is designed to provide: the world of nature, as it existed before the cities ever were."

She stared. "Not even a squirrel."

"Not even a squirrel, no."

"Where is this country of yours? Did you say it was in Arabia? One of the oil kingdoms?"

"No," he said. "Not in Arabia."

They went onward. The afternoon's heat was at its peak, now, and Thimiroi felt the moisture of the air clinging close against his skin, a strange and unusual sensation for him. Again they paused, after a while, to kiss, even more passionately than before.

"Come," Christine said. "Let's go home."

They hurried down the hillside, taking it practically at a jog. But they slowed as the Montgomery House came into view. Thimiroi thought of inviting her to his room once again, but the thought of Laliene hovering nearby—spying on him, scowling her disapproval as he entered into the same transgression for which she had so sternly censured Kleph—displeased him. Christine reminded him, though, that she had offered to play the piano for him, and wanted him to sing for her. Gladly, eagerly, Thimiroi accepted the invitation to go with her to her house.

But as they approached it he was dismayed to see Kleph standing on the steps of a big, rambling old house just opposite Christine's, on the uphill side of the street. She was talking to a sturdy square-shouldered man with a good-natured, open face, and she did not appear to notice Thimiroi.

Christine said, "Do you want to say hello to her?"

"Not really."

"She's one of your friends, isn't she? Someone from your country?"

"She's from my country, yes. But not exactly a friend. Just someone who's taking the same tour I am. Is that the house where she's staying?"

"Yes," Christine said. "She and another woman, and a tall somber-looking man. I saw them all with you, that night at the concert hall. They've rented the house for the whole month. That man's the owner, Oliver Wilson."

"Ah." Thimiroi drew his breath in sharply.

So that was the one. Oliver. Kleph's twentieth-century lover. Thimiroi felt a stab of despair. Looking across the way now at Kleph, deep in conversation with this Oliver, it seemed to him suddenly that Laliene's scorn for Kleph had not been misplaced, that it was foolish and pathetic and even a little sordid for any Traveler to indulge in such doomed and absurd romances as this. And yet he was on the verge of embarking on the same thing Kleph was doing. Was that what he really wanted? Or should he not leave such adventures to shallow, trivial people like Kleph?

Christine said, "You're looking troubled again."

"It's nothing. Nothing." Thimiroi gazed closely at her, and her warmth, her directness, her radiant joyous eyes, swept away all the sudden doubts that had come to engulf him. He had no right to condemn Kleph. And in any case what he might choose to do, or Kleph, was no concern of Laliene's. "Come," he said. He caught Christine lightly by the arm. "Let's go inside."

Just as he turned, Kleph did also, and for an instant their eyes met as they stood facing each other on opposite sides of the street. She gave him a startled look. Thimiroi smiled to her; but Kleph merely stared back intently in a curiously cold way. Then she was gone. Thimiroi shrugged.

He followed Christine into her house.

It was an old, comfortable-looking place with a great many small, dark, high-ceilinged rooms on the ground floor and a massive wooden staircase leading upstairs. The furnishings looked heavy and unstylish, as though they were already long out of date, but everything had an appealing, well-worn feel.

"My family's lived in this house for almost a hundred years," Christine said, as though reading his mind. "I was born here. I grew up here. I don't know what it's like to live anywhere else." She gestured toward the staircase. "The music room is upstairs."

"I know. Do you live here by yourself?"

"Basically. My sister and I inherited the house when my mother died, but she's hardly ever here. The last I heard from her, she was in Oaxaca."

"Wah-ha-ka?" Thimiroi said carefully.

"Oaxaca, yes. In Mexico, you know? She's studying Mexican handicrafts, she says. I think she's actually studying Mexican men, but that's her business, isn't it? She likes to travel. Before Mexico she was in Thailand, and before that it was Portugal, I think."

Mexico, Thimiroi thought. Thailand. Portugal. So many names, so many places. Such a complex society, this world of the twentieth century. His own world had fewer places, and they had different names. So much had changed, after the time of the Blue Death. So much had been swept away, never to return.

Christine said, "It's a musty old house, I know. But I love it. And I could never have afforded to buy one of my own. Everything's so fantastically expensive these days. If I hadn't happened to have lived here all along, I suppose I'd be living in one of those poky little studio apartments down by the river, paying umpty thousand dollars a month for one bedroom and a terrace the size of a postage stamp."

Desperately he tried to follow what she was saying. His implant helped, but not enough. Umpty thousand dollars? Studio apartment? Postage stamp? He got the sense of her words, but the literal meanings eluded him. How much was umpty? How big was a postage stamp?

The music room on the second floor was bright and spacious, with three large windows looking out into the garden and the street beyond. The piano itself, against the front wall between two of the windows, was larger than he expected, a splendid, imposing thing, with ponderous, ornately carved legs and a black, gleaming wooden case. Obviously it was old and very valuable and well cared for; and as he studied it he realized suddenly that this must not be any ordinary home musical instrument, but more likely one that a concert performer would use; and therefore Christine's lighthearted dismissal of his question about her having a musical career must almost certainly conceal bitter defeat, frustration, the deflection of a cherished dream. She had wanted and expected more from her music than life had been able to bring her.

"Play for me," he said. "The same piece you were playing the first time, when I happened to walk by."

"The Debussy, you mean?"

"I don't know its name."

Thimiroi hummed the melody that had so captured him. She nodded and sat down to play.

It was not quite as magical, the second time. But nothing ever was, he knew. And it was beautiful all the same, haunting, mysterious in its powerful simplicity.

"Will you sing for me now?" Christine asked.

"What should I sing?"

"A song of your own country?"

He thought a moment. How could he explain to her what music was like in his own time—not sound alone, but a cluster of all the arts, visual, olfactory, the melodic line rising out of a dozen different sensory concepts? But he could improvise, he supposed. He began to sing one of his own poems, putting a tune to it as he went. Christine, listening, closed her eyes, nodded, turned to the keyboard, played a few notes and a few more, gradually shaping them into an accompaniment for him. Thimiroi was amazed at the swiftness with which she caught the melody of his tune—stumbling only once or twice, over chordal structures that were obviously alien to her—and traveled along easily with it. By the time he reached the fifth cycle of the song, he and she were joined in an elegant harmony, as though they had played this song together many times instead of both improvising it as they went. And when he made the sudden startling key-shift that in his culture signalled the close of a song, she adapted to it almost instantaneously and stayed with him to the final note.

They applauded each other resoundingly.

Her eyes were shining with delight. "Oh, Thimiroi—Thimiroi—what a marvelous singer you are! And what a marvelous song!"

"And how cunningly you wove your accompaniment into it."

"That wasn't really hard."

"For you, perhaps. You have a great musical gift, Christine."

She reddened and looked away.

"What language were you singing in?" she asked, after a time.

"The language of my country."

"It was so strange. It isn't like any language I've ever heard. Why won't you tell me anything about where you come from, Thimiroi?"

"I will. Later."

"And what did the words mean?"

"It's a poem about—about journeying to far lands, and seeing great wonders. A very romantic poem, perhaps a little silly. But the poet himself is also very romantic and perhaps a little silly."

"What's his name?" she asked.

"Thimiroi."

"You?" she said, grinning broadly. "Is that what you are? A poet?"

"I sometimes write poetry, yes," he said, beginning to feel as uneasy as she had seemed when he was trying to praise her playing. They looked at each other awkwardly. Then he said, "May I try the piano?"

"Of course."

He sat down, peered at the keys, touched one of the white ones experimentally, then another, another. What were the black ones?

Modulators of some sort? No, no, their function was very much like that of the white ones, it seemed. And these pedals here—

He began to play.

He was dreadful at first, but quickly he came to understand the relationship of the notes and the range of the keyboard and the proper way of touching the keys. He played the piece that she had played for him before, exactly at first, then launching into a set of subtle variations that carried him farther and farther from the original, into the musical modes of his own time. The longer he played, the more keenly he appreciated the delicacy and versatility of this ancient instrument; and he knew that if he were to study it with some care, not merely guess his way along as he was doing now, he would be able to draw such wonders from it as even great composers like Cenbe or Palivandrin would find worthwhile. Once again he felt humbled by the achievements of this great lost civilization of the past. Which to brittle, heartless people like Hollia or Omerie must seem a mere simple primitive age. But they understood nothing. Nothing.

He stopped playing, and looked back at Christine.

She was staring at him in horror, her face pale, her eyes wide and stricken, tears streaking her cheeks.

"What's wrong?" he asked.

"The way you play—" she whispered. "I've never heard anyone play like that."

"It is all very bad, I know. But you must realize, I have had no formal training in this instrument, I am simply inventing a technique as I go—"

"No. Please. Don't tell me that. You mustn't tell me that!"

"Christine?"

And then he realized what the matter was. It was not that he had played badly; it was that he had played so well. She had devoted all her life to this instrument, and played it with great skill, and even so had never been able to attain a level of proficiency that gave her any real satisfaction. And he, never so much as having seen a piano in his life, could sit down at it and draw from it splendors beyond her fondest hope of achieving. His playing was unorthodox, of course, it was odd and even bizarre, but yet she had seen the surpassing mastery in it, and had been stunned and chagrined and crushed by it, and stood here now bewildered and confounded by this stranger she had brought into her own home—

I should have known better, Thimiroi thought. I should have realized that this is *her* art, and that I, with all the advantages that are mine purely by virtue of my having been born when I was, ought never to have presumed to invade her special territory with such a display of skills that are beyond her comprehension. Without even suspecting what I was doing, I have humiliated her.

"Christine," he murmured. "No. No, Christine."

Thimiroi went to her and pulled her close against him, and kissed the tears away, and spoke softly to her, calming her, reassuring her. He could never tell her the truth; but he could make her understand, at least, that he had not meant to hurt her. And after a time he felt the tension leave her, and felt her press herself tight to him, and then their lips met, and she looked up, smiling. And took him lightly by the hand, and drew him from the room and down the hall.

Afterward, as he was dressing, she touched the long, fading red scar on his arm and said, "Were you in some kind of accident?"

"An inoculation," he told her. "Against disease."

"I've never seen one like that before."

"No," he said. "I suppose you haven't."

"A disease of your country?"

"No," he said, after a time. "Of yours."

"But what kind of disease requires a vaccination like—"

"Do we have to talk of diseases just now, Christine."

"Of course not," she said, smiling ruefully. "How foolish of me. How absurd." She ran her fingers lightly, almost fondly, over the inoculation scar a second time. "Of all things for me to be curious about!" Softly she said, "You don't have to leave now, you know."

"But I must. I really must."

"Yes," she said. "I suppose you must." She accompanied him to the front door. "You'll call me, won't you? Very soon?"

"Of course," Thimiroi said.

Night had fallen. The air was mild and humid, but the sky was clear and the stars glittered brilliantly. He looked for the moon but could not find it.

How many days remain, he wondered?

Somewhere out there in the airless dark a lump of dead rock was falling steadily toward earth, falling, falling, inexorably coming this way. How far away was it now? How soon before it would come roaring over the horizon to bring unimaginable death to this place?

I must find a way of saving her, he told himself.

The thought was numbing, dizzying, intolerably disturbing.

Save her? How? Impossible. Impossible. It was something that he must not even allow himself to consider.

And yet—

Again it came. *I must find a way of saving her.*

There was a message for him at his hotel, just a few quick scrawled sentences:

Party at Lutheena's. We're all going. See you there?

Laliene's handwriting, which even in her haste was as beautiful as the finest calligraphy. Thimiroi crumpled the note and tossed it aside. Going to a party tonight was very close to the last thing he would want to do. Everyone in glittering clothes, making glittering conversation, trading sparkling anecdotes, no doubt, of their latest adventures among the simple sweaty blotchyskinned folk of this interestingly raucous and crude century—no. No. No. Let them trade their anecdotes without him. Let them sip their euphoriac and exchange their chatter and play their little games. He was going to bed. Very likely, without him there, they would all be talking about him. How oddly he had been behaving, how strange and uncouth he seemed to be becoming since their arrival in this era. Let them talk. What did it matter?

He wished Kleph had not seen him going into Christine's house, though.

But how would Kleph know whose house it was? And why would Kleph—Kleph, with her own Oliver Wilson entanglement preoccupying her—want to say anything to anyone about having seen some other member of the tour slipping away for an intimate hour with a twentieth-century person? Better for her to be silent. The subject was a delicate one. She would not want to raise it. She of all people would be unlikely to disapprove, or to want to bring down on him the disapproval of the others. No, Thimiroi thought. Kleph will say nothing. We are allies in this business, Kleph and I.

He slept, and dark dreams came that he could not abide: the remorseless meteor crossing the sky, the city aflame and shrieking, Christine's wonderful old house swept away by a searing blast of destruction, the piano lying tumbled in the street, split in half, golden strings spilling out.

Wearily Thimiroi dosed himself with the drug that banishes dreams, and lay down to sleep again. But now sleep evaded him. Very well: there was the other drug, the one that brings sleep. He hesitated to take it. The two drugs taken in the wrong order exacted a price; he would be jittery and off balance emotionally for the next two or three days. He was far enough off balance as it was already. So he lay still, hoping that he would drift eventually into sleep without recourse to more medication; and gradually his mind grew easier, gradually he began the familiar descent toward unconsciousness.

Suddenly the image of Laliene blazed in his mind.

It was so vivid that it seemed she was standing beside him in the darkness and light was streaming from her body. She was nude, and her breasts, her hips, her thighs, all had a throbbing incandescent glow. Thimiroi sat up, astonished, swept with waves of startling feverish excitement.

"Laliene?"

How radiant she looked! How splendid! Her eyes were glowing like beacons. Her crimson hair stood out about her head like a bright corona. The scent of her filled his nostrils. He trembled. His throat was dry, his lips seemed gummed together.

Wave after wave of intense, overpowering desire swept through him.

Helplessly Thimiroi rose, lurched across the room, reached gropingly toward her. This was madness, he knew, but there was no holding himself back.

The shimmering image retreated as he came near it. He stumbled, nearly tripped, regained his balance.

"Wait, Laliene," he cried hoarsely. His heart was pounding thunderously. It was almost impossible for him to catch his breath. He was choking with his need. "Come here, will you? Stop edging away like that."

"I'm not here, Thimiroi. I'm in my own room. Put your robe on and come visit me."

"What? You're not here?"

"Down the hall. Come, now. Hurry!"

"You are here. You have to be."

As though in a daze, brain swathed in thick layers of white cotton, he reached for her again. Like a lovestruck boy he yearned to draw her close, to cup her breasts in his hands, to run his fingers over those silken thighs, those satiny flanks—

"To my room," she whispered.

"Yes. Yes."

His flesh was aflame. Sweat rolled down his body. She danced before him like a shining will-o'-the-wisp. Frantically he struggled to comprehend what was happening. A vision? A dream? But he had drugged himself against dreams. And he was awake now. Surely he was awake. And yet he saw her—he wanted her—he wanted her beyond all measure—he was going to slip his robe on, and go to her suite, and she would be waiting for him there, and he would slip into her bed—into her arms—

No. No. No.

He fought it. He caught the side of some piece of furniture, and held it, anchoring himself, struggling to keep himself from going forward. His teeth chattered. Chills ran along his back and shoulders. The muscles in his arms and chest writhed and spasmed as he battled to stay where he was.

He was fully awake now, and he was beginning to understand. He remembered how Laliene had gone wandering around here the other day while he was brewing the tea—examining the works of art, so he had thought. But she could just as easily have been planting something. Which now was broadcasting monstrous compulsions into his mind.

He switched on the light, wincing as it flooded the room. Now Thimiroi could no longer see that mocking, beckoning image of Laliene, but he still felt her presence all around him, the heat of her body, the pungency of her fragrance, the strength of her urgent summons.

Somehow he managed to find the card with Christine's telephone number on it, and dialed it with tense, quivering fingers. The phone rang endlessly until, finally, he heard her sleepy voice, barely focused, saying, "Yes? Hello?"

"Christine? Christine, it's me, Thimiroi."

"What? Who? Don't you know it's four in the morn—" Then her tone changed. The sleepiness left it, and the irritation. "What's wrong, Thimiroi? What's happening?"

"I'll be all right. I need you to talk to me, that's all. I'm having a kind of an attack."

"No, Thimiroi!" He could feel the intensity of her concern. "What can I do? Shall I come over?"

"No. That's not necessary. Just talk to me. I need to stir up—cerebral activity. Do you understand? It's just an—an electrochemical imbalance. But if I talk—even if I listen to something—speak to me, say anything, recite poetry—"

"Poetry," she said. "All right. Let me think. '*Four score and seven years ago*—'" she began.

"Good," he said. "Even if I don't understand it, that's all right. Say anything. Just keep talking."

Already Laliene's aura was ebbing from the room. Christine continued to speak; and he broke in from time to time, simply to keep his mental level up. In a few minutes Thimiroi knew that he had defeated Laliene's plan. He slumped forward, breathing hard, letting his stiff, anguished muscles uncoil.

He still could feel the waves of mental force sweeping through the room. But they were pallid now, they were almost comical, they no longer were capable of arousing in him the obsessive obedience that they had been able to conjure into his sleeping mind.

Christine, troubled, still wanted to come to him; but Thimiroi told her that everything was fine, now, that she should go back to sleep, that he was sorry to have disturbed her. He would explain, he promised. Later. Later.

Fury overtook him the moment he put the receiver down.

Damn Laliene. Damn her! What did she think she was doing?

He searched through the sitting room, and then the bedroom, and the third room of the suite. But it was almost dawn before he found what he was looking for: the tiny silvery pellet, the minute erotic broadcaster, that she had hidden beneath one of his Sipulva tables. He pulled it loose and crushed it against the wall, and the last faint vestige of Laliene's presence went from the room like water swirling down a drain. Slowly Thimiroi's anger receded. He put on some music, one of Cenbe's early pieces, and listened quietly to it until he saw the first pale light of morning streaking the sky.

Casually, easily, with a wonderful recklessness he had not known he had in him, he said to Christine, "We go anywhere we want. Anywhen. They run tours for us, you see. We were in Canterbury in Chaucer's time, to make the pilgrimage. We went to Rome and then to Emperor Augustus' summer palace on the island of Capri, and he invited us to a grand banquet, thinking we were visitors from a great kingdom near India."

Christine was staring at him in a wide-eyed gaze, as though she were a child and he were telling her some fabulous tale of dragons and princes.

He had gone to her at midday, when the late May sun was immense overhead and the sky seemed like a great curving plate of burnished blue steel. She had let him in without a word, and for a long while they looked at each other in silence, their hands barely touching. She was very pale and her eyes were reddened from sleeplessness, with dark crescents beneath them. Thimiroi embraced her, and assured her that he was in no danger, that with her help he had been able to fight off the demon that had assailed him in the night. Then she took him upstairs, to the room on the second floor where they had made love the day before, and drew him down with her on the bed, almost shyly at first, and then, casting all reserve aside, seizing him eagerly, hungrily.

When finally they lay back, side by side, all passion slaked for the moment, Christine turned toward him and said, "Tell me now where your country is, Thimiroi."

And at last he began—calmly, unhesitatingly—to tell her about The Travel.

"We went to Canterbury in the autumn of 1347," he said. "Actually Chaucer was still only a boy, then. The poem was many years away. Of course we read him before we set out. We even looked at the original Old English text. I suppose the language would be strange even to you. '*When that Aprill with his shoures soote The droghte of March hath perced to the roote.*' I suppose we really should have gone in April ourselves, to be more authentic; but April was wet that year, as it usually is at that time in England, and the autumn was warm and brilliant, a season much like the one you are having here, a true vintage season. We are very fond of warm, dry weather, and rain depresses us."

"You could have gone in another year, then, and found a warmer, drier April," Christine said.

"No. The year had to be 1347. It isn't important why. And so we went in autumn, in beautiful October."

"Ah."

"We began in London, gathering in an inn on the south side of the river, just as Chaucer's pilgrims did, and we set out with a band of pilgrims that must have been much like his, even one who played a bagpipe the way his Miller did, and a woman who might almost have been the Wife of Bath—" Thimiroi closed his eyes a moment, letting the journey come rushing back from memory, sights and sounds, laughter, barking dogs, cool bitter ale, embroidered gowns, the mounds of straw in the stable, falling leaves, warm dry breezes. "And then, before that, first-century Capri. In the time of Augustus. In high summer, a perfect Mediterranean summer, still another vintage season. How splendid Capri is. Do you know it? No? An island off Italy, very steep, a mountaintop in the water, with strange grottos at its base and huge rocks all about. There comes a time every evening when the sky and the sea are the same color, a pale blue-gray, so that it is impossible to tell where one ends and the other begins, and you stand by the edge of the high cliff, looking outward into that gray haze, and it seems to you that all the world is completely still, that time is not moving at all."

"The—first century—?" Christine murmured.

"The reign of the Emperor Augustus, yes. A surprisingly short man, and very gentle and witty, extremely likable, although you can feel the ruthlessness of him just behind the gentleness. He has amazing eyes, utterly penetrating, with a kind of light coming from them. You look at him and you see Rome: the Empire embodied in one man, its beginning and its end, its greatness and its power."

"You speak of him as though he is still alive. 'He has amazing eyes,' you said."

"I saw him only a few months ago," said Thimiroi. "He handed me a cup of sweet red wine with his own hands, and recommended it, saying there certainly was nothing like it in my own land. He has a palace on Capri, nothing very grand—his stepson Tiberius, who was there also, would build a much greater one later on, so our guide told us—and he was there for the summer. We were guests under false pretenses, I suppose, ambassadors from a distant land, though he never would have guessed *how* distant. The year was—let me think—no, not the first century, not *your* first century, it was what you call B.C., the last century *before* the first century—I think the year was 19, the 19 *before*—such a muddle, these dating systems—"

"And in your country?" Christine asked. "What year is it now in your country, Thimiroi? 2600? 3100?"

He pondered that a moment. "We use a different system of reckoning. It is not at all analogous. The term would be meaningless to you."

"You can't tell me what year it is there?"

"Not in your kind of numbers, no. There was—a break in the pattern of numbering, long before our time. I could ask Kadro. He is our tour guide, Kadro. He knows how to compute the equivalencies."

She stared at him. "Couldn't you guess? Five hundred years? A thousand?"

"Perhaps it is something like that. But even if I knew, I would not tell you the exact span, Christine. It would be wrong. It is forbidden, absolutely forbidden." Thimiroi laughed. "Everything I have just told you is absolutely forbidden, do you know that? We must conceal the truth about ourselves to those we meet when we undertake The Travel. That is the rule. Of course, you don't believe a thing I've just been telling you, do you?"

Color flared in her cheeks. "Don't you think I do?" she cried.

Tenderly Thimiroi said, "There are two things they tell us about The Travel, Christine, before we set out for the first time. The first, they say, is that sooner or later you will feel some compulsion to reveal to a person of ancient times that you are a visitor from a future time. The second thing is that you will not be believed."

"But I believe you, Thimiroi!"

"Do you? Do you really?"

"Of course it all sounds so terribly strange, so fantastic—"

"Yes. Of course."

"But I want to believe you. And so I do believe you. The way you speak—the way you dress—the way you look—everything about you is *foreign*, Thimiroi, totally foreign beyond any ordinary kind of foreignness. It isn't Iran or India or Afghanistan that you come from, it has to be some other world, or some other time. Yes. Yes. Everything about you. The way you played the piano yesterday." She paused a moment. "The way you touch me in bed. You are like no man I have ever—like no man—" She faltered, reddened fiercely, looked away from him a moment. "Of course I believe that you are what you say you are. Of course I do!"

When he returned to the Montgomery House late that afternoon he went down the hall to Laliene's suite and rapped angrily at the door. Denvin opened it and peered out at him. He was dressed in peacock splendor, an outfit exceptional even for Denvin, a shirt with brilliant red stripes and golden epaulets, tight green trousers flecked with scarlet checks.

He gave Thimiroi a long cool malevolent glance and exclaimed, "Well! The prodigal returns!"

"How good to see you, Denvin. Am I interrupting anything?"

"Only a quiet little chat." Denvin turned. "Laliene! Our wandering poet is here!"

Laliene emerged from deeper within. Like Denvin she was elaborately clothed, wearing a pale topaz-hued gown fashioned of a myriad shimmering mirrors, shining metallic eye-shadow, gossamer finger-gloves. She looked magnificent. But for an instant, as her eyes met Thimiroi's, her matchless poise appeared to desert her, and she seemed startled, flustered, almost frightened. Then, regaining her equilibrium with a superb show of control, she gave him a cool smile and said, "So there you are. We tried to reach you before, but of course there was no finding you. Maitira, Antilimoin, and Fevra are here. We've just been with them. They've been holding open house all afternoon, and you were invited. I suppose it's still going on. Lesentru is due to arrive in about an hour, and Kuiane, and they say that Broyal and Hammin will be getting here tonight also."

"The whole clan," Thimiroi said. "That will be delightful. Laliene, may I speak with you privately?"

Again a flicker of distress from her. She glanced almost apologetically at Denvin.

"Well, excuse me!" Denvin said theatrically.

"Please," Laliene said. "For just a moment, Denvin."

"Certainly. Certainly, Laliene." He favored Thimiroi with a strange grimace as he went out.

"Very well," said Laliene, turning to face Thimiroi squarely. Her expression had hardened; she looked steely, now, and prepared for any sort of attack. "What is it, Thimiroi?"

He drew forth the little silvery pellet that he had found attached to the underside of the Sipulva table, and held it out to her in the palm of his hand.

"Do you know what this is, Laliene?"

"Some little broken toy, I assume. Why do you ask?"

"It's an erotic," he said. "I found it in my rooms, where someone had hidden it. It began broadcasting when I went to sleep last night. Sending out practically irresistible waves of sexual desire."

"How fascinating. I hope you were able to find someone to satisfy them with."

"The images I was getting, Laliene, were images of you. Standing naked next to my bed, whispering to me, inviting me to come down the hall and make love to you."

She smiled icily. "I had no idea you were still interested, Thimiroi!"

"Don't play games with me. Why did you plant this thing in my room, Laliene?"

"*I?*"

"I said, don't play games. You were in my room the other day. No one else of our group has been. The erotic was specifically broadcasting your image. How can there be any doubt that you planted it yourself, for the particular purpose of luring me into your bed?"

"You're being absurd, Thimiroi. Anyone could have planted it. Anyone. Do you think it's hard to get into these rooms? These people have no idea of security. You ask a chambermaid in the right way and you can enter anywhere. As for the images of me that were being broadcast to you, why, you know as well as I do that erotics don't broadcast images of specific individuals. They send out generalized waves of feeling, and the recipient supplies whatever image seems appropriate to him. In your case evidently it was my image that came up from your unconscious when—"

"Don't lie to me, Laliene."

Her eyes flashed. "I'm not lying. I deny planting anything in your room. Why on earth would I, anyway? Could going to bed with you, or anyone else, for that matter, possibly be that important to me that I would connive and sneak around and make use of some kind of mechanical amplifying device in order to achieve my purpose? Is that plausible, Thimiroi?"

"I don't know. What I do know is that what happened to me during the night happened to me, and that I found this when I searched my rooms." He thought for a moment to add, *And that you've been pressing yourself upon me ever since we began this trip, in the most embarrassing and irritating fashion.* But he did not have the heart to say that to her. "I believe that you hid this when you visited me for tea. What your reason may have been is something I can't begin to imagine."

"Of course you can't. Because I had no reason. And I didn't do it."

Thimiroi made no reply. Laliene's face was firmly set. Her gaze met his unwaveringly. She was certainly lying: he knew that beyond any question. But they were at an impasse. All he could do was accuse; he could not prove anything; he was stymied by her denial, and there was no way of carrying this further. She appeared to know that also. There was a long tense moment of silence between them, and then she said, "Are you finished with this, Thimiroi? Because there are more important things we should be discussing."

"Go ahead. What important things?"

"The plans for Friday night."

"Friday night," Thimiroi said, not understanding.

She looked at him scornfully. "Friday—tomorrow—is the last day of May. Or have you forgotten that?"

He felt a chill. "The meteor," he said.

"The meteor, yes. The event which we came to this place to see," Laliene said. "Do you recall?"

"So soon," Thimiroi said dully. "Tomorrow night."

"We will all assemble about midnight, or a little before, at the Sanciscos' house. The view will be best from there, according to Kadro. From their front rooms, upstairs. Kleph, Omerie, and Klia have invited everyone—everyone except Hollia and Hara, that is: Omerie is adamant about their not coming, because of something slippery that Hollia tried to do to him. Kleph would not discuss it, but I assume it had to do with trying to get the Sanciscos evicted, so that they could have the Wilson house for themselves. But all the rest of us will be there. And you are particularly included, Thimiroi. Kleph made a point of telling me that. Unless you have other plans for the evening, naturally."

"Is that what Kleph said? Or are you adding that part of it yourself, about my having other plans?"

"That is what Kleph said."

"I see."

"*Do* you have other plans?"

"What other plans could I possibly have, do you think? Where? With whom?"

Christine seemed startled to see him again so soon. She was still wearing an old pink robe that she had thrown on as he was leaving her house two hours before, and she looked rumpled and drowsy and confused. Behind him the sky held the pearl-gray of early twilight on this late spring evening, but she stood in the half-opened doorway blinking at him as though he had awakened her once again in the middle of the night.

"Thimiroi? You're back?"

"Let me in. Quickly, please."

"Is there something wrong? Are you in trouble?"

"Please."

He stepped past her into the vestibule and hastily pushed the door shut behind him. She gave him a baffled look. "I was just napping," she said. "I didn't think you'd be coming back this evening, and I had so little sleep last night, you know—"

"I know. We need to talk. This is urgent, Christine."

"Go into the parlor. I'll be with you in a moment."

She pointed to Thimiroi's left and vanished into the dim recesses at the rear of the entrance hall. Thimiroi went into the room she had indicated, a long, oppressively narrow chamber hung with heavy brocaded draperies and furnished with the sort of lowslung clumsy-looking couches and chairs, probably out of some even earlier era, that were everywhere in the house. He paced restlessly about the room. It was like being in a museum of forgotten styles. There was something eerie and almost hieratic about this mysterious furniture: the dark wood, the heavy legs jutting at curious angles, the coarse, intricately worked fabrics, the strange brass buttons running along the edges. Someone like Denvin would probably think it hideous. To him it was merely strange, powerful, haunting, wonderful in its way.

At last Christine appeared. She had been gone for what felt like hours: washing her face, brushing her hair, changing into a robe she evidently considered more seemly for receiving a visitor at nightfall. Her vanity was almost amusing. The world is about to come to an end, he thought, and she pauses to make herself fit for entertaining company.

But of course she could have no idea of why he was here.

He said, "Are you free tomorrow night?"

"Free? Tomorrow?" She looked uncertain. "Why—yes, yes, I suppose. Friday night. I'm free, yes. What did you have in mind, Thimiroi?"

"How well do you trust me, Christine?"

She did not reply for a moment. For the first time since that day they had had lunch together at the River Cafe, there was something other than fascination, warmth, even love for him, in her eyes. She seemed mystified, troubled, perhaps frightened. It was as if his sudden breathless arrival here this evening had reminded her of how truly strange their relationship was, and of how little she really knew about him.

"Trust you how?" she said finally.

"What I told you this afternoon, about Capri, about Canterbury, about The Travel—did you believe all that or not?"

She moistened her lips. "I suppose you're going to say that you were making it all up, and that you feel guilty now for having fed all that nonsense to a poor simple gullible woman like me."

"No."

"No what?"

"I wasn't making anything up. But do you believe that, Christine? Do you?"

"I said I did, this afternoon."

"But you've had a few hours to think about it. Do you still believe it?"

She made no immediate reply. At length she said, glancing at him warily, "I've been napping, Thimiroi. I haven't been thinking about anything at all. But since it seems to be so important to you: Yes. Yes, I think that what you told me, weird as it was, was the truth. There. If it was just a joke, I swallowed it. Does that make me a simpleton in your eyes?"

"So you trust me."

"Yes. I trust you."

"Will you go away with me, then? Leave here with me tomorrow, and possibly never come back?"

"*Tomorrow?*" The word seemed to have struck her like an explosion. She looked dazed. "Never—come—back—?"

"In all likelihood."

She put the palms of her hands together, rubbed them against each other, pressed them tight: a little ritual of hers, perhaps. When she looked up at him again her expression had changed: the confusion had cleared from her face and now she appeared merely puzzled, and even somewhat irritated.

In a sharp tone she said, "What is all this about, Thimiroi?"

He drew a deep breath. "Do you know why we chose the autumn of 1347 for our Canterbury visit?" he asked. "Because it was a season of extraordinarily fine weather, yes. But also because it was a peak time, looking down into a terrible valley, the last sweet moment before the coming of a great calamity. By the following summer the Black Death would be devouring England, and millions would die. We chose the timing of our visit to Augustus the same way. The year 19—19 B.C., it was—was the year he finally consolidated all imperial power in his grasp. Rome was his; he ruled it in a way that no one had ruled that nation before. After that there would be only anticlimax for him, and disappointments and losses; and indeed just after we went to him he would fall seriously ill, almost to the edge of death, and for a time it would seem to him that he had lost everything in the very moment of attaining it. But when we visited him in 19 B.C., it was the summit of his time."

"What does this have to do with—"

"This May, here, now, is another vintage season, Christine. This long golden month of unforgettable weather—it will end tomorrow, Christine, in terror, in destruction, a frightful descent from happiness into disaster, far steeper than either of the other two. That is why we are here, do you see? As spectators, as observers of the great irony—visiting your city at its happiest moment, and then, tomorrow, watching the catastrophe."

As he spoke, she grew pale and her lips began to quiver; and then color flooded into her face, as it will sometimes do when the full impact of terrible news arrives. Something close to panic was gleaming in her eyes.

"Are you saying that there's going to be nuclear war? That after all these years the bombs are finally going to go off?"

"Not war, no."

"What then?"

Without answering, Thimiroi drew forth his wallet and began to stack currency on the table in front of him, hundreds of dollars, perhaps thousands, all the strange little strips of green-and-black paper that they had supplied him with when he first had arrived here. Christine gaped in astonishment. He shoved the money toward her.

"Here," he said. "I'll get more tomorrow morning, and give you that too. Arrange a trip for us to some other country, France, Spain, England, wherever you'd like to go, it makes no difference which one, so long as it is far from here. You will understand how to do such things, with which I have had no experience. Buy airplane tickets—is that the right term, airplane tickets?—get us a hotel room, do whatever is necessary. But we must depart no later than this time tomorrow. When you pack, pack as though you may never return to this house: take your most precious things, the things you would not want to leave behind, but only as much as you can carry yourself. If you have money on deposit, take it out, or arrange for it to be transferred to some place of deposit in the country that we will be going to. Call me when everything is ready, and I'll come for you and we'll go together to the place where the planes take off."

Her expression was frozen, her eyes glazed, rigid. "You won't tell me what's going to happen?"

"I have already told you vastly too much. If I tell you more—and you tell others—and the news spreads widely, and the pattern of the future is greatly changed by the things that those people may do as a result of knowing what is to come—no. No. I do not dare, Christine. You are the only one I can save, and I can tell you no more than I have already told you. And you must tell no one else at all."

"This is like a dream, Thimiroi."

"Yes. But it is very real, I assure you."

Once again she stared. Her lips worked a moment before she could speak.

"I'm so terribly afraid, Thimiroi."

"I understand that. But you do believe me? Will you do as I ask? I swear to you, Christine, your only hope lies in trusting me. *Our* only hope."

"Yes," she said hesitantly.

"Then will you do as I ask?"

"Yes," she said, beginning the single syllable with doubt in her voice, and finishing it with sudden conviction. "But there's something I don't understand."

"What is that?"

"If something awful is going to happen here, why must we run off to England or Spain? Why not take me back to your own country, Thimiroi? Your own time."

"There is no way I can do that," he said softly.

"When you go back, then, what will happen to me?"

He took her hand in his. "I will not go back, Christine. I will stay here with you, in this era—in England, in France, wherever we may go—for the rest of my life. We will both be exiles. But we will be exiles together."

She asked him to stay with her at her house that night, and he refused. He could see that the refusal hurt her deeply; but there was much that he needed to do, and he could not do it there. They would have many other nights for spending together. Returning to his hotel, he went quickly to his rooms to contemplate the things that would have to be dealt with.

Everything that belonged to his own era, of course, packed and sent back via his suitcase: no question about that. He could keep some of his clothing with him here, perhaps, but none of the furniture, none of the artifacts, nothing that might betray the technology of a time yet unborn. The room would have to be bare when he left it. And he would have to requisition more twentieth-century money. He had no idea how much Christine might have above what he had already given her, nor how long it would last; but certainly they would need more as they began their new lives. As for the suitcase, his one remaining link to the epoch from which he came, he would have to destroy that. He would have to sever all ties. He would—

The telephone rang. The light jingling of its bell cut across his consciousness like a scream.

Christine, he thought. To tell him that she had reconsidered, that she saw now that this was all madness, that if he did not leave her alone she would call the police—

"Yes?" he said.

"Thimiroi! Oh, I *am* glad you're there." A warm, hearty, familiar masculine voice. "Laliene said I might have difficulty finding you, but I thought I'd ring your room anyway—"

"Antilimoin?"

"None other. We've just arrived. Ninth floor, the Presidential suite, whatever that may be. Maitira and Fevra are here with me, of course. Listen, old friend, we're having a tremendous blast tonight—oh, pardon me, that's a sick thing to say, isn't it?—a tremendous gathering, you know, a *soiree*, to enliven the night before the big night—do you think you can make it?"

"Well—"

"Laliene says you've been terribly standoffish lately, and I suppose she's right. But look, old friend, you can't spend the evening moping by yourself, you absolutely can't. Lesentru'll be here, do you know that? And Kuiane. Maybe even Broyal and Hammin, later on. And a rumor of Cenbe, too, though I suspect he won't show up until the very last minute, as usual. Listen, there are all sorts of stories to tell. You were in Canterbury, weren't you? And we've just done the Charlemagne thing. We have some splendid tips on what to see and what to avoid. You'll come, of course. Room 941, the end of the hall."

"I don't know if I—"

"Of course you will! Of course!"

Antilimoin's gusto was irresistible. It always was. The man was a ferociously social being: when he gave a party, attendance was never optional. And Thimiroi realized, after a moment, that it was better, perhaps, for him to go than to lurk here by himself, tensely awaiting the ordeals that tomorrow would bring. He had already brought more than enough suspicion upon himself. Antilimoin's party would be his farewell to his native time, to his friends, to everything that had been his life.

He spent a busy hour planning what had to be planned.

Then he dressed in his formal best—in the clothes, in fact, that he had planned to wear tomorrow night—and went upstairs. The party was going at full force. Antilimoin, dapper and elegant as always, greeted him with a hearty embrace, and Fevra and Maitira came gliding up from opposite sides of the room to kiss him, and Thimiroi saw, farther away, Lesentru and Kuiane deep in conversation with Lutheena, Denvin, and some others. Everyone seemed buoyant, excited, energetic. There was tension, too, the undercurrent of keen excitement that comes on the eve of a powerful experience.

Voices were pitched a little too high, gestures were a trifle too emphatic. A great screen on one wall was playing one of Cenbe's finest symphonias, but no one seemed to be watching or listening. Thimiroi glanced at it and shivered. Cenbe, of course: that connoisseur of disaster, assembling his masterpieces out of other people's tragedies—he was the perfect artist for this event. Doubtless he was in the city already, skulking around somewhere looking for the material he would need to complete his newest and surely finest work.

I will never see any of these people again after tonight, Thimiroi thought, and the concept was so difficult to accept that he repeated it to himself two or three more times, without being able to give it any more reality.

Laliene appeared beside him. There was no sign on her face of the earlier unpleasantness between them; her eyes were glowing and she was smiling warmly, even tenderly, as though they were lovers.

"I'm glad you came," she murmured. "I hoped you would."

"Antilimoin is very persuasive."

"You must have some tea. You look so tense, Thimiroi."

"Do I?"

"Is it because of our talk before?"

He shrugged. "Let's forget all about that, shall we?"

Laliene let the tips of her fingers rest lightly on his arm. "I should never have put that transmitter in your room. It was utterly stupid of me."

"It was, yes. But that's all ancient history."

Her face rose toward his. "Come have some tea with me."

"Laliene—"

Softly she said, "I wanted you to come to me so very badly. That was why I did it. You were ignoring me—you've ignored me ever since this trip began—oh, Thimiroi, Thimiroi, I'm trying to do the right thing, don't you see? And I want you to do the right thing too."

"What are you trying to tell me, Laliene?"

"Be careful, is what I'm trying to tell you."

"Careful of what?"

"Have some tea with me," she said.

"I'll have some tea," he told her. "But not, I think, with you."

Tears welled in her eyes. She turned her head to the side, but not so quickly that Thimiroi did not see them.

That was new, he thought. Tears in Laliene's eyes! He had never known her to be so overwrought. Too much euphoriac, he wondered? She kept her grip on his arm for a long moment, and then, smiling sadly, she released him and moved away.

"Thimiroi!" Lesentru called, turning and grinning broadly at him and waving his long thin arms. "How absolutely splendid to see you! Come, come, let's sip a little together!" He crossed the room as if swimming through air. "You look so gloomy, man! That can't be allowed. Lutheena! Fevra! Everybody! We must cheer Thimiroi up! We can't let anyone go around looking as bleak as this, not tonight."

They swept toward him from every direction, six, eight, ten of them, laughing, whooping, embracing him, holding fragrant cups of euphoriac tea out at him. It began almost to seem that the party was in his honor. Why were they making such a fuss over him? He was starting to regret having come here at all. He drank the tea that someone put in his hand, and almost at once there was another cup there. He drank that too.

Laliene was at his side again. Thimiroi was having trouble focusing his eyes.

"What did you mean?" he asked. "When you said to be careful."

"I'm not supposed to say. It would be improperly influencing the flow of events."

"Be improper, then. But stop talking in riddles."

"Are they such riddles, then?"

"To me they are."

"I think you know what I'm talking about," Laliene said.

"I do?"

They might have been all alone in the middle of the room. I have had too much euphoriac, he told himself. But I can still hold my own. I can still hold my own, yes.

Laliene said in a low whisper, leaning close, her breath warm against his cheek, "Tomorrow—where are you going to go tomorrow, Thimiroi?"

He looked at her, astounded, speechless.

"I know," she said.

"Get away from me."

"I've known all along. I've been trying to save you from—"

"You're out of your mind, Laliene."

"No, Thimiroi. *You* are!"

She clung to him. Everyone was gaping at them.

Terror seized him. I have to get out of here, he thought. Now. Go to Christine. Help her pack, and go with her to the airport. Right now. Whatever time it is, midnight, one in the morning, whatever. Before they can stop me. Before they *change* me.

"No, Thimiroi," Laliene cried. "Please—please—"

Furiously he pushed her away. She went sprawling to the floor, landing in a flurried heap at Antilimoin's feet. Everyone was yelling at once.

Laliene's voice came cutting through the confusion. "Don't do it, Thimiroi! *Don't do it!*"

He swung around and rushed toward the door, and through it, and wildly down the stairs, and through the quiet hotel lobby and out into the night. A brilliant crescent moon hung above him, and behind it the cold blaze of the stars in the clear darkness. Looking back, he saw no pursuers. He headed up the street toward Christine's, walking swiftly at first, then breaking into a light trot.

As he reached the corner, everything swirled and went strange around him. He felt a pang of inexplicable loss, and a sharp stab of wild fear, and a rush of anger without motive. The darkness closed bewilderingly around him, like a great glove. Then came a feeling of motion, swift and impossible to resist. He had a sense of being swept down a vast river toward an abyss that lay just beyond.

The effect lasted only a moment, but it was an endless moment, in which Thimiroi perceived the passage of time in sharp discontinuous segments, a burst of motion followed by a deep stillness and then another burst, and then stillness again. All color went from the world, even the muted colors of night: the sky was a startling blinding white, the buildings about him were black.

His eyes ached. His head was whirling.

He tried to move, but his movements were jerky and futile, as though he were fighting his way on foot through a deep tank of water. It must be the euphoriac, he told himself. I have had much too much. But I have had too much before, and I have never felt anything like—like—

Then the strangeness vanished as swiftly as it had come.

Everything was normal again, the whiteness gone from the sky, time flowing as it had always flowed, and he was running smoothly, steadily, down the street, like some sort of machine, arms and legs pumping, head thrown back.

Christine's house was dark. He rang the bell, and when there was no answer he hammered on the door.

"Christine! Christine, it's me, Thimiroi! Open the door, Christine! Hurry! Please!"

There was no response. He pounded on the door again.

This time a light went on upstairs.

"Here," he called. "I'm by the front door!"

Her window opened. Christine looked out and down at him.

"Who are you? What do you want? Do you know what time it is?"

"Christine!"

"Go away."

"But—Christine—"

"You have exactly two seconds to get away from here, whoever you are. Then I'm calling the police." Her voice was cold and angry. "They'll sober you up fast enough."

"Christine, I'm *Thimiroi*."

"Who? What kind of name is that? I don't know anybody by that name. I've never seen you before in my life." The window slammed shut. The light went out above him. Thimiroi stood frozen, amazed, dumbstruck.

Then he began to understand.

Laliene said, "We all knew, yes. We were told before we ever came here. Nothing is secret to those who operate The Travel. How could it be? They move freely through all of time. They see everything. We were warned in Canterbury that you were going to try an intervention, and that there would be a counter-intervention if you did. So I tried to stop you. To prevent you from getting yourself into trouble."

"By throwing your body at me?" Thimiroi said bitterly.

"By getting you to fall in love with me," she said. "So that you wouldn't want to get involved with *her*."

He shook his head in wonder. "All along, throughout the whole trip. Everything you did, aimed at ensnaring me into a romance, just as I thought. What I didn't realize was that you were simply trying to save me from myself."

"Yes."

"I suppose you didn't try hard enough," Thimiroi said. "No. No, that isn't it. You tried too hard."

"Did I?"

"Perhaps that was it. At any rate I didn't want you, not at any point. I wanted her the moment I saw her. It couldn't have been avoided, I suppose."

"I'm sorry, Thimiroi."

"That you failed?"

"That you have done such harm to yourself."

He stood there wordlessly for a time. "What will happen to me now?" he asked finally.

"You'll be sent back for rehabilitation, Kadro says."

"When?"

"It's up to you. You can stay and watch the show with the rest of us—you've paid for it, after all. There's no harm, Kadro says, in letting you remain in this era another few hours. Or you can let them have you right now."

For an instant despair engulfed him. Then he regained his control.

"Tell Kadro that I think I'll go now," he said.

"Yes," said Laliene. "That's probably the wisest thing."

He said, "Will Kleph be punished too?"

"I don't think so."

He felt a surge of anger. "Why not? Why is what I did any different from what she did? All right, I had a twentieth-century lover. So did Kleph. You know that. That Wilson man."

"It was different, Thimiroi."

"Different? How?"

"For Kleph it was just a little diversion, an illicit adventure. What she was doing was wrong, but it didn't imperil the basic structure of things. She doesn't propose to save this Wilson. She isn't going to intervene with the pattern. You were going to run off with yours, weren't you?

Live with her somewhere far from here, spare her from the calamity, possibly change all time to come? That couldn't be tolerated, Thimiroi. I'm astonished that you thought it would be. But of course you were in love."

Thimiroi was silent again. Then he said, "Will you do me one favor, at least?"

"What is that?"

"Send word to her. Her name's Christine Rawlins. She lives in the big old house right across the street from the one where the Sanciscos are. Tell her to go somewhere else tonight—to move into the Montgomery House, maybe, or even to leave the city. She can't stay where she is. Her house is almost certainly right in the path of—of—"

"I couldn't possibly do that," Laliene said quietly.

"No?"

"It would be intervention. It's the same thing you're being punished for."

"She'll die, though!" Thimiroi cried. "She doesn't deserve that. She's full of life, full of hopes, dreams—"

"She's been dead for hundreds of years," said Laliene coolly. "Giving her another day or two of life now won't matter. If the meteor doesn't get her, the plague will. You know that. You also know that I can't intervene for her. And you know that even if I tried, she'd never believe me. She'd have no reason to. No matter what you may have told her before, she knows nothing of it now. There's been a counter-intervention, Thimiroi. You understand that, don't you? She's never known you, now. Whatever may have happened between you and she has been unhappened."

Laliene's words struck him like knives.

"So you won't do a thing?"

"I can't," she said. "I'm sorry, Thimiroi. I tried to save you from this. For friendship's sake. For love's sake, even. But of course you wouldn't be swerved at all."

Kadro came into the room. He was dressed for the evening's big event already.

"Well?" he said. "Has Laliene explained the arrangement? You can stay on through tonight, or you can go back now."

Thimiroi looked at him, and back at Laliene, and to Kadro again. It was all very clear. He had gambled and lost. He had tried to do a foolish, romantic, impossible sort of thing, a twentieth-century sort of thing, for he was in many ways a twentieth-century sort of man; and it had failed, as of course, he realized now, it had been destined to do from the start. But that did not mean it had not been worth attempting. Not at all. Not at all.

"I understand," Thimiroi said. "I'll go back now."

The chairs had all been arranged neatly before the windows in the upstairs rooms. It was past midnight. There was euphoriac in the air, thick and dense. A quarter moon hung over the doomed city, but it was almost hidden now by the thickening clouds. The long season of clear skies was ending. The weather was changing, finally.

"It will be happening very soon now," Omerie said.

Laliene nodded. "I feel almost as though I've lived through it several times already."

"The same with me," said Kleph.

"Perhaps we have," said Klia, with a little laugh. "Who knows? We go round and round in time, and maybe we travel over the same paths more than once."

Denvin said, "I wonder where Thimiroi is now. And what they're doing to him."

"Let's not talk of Thimiroi," Antilimoin said. "It's too sad."

"He won't be able to Travel again, will he?" asked Maitira.

"Never again. Absolutely forbidden," Omerie said. "But he'll be lucky if that's the worst thing they throw at him. What he did was unforgivable. Unforgivable!"

"Antilimoin's right," said Laliene. "Let's not talk of Thimiroi."

Kleph moved closer to her. "You love him, don't you?"

"Loved," Laliene said.

"Here. Some more tea."

"Yes. Yes." Laliene smiled grimly. "He wanted me to send a warning to that woman of his, do you know? She lives right across the way. Her house will be destroyed by the shock wave, almost certainly."

Lutheena said, looking shocked, "You didn't think of doing it, did you?"

"Of course not. But I feel so sad about it, all the same. He loved her, you know. And I loved him. And so, for his sake, entirely for his sake—" Laliene shook her head. "But of course it was inconceivable. I suppose she's asleep right at this minute, not even suspecting—"

"Better the meteor than the Blue Death that follows," said Omerie. "Quicker. The quick deaths are the good ones. What's the point of hiding from the meteor only to die of the plague?"

"This is too morbid," Klia said. "I almost wish we hadn't come here. We could have skipped it and just gone on to Charlemagne's coronation—"

"We'll be there soon enough," said Kleph. "But we're here, now. And it's going to be wonderful—wonderful—"

"Places, everybody!" Kadro called. "It's almost time! Ten—nine—eight—"

Laliene held her breath. This all seemed so familiar, she thought. As though she had been through it many times already. In a moment the impact, and the tremendous sound, and the first flames rising, and the first stunned cries from the city, and the dark shapes moving around in the distance, blind, bewildered—and then the lurid sky, red as blood, the long unending shriek coming as though from a single voice—

"Now," said Kadro.

There was an astounding stillness overhead. The onrushing meteor might almost have been sucking all sound from the city toward which it plummeted. And after the silence the cataclysmic crash, the incredible impact, the earth itself recoiling with the force of the collision.

Poor Thimiroi, Laliene thought. And that poor woman, too.

Her heart overflowed with love and sorrow, and her eyes filled with tears, and she turned away from the window, unable to watch, unable to see. Then came the cries. And then the flames.

THE ASENION SOLUTION

This one was done basically as a lark. But there was a gesture of rec-onciliation buried in it, putting to an end a strange episode of unpleasant-ness between two basically even-tempered and good-natured people who happened to be very old friends.

The year 1989 marked Isaac Asimov's fiftieth anniversary as a pro-fessional writer. One day in the summer of 1988 I got a letter from the anthologist Martin H. Greenberg, who regarded Isaac virtually as his sec-ond father. Very quietly, Marty was going to assemble an anthology called Foundation's Friends, *made up of original stories based on themes that Isaac had made famous; it would be presented to Isaac in October of 1989, during the course of the festivities commemorating the fiftieth anniversary of the publication of his first story. Did I want to take part? Marty asked me.*

Don't be silly, I said. Of course I did.

And sat down and wrote "The Asenion Solution" in September of 1988—coincidentally, the same month when I had agreed to collaborate with Isaac on novel-length versions of his classic story "Nightfall" and two other celebrated Asimov novelettes.

The character I call "Ichabod Asenion" is only partially based on the real-world individual known as Isaac Asimov. Asenion is brilliant, yes, and lives in a Manhattan penthouse, and that was true of Asimov on both counts. But Asenion is described as ascetic and reclusive, two words that I suspect were never applied, even in jest, to Isaac Asimov. Asenion is a physicist; Isaac's scientific field was biochemistry before he deviated into writing books. And Asenion is a fanatic horticulturalist. Asimov—I'm only guessing here, but with some confidence—probably didn't know one plant from another, urban creature that he was, and he certainly didn't have time to tend to a greenhouse in his apartment, writing as he did three or four books a week. Asenion, then, is a kind of fantasy-Asimov, a figure made up of equal parts of fact and fiction.

The odd surname, though, is Asimovian, as a few insiders know. "Asenion" was a famous typographical error for "Asimov," attached to a fan letter of his that was published in one of the science-fiction magazines of the early 1940s. He took a lot of kidding about it, but remained genial enough to use the name himself in his Robot series. I figured it was good for one more go-round here.

And the gesture of reconciliation I was talking about a few paragraphs back?

It has to do with the plutonium-186 plot thread that you will find in the story that follows.

I knew Isaac Asimov from 1955 or so until his death in 1992, and in all that time there was only one disharmonious moment in what was otherwise a relationship of affection and mutual respect. It occurred when, at a science-fiction convention in New York about 1970, I made a joking reference to the imaginary isotope plutonium-186 during a panel discussion where Isaac was in the audience. I knew, of course, that a heavy element like plutonium couldn't have so light an isotope as that—that was the whole point of my playful remark. Isaac guffawed when he heard me speak of it. And went home and started writing a story I had requested from him for an anthology I was editing, a story in which he intended to come up with some plausible situation in which plutonium-186 actually could exist.

And so he did, but one thing led to another and the "story" turned into his first science-fiction novel in a decade and a half, The Gods Themselves. Well and good; I had inspired his return to the field. The only trouble was that Isaac had thought I was serious about plutonium-186, and took an extremely public, though gentle and loving, way of berating me for my scientific ignorance: he dedicated the book to me with a long introduction thanking me because my demonstration of scientific illiteracy at that convention had unwittingly inspired his novel.

I wasn't amused. I told him so. He was surprised that the dedication had irritated me, and told me so. We went around and around on it for a little while, and then each of us came to understand the other one's point. The offending dedication was removed from future editions of the book, the whole squabble was put away, and we went back to being good friends and high admirers of each other's work and intelligence, and eventually, through a set of circumstances nobody could have predicted, we even wound up becoming collaborators. But all those years I continued to suspect that Isaac still felt guilty/defensive/touchy/uneasy/wronged by our plutonium-186 contretemps.

So when the time came for me to write a story for a festschrift commemorating his fifty years as a professional author, I thought I'd send Isaac a signal that I carried no lingering bitterness over the misunderstanding, that in fact the whole thing now seemed to me a trifle that could be chuckled over. Thus I wrote "The Asenion Solution," yoking together Isaac's celebrated 1948 "thiotimoline" article with good old PU-186, by way of telling him that I bore no lasting resentment. It was fun to do, and, I hope, forever obliterated the one blemish on our long and harmonious friendship.

Foundation's Friends duly appeared on the anniversary of the beginning of Isaac's career and—though I wasn't at the publication party, 3000 miles from where I live—I hear that Isaac was greatly delighted by the book. Ray Bradbury did a preface for it and the contributors included Frederik Pohl, Robert Sheckley, Harry Harrison, Hal Clement, and a lot of other fine writers who had terrific fun running their own variations on Isaac's classic themes.

The clever jacket painting showed the various writers in the guise of robots—I'm the world-weary one in the middle, leaning on the bar, and that's Isaac himself in the samurai helmet down at lower right.

One thing I didn't expect, for a story that was just a prank. David Garnett chose it as one of the best science-fiction stories of 1989 for The Orbit Science Fiction Yearbook, a British anthology that he edited then. You never can tell about such things.

Fletcher stared bleakly at the small mounds of gray metal that were visible behind the thick window of the storage chamber.

"Plutonium-186," he muttered. "Nonsense! Absolute nonsense!"

"Dangerous nonsense, Lew" said Jesse Hammond, standing behind him. "Catastrophic nonsense."

Fletcher nodded. The very phrase, "plutonium-186," sounded like gibberish to him. There wasn't supposed to be any such substance. Plutonium-186 was an impossible isotope, too light by a good fifty neutrons. Or a bad fifty neutrons, considering the risks the stuff was creating as it piled up here and there around the world. But the fact that it was theoretically impossible for plutonium-186 to exist did not change the other, and uglier, fact that he was looking at three kilograms of it right this minute. Or that as the quantity of plutonium-186 in the world continued to increase, so did the chance of an uncontrollable nuclear reaction leading to an atomic holocaust.

"Look at the morning reports," Fletcher said, waving a sheaf of fax-prints at Hammond. "Thirteen grams more turned up at the nucleonics lab of Accra University. Fifty grams in Geneva. Twenty milligrams in—well, that little doesn't matter. But Chicago, Jesse, Chicago—three hundred grams in a single chunk!"

"Christmas presents from the Devil," Hammond muttered.

"Not the Devil, no. Just decent serious-minded scientific folk who happen to live in another universe where plutonium-186 is not only possible but also perfectly harmless. And who are so fascinated by the idea that *we're* fascinated by it that they keep on shipping the stuff to us in wholesale lots! What are we going to do with it all, Jesse? What in God's name are we going to do with it all?"

Raymond Nikolaus looked up from his desk at the far side of the room.

"Wrap it up in shiny red-and-green paper and ship it right back to them?" he suggested.

Fletcher laughed hollowly. "Very funny, Raymond. Very very funny."

He began to pace the room. In the silence the clicking of his shoes against the flagstone floor seemed to him like the ticking of a detonating device, growing louder, louder, louder...

He—they, all of them—had been wrestling with the problem all year, with an increasing sense of futility. The plutonium-186 had begun mysteriously to appear in laboratories all over the world—wherever supplies of one of the two elements with equivalent atomic weights existed. Gram for gram, atom for atom, the matching elements disappeared just as mysteriously: equal quantities of tungsten-186 or osmium-186.

Where was the tungsten and osmium going? Where was the plutonium coming from? Above all, how was it possible for a plutonium isotope whose atoms had only 92 neutrons in its nucleus to exist even for a fraction of a fraction of an instant? Plutonium was one of the heavier chemical elements, with a whopping 94 protons in the nucleus of each of its atoms. The closest thing to a stable isotope of plutonium was plutonium-244, in which 150 neutrons held those 94 protons together; and even at that, plutonium-244 had an inevitable habit of breaking down in radioactive decay, with a half-life of some 76 million years. Atoms of plutonium-186, if they could exist at all, would come dramatically apart in very much less than one 76-millionth of a second.

But the stuff that was turning up in the chemistry labs to replace the tungsten-186 and the osmium-186 had an atomic number of 94, no question about that. And element 94 was plutonium. That couldn't be disputed either. The defining characteristic of plutonium was the presence of 94 protons in its nucleus. If that was the count, plutonium was what that element had to be.

This impossibly light isotope of plutonium, this plutonium-186, had another impossible characteristic about it: not only was it stable, it was so completely stable that it wasn't even radioactive. It just sat there, looking exceedingly unmysterious, not even deigning to emit a smidgeon of energy. At least, not when first tested. But a second test revealed positron emission, which a third baffled look confirmed. The trouble was that the third measurement showed an even higher level of radioactivity than the second one. The fourth was higher than the third. And so on and so on.

Nobody had ever heard of any element, of whatever atomic number or weight, that started off stable and then began to demonstrate a steadily increasing intensity of radioactivity. No one knew what was likely to happen, either, if the process continued unchecked, but the possibilities seemed pretty explosive. The best suggestion anyone had was to turn it to powder and mix it with nonradioactive tungsten. That worked for a little while, until the tungsten turned radioactive too. After that graphite was used, with somewhat better results, to damp down the strange element's output of energy. There were no explosions. But more and more plutonium-186 kept arriving.

The only explanation that made any sense—and it did not make *very* much sense—was that it was coming from some unknown and perhaps even unknowable place, some sort of parallel universe, where the laws of nature were different and the binding forces of the atom were so much more powerful that plutonium-186 could be a stable isotope.

Why they were sending odd lumps of plutonium-186 here was something that no one could begin to guess. An even more important question was how they could be made to stop doing it. The radioactive breakdown of the plutonium-186 would eventually transform it into ordinary osmium or tungsten, but the twenty positrons that each plutonium nucleus emitted in the course of that process encountered and annihilated an equal number of electrons. Our universe could afford to lose twenty electrons here and there, no doubt. It could probably afford to go on losing electrons at a constant rate for an astonishingly long time without noticing much difference. But sooner or later the shift toward an overall positive charge that this electron loss created would create grave and perhaps incalculable problems of symmetry and energy conservation. Would the equilibrium of the universe break down? Would nuclear interactions begin to intensify? Would the stars—even the Sun—erupt into supernovas?

"This can't go on," Fletcher said gloomily.

Hammond gave him a sour look. "So? We've been saying that for six months now."

"It's time to do something. They keep shipping us more and more and more, and we don't have any idea how to go about telling them to cut it out."

"We don't even have any idea whether they really exist," Raymond Niklaus put in.

"Right now that doesn't matter. What matters is that the stuff is arriving constantly, and the more of it we have, the more dangerous it is. We don't have the foggiest idea of how to shut off the shipments. So we've got to find some way to get rid of it as it comes in."

"And what do you have in mind, pray tell?" Hammond asked.

Fletcher said, glaring at his colleague in a way that conveyed the fact that he would brook no opposition, "I'm going to talk to Asenion."

Hammond guffawed. "Asenion? You're crazy!"

"No. *He* is. But he's the only person who can help us."

It was a sad case, the Asenion story, poignant and almost incomprehensible. One of the finest minds atomic physics had ever known, a man to rank with Rutherford, Bohr, Heisenberg, Fermi, Meitner. A Harvard degree at twelve, his doctorate from M.I.T. five years later, after which he had poured forth a dazzling flow of technical papers that probed the deepest mysteries of the nuclear binding forces. As the twenty-first century entered its closing decades he had seemed poised to solve once and for all the eternal riddles of the universe. And then, at the age of 28, without having given the slightest warning, he walked away from the whole thing.

"I have lost interest," he declared. "Physics is no longer of any importance to me. Why should I concern myself with these issues of the way in which matter is constructed? How tiresome it all is! When one looks at the Parthenon, does one care what the columns are made of, or what sort of scaffolding was needing to put them in place? That the Parthenon exists, and is sublimely beautiful, is all that should interest us. So too with the universe. I see the universe, and it is beautiful and perfect. Why should I pry into the nature of its scaffolding? Why should anyone?"

And with that he resigned his professorship, burned his papers, and retreated to the 33rd floor of an apartment building on Manhattan's West Side, where he built an elaborate laboratory-greenhouse in which he intended to conduct experiments in advanced horticulture.

"Bromeliads," said Asenion. "I will create hybrid bromeliads. Bromeliads will be the essence and center of my life from now on."

Romelmeyer, who had been Asenion's mentor at Harvard, attributed his apparent breakdown to overwork, and thought that he would snap back in six or eight months. Jantzen, who had had the rare privilege of being the first to read his astonishing dissertation at M.I.T., took an equally sympathetic position, arguing that Asenion must have come to some terrifying impasse in his work that had compelled him to retreat dramatically from the brink of madness. "Perhaps he found himself looking right into an abyss of inconsistencies when he thought he was about to find the ultimate answers," Jantzen suggested. "What else could he do but run? But he won't run for long. It isn't in his nature."

Burkhardt, of Cal Tech, whose own work had been carried out in the sphere that Asenion was later to make his own, agreed with Jantzen's analysis. "He must have hit something really dark and hairy. But he'll wake up one morning with the solution in his head, and it'll be goodbye horticulture for him. He'll turn out a paper by noon that will revolutionize everything we think we know about nuclear physics, and that'll be that."

But Jesse Hammond, who had played tennis with Asenion every morning for the last two years of his career as a physicist, took a less charitable position. "He's gone nuts," Hammond said. "He's flipped out altogether, and he's never going to get himself together again."

"You think?" said Lew Fletcher, who had been almost as close to Asenion as Hammond, but who was no tennis player.

Hammond smiled. "No doubt of it. I began noticing a weird look in his eyes starting just about two years back. And then his playing started to turn weird too. He'd serve and not even look where he was serving. He'd double-fault without even caring. And you know what else? He didn't challenge me on a single out-of-bounds call the whole year. That was the key thing. Used to be, he'd fight me every call. Now he just didn't seem to care. He just let everything go by. He was completely indifferent. I said to myself, This guy must be flipping out."

"Or working on some problem that seems more important to him than tennis."

"Same thing," said Hammond. "No, Lew, I tell you—he's gone completely unglued. And nothing's going to glue him again."

That conversation had taken place almost a year ago. Nothing had happened in the interim to change anyone's opinion. The astounding arrival of plutonium-186 in the world had not brought forth any comment from Asenion's Manhattan penthouse. The sudden solemn discussions of fantastic things like parallel universes by otherwise reputable physicists had apparently not aroused him either. He remained closeted with his bromeliads, high above the streets of Manhattan.

Well, maybe he *is* crazy, Fletcher thought. But his mind can't have shorted out entirely. And he might just have an idea or two left in him—

Asenion said, "Well, you don't look a whole lot older, do you?"

Fletcher felt himself reddening. "Jesus, Ike, it's only been eighteen months since we last saw each other!"

"Is that all?" Asenion said indifferently. "It feels like a lot more to me."

He managed a thin, remote smile. He didn't look very interested in Fletcher or in whatever it was that had brought Fletcher to his secluded eyrie.

Asenion had always been an odd one, of course—aloof, mysterious, with a faint but unmistakable air of superiority about him that nearly everyone found instantly irritating. Of course, he *was* superior. But he had made sure that he let you know it, and never seemed to care that others found the trait less than endearing.

He appeared more remote than ever, now, stranger and more alien. Outwardly he had not changed at all: the same slender, debonair figure, surprisingly handsome, even striking. Though rumor had it that he had not left his penthouse in more than a year, there was no trace of indoor pallor about him. His skin still had its rich deep olive coloring, almost swarthy, a Mediterranean tone. His hair, thick and dark, tumbled down rakishly over his broad forehead. But there was something different about his dark, gleaming eyes. The old Asenion, however preoccupied he might have been with some abstruse problem of advanced physics, had nearly always had a playful sparkle in his eyes, a kind of amiable devilish glint. This man, this horticultural recluse, wore a different expression altogether—ascetic, mist-shrouded, *absent.* His gaze was as bright as ever, but the brightness was a cold one that seemed to come from some far-off star.

Fletcher said, "The reason I've come here—"

"We can go into all that later, can't we, Lew? First come into the greenhouse with me. There's something I want to show you. Nobody else has seen it yet, in fact."

"Well, if you—"

"Insist, yes. Come. I promise you, it's extraordinary."

He turned and led the way through the intricate pathways of the apartment. The sprawling many-roomed penthouse was furnished in the most offhand way, cheap student furniture badly cared for. Cats wandered everywhere, five, six, eight of them, sharpening their claws on the upholstery, prowling in empty closets whose doors stood ajar, peering down from the tops of bookcases containing jumbled heaps of coverless volumes. There was a rank smell of cat urine in the air.

But then suddenly Asenion turned a corridor and Fletcher, following just behind, found himself staring into what could have been an altogether different world. They had reached the entrance to the spectacular glass-walled extension that had been wrapped like an observation deck around the entire summit of the building. Beyond, dimly visible inside, Fletcher could see hundreds or perhaps thousands of strange-looking plants, some hanging from the ceiling, some mounted along the sides of wooden pillars, some rising in stepped array on benches, some growing out of beds set in the floor.

Asenion briskly tapped out the security-combination code on a diamond-shaped keyboard mounted in the wall, and the glass door slid silently back. A blast of warm humid air came forth.

"Quickly!" he said. "Inside!"

It was like stepping straight into the Amazon jungle. In place of the harsh, dry atmosphere of a Manhattan apartment in midwinter there was, abruptly, the dense moist sweet closeness of the tropics, enfolding them like folds of wet fabric. Fletcher almost expected to hear parrots screeching overhead.

And the plants! The bizarre plants, clinging to every surface, filling every available square inch!

Most of them followed the same general pattern, rosettes of broad shining strap-shaped leaves radiating outward from a central cup-shaped structure deep enough to hold several ounces of water. But beyond that basic area of similarity they differed wildly from one another. Some were tiny, some were colossal. Some were marked with blazing stripes of yellow and red and purple that ran the length of their thick, succulent leaves. Some were mottled with fierce blotches of shimmering, assertive, bewilderingly complicated combinations of color. Some, whose leaves were green, were a fiery scarlet or crimson, or a somber, mysterious blue, at the place where the leaves came together to form the cup. Some were armed with formidable teeth and looked ready to feed on unwary visitors. Some were topped with gaudy spikes of strangely shaped brilliant-hued flowers taller than a man, which sprang like radiant spears from their centers.

Everything glistened. Everything seemed poised for violent, explosive growth. The scene was alien and terrifying. It was like looking into a vast congregation of hungry monsters. Fletcher had to remind himself that these were merely plants, hothouse specimens that probably wouldn't last half an hour in the urban environment outside.

"These are bromeliads," Asenion said, shaping the word sensuously in his throat as though it were the finest word any language had ever produced. "Tropical plants, mainly. South and Central America is where most of them live. They tend to cling to trees, growing high up in the forks of branches, mainly. Some live at ground level, though. Such as the bromeliad you know best, which is the pineapple. But there are hundreds of others in this room. Thousands. And this is the humid room, where I keep the guzmanias and the vrieseas and some of the aechmeas. As we go around, I'll show you the tillandsias—they like it a lot drier—and the terrestrial ones, the hechtias and the dyckias, and then over on the far side—"

"Ike," Fletcher said quietly.

"You know I've never liked that name."

"I'm sorry. I forgot." That was a lie. Asenion's given name was Ichabod. Neither Fletcher nor anyone Fletcher knew had ever been able to bring himself to call him that. "Look, I think what you've got here is wonderful. Absolutely wonderful. But I don't want to intrude on your time, and there's a very serious problem I need to discuss with—"

"First the plants," Asenion said. "Indulge me." His eyes were glowing. In the half-light of the greenhouse he looked like a jungle creature himself, exotic, weird. Without a moment's hesitation, he pranced off down the aisle toward a group of oversized bromeliads near the outer wall. Willy-nilly, Fletcher followed.

Asenion gestured grandly.

"Here it is! Do you see? *Aechmea asenionii!* Discovered in northwestern Brazil two years ago—I sponsored the expedition myself—of course, I never expected them to name it for me, but you know how these things sometimes happen—"

Fletcher stared. The plant was a giant among giants, easily two meters across from leaf-tip to leaf-tip. Its dark green leaves were banded with jagged pale scrawls that looked like the hieroglyphs of some lost race. Out of the central cup, which was the size of a man's head and deep enough to drown rabbits in, rose the strangest flower Fletcher ever hoped to see, a thick yellow stalk of immense length from which sprang something like a cluster of black thunderbolts tipped with ominous red globes like dangling moons. A pervasive odor of rotting flesh came from it.

"The only specimen in North America!" Asenion cried. "Perhaps one of six or seven in the world. And I've succeeded in inducing it to bloom. There'll be seed, Lew, and perhaps there'll be offsets as well—I'll be able to propagate it, and cross it with others—can you imagine it crossed with *Aechmea chantinii*, Fletcher? Or perhaps an interspecific hybrid? With *Neoregelia carcharadon*, say? No. Of course you can't imagine it. What am I saying? But it would be spectacular beyond belief. Take my word for it."

"I have no doubt."

"It's a privilege, seeing this plant in bloom. But there are others here you must see too. The puyas—the pitcairnias—there's a clump of *Dyckia marnier-lapostollei* in the next room that you wouldn't believe—"

He bubbled with boyish enthusiasm. Fletcher forced himself to be patient. There was no help for it: he would simply have to take the complete tour.

It went on for what seemed like hours, as Asenion led him frantically from one peculiar plant to another, in room after room. Some were actually quite beautiful, Fletcher had to admit. Others seemed excessively flamboyant, or grotesque, or incomprehensibly ordinary to his untutored eye, or downright grotesque. What struck him most forcefully of all was the depth of Asenion's obsession. Nothing in the universe seemed to matter to him except this horde of exotic plants. He had given himself up totally to the strange world he had created here.

But at last even Asenion's manic energies seemed to flag. The pace had been merciless, and both he and Fletcher, drenched with sweat and gasping in the heat, paused for breath in a section of the greenhouse occupied by small gray gnarly plants that seemed to have no roots, and were held to the wall by barely visible wires.

Abruptly Asenion said, "All right. You aren't interested anyway. Tell me what you came here to ask me, and then get on your way. I have all sorts of things to do this afternoon."

"It's about plutonium-186," Fletcher began.

"Don't be idiotic. That's not a legitimate isotope. It can't possibly exist."

"I know," Fletcher said. "But it does."

Quickly, almost desperately, he outlined the whole fantastic story for the young physicist-turned-botanist. The mysterious substitution of a strange element for tungsten or osmium in various laboratories, the tests indicating that its atomic number was that of plutonium but its atomic weight was far too low, the absurd but necessary theory that the stuff was a gift from some parallel universe and—finally—the fact that the new element, stable when it first arrived, rapidly began to undergo radioactive decay in a startlingly accelerative way.

Asenion's saturnine face was a study in changing emotions as Fletcher spoke. He seemed bored and irritated at first, then scornful, then, perhaps, furious; but not a word did he utter, and gradually the fury ebbed, turning to distant curiosity and then, finally, a kind of fascination. Or so Fletcher thought. He realized that he might be altogether wrong in his interpretations of what was going on in the unique, mercurial mind of the other man.

When Fletcher fell silent Asenion said, "What are you most afraid of? Critical mass? Or cumulative electron loss?"

"We've dealt with the critical mass problem by powdering the stuff, shielding it in graphite, and scattering it in low concentrations to fifty different storage points. But it keeps on coming in—they love to send it to us, it seems. And the thought that every atom of it is giving off positrons that go around looking for electrons to annihilate—" Fletcher shrugged. "On a small scale it's a useful energy pump, I suppose, tungsten swapped for plutonium with energy gained in each cycle. But on a large scale, as we continue to transfer electrons from our universe to theirs—"

"Yes," Asenion said.

"So we need a way to dispose of—"

"Yes." He looked at his watch. "Where are you staying while you're in town, Fletcher?"

"The Faculty Club, as usual."

"Good. I've got some crosses to make and I don't want to wait any longer, on account of possible pollen contamination. Go over to the Club and keep yourself amused for a few hours. Take a shower. God knows you need one: you smell like something out of the jungle. Relax, have a drink, come back at five o'clock. We can talk about this again then." He shook his head. "Plutonium-186! What lunacy! It offends me just to say it out loud. It's like saying—saying—well, *Billbergia yukonensis*, or *Tillandsia bostoniae*. Do you know what I mean? No. No. Of course you don't." He waved his hands. "Out! Come back at five!"

It was a long afternoon for Fletcher. He phoned his wife, he phoned Jesse Hammond at the laboratory, he phoned an old friend and made a date for dinner. He showered and changed. He had a drink in the ornate lounge on the Fifth Avenue side of the Club.

But his mood was grim, and not merely because Hammond had told him that another four kilograms of Plutonium-186 had been reported from various regions that morning. Asenion's madness oppressed him.

There was nothing wrong with an interest in plants, of course. Fletcher kept a philodendron and something else, whose name he could never remember, in his own office. But to immerse yourself in one highly specialized field of botany with such intensity—it seemed sheer lunacy. No, Fletcher decided, even that was all right, difficult as it was for him to understand why anyone would want to spend his whole life cloistered with a bunch of eerie plants. What was hard for him to forgive was Asenion's renunciation of physics. A mind like that—the breadth of its vision—the insight Asenion had had into the greatest of mysteries—dammit, Fletcher thought, he had owed it to the world to stick to it! And instead, to walk away from everything, to hole himself up in a cage of glass—

Hammond's right, Fletcher told himself. Asenion really is crazy.

But it was useless to fret about it. Asenion was not the first supergenius to snap under contemplation of the Ultimate. His withdrawal from physics, Fletcher said sternly to himself, was a matter between Asenion and the universe. All that concerned Fletcher was getting Asenion's solution to the plutonium-186 problem; and then the poor man could be left with his bromeliads in peace.

About half past four Fletcher set out by cab to battle the traffic the short distance uptown to Asenion's place.

Luck was with him. He arrived at ten of five. Asenion's house-robot greeted him solemnly and invited him to wait. "The master is in the greenhouse," the robot declared. "He will be with you when he has completed the pollination."

Fletcher waited. And waited and waited.

Geniuses, he thought bitterly. Pains in the neck, all of them. Pains in the—

Just then the robot reappeared. It was half past six. All was blackness outside the window. Fletcher's dinner date was for seven. He would never make it.

"The master will see you now," said the robot.

Asenion looked limp and weary, as though he had spent the entire afternoon smashing up boulders. But the formidable edge seemed gone from him, too. He greeted Fletcher with a pleasant enough smile, offered a word or two of almost-apology for his tardiness, and even had the robot bring Fletcher a sherry. It wasn't very good sherry, but to get anything at all to drink in a teetotaler's house was a blessing, Fletcher figured.

Asenion waited until Fletcher had had a few sips. Then he said, "I have your answer."

"I knew you would."

There was a long silence.

"Thiotimoline," said Asenion finally.

"Thiotimoline?"

"Absolutely. Endochronic disposal. It's the only way. And, as you'll see, it's a *necessary* way."

Fletcher took a hasty gulp of the sherry. Even when he was in a relatively mellow mood, it appeared, Asenion was maddening. And mad. What was this new craziness now? Thiotimoline? How could that preposterous substance, as insane in its way as plutonium-186, have any bearing on the problem?

Asenion said, "I take it you know the special properties of thiotimoline?"

"Of course. Its molecule is distorted into adjacent temporal dimensions. Extends into the future, and, I think, into the past. Thiotimoline powder will dissolve in water one second *before* the water is added."

"Exactly," Asenion said. "And if the water isn't added, it'll go looking for it. In the future."

"What does this have to do with—"

"Look here," said Asenion. He drew a scrap of paper from his shirt pocket. "You want to get rid of something. You put it in this container here. You surround the container with a shell made of polymerized thiotimoline. You surround the shell with a water tank that will deliver water to the thiotimoline on a timed basis, and you set your timer so that the water is due to arrive a few seconds from now. But at the last moment the timing device withholds the water."

Fletcher stared at the younger man in awe.

Asenion said, "The water is always about to arrive, but never quite does. The thiotimoline making up the plastic shell is pulled forward one second into the future to encounter the water. The water has a high probability of being there, but not quite high enough. It's actually another second away from delivery, and always will be. The thiotimoline gets dragged farther and farther into the future. The world goes forward into the future at a rate of one second per second, but the thiotimoline's velocity is essentially infinite. And of course it carries with it the inner container, too."

"In which we have put our surplus plutonium-186."

"Or anything else you want to dispose of," said Asenion.

Fletcher felt dizzy. "Which will travel on into the future at an infinite rate—"

"Yes. And because the rate is infinite, the problem of the breakdown of thiotimoline into its stable isochronic form, which has hampered most time-transport experiments, isn't an issue. Something traveling through time at an infinite velocity isn't subject to little limitations of that kind. It'll simply keep going until it can't go any farther."

"But how does sending it into the future solve the problem?" Fletcher asked. "The plutonium-186 still stays in our universe, even if we've bumped it away from our immediate temporal vicinity. The electron loss continues. Maybe even gets worse, under temporal acceleration. We still haven't dealt with the fundamental—"

"You never were much of a thinker, were you, Fletcher?" said Asenion quietly, almost gently. But the savage contempt in his eyes had the force of a sun going nova.

"I do my best. But I don't see—"

Asenion sighed. "The thiotimoline will chase the water in the outer container to the end of time, carrying with it the plutonium in the inner container. To the end of time. *Literally.*"

"And?"

"What happens at the end of time, Fletcher?"

"Why—absolute entropy—the heat-death of the universe—"

"Precisely. The Final Entropic Solution. All molecules equally distributed throughout space. There will be no further place for the water-seeking thiotimoline to go. The end of the line is the end of the line. It, and the plutonium it's hauling with it, and the water it's trying to catch up with, will all plunge together over the entropic brink into anti-time."

"Anti-time," said Fletcher in a leaden voice. "Anti-time?"

"Naturally. Into the moment before the creation of the universe. Everything is in stasis. Zero time, infinite temperature. All the universal mass contained in a single incomprehensible body. Then the thiotimoline and the plutonium and the water arrive."

Asenion's eyes were radiant. His face was flushed. He waved his scrap of paper around as though it were the scripture of some new creed. "There will be a tremendous explosion. A Big Bang, so to speak. The beginning of all things. You—or should I say I?—will be responsible for the birth of the universe."

Fletcher, stunned, said after a moment, "Are you serious?"

"I am never anything but serious. You have your solution. Pack up your plutonium and send it on its way. No matter how many shipments you make, they'll all arrive at the same instant. And with the same effect. You have no choice, you know. The plutonium *must* be disposed of. And—" His eyes twinkled with some of the old Asenion playfulness. "The universe *must* be created, or else how will any of us get to be where we are? And this is how it was done. *Will* be done. Inevitable, ineluctable, unavoidable, mandatory. Yes? You see?"

"Well, no. yes. Maybe. That is, I think I do," said Fletcher, as if in a daze.

"Good. Even if you don't, you will."

"I'll need—to talk to the others—"

"Of course you will. That's how you people do things. That's why I'm here and you're there." Asenion shrugged. "Well, no hurry about it. Create the universe tomorrow, create it the week after next, what's the difference? It'll get done sooner or later. It has to, because it already has been done. You see?"

"Yes. Of course. Of—course. And now—if you'll excuse me—" Fletcher murmured. "I—ah—have a dinner appointment in a little while—"

"That can wait too, can't it?" said Asenion, smiling with sudden surprising amiability. He seemed genuinely glad to have been of assistance. "There's something I forgot to show you this afternoon. A remarkable plant, possibly unique—a nidularium, it is, Brazilian, not even named yet, as a matter of fact—just coming into bloom. And this one—wait till you see it, Fletcher, wait till you see it—"

WE ARE FOR THE DARK

Where do story ideas come from? the non-writer often asks. And the writer's usual answer is a bemused shrug. But in this instance I can reply very precisely.

My wife and I were visiting London in September of 1987 and of course we were spending virtually every evening at the theatre and some afternoons besides. On the next to last day of our stay we were at the National Theatre, on the south side of the Thames, to see Anthony Hopkins and Judi Dench in Antony and Cleopatra, *a wondrous, magical matinee performance. Act Five came around, Cleopatra's great catastrophe, and her serving-maid Iras signalled the beginning of the final act with lines long familiar to me:*

> *Finish, good lady; the bright day is done.*
> *And we are for the dark.*

A mysterious shiver ran through me at those words, we are for the *dark.* I had seen the play half a dozen times or more over the years, and *they had never seemed unusual to me before; but, hearing them now, I suddenly saw great vistas of black space opening before me. Later that splendid afternoon, strolling back across the bridge toward the heart of the city under brilliant summer sunshine, I found myself continuing to dwell on the vistas that Shakespeare's five words had evoked for me, and soon I was taking notes for a story that had absolutely nothing to do with the travails of Cleopatra or Antony.*

That was the engendering point. The other details followed quickly enough, all but the mechanism of the matter-transmission system around which the interstellar venture of the story was to be built. That had to wait until January of the following year. Now I was in Los Angeles, resting and reading before going out to dinner, and suddenly I found myself scribbling down stuff about the spontaneous conversion of matter into antimatter and a necessary balancing conversion in the opposite direction. Whether any such thing is actually the case is beyond my own scientific expertise, though I suspect it's nonsense, but at least the idea seemed plausible enough to work with, and very quickly I had built an entire method of faster-than-light travel out of it—one which is probably utterly unfeasible in the real universe but would serve well enough in my fictional one. I wrote the story in March of 1988 and Gardner Dozois published it in the October, 1988 Isaac Asimov's Science Fiction Magazine. For me it had some of the sweep and grandeur that first had drawn me to science fiction as a reader more than forty years before, and it pleased me greatly on that account. I thought that it might attract some attention among readers, but, oddly, it seemed to pass almost unnoticed—no awards nominations, no year's-best selection. Which puzzled me; but eventually I put the matter out of mind. Stories of mine that I had thought of as quite minor indeed had gone on to gain not only awards nominations but, more than once, the awards themselves; stories that had seemed to me to be failures when I wrote them had been reprinted a dozen times over in later years; and, occasionally, a story that moved me profoundly as I composed it had gone straight from publication to oblivion almost as if it had never existed at all. We Are for the Dark seems to have been one of those, though I still have hope for its rediscovery.

But the moral is clear, at least to me: write what satisfies you and let the awards and anthologizations take care of themselves, because there's no way of predicting what kind of career a story will have. Strive always to do your best, and, when you believe that you have, allow yourself the pleasure of your own approval. If readers happen to share your delight in your own work, that's a bonus in which to rejoice, but it's folly ever to expect others to respond to your work in the same way you do yourself.

Great warmth comes from him, golden cascades of bright, nurturing energy. The Master is often said to be like a sun, and so he is, a luminous creature, a saint, a sun indeed. But warmth is not the only thing that emanates from suns. They radiate at many frequencies of the spectrum, hissing and crackling and glaring like furnaces as they send forth the angry power that withers, the power that kills. The moment I enter the Master's presence I feel that other force, that terrible one, flowing from him. The air about him hums with it, though the warmth of him, the benevolence, is evident also. His power is frightful. And yet all he is is a man, a very old one at that, with a smooth round hairless head and pale, mysteriously gentle eyes. Why should I fear him? My faith is strong. I love the Master. We all love him.

This is only the fifth time I have met him. The last was seven years ago, at the time of the Altair launch. We of the other House rarely have reason to come to the Sanctuary, or they to us. But he recognizes me at once, and calls me by name, and pours cool clear golden wine for me with his own hand. As I expect, he says nothing at first about his reason for summoning me. He talks instead of his recent visit to the Capital, where great swarms of ragged hungry people trotted tirelessly alongside his palanquin as he was borne in procession, begging him to send them into the Dark. "Soon, soon, my children," is what he tells me now that he told them then. "Soon we will all go to our new dwelling-places in the stars." And he wept, he says, for sheer joy, feeling the intensity of their love for him, feeling their longing for the new worlds to which we alone hold the keys. It seems to me that he is quietly weeping now, telling me these things.

Behind his desk is a star-map of extraordinary vividness and detail, occupying the rear wall of his austere chamber. Indeed, it is the rear wall: a huge curving shield of some gleaming dark substance blacker than night, within which I can see our galaxy depicted, its glittering core, its spiralling arms. Many of the high-magnitude stars shine forth clearly in their actual colors. Beyond, sinking into the depths of the dark matrix in a way that makes the map seem to stretch outward to infinity, are the neighboring galaxies, resting in clouds of shimmering dust. More distant clusters and nebulae are visible still farther from the map's center. As I stare, I feel myself carried on and on to the outermost ramparts of the universe. I compliment him on the ingenuity of the map, and on its startling realism.

But that seems to be a mistake. "Realism? This map?" the Master cries, and the energies flickering around him grow fierce and sizzling once again. "This map is nothing: a crazy hodgepodge. A lunacy. Look, this star sent us its light twelve billion years ago, and that one six billion years ago, and this other one twenty-three years ago, and we're seeing them all at once. But this one didn't even exist when that one started beaming its light at us. And this one may have died five billion years ago, but we won't know it for five billion more." His voice, usually so soft, is rising now and there is a dangerous edge on it. I have never seen him this angry. "So what does this map actually show us? Not the absolute reality of the universe but only a meaningless ragbag of subjective impressions. It shows the stars as they happen to appear to us just at this minute and we pretend that that is the actual cosmos, the true configuration." His face has grown flushed. He pours more wine. His hand is trembling, suddenly, and I think he will miss the rim of the glass, but no: his control is perfect. We drink in silence. Another moment and he is calm again, benign as the Buddha, bathing me in the glow and lustre of his spirit.

"Well, we must do the best we can within our limitations," he says gently. "For the closer spans the map is not so useless." He touches something on his desk and the star-map undergoes a dizzying shift, the outer clusters dropping away and the center of our own galaxy coming up until it fills the whole screen. Another flick of his finger and the inner realm of the galaxy stands out in bright highlighting: that familiar sphere, a hundred light-years in diameter, which is the domain of our Mission. A network of brilliant yellow lines cuts across the heart of it from star to star, marking the places where we have chosen to place our first receiver stations. It is a pattern I could trace from memory, and, seeing it now, I feel a sense of comfort and well-being, as though I am looking at a map of my native city.

Now, surely, he will begin to speak of Mission matters, he will start working his way round to the reason for my being here. But no, no, he wants to tell me of a garden of aloes he has lately seen by the shores of the Mediterranean, twisted spiky green rosettes topped by flaming red torches of blooms, and then of his visit to a lake in East Africa where pink flamingos massed in millions, so that all the world seemed pink, and then of a pilgrimage he has undertaken in the highest passes of the Sierra Nevada, where gnarled little pines ten thousand years old endure the worst that winter can hurl at them. As he speaks, his face grows more animated, his eyes taken on an eager sparkle. His great age drops away from him: he seems younger by thirty, forty, fifty years. I had not realized he was so keen a student of nature. "The next time you are in my country," I tell him, "perhaps you will allow me to show you the place along the southern shore where the fairy penguins come to nest in summer. In all the world I think that is the place I love the best."

He smiles. "You must tell me more about that some time." But his tone is flat, his expression has gone slack. The effort of this little talk must have exhausted him. "This Earth of ours is so beautiful," he says. "Such marvels, such splendors."

What can he mean by that? Surely he knows that only a few scattered islands of beauty remain, rare fortunate places rising above the polluted seas or sheltered from the tainted air, and that everything else is soiled, stained, damaged, corroded beyond repair by one sort of human folly or another.

"Of course," he says, "I would leave it in a moment, if duty beckoned me into the Dark. I would not hesitate. That I could never return would mean nothing to me." For a time he is silent. Then he draws a disk from a drawer of his desk and slides it toward me. "This music has given me great pleasure. Perhaps it will please you also. We'll talk again in a day or two."

The map behind him goes blank. His gaze, though it still rests on me, is blank now also.

So the audience is over, and I have learned nothing. Well, indirection has always been his method. I understand now that whatever has gone wrong with the Mission—for surely something has, why else would I be here?—is not only serious enough to warrant calling me away from my House and my work, but is so serious that the Master feels the need of more than one meeting to convey its nature to me. Of course I am calm. Calmness is inherent in the character of those who serve the Order. Yet there is a strangeness about all this that troubles me as I have never been troubled before in the forty years of my service.

Outside, the night air is warm, and still humid from earlier rain. The Master's lodge sits by itself atop a lofty stepped platform of pink granite, with the lesser buildings of the Order arrayed in a semi-circle below it on the side of the great curving hill. As I walk toward the hostelry where I am staying, novitiates and even some initiates stare at me as though they would like to prostrate themselves before me. They revere me as I revere the Master. They would touch the hem of my robe, if they could. I nod and smile. Their eyes are hungry, God-haunted, star-haunted.

"Lord Magistrate," they murmur. "God be with you, your grace. God be with you." One novitiate, a gaunt boy, all cheekbones and eyebrows, dares to run to my side and ask me if the Master is well. "Very well," I tell him. A girl, quivering like a bowstring, says my name over and over as though it alone can bring her salvation. A plump monkish-looking man in a gray robe much too heavy for this hot climate looks toward me for a blessing, and I give him a quick gesture and walk swiftly onward, sealing my attention now inward and heavenward to free myself of their supplications as I stride across the terraced platform to my lodging.

There is no moon tonight, and against the blackness of the high-lands sky the stars shine forth resplendently by the tens of thousands. I feel those stars in all their multitudes pressing close about me, enclos-ing me, enfolding me, and I know that what I feel is the presence of God. I imagine even that I see the distant nebulas, the far-off island universes. I think of our little ships, patiently sailing across the great Dark toward the remote precincts of our chosen sphere of settlement, carrying with them the receivers that will, God willing, open all His heavens to us. My throat is dry. My eyes are moist. After forty years I have lost none of my ability to feel the wonder of it.

In my spacious and lavishly appointed room in the hostelry I kneel and make my devotions, and pray, as ever, to be brought ever closer to Him. In truth I am merely the vehicle by which others are allowed to approach Him, I know: the bridge through which they cross to Him. But in my way I serve God also, and to serve Him is to grow closer to Him. My task for these many years has been to send voyagers to the far worlds of His realm. It is not for me to go that way myself: that is my sacrifice, that is my glory. I have no regret over remaining Earthbound: far from it! Earth is our great mother. Earth is the mother of us all. Troubled as she is, blighted as she now may be, dying, even, I am con-tent to stay here, and more than content. How could I leave? I have my task, and the place of my task is here, and here I must remain.

I meditate upon these things for a time.

Afterward I oil my body for sleep and pour myself a glass of the fine brandy I have brought with me from home. I go to the wall dis-penser and allow myself thirty seconds of ecstasy. Then I remember the disk the Master gave me, and decide to play it before bed. The music, if that is what it is, makes no impression on me whatever. I hear one note, and the next, and the one after that, but I am unable to put them together into any kind of rhythmic or melodic pattern. When it ends I play it again. Again I can hear only random sound, neither pleasant nor unpleasant, merely incomprehensible.

✹

The next morning they conduct me on a grand tour of the Sanctuary complex to show me everything that has been constructed here since my last visit. The tropical sunlight is brilliant, dazzling, so strong that it bleaches the sky to a matte white, against which the colorful domes and pavilions and spires of the complex stand out in strange clarity and the lofty green bowl of surrounding hills, thick and lush with flowering trees bedecked in yellow and purple, takes on a heavy, looming quality.

Kastel, the Lord Invocator, is my chief guide, a burly, redfaced man with small, shrewd eyes and a deceptively hearty manner. With us also are a woman from the office of the Oracle and two subAdjudicators. They hurry me, though with the utmost tact, from one building to the next. All four of them treat me as though I were something extremely fragile, made of the most delicate spun glass—or, perhaps, as though I were a bomb primed to explode at the touch of a breath.

"Over here on the left," says Kastel, "is the new observatory, with the finest scanning equipment ever devised, providing continuous input from every region of the Mission. The scanner itself, I regret to say, Lord Magistrate, is out of service this morning. There, of course, is the shrine of the blessed Haakon. Here we see the computer core, and this, behind it under the opaque canopy, is the recently completed stellarium."

I see leaping fountains, marble pavements, alabaster walls, gleaming metallic facades. They are very proud of what they have constructed here. The House of the Sanctuary has evolved over the decades, and by now has come to combine in itself aspects of a pontifical capital, a major research facility, and the ultimate sybaritic resort. Everything is bright, shining, startlingly luxurious. It is at once a place of great symbolic power, a potent focus of spiritual authority as overwhelming in its grandeur as any great ceremonial center of the past—ranking with the Vatican, the Potala, the shrine at Delphi, the grand temple of the Aztecs—and an efficient command post for the systematic exploration of the universe. No one doubts that the Sanctuary is the primary House of the Order—how could it be anything else?—but the splendors of this mighty eyrie underscore that primacy beyond all question. In truth I prefer the starker, more disciplined surroundings of my own desert domain, ten thousand kilometers away. But the Sanctuary is certainly impressive in its way.

"And that one down there?" I ask, more for politeness' sake than anything else. "The long flat-roofed building near that row of palms?"

"The detention center, Lord Magistrate," replies one of the subAdjudicators.

I give him a questioning look.

"People from the towns below constantly come wandering in here," he explains. "Trespassers, I mean." His expression is cold. Plainly the intruders of which he speaks are annoyances to him; or is it my question that bothers him? "They hope they can talk us into shipping them out, you understand. Or think that the actual transmitters are somewhere on the premises and they can ship themselves out when nobody's looking. We keep them for a while, so that they'll learn that trying to break in here isn't acceptable. Not that it does much good. They keep on coming. We've caught at least twenty so far this week."

Kastel laughs. "We try to teach them a thing or two, all right! But they're too stupid to learn."

"They have no chance of getting past the perimeter screen," says the woman from the Oracle's office. "We pick them up right away. But as Joseph says, they keep on coming all the same." She shivers. "They look so dirty! And mean, and frightening. I don't think they want to be shipped out at all. I think they're just bandits who come up here to try to steal from us, and when they're caught they give us a story about wanting to be colonists. We're much too gentle with them, let me tell you. If we started dealing with them like the thieves they are, they wouldn't be so eager to come creeping around in here."

I find myself wondering just what does happen to the detainees in the detention center. I suspect that they are treated a good deal less gently than the woman from the Oracle's office thinks, or would have me believe. But I am only a guest here. It's not my place to make inquiries into their security methods.

It is like another world up here above the clouds. Below is the teeming Earth, dark and troubled, cult-ridden, doom-ridden, sweltering and stewing in its own corruption and decay; while in this airy realm far above the crumbling and sweltering cities of the plain these votaries of the Order, safe behind their perimeter screen, go quietly about their task of designing and clarifying the plan that is carrying mankind's best outward into God's starry realm. The contrast is vast and jarring: pink marble terraces and fountains here, disease and squalor and despair below.

And yet, is it any different at my own headquarters on the Australian plains? In our House we do not go in for these architectural splendors, no alabaster, no onyx, just plain green metal shacks to house our equipment and ourselves. But we keep ourselves apart from the hungry sweaty multitudes in hieratic seclusion, a privileged caste, living simply but well, undeniably well, as we perform our own task of selecting those who are to go to the stars and sending them forth on their unimaginable journeys. In our own way we are as remote from the pressures and torments of mankind as these coddled functionaries of the Sanctuary. We know nothing of the life beyond our own Order. Nothing. Nothing.

The Master says, "I was too harsh yesterday, and even blasphemous." The map behind him is aglow once again, displaying the inner sphere of the galaxy and the lines marking the network of the Mission, as it had the day before. The Master himself is glowing too, his soft skin ruddy as a baby's, his eyes agleam. How old is he? A hundred fifty? Two hundred? "The map, after all, shows us the face of God," he says. "If the map is inadequate, it simply reveals the inadequacies of our own perceptions. But should we condemn it, then? Hardly, any more than we should condemn ourselves for not being gods. We should revere it, rather, flawed though it may be, because it is the best approximation that we can ever make of the reality of the Divine."

"The face of God?"

"What is God, if not the Great Totality? And how can we expect to see and comprehend the Totality of the Totality in a single glance?" The Master smiles. These are not thoughts that he has just had for the first time, nor can his complete reversal of yesterday's outburst be a spontaneous one. He is playing with me. "God is eternal motion through infinite space. He is the cosmos as it was twelve billion years ago and as it was twelve billion years from now, all in the same instant. This map you see here is our pitiful attempt at a representation of something inherently incapable of being represented; but we are to be praised for making an attempt, however foredoomed, at doing that which cannot be done."

I nod. I stare. What could I possibly say?

"When we experience the revelation of God," the Master continues softly, "what we receive is not the communication of a formula about a static world, which enables us to be at rest, but rather a sense of the power of the Creator, which sets us in motion even as He is in motion."

I think of Dante, who said, "In His will is our peace." Is there a contradiction here? How can "motion" be "peace"? Why is the Master telling me all this? Theology has never been my specialty, nor the specialty of my House in general, and he knows that. The abstruse nature of this discussion is troublesome to me. My eyes rest upon the Master, but their focus changes, so that I am looking beyond him, to red Antares and blue Rigel and fiery blue-white Vega, blazing at me from the wall.

The Master says, "Our Mission, you must surely agree, is an aspect of God's great plan. It is His way of enabling us to undertake the journey toward Him."

"Of course."

"Then whatever thwarts the design of the Mission must be counter to the will of God, is that not so?"

It is not a question. I am silent again, waiting.

He gestures toward the screen. "I would think that you know this pattern of lights and lines better than you do that of the palm of your hand."

"So I do."

"What about this one?"

The Master touches a control. The pattern suddenly changes: the bright symmetrical network linking the inner stars is sundered, and streaks of light now skid wildly out of the center toward the far reaches of the galaxy, like errant particles racing outward in a photomicrograph of an atomic reaction. The sight is a jarring one: balance overthrown, the sky untuned, discordancy triumphant. I wince and lean back from it as though he has slapped my face.

"Ah. You don't like it, eh?"

"Your pardon. It seems like a desecration."

"It is," he says. "Exactly so."

I feel chilled. I want him to restore the screen to its proper state. But he leaves the shattered image where it is.

He says, "This is only a probability projection, you understand. Based on early fragmentary reports from the farther outposts, by way of the Order's relay station on Lalande 21185. We aren't really sure what's going on out there. What we hope, naturally, is that our projections are inaccurate and that the plan is being followed after all. Harder data will be here soon."

"Some of those lines must reach out a thousand light-years!"

"More than that."

"Nothing could possibly have gotten so far from Earth in just the hundred years or so that we've been—"

"These are projections. Those are vectors. But they seem to be telling us that some carrier ships have been aimed beyond the predetermined targets, and are moving through the Dark on trajectories far more vast than anything we intend."

"But the plan—the Mission—"

His voice begins to develop an edge again. "Those whom we, acting through your House, have selected to implement the plan are very far from home, Lord Magistrate. They are no longer subject to our control. If they choose to do as they please once they're fifty light-years away, what means do we have of bringing them into check?"

"I find it very hard to believe that any of the colonists we've sent forth would be capable of setting aside the ordinances of Darklaw," I say, with perhaps too much heat in my voice.

What I have done, I realize, is to contradict him. Contradicting the Master is never a good idea. I see the lightnings playing about his head, though his expression remains mild and he continues to regard me benignly. Only the faintest of flushes on his ancient face betrays his anger. He makes no reply. I am getting into deep waters very quickly.

"Meaning no disrespect," I say, "but if this is, as you say, only a probability projection—"

"All that we have devoted our lives to is in jeopardy now," he says quietly. "What are we to do? What are we to do, Lord Magistrate?"

We have been building our highway to the stars for a century now and a little more, laying down one small paving-block after another. That seems like a long time to those of us who measure our spans in tens of years, and we have nibbled only a small way into the great darkness; but though we often feel that progress has been slow, in fact we have achieved miracles already, and we have all of eternity to complete our task.

In summoning us toward Him, God did not provide us with magical chariots. The inflexible jacket of the relativistic equations constrains us as we work. The speed of light remains our limiting factor while we establish our network. Although the Velde Effect allows us to deceive it and in effect to sidestep it, we must first carry the Velde receivers to the stars, and for that we can use only conventional spacegoing vehicles. They can approach the velocity of light, they may virtually attain it, but they can never exceed it: a starship making the outward journey to a star forty light-years from Earth must needs spend some forty years, and some beyond, in the doing of it. Later, when all the sky is linked by our receivers, that will not be a problem. But that is later.

The key to all that we do is the matter/antimatter relationship. When He built the universe for us, He placed all things in balance. The basic constituents of matter come in matched pairs: for each kind of particle there is an antiparticle, identical in mass but otherwise wholly opposite in all properties, mirror images in such things as electrical charge and axis of spin. Matter and antimatter annihilate one another upon contact, releasing tremendous energy. Conversely, any sufficiently strong energy field can bring about the creation of pairs of particles and antiparticles in equal quantities, though mutual annihilation will inevitably follow, converting the mass of the paired particles back into energy.

Apparently there is, and always has been since the Creation, a symmetry of matter and antimatter in the universe, equal quantities of each—a concept that has often been questioned by physicists, but which we believe now to be God's true design. Because of the incompatibility of matter and antimatter in the same vicinity, there is very little if any antimatter in our galaxy, which leads us to suppose that if symmetry is conserved, it must be through the existence of entire galaxies of antimatter, or even clusters of galaxies, at great distances from our own. Be that as it may: we will probably have no way of confirming or denying that for many thousands of years.

But the concept of symmetry is the essential thing. We base our work on Velde's Theorem, which suggests that the spontaneous conversion of matter into antimatter may occur at any time—though in fact it is an event of infinitesimal probability—but it must inescapably be accompanied by a simultaneous equal decay of antimatter into matter somewhere else, anywhere else, in the universe. About the same time that Velde offered this idea—that is, roughly a century and a half ago—Wilf demonstrated the feasibility of containment facilities capable of averting the otherwise inevitable mutual annihilation of matter and antimatter, thus making possible the controlled transformation of particles into their antiparticles. Finally came the work of Simtow, linking

Wilf's technical achievements with Velde's theoretical work and giving us a device that not only achieved controlled matter/antimatter conversion but also coped with the apparent randomness of Velde symmetry-conservation.

Simtow's device tunes the Velde Effect so that conversion of matter into antimatter is accompanied by the requisite balancing transformation of antimatter into matter, not at some random site anywhere in the universe, *but at a designated site*. Simtow was able to induce particle decay at one pole of a closed system in such a way that a corresponding but opposite decay occurs at the other. Wilf containment fields were employed at both ends of the system to prevent annihilation of the newly converted particles by ambient particles of the opposing kind.

The way was open now, though it was some time before we realized it, for the effective instanteous transmission of matter across great distances. That was achieved by placing the receiving pole of a Simtow transformer at the intended destination. Then an intricate three-phase cycle carried out the transmission.

In the first phase, matter is converted into antimatter at the destination end in an untuned reaction, and stored in a Wilf containment vessel. This, following Velde's conservation equations, presumably would induce spontaneous transformation of an equivalent mass of antimatter into matter in one of the unknown remote antimatter galaxies, where it would be immediately annihilated.

In the second phase, matter is converted to antimatter at the transmitting end, this time employing Simtow tuning so that the corresponding Velde-law transformation of the previously stored antimatter takes place not at some remote and random location but within the Wilf field at the designated receiving pole, which may be situated anywhere in the universe. What this amounts to, essentially, is the instantaneous particle-by-particle duplication of the transmitted matter at the receiving end.

The final step is to dispose of the unwanted antimatter that has been created at the transmission end. Since it is unstable outside the Wilf containment vessel, its continued existence in an all-matter system is pointless as well as untenable. Therefore it is annihilated under controlled circumstances, providing a significant release of energy that can be tapped to power a new cycle of the transmission process.

What is accomplished by all this? A certain quantity of matter at the transmission end of the system is destroyed; an exact duplicate of it is created, essentially simultaneously, at the receiving end. It made no difference, the early experimenters discovered, what was being put through the system: a stone, a book, a potted geranium, a frog. Whatever went in here came out there, an apparently perfect replica, indistinguishable in all respects from the original. Whether the two poles were situated at opposite ends of the same laboratory, or in different continents, or on Earth and Mars, the transmission was instant and total. What went forth alive came out alive. The geranium still bloomed and set seed; the frog still stared and leaped and gobbled insects. A mouse was sent, and thrived, and went on to live and die a full mouse-life. A pregnant cat made the journey and was delivered, three weeks later, of five healthy kittens. A dog—an ape—a man—

A man, yes. Has anyone ever made a bolder leap into the darkness than God's great servant Haakon Christiansen, the blessed Haakon whom we all celebrate and revere? He gambled everything on one toss of the dice, and won, and by his victory made himself immortal and gave us a gift beyond price.

His successful voyage opened the heavens. All we needed to do now was set up receiving stations. The Moon, Mars, the moons of Jupiter and Saturn, were only an eyeblink away. And then? Then? Why, of course, what remained but to carry our receivers to the stars?

For hours I wander the grounds of the Sanctuary, alone, undisturbed, deeply troubled. It is as if a spell of silence and solitude surrounds and protects me. No one dares approach me, neither as a supplicant of some sort nor to offer obeisance nor merely to see if I am in need of any service. I suppose many eyes are studying me warily from a distance, but in some way it must be obvious to all who observe me that I am not to be intruded upon. I must cast a forbidding aura today. In the brilliance of the tropic afternoon a darkness and a chill have settled over my soul. It seems to me that the splendid grounds are white with snow as far as I can see, snow on the hills, snow on the lawns, snow piled high along the banks of the sparkling streams, a sterile whiteness all the way to the rim of the world.

I am a dour man, but not a melancholy or tormented one. Others mistake my disciplined nature for something darker, seeing in me an iciness of spirit, a somberness, a harshness that masks some pervasive anguish of the heart. It is not so. If I have renounced the privilege of going to the stars, which could surely have been mine, it is not because I love the prospect of ending my days on this maimed and ravaged world of ours, but because I feel that God demands this service of me, that I remain here and help others to go forth. If I am hard and stern, it is because I can be nothing else, considering the choices I have made in shaping my course: I am a priest and a magistrate and a soldier of sorts, all in one. I have passed a dedicated and cloistered life. Yet I understand joy. There is a music in me. My senses are fully alive, all of them. From the outside I may appear unyielding and grim, but it is only because I have chosen to deny myself the pleasure of being ordinary, of being slothful, of being unproductive. There are those who misunderstand that in me, and see me as some kind of dismal monastic, narrow and fanatical, a gloomy man, a desolate man, one whom the commonplace would do well to fear and to shun. I think they are wrong. Yet this day, contemplating all that the Master has just told me and much that he has only implied, I am swept with such storms of foreboding and distress that I must radiate a frightful bleakness which warns others away. At any rate for much of this afternoon they all leave me alone to roam as I please.

The Sanctuary is a self-sufficient world. It needs nothing from outside. I stand near the summit of the great hill, looking down on children playing, gardeners setting out new plantings, novitiates sitting crosslegged at their studies on the lawn. I look toward the gardens and try to see color, but all color has leached away. The sun has passed beyond the horizon, here at this high altitude, but the sky is luminous. It is like a band of hot metal, glowing white. It devours everything: the edges of the world are slowly being engulfed by it. Whiteness is all, a universal snowy blanket.

For a long while I watch the children. They laugh, they shriek, they run in circles and fall down and rise again, still laughing. Don't they feel the sting of the snow? But the snow, I remind myself, is not there. It is illusionary snow, metaphorical snow, a trick of my troubled soul, a snowfall of the spirit. For the children there is no snow. I choose a little girl, taller and more serious than the others, standing somewhat to one side, and pretend that she is my own child. A strange idea, myself as a father, but pleasing. I could have had children. It might not have meant a very different life from the one I have had. But it was not what I chose.

Now I toy with the fantasy for a time, enjoying it. I invent a name for the girl; I picture her running to me up the grassy slope; I see us sitting quietly together, poring over a chart of the sky. I tell her the names of the stars, I show her the constellations. The vision is so compelling that I begin to descend the slope toward her. She looks up at me while I am still some distance from her. I smile. She stares, solemn, uncertain of my intentions. Other children nudge her, point, and whisper. They draw back, edging away from me. It is as if my shadow has fallen upon them and chilled them as they played. I nod and move on, releasing them from its darkness.

A path strewn with glossy green leaves takes me to an overlook point at the cliff's edge, where I can see the broad bay far below, at the foot of Sanctuary Mountain. The water gleams like a burnished shield, or perhaps it is more like a huge shimmering pool of quicksilver. I imagine myself leaping from the stone balcony where I stand and soaring outward in a sharp smooth arc, striking the water cleanly, knifing down through it, vanishing without a trace.

Returning to the main Sanctuary complex, I happen to glance downslope toward the long narrow new building that I have been told is the detention center. A portcullis at its eastern end has been hoisted and a procession of prisoners is coming out. I know they are prisoners because they are roped together and walk in a sullen, slack way, heads down, shoulders slumped.

They are dressed in rags and tatters, or less than that. Even from fairly far away I can see cuts and bruises and scabs on them, and one has his arm in a sling, and one is bandaged so that nothing shows of his face but his glinting eyes. Three guards walk alongside them, carelessly dangling neural truncheons from green lanyards. The ropes that bind the prisoners are loosely tied, a perfunctory restraint. It would be no great task for them to break free and seize the truncheons from the captors. But they seem utterly beaten down; for them to make any sort of move toward freedom is probably as unlikely as the advent of an army of winged dragons swooping across the sky.

They are an incongruous and disturbing sight, these miserable prisoners plodding across this velvet landscape. Does the Master know that they are here, and that they are so poorly kept? I start to walk toward them. The Lord Invocator Kastel, emerging suddenly from nowhere as if he had been waiting behind a bush, steps across my path and says, "God keep you, your grace. Enjoying your stroll through the grounds?"

"Those people down there—"

"They are nothing, Lord Magistrate. Only some of our thieving rabble, coming out for a little fresh air."

"Are they well? Some of them look injured."

Kastel tugs at one ruddy fleshy jowl. "They are desperate people. Now and then they try to attack their guards. Despite all precautions we can't always avoid the use of force in restraining them."

"Of course. I quite understand," I say, making no effort to hide my sarcasm. "Is the Master aware that helpless prisoners are being beaten within a thousand meters of his lodge?"

"Lord Magistrate—!"

"If we are not humane in all our acts, what are we, Lord Invocator Kastel? What example do we set for the common folk?"

"It's these common folk of yours," Kastel says sharply—I have not heard that tone from him before—"who ring this place like an army of filthy vermin, eager to steal anything they can carry away and destroy everything else. Do you realize, Lord Magistrate, that this mountain rises like a towering island of privilege above a sea of hungry people? That within a sixty-kilometer radius of these foothills there are probably thirty million empty bellies? That if our perimeter defenses were to fail, they'd sweep through here like locusts and clean the place out? And probably slaughter every last one of us, up to and including the Master."

"God forbid."

"God created them. He must love them. But if this House is going to carry out the work God intended for us, we have to keep them at bay. I tell you, Lord Magistrate, leave these grubby matters of administration to us. In a few days you'll go flying off to your secluded nest in the Outback, where your work is undisturbed by problems like these. Whereas we'll still be here, in our pretty little mountain paradise, with enemies on every side. If now and then we take some action that you might not consider entirely humane, I ask you to remember that we guard the Master here, who is the heart of the Mission." He allows me, for a moment, to see the contempt he feels for my qualms. Then he is all affability and concern again. In a completely different tone he says, "The observatory's scanning equipment will be back in operation again tonight. I want to invite you to watch the data come pouring in from every corner of space. It's an inspiring sight, Lord Magistrate."

"I would be pleased to see it."

"The progress we've made, Lord Magistrate—the way we've moved out and out, always in accordance with the divine plan—I tell you, I'm not what you'd call an emotional man, but when I see the track we're making across the Dark my eyes begin to well up, let me tell you. My eyes begin to well up."

His eyes, small and keen, study me for a reaction.

Then he says, "Everything's all right for you here?"

"Of course, Lord Invocator."

"Your conversations with the Master—have they met with your expectations?"

"Entirely so. He is truly a saint."

"Truly, Lord Magistrate. Truly."

"Where would the Mission be without him?"

"Where will it be," says Kastel thoughtfully, "when he is no longer here to guide us?"

"May that day be far from now."

"Indeed," Kastel says. "Though I have to tell you, in all confidence, I've started lately to fear—"

His voice trails off.

"Yes?"

"The Master," he whispers. "Didn't he seem different to you, somehow?"

"Different?"

"I know it's years since you last saw him. Perhaps you don't remember him as he was."

"He seemed lucid and powerful to me, the most commanding of men," I reply.

Kastel nods. He takes me by the arm and gently steers me toward the upper buildings of the Sanctuary complex, away from those ghastly prisoners, who are still shuffling about like walking corpses in front of their jail. Quietly he says, "Did he tell you that he thinks someone's interfering with the plan? That he has evidence that some of the receivers are being shipped far beyond the intended destinations?"

I look at him, wide-eyed.

"Do you really expect me to violate the confidential nature of the Master's audiences with me?"

"Of course not! Of course not, Lord Magistrate. But just between you and me—and we're both important men in the Order, it's essential that we level with each other at all times—I can admit to you that I'm pretty certain what the Master must have told you. Why else would he have sent for you? Why else pull you away from your House and interrupt what is now the key activity of the Mission? He's obsessed with this idea that there have been deviations from the plan. He's reading God knows what into the data. But I don't want to try to influence you. It's absurd to think that a man of your supreme rank in the second House of the Order can't analyze the situation unaided. You come tonight, you look at what the scanner says, you make up your own mind. That's all I ask. All right, Lord Magistrate? All right?"

He walks away, leaving me stunned and shocked. The Master insane? Or the Lord Invocator disloyal? Either one is unthinkable.

I will go to the observatory tonight, yes.

Kastel, by approaching me, seems to have broken the mysterious spell of privacy that has guarded me all afternoon. Now they come from all sides, crowding around me as though I am some archangel—staring, whispering, smiling hopefully at me. They gesture, they kneel. The bravest of them come right up to me and tell me their names, as though I will remember them when the time comes to send the next settlers off to the worlds of Epsilon Eridani, of Castor C, of Ross 154, of Wolf 359. I am kind with them, I am gracious, I am warm. It costs me nothing; it gives them happiness. I think of those bruised and slumpshouldered prisoners sullenly parading in front of the detention center. For them I can do nothing; for these, the maids and gardeners and acolytes and novitiates of the Sanctuary, I can at least provide a flicker of hope. And, smiling at them, reaching my hands toward them, my own mood lightens. All will be well. God will prevail, as ever. The Kastels of this world cannot dismay me.

I see the little girl at the edge of the circle, the one whom I had taken, for a strange instant, to be my daughter. Once again I smile at her. Once again she gives me a solemn stare, and edges away. There is laughter. "She means no disrespect," a woman says. "Shall I bring her to you, your grace?" I shake my head. "I must frighten her," I say. "Let her be." But the girl's stare remains to haunt me, and I see snow about me once more, thickening in the sky, covering the lush gardens of the Sanctuary, spreading to the rim of the world and beyond.

In the observatory they hand me a polarizing helmet to protect my eyes. The data flux is an overpowering sight: hot pulsing flares, like throbbing suns. I catch just a glimpse of it while still in the vestibule. The world, which has thawed for me, turns to snow yet again. It is a total white-out, a flash of photospheric intensity that washes away all surfaces and dechromatizes the universe.

"This way, your grace. Let me assist you."

Soft voices. Solicitous proximity. To them, I suppose, I am an old man. Yet the Master was old before I was born. Does he ever come here?

I hear them whispering: "The Lord Magistrate—the Lord Magistrate—"

The observatory, which I have never seen before, is one huge room, an eight-sided building as big as a cathedral, very dark and shadowy within, massive walls of some smooth moist-looking greenish stone, vaulted roof of burnished red metal, actually not a roof at all but an intricate antenna of colossal size and complexity, winding round and round and round upon itself. Spidery catwalks run everywhere to link the various areas of the great room. There is no telescope. This is not that sort of observatory. This is the central gathering-point for three rings of data-collectors, one on the Moon, one somewhere beyond the orbit of Jupiter, one eight light-years away on a world of the star Lalande 21185. They scan the heavens and pump a stream of binary digits toward this building, where the data arrives in awesome convulsive actinic spurts, like thunderbolts hurled from Olympus.

There is another wall-sized map of the Mission here, the same sort of device that I saw in the Master's office, but at least five times as large. It too displays the network of the inner stars illuminated in bright yellow lines. But it is the old pattern, the familiar one, the one we have worked with since the inception of the program. This screen shows none of the wild divagations and bizarre trajectories that marked the image the Master showed me in my last audience with him.

"The system's been down for four days," a voice at my elbow murmurs: one of the astronomers, a young one, who evidently has been assigned to me. She is dark-haired, snub-nosed, bright-eyed, a pleasant-faced girl. "We're just priming it now, bringing it up to realtime level. That's why the flares are so intense. There's a terrific mass of data backed up in the system and it's all trying to get in here at once."

"I see."

She smiles. "If you'll move this way, your grace—"

She guides me toward an inner balcony that hangs suspended over a well-like pit perhaps a hundred meters deep. In the dimness far below I see metal arms weaving in slow patterns, great gleaming disks turning rapidly, mirrors blinking and flashing. My astronomer explains that this is the main focal limb, or some such thing, but the details are lost on me. The whole building is quivering and trembling here, as though it is being pounded by a giant's hand. Colors are changing: the spectrum is being tugged far off to one side. Gripping the rail of the balcony, I feel a terrible vertigo coming over me. It seems to me that the expansion of the universe has suddenly been reversed, that all the galaxies are converging on this point, that I am standing in a vortex where floods of ultraviolet light, x-rays, and gamma rays come rushing in from all points of the cosmos at once. "Do you notice it?" I hear myself asking. "The violet-shift? Everything running backwards toward the center?"

"What's that, your grace?"

I am muttering incoherently. She has not understood a word, thank God! I see her staring at me, worried, perhaps shocked. But I pull myself together, I smile, I manage to offer a few rational-sounding questions. She grows calm. Making allowances for my age, perhaps, and for my ignorance of all that goes on in this building. I have my own area of technical competence, she knows—oh, yes, she certainly knows that!—but she realizes that it is quite different from hers.

From my vantage point overlooking the main focal limb I watch with more awe than comprehension as the data pours in, is refined and clarified, is analyzed, is synthesized, is registered on the various display units arrayed on the walls of the observatory. The young woman at my side keeps up a steady whispered flow of commentary, but I am distracted by the terrifying patterns of light and shadow all about me, by sudden and unpredictable bursts of high-pitched sound, by the vibrations of the building, and I miss some of the critical steps in her explanations and rapidly find myself lost. In truth I understand almost nothing of what is taking place around me. No doubt it is significant. The place is crowded with members of the Order, and high ones at that, everyone at least an initiate, several wearing the armbands of the inner levels of the primary House, the red, the green, even a few amber. Lord Invocator Kastel is here, smiling smugly, embracing people like a politician, coming by more than once to make sure I appreciate the high drama of this great room. I nod, I smile, I assure him of my gratitude.

Indeed it is dramatic. Now that I have recovered from my vertigo I find myself looking outward rather than down, and my senses ride heavenward as though I myself am traveling to the stars.

This is the nerve-center of our Mission, this is the grand sensorium by which we keep track of our achievement.

The Alpha Centauri system was the starting-point, of course, when we first began seeding the stars with Velde receivers, and then Barnard's Star, Wolf 359, Lalande 21185, and so on outward and outward, Sirius, Ross 154, Epsilon Indi—who does not know the names?—to all the stars within a dozen light-years of Earth. Small unmanned starships, laser-powered robot drones, unfurling great lightsails and gliding starward on the urgent breath of photonic winds that we ourselves stirred up. Light was their propulsive force, and its steady pressure afforded constant acceleration, swiftly stepping up the velocity of our ships until it approached that of light.

Then, as they neared the stars that were their destinations, scanning for planets by one method or another, plotting orbital deviations or homing in on infrared radiation or measuring Doppler shifts—finding worlds, and sorting them to eliminate the unlivable ones, the gas giants, the ice-balls, the formaldehyde atmospheres—

One by one our little vessels made landfall on new Earths. Silently opened their hatches. Sent forth the robots who would set up the Velde receivers that would be our gateways. One by one, opening the heavens.

And then—the second phase, the fabricating devices emerging, going to work, tiny machines seeking out carbon, silicon, nitrogen, oxygen, and the rest of the necessary building-blocks, stacking up the atoms in the predesignated patterns, assembling new starships, new laser banks, new Velde receivers. Little mechanical minds giving the orders, little mechanical arms doing the work. It would take some fifteen years for one of our ships to reach a star twelve light-years away. But it would require much less than that for our automatic replicators to construct a dozen twins of that ship at the landing point and send them in a dozen directions, each bearing its own Velde receiver to be established on some farther star, each equipped to replicate itself just as quickly and send more ships onward. Thus we built our receiver network, spreading our highway from world to world across a sphere that by His will and our choice would encompass only a hundred light-years in the beginning. Then from our transmitters based on Earth we could begin to send—instantly, miraculously—the first colonists to the new worlds within our delimited sphere.

And so have we done. Standing here with my hands gripping the metal rail of the observatory balcony, I can in imagination send my mind forth to our colonies in the stars, to those tiny far-flung outposts peopled by the finest souls Earth can produce, men and women whom I myself have helped to choose and prepare and hurl across the gulf of night, pioneers sworn to Darklaw, bound by the highest of oaths not to repeat in the stars the errors we have made on Earth. And, thinking now of everything that our Order has achieved and all that we will yet achieve, the malaise that has afflicted my spirit since I arrived at the Sanctuary lifts, and a flood of joy engulfs me, and I throw my head back, I stare toward the maze of data-gathering circuitry far above me, I let the full splendor of the Project invade my soul.

It is a wondrous moment, but short-lived. Into my ecstasies come intrusive sounds: mutterings, gasps, the scurrying of feet. I snap to attention. All about me, there is sudden excitement, almost a chaos. Someone is sobbing. Someone else is laughing. It is a wild, disagreeable laughter that is just this side of hysteria. A furious argument has broken out across the way: the individual words are blurred by echo but the anger of their inflection is unmistakable.

"What's happening?" I ask the astronomer beside me.

"The master chart," she says. Her voice has become thick and hoarse. There is a troubled gleam in her eyes. "It's showing the update now—the new information that's just come in—"

She points. I stare at the glowing star-map. The familiar pattern of the Mission network has been disrupted, now, and what I see, what they all see, is that same crazy display of errant tracks thrusting far out beyond our designated sphere of colonization that I beheld on the Master's own screen two days before.

The most tactful thing I can do, in the difficult few days that follow, is to withdraw to my quarters and wait until the Sanctuary people have begun to regain their equilibrium. My being here among them now must be a great embarrassment for them. They are taking this apparent deviation from the Mission's basic plan as a deep humiliation and a stinging rebuke upon their House. They find it not merely profoundly disquieting and improper, as I do, but a mark of shame, a sign that God himself has found inadequate the plan of which they are the designers and custodians, and has discarded it. How much more intense their loss of face must be for all this to be coming down upon them at a time when the Lord Magistrate of the Order's other high House is among them to witness their disgrace.

It would be even more considerate of me, perhaps, to return at once to my own House's headquarters in Australia and let the Sanctuary people sort out their position without my presence to distract and reproach them. But that I cannot do. The Master wants me here. He has called me all the way from Australia to be with him at the Sanctuary in this difficult time. Here I must stay until I know why.

So I keep out of the way. I ask for my meals in my chambers instead of going to the communal hall. I spend my days and nights in prayer and meditation and reading. I sip brandy and divert myself with music. I take pleasure from the dispenser when the need comes over me. I stay out of sight and await the unfolding of events.

But my isolation is shortlived. On the third day after my retreat into solitude Kastel comes to me, pale and shaken, all his hearty condescension gone from him now.

"Tell me," he says hoarsely, "what do you make of all this? Do you think the data's genuine?"

"What reason do I have to think otherwise?"

"But suppose"—he hesitates, and his eyes do not quite meet mine—"suppose the Master has rigged things somehow so that we're getting false information?"

"Would that be possible? And why would he do such a monstrous thing in the first place?"

"I don't know."

"Do you really have so little regard for the Master's honesty? Or is it his sanity that you question?"

He turns crimson.

"God forbid, either one!" he cries. "The Master is beyond all censure. I wonder only whether he has embarked upon some strange plan beyond our comprehension, absolutely beyond our understanding, which in the execution of his unfathomable purpose requires him to deceive us about the true state of things in the heavens."

Kastel's cautious, elaborately formal syntax offends my ear. He did not speak to me in such baroque turns and curlicues when he was explaining why it was necessary to beat the prisoners in the detention center. But I try not to let him see my distaste for him. Indeed he seems more to be pitied than detested, a frightened and bewildered man.

"Why don't you ask the Master?" I say.

"Who would dare? But in any case the Master has shut himself away from us all since the other night."

"Ah. Then ask the Oracle."

"The Oracle offers only mysteries and redundancies, as usual."

"I can't offer anything better," I tell him. "Have faith in the Master. Accept the data of your own scanner until you have solid reason to doubt it. Trust God."

Kastel, seeing I can tell him nothing useful, and obviously uneasy now over having expressed these all but sacrilegious suppositions about the Master to me, asks a blessing of me, and I give it, and he goes. But others come after him, one by one—hesitantly, even fearfully, as though expecting me to turn them away in scorn. High and low, haughty and humble, they seek audiences with me. I understand now what is happening. With the Master in seclusion, the community is leaderless in this difficult moment. On him they dare not intrude under any circumstances, if he has given the sign that he is not to be approached. I am the next highest ranking member of the hierarchy currently in residence at the Sanctuary. That I am of another House, and that between the Master and me lies an immense gulf of age and primacy, does not seem to matter to them just now. So it is to me that they come, asking for guidance, comfort, whatever. I give them what I can—platitudes, mainly—until I begin to feel hollow and cynical. Toward evening the young astronomer comes to me, she who had guided me through the observatory on the night of the great revelation. Her eyes are red and swollen, with dark rings below them. By now I have grown expert at offering these Sanctuary people the bland reassurances that are the best I can provide for them, but as I launch into what has become my standard routine I see that it is doing more harm to her than good— she begins to tremble, tears roll down her cheeks, she shakes her head and looks away, shivering—and suddenly my own facade of spiritual authority and philosophical detachment crumbles, and I am as troubled and confused as she is. I realize that she and I stand at the brink of the same black abyss. I begin to feel myself toppling forward into it. We reach for each other and embrace in a kind of wild defiance of our fears. She is half my age. Her skin is smooth, her flesh is firm. We each grasp for whatever comfort we can find. Afterward she seems stunned, numbed, dazed. She dresses in silence.

"Stay," I urge her. "Wait until morning."

"Please, your grace—no—no—"

But she manages a faint smile. Perhaps she is trying to tell me that though she is amazed by what we have done she feels no horror and perhaps not even regret. I hold the tips of her fingers in my hands for a moment, and we kiss quickly, a dry, light, chaste kiss, and she goes.

Afterward I experience a strange new clarity of mind. It is as if this unexpected coupling has burned away a thick fog of the soul and allowed me to think clearly once again.

In the night, which for me is a night of very little sleep, I contemplate the events of my stay at the House of Sanctuary and I come to terms, finally, with the obvious truth that I have tried to avoid for days. I remember the Master's casual phrase at my second audience with him, as he told me of his suspicion that certain colonists must be deviating from the tenets of Darklaw: "Those whom we, *acting through your House*, have selected..." Am I being accused of some malfeasance? Yes. Of course. I am the one who chose the ones who have turned away from the plan. It has been decided that the guilt is to fall upon me. I should have seen it much earlier, but I have been distracted, I suppose, by troublesome emotions. Or else I have simply been unwilling to see.

I decide to fast today. When they bring me my morning meal-tray they will find a note from me, instructing them not to come to me again until I notify them.

I tell myself that this is not so much an act of penitence as one of purgation. Fasting is not something that the Order asks of us. For me it is a private act, one which I feel brings me closer to God. In any case my conscience is clear; it is simply that there are times when I think better on an empty stomach, and I am eager now to maintain and deepen that lucidity of perception that came upon me late the previous evening. I have fasted before, many times, when I felt a similar need. But then, when I take my morning shower, I dial it cold. The icy water burns and stings and flays; I have to compel myself to remain under it, but I do remain, and I hold myself beneath the shower head much longer than I might ordinarily have stayed there. That can only be penitence. Well, so be it. But penitence for what? I am guilty of no fault. Do they really intend to make me the scapegoat? Do I intend to offer myself to expiate the general failure? Why should I? Why do I punish myself now?

All that will be made known to me later. If I have chosen to impose a day of austerity and discomfort upon myself, there must be a good reason for it, and I will understand in good time.

Meanwhile I wear nothing but a simple linen robe of a rough texture, and savor the roughness against my skin. My stomach, by midmorning, begins to grumble and protest, and I give it a glass of water, as though to mock its needs. A little later the vision of a fine meal assails me, succulent grilled fish on a shining porcelain plate, cool white wine in a sparkling crystal goblet. My throat goes dry, my head throbs. But instead of struggling against these tempting images I encourage them, I invite my traitor mind to do its worst: I add platters of gleaming red grapes to the imaginary feast, cheeses, loaves of bread fresh from the oven. The fish course is succeeded by roast lamb, the lamb by skewers of beef, the wine in the glass is now a fine red Coonawarra, there is rare old port to come afterward. I fantasize such gluttonies that they become absurd, and I lose my appetite altogether.

The hours go by and I begin to drift into the tranquility that for me is the first sign of the presence of God close at hand. Yet I find myself confronting a barrier. Instead of simply accepting His advent and letting Him engulf me, I trouble myself with finicky questions. Is He approaching me, I wonder? Or am I moving toward Him? I tell myself that the issue is an empty one. He is everywhere. It is the power of God which sets us in motion, yes, but He is motion incarnate. It is pointless to speak of my approaching Him, or His approaching me: those are two ways of describing the same thing. But while I contemplate such matters my mind itself holds me apart from Him.

I imagine myself in a tiny ship, drifting toward the stars. To make such a voyage is not what I desire; but it is a useful focus for my reverie. For the journey to the stars and the journey toward God are one thing and the same. It is the journey into reality.

Once, I know, these things were seen in a different light. But it was inevitable that as we began to penetrate the depths of space we would come to see the metaphysical meaning of the venture on which we had embarked. And if we had not, we could not have proceeded. The curve of secular thought had extended as far as it could reach, from the seventeenth century to the twenty-first, and had begun to crack under its own weight; just when we were beginning to believe that *we* were God, we rediscovered the understanding that we were not. The universe was too huge for us to face alone. That new ocean was so wide, and our boats so very small.

I urge my little craft onward. I set sail at last into the vastness of the Dark. My voyage has begun. God embraces my soul. He bids me be welcome in His kingdom. My heart is eased.

Under the Master's guidance we have all come to know that in our worldly lives we see only distortions—shadows on the cave wall. But as we penetrate the mysteries of the universe we are permitted to perceive things as they really are. The entry into the cosmos is the journey into the sublime, the literal attainment of heaven. It is a post-Christian idea: voyages must be undertaken, motion must never cease, we must seek Him always. In the seeking is the finding.

Gradually, as I reflect on these things yet again, the seeking ends for me and the finding begins, and my way becomes clear. I will resist nothing. I will accept everything. Whatever is required of me, that will I do, as always.

It is night, now. I am beyond any hunger and I feel no need for sleep. The walls of my chamber seem transparent to me and I can cast my vision outward to all the world, the heavy surging seas and the close blanket of the sky, the mountains and valleys, the rivers, the fields. I feel the nearness of billions of souls. Each human soul is a star: it glows with unique fire, and each has its counterpart in the heavens. There is one star that is the Master, and one that is Kastel, and one that is the young astronomer who shared my bed. And somewhere there is a star that is me. My spirit goes outward at last, it roves the distant blackness, it journeys on and on, to the ends of the universe. I soar above the Totality of the Totality. I look upon the face of God.

When the summons comes from the Master, shortly before dawn, I go to him at once. The rest of the House of Sanctuary sleeps. All is silent. Taking the garden path uphill, I experience a marvelous precision of sight: as though by great magnification I perceive the runnels and grooves on each blade of grass, the minute jagged teeth left by the mower as it bit it short, the glistening droplets of dew on the jade surface. Blossoms expand toward the pale new light now streaming out of the east as though they are coming awake. On the red earth of the path, strutting like dandies in a summer parade, are little shining scarlet-backed beetles with delicate black legs that terminate in intricate hairy feet. A fine mist rises from the ground. Within the silence I hear a thousand tiny noises.

The Master seems to be bursting with youthful strength, vitality, a mystic energy. He sits motionless, waiting for me to speak. The star-screen behind him is darkened, an ebony void, infinitely deep. I see the fine lines about his eyes and the corners of his mouth. His skin is pink, like a baby's. He could be six weeks old, or six thousand years.

His silence is immense.

"You hold me responsible?" I say at last.

He stares for a long while. "Don't you?"

"I am the Lord Magistrate of Senders. If there has been a failure, the fault must be mine."

"Yes. The fault must be yours."

He is silent again.

It is very easy, accepting this, far easier than I would have thought only the day before.

He says after a time, "What will you do?"

"You have my resignation."

"From your magistracy?"

"From the Order," I say. "How could I remain a priest, having been a Magistrate?"

"Ah. But you must."

The pale gentle eyes are inescapable.

"Then I will be a priest on some other world," I tell him. "I could never stay here. I respectfully request release from my vow of renunciation."

He smiles. I am saying exactly the things he hoped I would say.

"Granted."

It is done. I have stripped myself of rank and power. I will leave my House and my world; I will go forth into the Dark, although long ago I had gladly given that great privilege up. The irony is not lost on me. For all others it is heart's desire to leave Earth, for me it is merely the punishment for having failed the Mission. My penance will be my exile and my exile will be my penance. It is the defeat of all my work and the collapse of my vocation. But I must try not to see it that way. This is the beginning of the next phase of my life, nothing more. God will comfort me. Through my fall He has found a way of calling me to Him.

I wait for a gesture of dismissal, but it does not come.

"You understand," he says after a time, "that the Law of Return will hold, even for you?"

He means the prime tenet of Darklaw, the one that no one has ever violated. Those who depart from Earth may not come back to it. Ever. The journey is a one-way trip.

"Even for me," I say. "Yes. I understand."

✹

I stand before a Velde doorway like any other, one that differs in no way from the one that just a short time before had carried me instantaneously halfway around the world, home from Sanctuary to the House of Senders. It is a cubicle of black glass, four meters high, three meters wide, three meters deep. A pair of black-light lenses face each other like owlish eyes on its inner sides. From the rear wall jut the three metal cones that are the discharge points.

How many journeys have I made by way of transmitting stations such as this one? Five hundred? A thousand? How many times have I been scanned, measured, dissected, stripped down to my component baryons, replicated: annihilated *here*, created *there*, all within the same moment? And stepped out of a receiver, intact, unchanged, at some distant point, Paris, Karachi, Istanbul, Nairobi, Dar-esSalaam?

This doorway is no different from the ones through which I stepped those other times. But this journey will be unlike all those others. I have never left Earth before, not even to go to Mars, not even to the Moon. There has been no reason for it. But now I am to leap to the stars. Is it the scope of the leap that I fear? But I know better. The risks are not appreciably greater in a journey of twenty light-years than in one of twenty kilometers.

Is it the strangeness of the new worlds which I will confront that arouses this uneasiness in me? But I have devoted my life to building those worlds. What is it, then? The knowledge that once I leave this House I will cease to be Lord Magistrate of the Senders, and become merely a wandering pilgrim?

Yes. Yes, I think that that is it. My life has been a comfortable one of power and assurance, and now I am entering the deepest unknown, leaving all that behind, leaving everything behind, giving up my House, relinquishing my magistracy, shedding all that I have been except for my essence itself, from which I can never be parted. It is a great severance. Yet why do I hesitate? I have asked so many others, after all, to submit to that severance. I have bound so many others, after all, by the unbending oaths of Darklaw. Perhaps it takes more time to prepare oneself than I have allowed. I have given myself very short notice indeed.

But the moment of uneasiness passes. All about me are friendly faces, men and women of my House, come to bid me a safe journey.

Their eyes are moist, their smiles are tender. They know they will never see me again. I feel their love and their loyalty, and it eases my soul.

Ancient words drift through my mind.

Into thy hands, O Lord, I commend my spirit.

Yes. And my body also.

Lord, thou hast been our refuge: from one generation to another. Before the mountains were brought forth, or ever the earth and the world were made: thou art God from everlasting, and world without end.

Yes. And then:

The heavens declare the glory of God: and the firmament showeth His handiwork.

There is no sensation of transition. I was there; now I am here. I might have traveled no further than from Adelaide to Melbourne, or from Brisbane to Cairns. But I am very far from home now. The sky is amber, with swirls of blue. On the horizon is a great dull warm red mass, like a gigantic glowing coal, very close by. At the zenith is a smaller and brighter star, much more distant.

This world is called Cuchulain. It is the third moon of the subluminous star Gwydion, which is the dark companion of Lalande 21185. I am eight light-years from Earth. Cuchulain is the Order's prime outpost in the stars, the home of Second Sanctuary. Here is where I have chosen to spend my years of exile. The fallen magistrate, the broken vessel.

The air is heavy and mild. Crazy whorls of thick green ropy vegetation entangle everything, like a furry kelp that has infested the land. As I step from the Velde doorway I am confronted by a short, crisp little man in dark priestly robes. He is tonsured and wears a medallion of high office, though it is an office two or three levels down from the one that had been mine.

He introduces himself as Procurator-General Guardiano. Greeting me by name, he expresses his surprise at my most unexpected arrival in his diocese. Everyone knows that those who serve at my level of the Order must renounce all hope of emigration from Earth.

"I have resigned my magistracy," I tell him. "No," I say. "Actually I've been dismissed. For cause. I've been reassigned to the ordinary priesthood."

He stares, plainly shocked and stunned.

"It is still an honor to have you here, your grace," he says softly, after a moment.

I go with him to the chapter house, not far away. The gravitational pull here is heavier than Earth's, and I find myself leaning forward as I walk and pulling my feet after me as though the ground is sticky. But such incidental strangenesses as this are subsumed, to my surprise, by a greater familiarity: this place is not as alien as I had expected. I might merely be in some foreign land, and not on another world. The full impact of my total and final separation from Earth, I know, will not hit me until later.

We sit together in the refectory, sipping glass after glass of a sweet strong liqueur. Procurator-General Guardiano seems flustered by having someone of my rank appear without warning in his domain, but he is handling it well. He tries to make me feel at home. Other priests of the higher hierarchy appear—the word of my arrival must be traveling fast—and peer into the room. He waves them away. I tell him, briefly, the reasons for my downfall. He listens gravely and says, "Yes. We know that the outer worlds are in rebellion against Darklaw."

"Only the outer worlds?"

"So far, yes. It's very difficult for us to get reliable data."

"Are you saying that they've closed the frontier to the Order?"

"Oh, no, nothing like that. There's still free transit to every colony, and chapels everywhere. But the reports from the outer worlds are growing increasingly mysterious and bizarre. What we've decided is that we're going to have to send an Emissary Plenipotentiary to some of the rebel worlds to get the real story."

"A spy, you mean?"

"A spy? No. Not a spy. A teacher. A guide. A prophet, if you will. One who can bring them back to the true path." Guardiano shakes his head. "I have to tell you that all this disturbs me profoundly, this repudiation of Darklaw, these apparent breaches of the plan. It begins to occur to me—though I know the Master would have me strung up for saying any such thing—that we may have been in error from the beginning." He gives me a conspiratorial look. I smile encouragingly. He goes on, "I mean, this whole elitist approach of ours, the Order maintaining its monopoly over the mechanism of matter transmission, the Order deciding who will go to the stars and who will not, the Order attempting to create new worlds in our own image—" He seems to be talking half to himself. "Well, apparently it hasn't worked, has it? Do I dare say it? They're living just as they please, out there. We can't control them at long range. Your own personal tragedy is testimony to that. And yet, and yet—to think that we would be in such a shambles, and that a Lord Magistrate would be compelled to resign, and go into exile—exile, yes, that's what it is!—"

"Please," I say. His ramblings are embarrassing; and painful, too, for there may be seeds of truth in them. "What's over is over. All I want now is to live out my years quietly among the people of the Order on this world. Just tell me how I can be of use. Any work at all, even the simplest—"

"A waste, your grace. An absolute shameful waste."

"Please."

He fills my glass for the fourth or fifth time. A crafty look has come into his eyes. "You would accept any assignment I give you?"

"Yes. Anything."

"Anything?" he says.

I see myself sweeping the chapel house stairs, polishing sinks and tables, working in the garden on my knees.

"Even if there is risk?" he says. "Discomfort?"

"Anything."

He says, "You will be our Plenipotentiary, then."

There are two suns in the sky here, but they are not at all like Cuchulain's two, and the frosty air has a sharp sweet sting to it that is like nothing I have ever tasted before, and everything I see is haloed by a double shadow, a rim of pale red shading into deep, mysterious azure. It is very cold in this place. I am fourteen light-years from Earth.

A woman is watching me from just a few meters away. She says something I am unable to understand.

"Can you speak Anglic?" I reply.

"Anglic. All right." She gives me a chilly, appraising look. "What are you? Some kind of priest?"

"I was Lord Magistrate of the House of Senders, yes."

"Where?"

"Earth."

"On *Earth*? Really?"

I nod. "What is the name of this world?"

"Let me ask the questions," she says. Her speech is odd, not so much a foreign accent as a foreign intonation, a curious singsong, vaguely menacing. Standing face to face just outside the Velde station, we look each other over. She is thick-shouldered, deep-chested, with a flat-featured face, close-cropped yellow hair, green eyes, a dusting of light red freckles across her heavy cheekbones. She wears a heavy blue jacket, fringed brown leggings, blue leather boots, and she is armed. Behind her I see a muddy road cut through a flat snowy field, some low rambling metal buildings with snow piled high on their roofs, and a landscape of distant jagged towering mountains whose sharp black spires are festooned with double-shadowed glaciers. An icy wind rips across the flat land. We are a long way from those two suns, the fierce blue-white one and its cooler crimson companion. Her eyes narrow and she says, "Lord Magistrate, eh? The House of Senders. Really?"

"This was my cloak of office. This medallion signified my rank in the Order."

"I don't see them."

"I'm sorry. I don't understand."

"You have no rank here. You hold no office here."

"Of course," I say. "I realize that. Except such power as Darklaw confers on me."

"Darklaw?"

I stare at her in some dismay. "Am I beyond the reach of Darklaw so soon?"

"It's not a word I hear very often. Shivering, are you? You come from a warmer place?"

"Earth," I say. "South Australia. It's warm there, yes."

"Earth. South Australia." She repeats the words as though they are mere noises to her. "We have some Earthborn here, still. Not many. They'll be glad to see you, I suppose. The name of this world is Zima."

"Zima." A good strong sound. "What does that mean?"

"Mean?"

"The name must mean something. This planet wasn't named Zima just because someone liked the way it sounded."

"Can't you see why?" she asks, gesturing toward the far-off ice-shrouded mountains.

"I don't understand."

"Anglic is the only language you speak?"

"I know some Espanol and some Deutsch."

She shrugs. "Zima is Russkiye. It means Winter."

"And this is wintertime on Winter?"

"It is like this all the year round. And so we call the world Zima."

"Zima," I say. "Yes."

"We speak Russkiye here, mostly, though we know Anglic too. Everybody knows Anglic, everywhere in the Dark. It is necessary. You really speak no Russkiye?"

"Sorry."

"Ty shto, s pizdy sarvalsa?" she says, staring at me.

I shrug and am silent.

"Bros' dumat' zhopay!"

I shake my head sadly.

"Idi v zhopu!"

"No," I say. "Not a word."

She smiles, for the first time. "I believe you."

"What were you saying to me in Russkiye?"

"Very abusive things. I will not tell you what they were. If you understood, you would have become very angry. They were filthy things, mockery. At least you would have laughed, hearing such vile words. I am named Marfa Ivanovna. You must talk with the boyars. If they think you are a spy, they will kill you."

I try to hide my astonishment, but I doubt that I succeed. *Kill?* What sort of world have we built here? Have these Zimans reinvented the middle ages?

"You are frightened?" she asks.

"Surprised," I say."

"You should lie to them, if you are a spy. Tell them you come to bring the Word of God, only. Or something else that is harmless. I like you. I would not want them to kill you."

A spy? No. As Guardiano would say, I am a teacher, a guide, a prophet, if you will. Or as I myself would say, I am a pilgrim, one who seeks atonement, one who seeks forgiveness.

"I'm not a spy, Marfa Ivanovna," I say.

"Good. Good. Tell them that." She puts her fingers in her mouth and whistles piercingly, and three burly bearded men in fur jackets appear as though rising out of the snowbanks. She speaks with them a long while in Russkiye. Then she turns to me. "These are the boyars Ivan Dimitrovich, Pyotr Pyotrovich, and Ivan Pyotrovich. They will conduct you to the voivode Ilya Alexandrovich, who will examine you. You should tell the voivode the truth."

"Yes," I say. "What else is there to tell?"

Guardiano had told me before I left Cuchulain, of course, that the world I was going to had been settled by emigrants from Russia. It was one of the first to be colonized, in the early years of the Mission. One would expect our Earthly ways to begin dropping away, and something like an indigenous culture to have begun evolving, in that much time. But I am startled, all the same, by how far they have drifted. At least Marfa Ivanova—who is, I imagine, a third-generation Ziman—knows what Darklaw is. But is it observed? They have named their world Winter, at any rate, and not New Russia or New Moscow or something like that, which Darklaw would have forbidden. The new worlds in the stars must not carry such Earthly baggage with them. But whether they follow any of the other laws, I cannot say. They have reverted to their ancient language here, but they know Anglic as well, as they should. The robe of the Order means something to her, but not, it would seem, a great deal. She speaks of spies, of killing. Here at the outset of my journey I can see already that there will be many surprises for me as I make my way through the Dark.

The voivode Ilya Alexandrovich is a small, agile-looking man, brown-faced, weatherbeaten, with penetrating blue eyes and a great shock of thick, coarse white hair. He could be any age at all, but from his vigor and seeming reserves of power I guess that he is about forty. In a harsh climate the face is quickly etched with the signs of age, but this man is probably younger than he looks.

Voivode, he tells me, means something like "mayor," or "district chief." His office, brightly lit and stark, is a large ground-floor room in an unassuming two-story aluminum shack that is, I assume, the town hall. There is no place for me to sit. I stand before him, and the three husky boyars, who do not remove their fur jackets, stand behind me, arms folded ominously across their breasts.

I see a desk, a faded wall map, a terminal. The only other thing in the room is the immense bleached skull of some alien beast on the floor beside his desk. It is an astounding sight, two meters long and a meter high, with two huge eye-sockets in the usual places and a third set high between them, and a pair of colossal yellow tusks that rise straight from the lower jaw almost to the ceiling. One tusk is chipped at the tip, perhaps six centimeters broken off. He sees me staring at it. "You ever see anything like that?" he asks, almost belligerently.

"Never. What is it?"

"We call it a bolshoi. Animal of the northern steppe, very big. You see one five kilometers away and you shit your trousers, I tell you for true." He grins. "Maybe we send one back to Earth some day to show them what we have here. Maybe."

His Anglic is much more heavily accented than Marfa Ivanovna's, and far less fluent. He seems unable to hold still very long. The district that he governs, he tells me, is the largest on Zima. It looks immense indeed on his map, a vast blue area, a territory that seems to be about the size of Brazil. But when I take a closer look I see three tiny dots clustered close together in the center of the blue zone. They are, I assume, the only villages. He follows my gaze and strides immediately across the room to tap the map. "This is Tyomni," he says. "That is this village. This one here, it is Doch. This one, Sin. In this territory we have six thousand people altogether. There are two other territories, here and here." He points to regions north and south of the blue zone. A yellow area and a pink one indicate the other settlements, each with two towns. The whole human population of this planet must be no more than ten thousand.

Turning suddenly toward me, he says, "You are big priest in the Order?"

"I was Lord Magistrate, yes. The House of Senders."

"Senders. Ah. I know Senders. The ones who choose the colonists. And who run the machinery, the transmitters."

"That's right."

"And you are the bolshoi Sender? The big man, the boss, the captain?"

"I was, yes. This robe, this medallion, those are signs of my office."

"A very big man. Only instead of sending, you are sent."

"Yes," I say.

"And you come here, why? Nobody from Earth comes here in ten, fifteen years." He no longer makes even an attempt to conceal his suspicions, or his hostility. His cold eyes flare with anger. "Being boss of Senders is not enough for you? You want to tell us how to run Zima? You want to run Zima yourself?"

"Nothing of that sort, believe me."

"Then what?"

"Do you have a map of the entire Dark?"

"The Dark," he says, as though the word is unfamiliar to him. Then he says something in Russkiye to one of the boyars. The man leaves the room and returns, a few moments later, with a wide, flat black screen that turns out to be a small version of the wall screen in the Master's office. He lights it and they all look expectantly at me.

The display is a little different from the one I am accustomed to, since it centers on Zima, not on Earth, but the glowing inner sphere that marks the location of the Mission stars is easy enough to find. I point to that sphere and I remind them, apologizing for telling them what they already know, that the great plan of the Mission calls for an orderly expansion through space from Earth in a carefully delimited zone a hundred light-years in diameter. Only when that sphere has been settled are we to go farther, not because there are any technical difficulties in sending our carrier ships a thousand light-years out, or ten thousand, but because the Master has felt from the start that we must assimilate our first immense wave of outward movement, must pause and come to an understanding of what it is like to have created a galactic empire on so vast a scale, before we attempt to go onward into the infinity that awaits us. Otherwise, I say, we risk falling victim to a megalomaniacal centrifugal dizziness from which we may never recover. And so Darklaw forbids journeys beyond the boundary.

They watch me stonily throughout my recital of these overfamiliar concepts, saying nothing.

I go on to tell them that Earth now is receiving indications that voyages far beyond the hundred-light-year limit have taken place.

Their faces are expressionless.

"What is that to us?" the voivode asks.

"One of the deviant tracks begins here," I say.

"Our Anglic is very poor. Perhaps you can say that another way."

"When the first ship brought the Velde receiver to Zima, it built replicas of itself and of the receiver, and sent them onward to other stars farther from Earth. We've traced the various trajectories that lead beyond the Mission boundaries, and one of them comes out of a world that received its Velde equipment from a world that got its equipment from here. A granddaughter world, so to speak."

"This has nothing to do with us, nothing at all," the voivode says coolly.

"Zima is only my starting point," I say. "It may be that you are in contact with these outer worlds, that I can get some clue from you about who is making these voyages, and why, and where he's setting out from."

"We have no knowledge of any of this."

I point out, trying not to do it in any overbearing way, that by the authority of Darklaw vested in me as a Plenipotentiary of the Order he is required to assist me in my inquiry. But there is no way to brandish the authority of Darklaw that is not overbearing, and I see the voivode stiffen at once, I see his face grow black, I see very clearly that he regards himself as autonomous and his world as independent of Earth.

That comes as no surprise to me. We were not so naive, so innocent of historical precedent, as to think we could maintain control over the colonies. What we wanted was quite the opposite, new Earths free of our grasp—cut off, indeed, by an inflexible law forbidding all contact between mother world and colony once the colony has been established—and free, likewise, of the compulsion to replicate the tragic mistakes that the old Earth had made. But because we had felt the hand of God guiding us in every way as we led mankind forth into the Dark, we believed that God's law as we understood it would never be repudiated by those whom we had given the stars. Now, seeing evidence that His law is subordinate out here to the will of wilful men, I fear for the structure that we have devoted our lives to building.

"If this is why you really have come," the voivode says, "then you have wasted your time. But perhaps I misunderstand everything you say. My Anglic is not good. We must talk again." He gestures to the boyars and says something in Russkiye that is unmistakably a dismissal. They take me away and give me a room in some sort of dreary lodging-house overlooking the plaza at the center of town. When they leave, they lock the door behind them. I am a prisoner.

It is a harsh land. In the first few days of my internment there is a snowstorm every afternoon. First the sky turns metal-gray, and then black. Then hard little pellets of snow, driven by the rising wind, strike the window. Then it comes down in heavy fluffy flakes for several hours. Afterwards machines scuttle out and clear the pathways. I have never before been in a place where they have snow. It seems quite beautiful to me, a kind of benediction, a cleansing cover.

This is a very small town, and there is wilderness all around it. On the second day and again on the third, packs of wild beasts go racing through the central plaza. They look something like huge dogs, but they have very long legs, almost like those of horses, and their tails are tipped with three pairs of ugly-looking spikes. They move through the town like a whirlwind, prowling in the trash, butting their heads against the closed doors, and everyone gets quickly out of their way.

Later on the third day there is an execution in the plaza, practically below my window. A jowly, heavily bearded man clad in furs is led forth, strapped to a post, and shot by five men in uniforms. For all I can tell, he is one of the three boyars who took me to the voivode on my first day. I have never seen anyone killed before, and the whole event has such a strange, dreamlike quality for me that the shock and horror and revulsion do not strike me until perhaps half an hour later.

It is hard for me to say which I find the most alien, the snowstorms, the packs of fierce beasts running through the town, or the execution.

My food is shoved through a slot in the door. It is rough, simple stuff, stews and soups and a kind of gritty bread. That is all right. Not until the fourth day does anyone come to see me. My first visitor is Marfa Ivanovna, who says, "They think you're a spy. I told you to tell them the truth."

"I did."

"Are you a spy?"

"You know that I'm not."

"Yes," she says. "I know. But the voivode is troubled. He thinks you mean to overthrow him."

"All I want is for him to give me some information. Then I'll be gone from here and won't ever return."

"He is a very suspicious man."

"Let him come here and pray with me, and see what my nature is like. All I am is a servant of God. Which I hope is true of the voivode as well."

"He is thinking of having you shot," Marfa Ivanovna says.

"Let him come to me and pray with me," I tell her.

※

The voivode comes to me, not once but three times. We do no pray-ing—in truth, any mention of God, or Darklaw, or even the Mission, seems to make him uncomfortable—but gradually we begin to under-stand each other. We are not that different. He is a hard, dedicated, cautious man governing a harsh troublesome land. I have been called hard and dedicated and cautious myself. My nature is not as suspicious as his, but I have not had to contend with snowstorms and wild beasts and the other hazards of this place. Nor am I Russian. They seem to be suspicious from birth, these Russians. And they have lived apart from Earth a long while. That too is Darklaw: we would not have the new worlds contaminated with our plagues of the spirit or of the flesh, nor do we want alien plagues of either kind carried back from them to us. We have enough of our own already.

I am not going to be shot. He makes that clear. "We talked of it, yes. But it would be wrong."

"The man who was? What did he do?"

"He took that which was not his," says the voivode, and shrugs. "He was worse than a beast. He could not be allowed to live among us."

Nothing is said of when I will be released. I am left alone for two more days. The coarse dull food begins to oppress me, and the solitude. There is another snowstorm, worse than the last. From my window I see ungainly birds something like vultures, with long naked yellow necks and drooping reptilian tails, circling in the sky. Finally the voivode comes a second time, and simply stares at me as though expecting me to blurt out some confession. I look at him in puzzlement, and after long silence he laughs explosively and summons an aide, who brings in a bottle of a clear fiery liquor. Two or three quick gulps and he becomes expansive, and tells me of his childhood. His father was voivode before him, long ago, and was killed by a wild animal while out hunting. I try to imagine a world that still has dangerous animals roaming freely. To me it is like a world where the gods of primitive man are real and alive, and go disguised among mortals, striking out at them randomly and without warning.

Then he asks me about myself, wanting to know how old I was when I became a priest of the Order, and whether I was as religious as a boy as I am now. I tell him what I can, within the limits placed on me by my vows. Perhaps I go a little beyond the limits, even. I explain about my early interest in technical matters, my entering the Order at seventeen, my life of service.

The part about my religious vocation seems odd to him. He appears to think I must have undergone some sudden conversion midway through my adolescence. "There has never been a time when God has not been present at my side," I say.

"How very lucky you are," he says.

"Lucky?"

He touches his glass to mine.

"Your health," he says. We drink. Then he says, "What does your Order really want with us, anyway?"

"With you? We want nothing with you. Three generations ago we gave you your world; everything after that is up to you."

"No. You want to dictate how we shall live. You are people of the past, and we are people of the future, and you are unable to understand our souls."

"Not so," I tell him. "Why do you think we want to dictate to you? Have we interfered with you up till now?"

"You are here now, though."

"Not to interfere. Only to gain information."

"Ah. Is this so?" He laughs and drinks. "Your health," he says again.

He comes a third time a couple of days later. I am restless and irritable when he enters; I have had enough of this imprisonment, these groundless suspicions, this bleak and frosty world; I am ready to be on my way. It is all I can do to keep from bluntly demanding my freedom. As it is I am uncharacteristically sharp and surly with him, answering in quick snarling monosyllables when he asks me how I have slept, whether I am well, is my room warm enough. He gives me a look of surprise, and then one of thoughtful appraisal, and then he smiles. He is in complete control, and we both know it.

"Tell me once more," he says, "why you have come to us."

I calm myself and run through the whole thing one more time. He nods. Now that he knows me better, he tells me, he begins to think that I may be sincere, that I have not come to spy, that I actually would be willing to chase across the galaxy this way in pursuit of an ideal. And so on in that vein for a time, both patronizing and genuinely friendly almost in the same breath.

Then he says, "We have decided that it is best to send you onward."

"Where?"

"The name of the world is Entrada. It is one of our daughter worlds, eleven light-years away, a very hot place. We trade our precious metals for their spices. Someone came from there not long ago and told us of a strange man named Oesterreich, who passed through Entrada and spoke of undertaking journeys to new and distant places. Perhaps he can provide you with the answers that you seek. If you can find him."

"Oesterreich?"

"That is the name, yes."

Can you tell me any more about him than that?"

"What I have told you is all that I know."

He stares at me truculently, as if defying me to show that he is lying. But I believe him.

"Even for that much assistance, I am grateful," I say.

"Yes. Never let it be said that we have failed to offer aid to the Order." He smiles again. "But if you ever come to this world again, you understand, we will know that you were a spy after all. And we will treat you accordingly."

Marfa Ivanovna is in charge of the Velde equipment. She positions me within the transmitting doorway, moving me about this way and that to be certain that I will be squarely within the field. When she is satisfied, she says, "You know, you ought not ever come back this way."

"I understand that."

"You must be a very virtuous man. Ilya Alexandrovitch came very close to putting you to death, and then he changed his mind. This I know for certain. But he remains suspicious of you. He is suspicious of everything the Order does."

"The Order has never done anything to injure him or anyone else on this planet, and never will."

"That may be so," says Marfa Ivanovna. "But still, you are lucky to be leaving here alive. You should not come back. And you should tell others of your sort to stay away from Zima too. We do not accept the Order here."

I am still pondering the implications of that astonishing statement when she does something even more astonishing. Stepping into the cubicle with me, she suddenly opens her fur-trimmed jacket, revealing full round breasts, very pale, dusted with the same light red freckles that she has on her face. She seizes me by the hair and presses my head against her breasts, and holds it there a long moment. Her skin is very warm. It seems almost feverish.

"For luck," she says, and steps back. Her eyes are sad and strange. It could almost be a loving look, or perhaps a pitying one, or both. Then she turns away from me and throws the switch.

✹

Entrada is torrid and moist, a humid sweltering hothouse of a place so much the antithesis of Zima that my body rebels immediately against the shift from one world to the other. Coming forth into it, I feel the heat rolling toward me like an implacable wall of water. It sweeps up and over me and smashes me to my knees. I am sick and numb with displacement and dislocation. It seems impossible for me to draw a breath. The thick, shimmering, golden-green atmosphere here is almost liquid; it crams itself into my throat, it squeezes my lungs in an agonizing grip. Through blurring eyes I see a tight green web of jungle foliage rising before me, a jumbled vista of corrugated-tin shacks, a patch of sky the color of shallow sea-water, and, high above, a merciless, throbbing, weirdly elongated sun shaped like no sun I have ever imagined. Then I sway and fall forward and see nothing more.

I lie suspended in delirium a long while. It is a pleasing restful time, like being in the womb. I am becalmed in a great stillness, lulled by soft voices and sweet music. But gradually consciousness begins to break through. I swim upward toward the light that glows somewhere above me, and my eyes open, and I see a serene friendly face, and a voice says, "It's nothing to worry about. Everyone who comes here the way you did has a touch of it, the first time. At your age I suppose it's worse than usual."

Dazedly I realize that I am in mid-conversation.

"A touch of what?" I ask.

The other, who is a slender gray-eyed woman of middle years wearing a sort of Indian sari, smiles and says, "Of the Falling. It's a lambda effect. But I'm sorry. We've been talking for a while, and I thought you were awake. Evidently you weren't."

"I am now," I tell her. "But I don't think I've been for very long."

Nodding, she says, "Let's start over. You're in Traveler's Hospice. The humidity got you, and the heat, and the lightness of the gravity. You're all right now."

"Yes."

"Do you think you can stand?"

"I can try," I say.

She helps me up. I feel so giddy that I expect to float away. Carefully she guides me toward the window of my room. Outside I see a veranda and a close-cropped lawn. Just beyond, a dark curtain of dense bush closes everything off. The intense light makes everything seem very near; it is as if I could put my hand out the window and thrust it into the heart of that exuberant jungle.

"So bright—the sun—" I whisper.

In fact there are two whitish suns in the sky, so close to each other that their photospheres overlap and each is distended by the other's gravitational pull, making them nearly oval in shape. Together they seem to form a single egg-shaped mass, though even the one quick dazzled glance I can allow myself tells me that this is really a binary system, discrete bundles of energy forever locked together.

Awed and amazed, I touch my fingertips to my cheek in wonder, and feel a thick coarse beard there that I had not had before.

The woman says, "Two suns, actually. Their centers are only about a million and a half kilometers apart, and they revolve around each other every seven and a half hours. We're the fourth planet out, but we're as far from them as Neptune is from the Sun."

But I have lost interest for the moment in astronomical matters. I rub my face, exploring its strange new shagginess. The beard covers my cheeks, my jaws, much of my throat.

"How long have I been unconscious?" I ask.

"About three weeks."

"Your weeks or Earth weeks?"

"We use Earth weeks here."

"And that was just a light case? Does everybody who gets the Falling spend three weeks being delirious?"

"Sometimes much more. Sometimes they never come out of it."

I stare at her. "And it's just the heat, the humidity, the lightness of the gravity? They can knock you down the moment you step out of the transmitter and put you under for weeks? I would think it should take something like a stroke to do that."

"It *is* something like a stroke," she says. "Did you think that traveling between stars is like stepping across the street? You come from a low-lambda world to a high-lambda one without doing your adaptation drills and of course the change is going to knock you flat right away. What did you expect?"

High-lambda? Low-lambda?

"I don't know what you're talking about," I say.

"Didn't they tell you on Zima about the adaptation drills before they shipped you here?"

"Not a thing."

"Or about lambda differentials?"

"Nothing," I say.

Her face grows very solemn. "Pigs, that's all they are. They should have prepared you for the jump. But I guess they didn't care whether you lived or died."

I think of Marfa Ivanovna, wishing me luck as she reached for the switch. I think of that strange sad look in her eyes. I think of the voivode Ilya Alexandrovitch, who might have had me shot but decided instead to offer me a free trip off his world, a one-way trip. There is much that I am only now beginning to understand, I see, about this empire that Earth is building in what we call the Dark. We are building it in the dark, yes, in more ways than one.

"No," I say. "I guess they didn't care."

They are friendlier on Entrada, no question of that. Interstellar trade is important here and visitors from other worlds are far more common than they are on wintry Zima. Apparently I am free to live at the hospice as long as I wish. The weeks of my stay have stretched now into months, and no one suggests that it is time for me to be moving along.

I had not expected to stay here so long. But gathering the information I need has been a slow business, with many a maddening detour and delay.

At least I experience no further lambda problems. Lambda, they tell me, is a planetary force that became known only when Velde jumps between solar systems began. There are high-lambda worlds and low-lambda worlds, and anyone going from one kind to the other without proper preparation is apt to undergo severe stress. It is all news to me. I wonder if the Order on Earth is aware at all of these difficulties. But perhaps they feel that matters which may arise during journeys *between* worlds of the Dark are of no concern to us of the mother world.

They have taken me through the adaptation drills here at the hospice somehow while I was still unconscious, and I am more or less capable now of handling Entradan conditions. The perpetual steambath heat, which no amount of air conditioning seems really to mitigate, is hard to cope with, and the odd combination of heavy atmosphere and light gravity puts me at risk of nausea with every breath, though after a time I get the knack of pulling shallow nips of air. There are allergens borne on every breeze, too, pollen of a thousand kinds and some free-floating alkaloids, against which I need daily medication. My face turns red under the force of the double sun, and the skin of my cheeks gets strangely soft, which makes my new beard an annoyance. I rid myself of it. My hair acquires an unfamiliar silver sheen, not displeasing, but unexpected. All this considered, though, I can manage here.

Entrada has a dozen major settlements and several hundred thousand people. It is a big world, metal-poor and light, on which a dozen small continents and some intricate archipelagoes float in huge warm seas. The whole planet is tropical, even at the poles: distant though it is from its suns, it would probably be inhospitable to human life if it were very much closer. The soil of Entrada has the lunatic fertility that we associate with the tropics, and agriculture is the prime occupation here. The people, drawn from many regions of Earth, are attractive and outgoing, with an appealingly easy manner.

It appears that they have not drifted as far from Darklaw here as the Zimans have.

Certainly the Order is respected. There are chapels everywhere and the people use them. Whenever I enter one there is a little stir of excitement, for it is generally known that I was Lord Magistrate of the Senders during my time on Earth, and that makes me a celebrity, or a curiosity, or both. Many of the Entradans are Earthborn themselves—emigration to this world was still going on as recently as eight or ten years ago—and the sight of my medallion inspires respect and even awe in them. I do not wear my robe of office, not in this heat. Probably I will never wear it again, no matter what climate I find myself in when I leave here. Someone else is Lord Magistrate of the House of Senders now, after all. But the medallion alone is enough to win me a distinction here that I surely never had on Zima.

I think, though, that they pick and choose among the tenets of Darklaw to their own satisfaction on Entrada, obeying those which suit them and casting aside anything that seems too constricting. I am not sure of this, but it seems likely. To discuss such matters with anyone I have come to know here is, of course, impossible. The people I have managed to get to know so far, at the hospice, at the chapel house in town, at the tavern where I have begun to take my meals, are pleasant and sociable. But they become uneasy, even evasive, whenever I speak of any aspect of Earth's migration into space. Let me mention the Order, or the Master, or anything at all concerning the Mission, and they begin to moisten their lips and look uncomfortable. Clearly things are happening out here, things never envisioned by the founders of the Order, and they are unwilling to talk about them with anyone who himself wears the high medallion.

It is a measure of the changes that have come over me since I began this journey that I am neither surprised nor dismayed by this.

Why should we have believed that we could prescribe a single code of law that would meet the needs of hundreds of widely varying worlds? Of course they would modify our teachings to fit their own evolving cultures, and some would probably depart entirely from that which we had created for them. It was only to be expected. Many things have become clear to me on this journey that I did not see before, that, indeed, I did not so much as pause to consider. But much else remains mysterious.

I am at the busy waterfront esplanade, leaning over the rail, staring out toward Volcano Isle, a dim gray peak far out to sea. It is midmorning, before the full heat of noon has descended. I have been here long enough so that I think of this as the cool time of the day.

"Your grace?" a voice calls. "Lord Magistrate?"

No one calls me those things here.

I glance down to my left. A dark-haired man in worn seaman's clothes and a braided captain's hat is looking up at me out of a rowboat just below the sea-wall. He is smiling and waving. I have no idea who he is, but he plainly wants to talk with me, and anything that helps me break the barrier that stands between me and real knowledge of this place is to be encouraged.

He points to the far end of the harbor, where there is a ramp leading from the little beach to the esplanade, and tells me in pantomime that he means to tie up his boat and go ashore. I wait for him at the head of the ramp, and after a few moments he comes trudging up to greet me. He is perhaps fifty years old, trim and sun-bronzed, with a lean weatherbeaten face.

"You don't remember me," he says.

"I'm afraid not."

"You personally interviewed me and approved my application to emigrate, eighteen years ago. Sandys. Lloyd Sandys." He smiles hopefully, as though his name alone will open the floodgates of my memory.

When I was Lord Magistrate I reviewed five hundred emigrant dossiers a week, and interviewed ten or fifteen applicants a day myself, and forgot each one the moment I approved or rejected them. But for this man the interview with the Lord Magistrate of the Senders was the most significant moment of his life.

"Sorry," I say. "So many names, so many faces—"

"I would have recognized you even if I hadn't already heard you were here. After all these years, you've hardly changed at all, your grace." He grins. "So now you've come to settle on Entrada yourself?"

"Only a short visit."

"Ah." He is visibly disappointed. "You ought to think of staying. It's a wonderful place, if you don't mind a little heat. I haven't regretted coming here for a minute."

He takes me to a seaside tavern where he is obviously well known, and orders lunch for both of us: skewers of small corkscrew-shaped creatures that look and taste a little like squid, and a flask of a strange but likable emerald-colored wine with a heavy, musky, spicy flavor. He tells me that he has four sturdy sons and four strapping daughters, and that he and his wife run a harbor ferry, short hops to the surrounding islands of this archipelago, which is Entrada's main population center. There still are traces of Melbourne in his accent. He seems very happy. "You'll let me take you on a tour, won't you?" he asks. "We've got some very beautiful islands out there, and you can't get to see them by Velde jumps."

I protest that I don't want to take him away from his work, but he shrugs that off. Work can always wait, he says. There's no hurry, on a world where anyone can dip his net in the sea and come up with a good meal. We have another flask of wine. He seems open, genial, trustworthy. Over cheese and fruit he asks me why I've come here.

I hesitate.

"A fact-finding mission," I say.

"Ah. Is that really so? Can I be of any help, d'ye think?"

✹

It is several more winy lunches, and a little boat-trip to some nearby islands fragrant with masses of intoxicating purple blooms, before I am willing to begin taking Sandys into my confidence. I tell him that the Order has sent me into the Dark to study and report on the ways of life that are evolving on the new worlds. He seems untroubled by that, though Ilya Alexandrovitch might have had me shot for such an admission.

Later, I tell him about the apparent deviations from the planned scope of the Mission that are the immediate reason for my journey.

"You mean, going out beyond the hundred-light-year zone?"

"Yes."

"That's pretty amazing, that anyone would go there."

"We have indications that it's happening."

"Really," he says.

"And on Zima," I continue, "I picked up a story that somebody here on Entrada has been preaching ventures into the far Dark. You don't know anything about that, do you?"

His only overt reaction is a light frown, quickly erased. Perhaps he has nothing to tell me. Or else we have reached the point, perhaps, beyond which he is unwilling to speak.

But some hours later he revives the topic himself. We are on our way back to harbor, sunburned and a little tipsy from an outing to one of the prettiest of the local islands, when he suddenly says, "I remember hearing something about that preacher you mentioned before."

I wait, not saying anything.

"My wife told me about him. There was somebody going around talking about far voyages, she said." New color comes to his face, a deep red beneath the bronze. "I must have forgotten about it when we were talking before." In fact he must know that I think him disingenuous for withholding this from me all afternoon. But I make no attempt to call him on that. We are still testing each other.

I ask him if he can get more information for me, and he promises to discuss it with his wife. Then he is absent for a week, making a circuit of the outer rim of the archipelago to deliver freight. When he returns, finally, he brings with him an unusual golden brandy from one of the remote islands as a gift for me, but my cautious attempt to revive our earlier conversation runs into a familiar sort of Entradan evasiveness. It is almost as though he doesn't know what I'm referring to.

At length I say bluntly, "Have you had a chance to talk to your wife about that preacher?"

He looks troubled. "In fact, it slipped my mind."

"Ah."

"Tonight, maybe—"

"I understand that the man's name is Oesterreich," I say.

His eyes go wide.

"You know that, do you?"

"Help me, will you, Sandys? I'm the one who sent you to this place, remember? Your whole life here wouldn't exist but for me."

"That's true. That's very true."

"Who's Oesterreich?"

"I never knew him. I never had any dealings with him."

"Tell me what you know about him."

"A crazy man, he was."

"Was?"

"He's not here any more."

I uncork the bottle of rare brandy, pour a little for myself, a more generous shot for Sandys.

"Where'd he go?" I ask.

He sips, reflectively. After a time he says, "I don't know, your grace. That's God's own truth. I haven't seen or heard of him in a couple of years. He chartered one of the other captains here, a man named Feraud, to take him to one of the islands, and that's the last I know."

"Which island?"

"I don't know."

"Do you think Feraud remembers?"

"I could ask him," Sandys says.

"Yes. Ask him. Would you do that?"

"I could ask him, yes," he says.

So it goes, slowly. Sandys confers with his friend Feraud, who hesitates and evades, or so Sandys tells me; but eventually Feraud finds it in him to recall that he had taken Oesterreich to Volcano Isle, three hours' journey to the west. Sandys admits to me, now that he is too deep in to hold back, that he himself actually heard Oesterreich speak several times, that Oesterreich claimed to be in possession of some secret way of reaching worlds immensely remote from the settled part of the Dark.

"And do you believe that?"

"I don't know. He seemed crazy to me."

"Crazy how?"

"The look in his eye. The things he said. That it's our destiny to reach the rim of the universe. That the Order holds us back out of its own timidity. That we must follow the Goddess Avatar, who beckons us onward to—"

"*Who?*"

His face flushes bright crimson. "The Goddess Avatar. I don't know what she is, your grace. Honestly. It's some cult he's running, some new religion he's made up. I told you he's crazy. I've never believed any of this."

There is a pounding in my temples, and a fierce ache behind my eyes. My throat has gone dry and not even Sandys' brandy can soothe it.

"Where do you think Oesterreich is now?"

"I don't know." His eyes are tormented. "Honestly. Honestly. I think he's gone from Entrada."

"Is there a Velde transmitter station on Volcano Isle?"

He thinks for a moment. "Yes. Yes, there is."

"Will you do me one more favor?" I ask. "One thing, and then I won't ask any more."

"Yes?"

"Take a ride over to Volcano Isle tomorrow. Talk with the people who run the Velde station there. See if you can find out where they sent Oesterreich."

"They'll never tell me anything like that."

I put five shining coins in front of him, each one worth as much as he can make in a month's ferrying.

"Use these," I say. "If you come back with the answer, there are five more for you."

"Come with me, your grace. You speak to them."

"No."

"You ought to see Volcano Isle. It's a fantastic place. The center of it blew out thousands of years ago, and people live up on the rim, around a lagoon so deep nobody's been able to find the bottom. I was meaning to take you there anyway, and—"

"You go," I say. "Just you."

After a moment he pockets the coins. In the morning I watch him go off in one of his boats, a small hydrofoil skiff. There is no word from him for two days, and then he comes to me at the hospice, looking tense and unshaven.

"It wasn't easy," he says.

"You found out where he went?"

"Yes."

"Go on," I urge, but he is silent, lips working but nothing coming out. I produce five more of the coins and lay them before him. He ignores them. This is some interior struggle.

He says, after a time, "We aren't supposed to reveal anything about anything of this. I told you what I've already told you because I owe you. You understand that?"

"Yes."

"You mustn't ever let anyone know who gave you the information."

"Don't worry," I say.

He studies me for a time. Then he says, "The name of the planet where Oesterreich went is Eden. It's a seventeen-light-year hop. You won't need lambda adjustment, coming from here. There's hardly any differential. All right, your grace? That's all I can tell you." He stares at the coins and shakes his head. Then he runs out of the room, leaving them behind.

Eden turns out to be no Eden at all. I see a spongy, marshy landscape, a gray sodden sky, a raw, half-built town. There seem to be two suns, a faint yellow-white one and a larger reddish one. A closer look reveals that the system here is like the Lalande one: the reddish one is not really a star but a glowing substellar mass about the size of Jupiter. Eden is one of its moons. What we like to speak of in the Order as the new Earths of the Dark are in fact scarcely Earthlike at all, I am coming to realize: all they have in common with the mother world is a tolerably breathable atmosphere and a manageable gravitational pull. How can we speak of a world as an Earth when its sun is not yellow but white or red or green, or there are two or three or even four suns in the sky all day and all night, or the primary source of warmth is not even a sun but a giant planet-like ball of hot gas?

"Settler?" they ask me, when I arrive on Eden.

"Traveler," I reply. "Short-term visit."

They scarcely seem to care. This is a difficult world and they have no time for bureaucratic formalities. So long as I have money, and I do—at least these strange daughter worlds of ours still honor our currency—I am, if not exactly welcome, then at least permitted.

Do they observe Darklaw here? When I arrive I am wearing neither my robe of office nor my medallion, and it seems just as well. The Order appears not to be in favor, this far out. I can find no sign of our chapels or other indications of submission to our rule. What I do find, as I wander the rough streets of this jerry-rigged town on this cool, rainswept world, is a chapel of some other kind, a white geodesic dome with a mysterious symbol—three superimposed six-pointed stars—painted in black on its door.

"Goddess save you," a woman coming out says brusquely to me, and shoulders past me in the rain.

They are not even bothering to hide things, this far out on the frontier.

I go inside. The walls are white and an odd, disturbing mural is painted on one of them. It shows what seems to be a windowless ruined temple drifting in blue starry space, with all manner of objects and creatures floating near it, owls, skulls, snakes, masks, golden cups, bodiless heads. It is like a scene viewed in a dream. The temple's alabaster walls are covered with hieroglyphics. A passageway leads inward and inward and inward, and at its end I can see a tiny view of an eerie landscape like a plateau at the end of time.

There are half a dozen people in the room, each facing in a different direction, reading aloud in low murmurs. A slender dark-skinned man looks up at me and says, "Goddess save you, father. How does your journey go?"

"I'm trying to find Oesterreich. They said he's here."

A couple of the other readers look up. A woman with straw-colored hair says, "He's gone Goddessward."

"I'm sorry. I don't under—"

Another woman, whose features are tiny and delicately modeled in the center of a face vast as the map of Russia, breaks in to tell me, "He was going to stop off on Phosphor first. You may be able to catch up with him there. Goddess save you, father."

I stare at her, at the mural of the stone temple, at the other woman. "Thank you," I say. "Goddess save you," my voice adds.

I buy passage to Phosphor. It is sixty-seven light-years from Earth. The necessary lambda adjustment costs nearly as much as the transit fee itself, and I must spend three days going through the adaptation process before I can leave.

Then, Goddess save me, I am ready to set out from Eden for whatever greater strangeness awaits me beyond.

As I wait for the Simtow reaction to annihilate me and reconstruct me in some unknown place, I think of all those who passed through my House over the years as I selected the outbound colonists—and how I and the Lord Magistrates before me had clung to the fantasy that we were shaping perfect new Earths out there in the Dark, that we were composing exquisite symphonies of human nature, filtering out all of the discordances that had marred all our history up till now. Without ever going to the new worlds ourselves to view the results of our work, of course, because to go would mean to cut ourselves off forever, by Darklaw's own constricting terms, from our House, from our task, from Earth itself. And now, catapulted into the Dark in a moment's convulsive turn, by shame and guilt and the need to try to repair that which I had evidently made breakable instead of imperishable, I am learning that I have been wrong all along, that the symphonies of human nature that I had composed were built out of the same old tunes, that people will do what they will do unconstrained by abstract regulations laid down for them *a priori* by others far away. The tight filter of which the House of Senders is so proud is no filter at all. We send our finest ones to the stars and they turn their backs on us at once. And, pondering these things, it seems to me that my soul is pounding at the gates of my mind, that madness is pressing close against the walls of my spirit—a thing which I have always dreaded, the thing which brought me to the cloisters of the Order in the first place.

Black light flashes in my eyes and once more I go leaping through the Dark.

"He isn't here," they tell me on Phosphor. There is a huge cool red sun here, and a hot blue one a couple of hundred solar units away, close enough to blaze like a brilliant beacon in the day sky. "He's gone on to Entropy. Goddess save you."

"Goddess save you," I say.

There are triple-triangle signs on every doorfront in Phosphor's single city. The city's name is Jerusalem. To name cities or worlds for places on Earth is forbidden. But I know that I have left Darklaw far behind here.

Entropy, they say, is ninety-one light-years from Earth. I am approaching the limits of the sphere of settlement.

Oesterreich has a soft, insinuating voice. He says, "You should come with me. I really would like to take a Lord Magistrate along when I go to her."

"I'm no longer a Lord Magistrate."

"You can't ever stop being a Lord Magistrate. Do you think you can take the Order off just by putting your medallion in your suitcase?"

"Who is she, this Goddess Avatar everybody talks about?"

Oesterreich laughs. "Come with me and you'll find out."

He is a small man, very lean, with broad, looming shoulders that make him appear much taller than he is when he is sitting down. Maybe he is forty years old, maybe much older. His face is paper-white, with perpetual bluish stubble, and his eyes have a black troublesome gleam that strikes me as a mark either of extraordinary intelligence or of pervasive insanity, or perhaps both at once. It was not difficult at all for me to find him, only hours after my arrival on Entropy. The planet has a single village, a thousand settlers. The air is mild here, the sun yellow-green. Three huge moons hang just overhead in the daytime sky, as though dangling on a clothesline.

I say, "Is she real, this goddess of yours?"

"Oh, she's real, all right. As real as you or me."

"Someone we can walk up to and speak with?"

"Her name used to be Margaret Benevente. She was born in Geneva. She emigrated to a world called Three Suns about thirty years ago."

"And now she's a goddess."

"No. I never said that."

"What is she, then?"

"She's the Goddess Avatar."

"Which means what?"

He smiles. "Which means she's a holy woman in whom certain fundamental principles of the universe have been incarnated. You want to know any more than that, you come with me, eh? Your grace."

"And where is she?"

"She's on an uninhabited planet about five thousand light-years from here right now."

I am dealing with a lunatic, I tell myself. That gleam is the gleam of madness, yes.

"You don't believe that, do you?" he asks.

"How can it be possible?"

"Come with me and you'll find out."

"Five thousand light-years—" I shake my head. "No. No."

He shrugs. "So don't go, then."

There is a terrible silence in the little room. I feel impaled on it. Thunder crashes outside, finally, breaking the tension. Lightning has been playing across the sky constantly since my arrival, but there has been no rain.

"Faster-than-light travel is impossible," I say inanely. "Except by way of Velde transmission. You know that. If we've got Velde equipment five thousand light-years from here, we would have had to start shipping it out around the time the Pyramids were being built in Egypt."

"What makes you think we get there with Velde equipment?" Oesterreich asks me.

He will not explain. Follow me and you'll see, he tells me. Follow me and you'll see.

The curious thing is that I like him. He is not exactly a likable man—too intense, too tightly wound, the fanaticism carried much too close to the surface—but he has a sort of charm all the same. He travels from world to world, he tells me, bringing the new gospel of the Goddess Avatar. That is exactly how he says it, "the new gospel of the Goddess Avatar," and I feel a chill when I hear the phrase. It seems absurd and frightening both at once. Yet I suppose those who brought the Order to the world a hundred fifty years ago must have seemed just as strange and just as preposterous to those who first heard our words.

Of course, we had the Velde equipment to support our philosophies.

But these people have—what? The strength of insanity? The clear cool purposefulness that comes from having put reality completely behind them?

"You were in the Order once, weren't you?" I ask him.

"You know it, your grace."

"Which House?"

"The Mission," he says.

"I should have guessed that. And now you have a new mission, is that it?"

"An extension of the old one. Mohammed, you know, didn't see Islam as a contradiction of Judaism and Christianity. Just as the next level of revelation, incorporating the previous ones."

"So you would incorporate the Order into your new belief?"

"We would never repudiate the Order, your grace."

"And Darklaw? How widely is that observed, would you say, in the colony worlds?"

"I think we've kept much of it," Oesterreich says. "Certainly we keep the part about not trying to return to Earth. And the part about spreading the Mission outward."

"Beyond the boundaries decreed, it would seem."

"This is a new dispensation," he says.

"But not a repudiation of the original teachings?"

"Oh, no," he says, and smiles. "Not a repudiation at all, your grace."

He has that passionate confidence, that unshakable assurance, that is the mark of the real prophet and also of the true madman. There is something diabolical about him, and irresistible. In these conversations with him I have so far managed to remain outwardly calm, even genial, but the fact is that I am quaking within. I really do believe he is insane. Either that or an utter fraud, a cynical salesman of the irrational and the unreal, and though he is flippant he does not seem at all cynical. A madman, then. Is his condition infectious? As I have said, the fear of madness has been with me all my life; and so my harsh discipline, my fierce commitment, my depth of belief. He threatens all my defenses.

"When do you set out to visit your Goddess Avatar?" I ask.

"Whenever you like, your grace."

"You really think I'm going with you?"

"Of course you are. How else can you find out what you came out here to learn?"

"I've learned that the colonies have fallen away from Darklaw. Isn't that enough?"

"But you think we've all gone crazy, right?"

"When did I say that?"

"You didn't need to say it."

"If I send word to Earth of what's happened, and the Order chooses to cut off all further technical assistance and all shipments of manufactured goods—?"

"They won't do that. But even if they do—well, we're pretty much self-sufficient out here now, and getting more so every year—"

"And further emigration from Earth?"

"That would be your loss, not ours, your grace. Earth needs the colonies as a safety valve for her population surplus. We can get along without more emigrants. We know how to reproduce, out here." He grins at me. "This is foolish talk. You've come this far. Now go the rest of the way with me."

I am silent.

"Well?"

"Now, you mean?"

"Right now."

There is only one Velde station on Entropy, about three hundred meters from the house where I have been talking with Oesterreich. We go to it under a sky berserk with green lightning. He seems not even to notice.

"Don't we have to do lambda drills?" I ask.

"Not for this hop," Oesterreich says. "There's no differential between here and there." He is busy setting up coordinates.

"Get into the chamber, your grace."

"And have you send me God knows where by myself?"

"Don't be foolish. Please."

It may be the craziest thing I have ever done. But I am the servant of the Order; and the Order has asked this of me. I step into the chamber.

No one else is with us. He continues to press keys, and I realize that he is setting up an automatic transfer, requiring no external operator. When he is done with that he joins me, and there is the moment of flash.

We emerge into a cool, dry world with an Earthlike sun, a sea-green sky, a barren, rocky landscape. Ahead of us stretches an empty plateau broken here and there by small granite hillocks that rise like humped islands out of the flatness.

"Where are we?" I ask.

"Fifty light-years from Entropy, and about eighty-five light-years from Earth."

"What's the name of this place?"

"It doesn't have one. Nobody lives here. Come, now we walk a little."

We start forward. The ground has the look that comes of not having felt rain for ten or twenty years, but tough little tussocks of a grayish jagged-looking grass are pushing up somehow through the hard, stony red soil. When we have gone a hundred meters or so the land begins to drop away sharply on my left, so that I can look down into a broad, flat valley about three hundred meters below us. A solitary huge beast, somewhat like an elephant in bulk and manner, is grazing quietly down there, patiently prodding at the ground with its rigid two-pronged snout.

"Here we are," Oesterreich says.

We have reached the nearest of the little granite islands. When we walk around it, I see that its face on the farther side is fissured and broken, creating a sort of cave. Oesterreich beckons and we step a short way into it.

To our right, against the wall of the cave, is a curious narrow three-sided framework, a kind of tapering doorway, with deep darkness behind it. It is made of an odd glossy metal, or perhaps a plastic, with a texture that is both sleek and porous at the same time. There are hieroglyphs inscribed on it that seem much like those I saw on the wall of the stone temple in the mural in the Goddess-chapel on Phosphor, and to either side of it, mounted in the cave wall, are the triple six-pointed stars that are the emblem of Oesterreich's cult.

"What is this here?" I say, after a time.

"It's something like a Velde transmitter."

"It isn't anything like a Velde transmitter."

"It works very much like a Velde transmitter," he says. "You'll see when we step into its field. Are you ready?"

"Wait."

He nods. "I'm waiting."

"We're going to let this thing send us somewhere?"

"That's right, your grace."

"What is it? Who built it?"

"I've already told you what it is. As for who built it, I don't have any idea. Nobody does. We think it's five or ten million years old, maybe. It could be older than that by a factor of ten. Or a factor of a hundred. We have no way of judging."

After a long silence I say, "You're telling me that it's an alien device?"

"That's right."

"We've never discovered any sign of intelligent alien life anywhere in the galaxy."

"There's one right in front of you," Oesterreich says. "It isn't the only one."

"You've found aliens?"

"We've found their matter-transmitters. A few of them, anyway. They still work. Are you ready to jump now, your grace?"

I stare blankly at the three-sided doorway.

"Where to?"

"To a planet about five hundred light-years from here, where we can catch the bus that'll take us to the Goddess Avatar."

"You're actually serious?"

"Let's go, your grace."

"What about lambda effects?"

"There aren't any. Lambda differentials are a flaw in the Velde technology, not in the universe itself. This system gets us around without any lambda problems at all. Of course, we don't know how it works. Are you ready?"

"All right," I say helplessly.

He beckons to me and together we step toward the doorway and simply walk through it, and out the other side into such astonishing beauty that I want to fall down and give praise. Great feathery trees rise higher than sequoias, and a milky waterfall comes tumbling down the flank of an ebony mountain that fills half the sky, and the air quivers with a diamond-bright haze. Before me stretches a meadow like a scarlet carpet, vanishing into the middle distance. There is a Mesozoic richness of texture to everything: it gleams, it shimmers, it trembles in splendor.

A second doorway, identical to the first, is mounted against an enormous boulder right in front of us. It too is flanked by the triple star emblem.

"Put your medallion on," Oesterreich tells me.

"My medallion?" I say, stupidly.

"Put it on. The Goddess Avatar will wonder why you're with me, and that'll tell her."

"Is she here?"

"She's on the next world. This is just a way station. We had to stop here first. I don't know why. Nobody does. Ready?"

"I'd like to stay here longer."

"You can come back some other time," he says. "She's waiting for you. Let's go."

"Yes," I say, and fumble in my pocket and find my medallion, and put it around my throat. Oesterreich winks and puts his thumb and forefinger together approvingly. He takes my hand and we step through.

She is a lean, leathery-looking woman of sixty or seventy years with hard bright blue eyes. She wears a khaki jacket, an olive-drab field hat, khaki shorts, heavy boots. Her graying hair is tucked behind her in a tight bun. Standing in front of a small tent, tapping something into a hand terminal, she looks like an aging geology professor out on a field trip in Wyoming. But next to her tent the triple emblem of the Goddess is displayed on a sandstone plaque.

This is a Mesozoic landscape too, but much less lush than the last one: great red-brown cliffs sparsely peppered with giant ferns and palms, four-winged insects the size of dragons zooming overhead, huge grotesque things that look very much like dinosaurs warily circling each other in a stony arroyo out near the horizon. I see some other tents out there too. There is a little colony here. The sun is reddish-yellow, and large.

"Well, what do we have here?" she says. "A Lord Magistrate, is it?"

"He was nosing around on Zima and Entrada, trying to find out what was going on."

"Well, now he knows." Her voice is like flint. I feel her contempt, her hostility, like something palpable. I feel her strength, too, a cold, harsh, brutal power. She says, "What was your house, Lord Magistrate?"

"Senders."

She studies me as if I were a specimen in a display case. In all my life I have known only one other person of such force and intensity, and that is the Master. But she is nothing like him.

"And now the Sender is sent?"

"Yes," I say. "There were deviations from the plan. It became necessary for me to resign my magistracy."

"We weren't supposed to come out this far, were we?" she asks. "The light of that sun up there won't get to Earth until the seventy-third century, do you know that? But here we are. Here we are!" She laughs, a crazed sort of cackle. I begin to wonder if they intend to kill me. The aura that comes from her is terrifying. The geology professor I took her for at first is gone: what I see now is something strange and fierce, a prophet, a seer. Then suddenly the fierceness vanishes too and something quite different comes from her: tenderness, pity, even love. The strength of it catches me unawares and I gasp at its power. These shifts of hers are managed without apparent means; she has spoken only a few words, and all the rest has been done with movement, with posture, with expression. I know that I am in the presence of some great charismatic. She walks over to me and with her face close to mine says, "We spoiled your plan, I know. But we too follow the divine rule. We discovered things that nobody had suspected, and everything changed for us. Everything."

"Do you need me, Lady?" Oesterreich asks.

"No. Not now." She touches the tips of her fingers to my medallion of office, rubbing it lightly as though it is a magic talisman. Softly she says, "Let me take you on a tour of the galaxy, Lord Magistrate."

One of the alien doorways is located right behind her tent. We step through it hand in hand, and emerge on a dazzling green hillside looking out over a sea of ice. Three tiny blue-white suns hang like diamonds in the sky. In the trembling air they look like the three six-pointed stars of the emblem. "One of their capital cities was here once," she says. "But it's all at the bottom of that sea now. We ran a scan on it and saw the ruins, and some day we'll try to get down there." She beckons and we step through again, and out onto a turbulent desert of iron-hard red sand, where heavily armored crabs the size of footballs go scuttling sullenly away as we appear. "We think there's another city under here," she says. Stooping, she picks up a worn shard of gray pottery and puts it in my hand. "That's an artifact millions of years old.

We find them all over the place." I stare at it as if she has handed me a small fragment of the core of a star. She touches my medallion again, just a light grazing stroke, and leads me on into the next doorway, and out onto a world of billowing white clouds and soft dewy hills, and onward from there to one where trees hang like ropes from the sky, and onward from there, and onward from there— "How did you find all this?" I ask, finally.

"I was living on Three Suns. You know where that is? We were exploring the nearby worlds, trying to see if there was anything worthwhile, and one day I stepped out of a Velde unit and found myself looking at a peculiar three-sided kind of doorway right next to it, and I got too close and found myself going through into another world entirely. That was all there was to it."

"And you kept on going through one doorway after another?"

"Fifty of them. I didn't know then how to tune for destination, so I just kept jumping, hoping I'd get back to my starting point eventually. There wasn't any reason in the world why I should. But after six months I did. The Goddess protects me."

"The Goddess," I say.

She looks at me as though awaiting a challenge. But I am silent.

"These doorways link the whole galaxy together like the Paris Metro," she says after a moment. "We can go everywhere with them. *Everywhere.*"

"And the Goddess? Are the doorways Her work?"

"We hope to find that out some day."

"What about this emblem?" I ask, pointing to the six-pointed stars beside the gateway. "What does that signify?"

"Her presence," she says. "Come. I'll show you."

We step through once more, and emerge into night. The sky on this world is the blackest black I have ever seen, with comets and shooting stars blazing across it in almost comic profusion. There are two moons, bright as mirrors. A dozen meters to one side is the white stone temple of the chapel mural I saw on Eden, marked with the same hieroglyphs that are shown on the painting there and that are inscribed on all the alien doorways. It is made of cyclopean slabs of white stone that look as if they were carved billions of years ago. She takes my arm and guides me through its squared-off doorway into a high-vaulted inner chamber where the triple six-pointed triangle, fashioned out of the glossy doorway material, is mounted on a stone altar.

"This is the only building of theirs we've ever found," she says. Her eyes are gleaming. "It must have been a holy place. Can you doubt it? You can feel the power."

"Yes."

"Touch the emblem."

"What will happen to me if I do?"

"Touch it," she says. "Are you afraid?"

"Why should I trust you?"

"Because the Goddess has used me to bring you to this place. Go on. Touch."

I put my hand to the smooth cool alien substance, and instantly I feel the force of revelation flowing through me, the unmistakable power of the Godhead. I see the multiplicity of worlds, an infinity of them circling an infinity of suns. I see the Totality. I see the face of God clear and plain. It is what I have sought all my life and thought that I had already found; but I know at once that I am finding it for the first time. If I had fasted for a thousand years, or prayed for ten thousand, I could not have felt anything like that. It is the music out of which all things are built. It is the ocean in which all things float. I hear the voice of every god and goddess that ever had worshippers, and it is all one voice, and it goes coursing through me like a river of fire.

After a moment I take my hand away. And step back, trembling, shaking my head. This is too easy. One does not reach God by touching a strip of smooth plastic.

She says, "We mean to find them. They're still alive somewhere. How could they not be? And who could doubt that we were meant to follow them and find them? And kneel before them, for they are Whom we seek. So we'll go on and on, as far as we need to go, in search of them. To the farthest reaches, if we have to. To the rim of the universe and then beyond. With these doorways there are no limits. We've been handed the key to everywhere. We are for the Dark, all of it, on and on and on, not the little hundred-light-year sphere that your Order preaches, but the whole galaxy and even beyond. Who knows how far these doorways reach? The Magellanic Clouds? Andromeda? M33? They're waiting for us out there. As they have waited for a billion years."

So she thinks she can hunt Him down through doorway after doorway. Or Her. Whichever. But she is wrong. The One who made the universe made the makers of the doorways also.

"And the Goddess—?" I say.

"The Goddess is the Unknown. The Goddess is the Mystery toward which we journey. You don't feel Her presence?"

"I'm not sure."

"You will. If not now, then later. She'll greet us when we arrive. And embrace us, and make us all gods."

I stare a long while at the six-pointed stars. It would be simple enough to put forth my hand again and drink in the river of revelation a second time. But there is no need. That fire still courses through me. It always will, drawing me onward toward itself. Whatever it may be, there is no denying its power.

She says, "I'll show you one more thing, and then we'll leave here."

We continue through the temple and out the far side, where the wall has toppled. From a platform amid the rubble we have an unimpeded view of the heavens. An immense array of stars glitters above us, set out in utterly unfamiliar patterns. She points straight overhead, where a Milky Way in two whirling strands spills across the sky.

"That's Earth right up there," she says. "Can you see it? Going around that little yellow sun, only a hundred thousand light-years away? I wonder if they ever paid us a visit. We won't know, will we, until we turn up one of their doorways somewhere in the Himalayas, or under the Antarctic ice, or somewhere like that. I think that when we finally reach them, they'll recognize us. It's interesting to think about, isn't it." Her hand rests lightly on my wrist. "Shall we go back now, Lord Magistrate?"

So we return, in two or three hops, to the world of the dinosaurs and the giant dragonflies. There is nothing I can say. I feel storms within my skull. I feel myself spread out across half the universe.

Oesterreich waits for me now. He will take me back to Phosphor, or Entropy, or Entrada, or Zima, or Cuchulain, or anywhere else I care to go.

"You could even go back to Earth," the Goddess Avatar says. "Now that you know what's happening out here. You could go back home and tell the Master all about it."

"The Master already knows, I suspect. And there's no way I can go home. Don't you understand that?"

She laughs lightly. "Darklaw, yes. I forgot. The rule is that no one goes back. We've been catapulted out here to be cleansed of original sin, and to return to Mother Earth would be a crime against the laws of thermodynamics. Well, as you wish. You're a free man."

"It isn't Darklaw," I say. "Darklaw doesn't bind anyone any more."

I begin to shiver. Within my mind shards and fragments are falling from the sky: the House of Senders, the House of the Sanctuary, the whole Order and all its laws, the mountains and valleys of Earth, the body and fabric of Earth. All is shattered; all is made new; I am infinitely small against the infinite greatness of the cosmos. I am dazzled by the light of an infinity of suns.

And yet, though I must shield my eyes from that fiery glow, though I am numbed and humbled by the vastness of that vastness, I see that there are no limits to what may be attained, that the edge of the universe awaits me, that I need only reach and stretch, and stretch and reach, and ultimately I will touch it.

I see that even if she has made too great a leap of faith, even if she has surrendered herself to assumptions without basis, she is on the right path. The quest is unattainable because its goal is infinite. But the way leads ever outward. There is no destination, only a journey. And she has traveled farther on that journey than anyone.

And me? I had thought I was going out into the stars to spin out the last of my days quietly and obscurely, but I realize now that my pilgrimage is nowhere near its end. Indeed it is only beginning. This is not any road that I ever thought I would take. But this is the road that I am taking, all the same, and I have no choice but to follow it, though I am not sure yet whether I am wandering deeper into exile or finding my way back at last to my true home.

What I cannot help but see now is that our Mission is ended and that a new one has begun; or, rather, that this new Mission is the continuation and culmination of ours. Our Order has taught from the first that the way to reach God is to go to the stars. So it is. And so we have done. We have been too timid, limiting ourselves to that little ball of space surrounding Earth. But we have not failed. We have made possible everything that is to follow after.

I hand her my medallion. She looks at it the way I looked at that bit of alien pottery on the desert world, and then she starts to hand it back to me, but I shake my head.

"For you," I say. "A gift. An offering. It's of no use to me now."

293

She is standing with her back to the great reddish-yellow sun of this place, and it seems to me that light is streaming from her as it does from the Master, that she is aglow, that she is luminous, that she is herself a sun.

"Goddess save you, Lady," I say quietly.

All the worlds of the galaxy are whirling about me. I will take this road and see where it leads, for now I know there is no other.

"Goddess save you," I say. "Goddess save you, Lady."

LION TIME IN TIMBUCTOO

As I explained earlier in this volume in the introduction to Enter a Soldier. Later: Enter Another, *shared-world anthologies, for which several writers produced stories set in a world of another writer's devising, were an odd and ubiquitous manifestation of the hyperfrenzied science-fiction publishing world of the late 1980s. I noted back there that I had taken part in these activities both as editor and writer almost from the beginning, though by the end of that decade I had decided to do so no longer.*

It was hard for any active writer of the time to resist the siren call of the shared world. I involved myself in a number of the new series, and even walked away with two Hugos for my participation, one in 1987 for "Gilgamesh in the Outback" *from the* Heroes in Hell *series, and one in 1990 for* "Enter a Soldier" *from my own* Time Gate *series. By then I was beginning to tire of the whole idea of working this way, since many of the newer shared-world projects were haphazardly conceived and hazily edited and the results were less than admirable. But before I quit the game I assembled one more shared-world book of my own devising, the anthology* Beyond the Gate of Worlds, *which Tor Books would publish in 1991. I based it on an alternative-history novel I had written nearly thirty years before,* The Gate of Worlds, *the premise of which was that the Black Death of 1348 had wiped out nearly all the population of Western Europe instead of just one fourth, and that the survivors had been unable to resist the westward march of the expansionist Ottoman Turks. All of Europe thus had become Turkish-speaking and Moslem; the Renaissance had never happened; nor had the European conquest of the New World and Africa taken place, and the Aztec*

295

and Inca empires had remained intact on into the twentieth century, as had the black kingdoms of Africa.

The Gate of Worlds itself was the story of the adventures of a young British boy in Aztec North America. Back in the 1960s I had intended it to be the first of a trilogy, with the second volume taking place in Africa and the third in England, but I never did get around to writing the other two books. The basic story situation, though, remained in my mind and continued to tempt me. And so, in October, 1989, I finally did get to tell the African part of the story, by writing the first third of the Gate of Worlds *shared-world anthology myself—the novella "Lion Time in Timbuctoo." (Chelsea Quinn Yarbro and John Brunner did the other two sections of the book.) Prior to the publication of the Tor anthology* Asimov's Science Fiction *published my story in magazine form in its October, 1990 issue, and Axolotl Press of Oregon did it as a one-volume limited-edition book about the same time. I admire it for its evocation of place and for what I think is a successful depiction of life in the capital of a powerful African kingdom of a considerably altered twentieth century.*

I n the dry stifling days of early summer the Emir lay dying, the king, the imam, Big Father of the Songhay, in his cool dark mud-walled palace in the Sankore quarter of Old Timbuctoo. The city seemed frozen, strange though it was to think of freezing in this season of killing heat that fell upon you like a wall of hot iron. There was a vast stasis, as though everything were entombed in ice. The river was low and sluggish, moving almost imperceptibly in its bed with scarcely more vigor than a sick weary crocodile. No one went out of doors, no one moved indoors, everyone sat still, waiting for the old man's death and praying that it would bring the cooling rains.

In his own very much lesser palace alongside the Emir's, Little Father sat still like all the rest, watching and waiting. His time was coming now at last. That was a sobering thought. How long had he been the prince of the realm? Twenty years? Thirty? He had lost count. And now finally to rule, now to be the one who cast the omens and uttered the decrees and welcomed the caravans and took the high seat in the Great Mosque. So much toil, so much responsibility: but the Emir was not yet dead. Not yet. Not quite.

"Little Father, the ambassadors are arriving."

In the arched doorway stood Ali Pasha, bowing, smiling. The vizier's face, black as ebony, gleamed with sweat, a dark moon shining against the lighter darkness of the vestibule. Despite his name, Ali Pasha was pure Songhay, black as sorrow, blacker by far than Little Father, whose blood was mixed with that of would-be conquerors of years gone by. The aura of the power that soon would be his was glistening and crackling around Ali Pasha's head like midwinter lightning: for Ali Pasha was the future Grand Vizier, no question of it. When Little Father became king, the old Emir's officers would resign and retire. An Emir's ministers did not hold office beyond his reign. In an earlier time they would have been lucky to survive the old Emir's death at all.

Little Father, fanning himself sullenly, looked up to meet his vizier's insolent grin.

"Which ambassadors, Ali Pasha?"

"The special ones, here to attend Big Father's funeral. A Turkish. A Mexican. A Russian. And an English."

"An English? Why an English?"

"They are a very proud people, now. Since their independence. How could they stay away? This is a very important death, Little Father."

"Ah. Ah, of course." Little Father contemplated the fine wooden Moorish grillwork that bedecked the doorway. "Not a Peruvian?"

"A Peruvian will very likely come on the next riverboat, Little Father. And a Maori one, and they say a Chinese. There will probably be others also. By the end of the week the city will be filled with dignitaries. This is the most important death in some years."

"A Chinese," Little Father repeated softly, as though Ali Pasha had said an ambassador from the Moon was coming. A Chinese! But yes, yes, this was a very important death. The Songhay Empire was no minor nation. Songhay controlled the crossroads of Africa; all caravans journeying between desert north and tropical south must pass through Songhay. The Emir of Songhay was one of the grand kings of the world.

Ali Pasha said acidly, "The Peruvian hopes that Big Father will last until the rains come, I suppose. And so he takes his time getting here. They are people of a high country, these Peruvians. They aren't accustomed to our heat."

"And if he misses the funeral entirely, waiting for the rains to come?"

Ali Pasha shrugged. "Then he'll learn what heat really is, eh, Little Father? When he goes home to his mountains and tells the Grand Inca that he didn't get here soon enough, eh?" He made a sound that was something like a laugh, and Little Father, experienced in his vizier's sounds, responded with a gloomy smile.

"Where are these ambassadors now?"

"At Kabara, at the port hostelry. Their riverboat has just come in. We've sent the royal barges to bring them here."

"Ah. And where will they stay?"

"Each at his country's embassy, Little Father."

"Of course. Of course. So no action is needed from me at this time concerning these ambassadors, eh, Ali Pasha?"

"None, Little Father." After a pause the vizier said, "The Turk has brought his daughter. She is very handsome." This with a rolling of the eyes, a baring of the teeth. Little Father felt a pang of appetite, as Ali Pasha had surely intended. The vizier knew his prince very well, too. "Very handsome, Little Father! In a white way, you understand."

"I understand. The English, did he bring a daughter too?"

"Only the Turk," said Ali Pasha.

"Do you remember the Englishwoman who came here once?" Little Father asked.

"How could I forget? The hair like strands of fine gold. The breasts like milk. The pale pink nipples. The belly-hair down below, like fine gold also."

Little Father frowned. He had spoken often enough to Ali Pasha about the Englishwoman's milky breasts and pale pink nipples. But he had no recollection of having described to him or to anyone else the golden hair down below. A rare moment of carelessness, then, on Ali Pasha's part; or else a bit of deliberate malice, perhaps a way of testing Little Father. There were risks in that for Ali Pasha, but surely Ali Pasha knew that. At any rate it was a point Little Father chose not to pursue just now. He sank back into silence, fanning himself more briskly.

Ali Pasha showed no sign of leaving. So there must be other news.

The vizier's glistening eyes narrowed. "I hear they will be starting the dancing in the marketplace very shortly."

Little Father blinked. Was there some crisis in the king's condition, then? Which everyone knew about but him?

"The death dance, do you mean?"

"That would be premature, Little Father," said Ali Pasha unctuously. "It is the life dance, of course."

"Of course. I should go to it, in that case."

"In half an hour. They are only now assembling the formations. You should go to your father, first."

"Yes. So I should. To the Emir, first, to ask his blessing; and then to the dance."

Little Father rose.

"The Turkish girl," he said. "How old is she, Ali Pasha?"

"She might be eighteen. She might be twenty."

"And handsome, you say?"

"Oh, yes. Yes, very handsome, Little Father!"

There was an underground passageway connecting Little Father's palace to that of Big Father; but suddenly, whimsically, Little Father chose to go there by the out-of-doors way. He had not been out of doors in two or three days, since the worst of the heat had descended on the city. Now he felt the outside air hit him like the blast of a furnace as he crossed the courtyard and stepped into the open. The whole city was like a smithy these days, and would be for weeks and weeks more, until the rains came. He was used to it, of course, but he had never come to like it. No one ever came to like it except the deranged and the very holy, if indeed there was any difference between the one and the other.

Emerging onto the portico of his palace, Little Father looked out on the skyline of flat mud roofs before him, the labyrinth of alleys and connecting passageways, the towers of the mosques, the walled mansions of the nobility. In the hazy distance rose the huge modern buildings of the New City. It was late afternoon, but that brought no relief from the heat. The air was heavy, stagnant, shimmering. It vibrated like a live thing. All day long the myriad whitewashed walls had been soaking up the heat, and now they were beginning to give it back.

Atop the vibration of the air lay a second and almost tangible vibration, the tinny quivering sound of the musicians tuning up for the dance in the marketplace. The life dance, Ali Pasha had said. Perhaps so; but Little Father would not be surprised to find some of the people dancing the death dance as well, and still others dancing the dance of the changing of the king. There was little linearity of time in Old Timbuctoo; everything tended to happen at once. The death of the old king and the ascent of the new one were simultaneous affairs, after all: they were one event. In some countries, Little Father knew, they used to kill the king when he grew sick and feeble, simply to hurry things along. Not here, though. Here they danced him out, danced the new king in. This was a civilized land. An ancient kingdom, a mighty power in the world. He stood for a time, listening to the music in the marketplace, wondering if his father in his sickbed could hear it, and what he might be thinking, if he could. And he wondered too how it would feel when his own time came to lie abed listening to them tuning up in the market for the death dance. But then Little Father's face wrinkled in annoyance at his own foolishness. He would rule for many years; and when the time came to do the death dance for him out there he would not care at all. He might even be eager for it.

Big Father's palace rose before him like a mountain. Level upon level sprang upward, presenting a dazzling white facade broken only by the dark butts of the wooden beams jutting through the plaster and the occasional grillwork of a window. His own palace was a hut compared with that of the Emir. Implacable blue-veiled Tuareg guards stood in the main doorway. Their eyes and foreheads, all that was visible of their coffee-colored faces, registered surprise as they saw Little Father approaching, alone and on foot, out of the aching sunblink of the afternoon; but they stepped aside. Within, everything was silent and dark. Elderly officials of the almost-late Emir lined the hallways, grieving soundlessly, huddling into their own self-pity. They looked toward Little Father without warmth, without hope, as he moved past them. In a short while he would be king, and they would be nothing. But he wasted no energy on pitying them. It wasn't as though they would be fed to the royal lions in the imperial pleasure-ground, after all, when they stepped down from office. Soft retirements awaited them. They had had their greedy years at the public trough; when the time came for them to go, they would move along to villas in Spain, in Greece, in the south of France, in chilly remote Russia, even, and live comfortably on the fortunes they had embezzled during Big Father's lengthy reign. Whereas he, he, he, he was doomed to spend all his days in this wretched blazing city of mud, scarcely even daring ever to go abroad for fear they would take his throne from him while he was gone.

The Grand Vizier, looking twenty years older than he had seemed when Little Father had last seen him a few days before, greeted him formally at the head of the Stairs of Allah and said, "The imam your father is resting on the porch, Little Father. Three saints and one of the Tijani are with him."

"Three saints? He must be very near the end, then!"

"On the contrary. We think he is rallying."

"Allah let it be so," said Little Father.

Servants and ministers were everywhere. The place reeked of incense. All the lamps were lit, and they were flickering wildly in the conflicting currents of the air within the palace, heat from outside meeting the cool of the interior in gusting wafts. The old Emir had never cared much for electricity.

Little Father passed through the huge, musty, empty throne room, bedecked with his father's hunting trophies, the 20-foot-long crocodile skin, the superb white oryx head with horns like scimitars, the hippo skulls, the vast puzzled-looking giraffe. The rich gifts from foreign monarchs were arrayed here too, the hideous Aztec idol that King Moctezuma had sent a year or two ago, the brilliant feather cloaks from the Inca Capac Yupanqui of Peru, the immense triple-paneled gilded painting of some stiff-jointed Christian holy men with which the Czar Vladimir had paid his respects during a visit of state a decade back, and the great sphere of ivory from China on which some master craftsman had carved a detailed map of the world, and much more, enough to fill half a storehouse. Little Father wondered if he would be able to clear all this stuff out when he became Emir.

In his lifetime Big Father had always preferred to hold court on his upstairs porch, rather than in this dark, cluttered, and somehow sinister throne room; and now he was doing his dying on the porch as well. It was a broad square platform, open to the skies but hidden from the populace below, for it was at the back of the palace facing toward the distant river and no one in the city could look into it.

The dying king lay swaddled, despite the great heat, in a tangle of brilliant blankets of scarlet and turquoise and lemoncolored silk on a rumpled divan to Little Father's left. He was barely visible, a pale sweaty wizened face and nothing more, amid the rumpled bedclothes. To the right was the royal roof-garden, a mysterious collection of fragrant exotic trees and shrubs planted in huge square porcelain vessels from Japan, another gift of the bountiful Czar. The dark earth that filled those blue-and-white tubs had been carried in panniers by donkeys from the banks of the Niger, and the plants were watered every evening at sunset by prisoners, who had to haul great leather sacks of immense weight to this place and were forbidden by the palace guards to stumble or complain. Between the garden and the divan was the royal viewing-pavilion, a low structure of rare satin-smooth woods upon which the Emir in better days would sit for hours, staring out at the barren sun-hammered sandy plain, the pale tormented sky, the occasional wandering camel or hyena, the gnarled scrubby bush that marked the path of the river, six or seven miles away. The cowrie-studded ebony scepter of high office was lying abandoned on the floor of the pavilion, as though nothing more than a cast-off toy.

Four curious figures stood now at the foot of the Emir's divan. One was the Tijani, a member of the city's chief fraternity of religious laymen. He was a man of marked Arab features, dressed in a long white robe over droopy yellow pantaloons, a red turban, a dozen or so strings of amber beads. Probably he was a well-to-do merchant or shopkeeper in daily life. He was wholly absorbed in his orisons, rocking back and forth in place, crooning indefatigably to his hundred-beaded rosary, working hard to efface the Emir's sins and make him fit for Paradise. His voice was thin as feathers from overuse, a low eroded murmur that scarcely halted even for breath. He acknowledged Little Father's arrival with the merest flick of an eyebrow, without pausing in his toil.

The other three holy men were marabouts, living saints, two black Songhay and a man of mixed blood. They were weighted down with leather packets of grigri charms hanging in thick mounds around their necks and girded by other charms by the dozen around their wrists and hips, and they had the proper crazy glittering saint-look in their eyes, the true holy baraka. It was said that saints could fly, could raise the dead, could make the rains come and the rivers rise. Little Father doubted all of that, but he was one who tended to keep his doubts to himself. In any case the city was full of such miracle-workers, dozens of them, and the tombs of hundreds more were objects of veneration in the poorer districts. Little Father recognized all three of these: he had seen them now and then hovering around the Sankore Mosque or sometimes the other and greater one at Dyingerey Ber, striking saint-poses on one leg or with arms outflung, muttering saint-gibberish, giving passersby the saint-stare. Now they stood lined up in grim silence before the Emir, making cryptic gestures with their fingers. Even before Big Father had fallen ill, these three had gone about declaring that he was doomed shortly to be taken by a vampire, as various recent omens indisputably proved—a flight of owls by day, a flight of vultures by night, the death of a sacred dove that lived on the minaret of the Great Mosque. For them to be in the palace at all was remarkable; for them to be in the presence of the king was astounding. Someone in the royal entourage must be at the point of desperation, Little Father concluded.

He knelt at the bedside.

"Father?"

The Emir's eyes were glassy. Perhaps he was becoming a saint too.

"Father, it's me. They said you were rallying. I know you're going to be all right soon."

Was that a smile? Was that any sort of reaction at all?

"Father, it'll be cooler in just a few weeks. The rains are already on the way. Everybody's saying so. You'll feel better when the rains come."

The old man's cheeks were like parchment. His bones were showing through. He was eighty years old and he had been Emir of Songhay for fifty of those years. Electricity hadn't even been invented when he became king, nor the motorcar. Even the railroad had been something new and startling.

There was a claw-like hand suddenly jutting out of the blankets. Little Father touched it. It was like touching a piece of worn leather. By the time the rains had reached Timbuctoo, Big Father would have made the trip by ceremonial barge to the old capital of Gao, two hundred miles down the Niger, to take his place in the royal cemetery of the Kings of Songhay.

Little Father went on murmuring encouragement for another few moments, but it was apparent that the Emir wasn't listening. A stray burst of breeze brought the sound of the marketplace music, growing louder now. Could he hear that? Could he hear anything? Did he care? After a time Little Father rose, and went quickly from the palace.

In the marketplace the dancing had already begun. They had shoved aside the booths of the basket-weavers and the barbers and the slipper-makers and the charm-peddlers, the dealers in salt and fruit and donkeys and rice and tobacco and meat, and a frenetic procession of dancers was weaving swiftly back and forth across the central square from the place of the milk vendors at the south end to the place of the wood vendors at the north when Little Father and Ali Pasha arrived.

"You see?" Ali Pasha asked. "The life dance. They bring the energy down from the skies to fill your father's veins."

There was tremendous energy in it, all right. The dancers pounded the sandy earth with their bare feet, they clapped their hands, they shouted quick sharp punctuations of wordless sound, they made butting gestures with their outflung elbows, they shook their heads convulsively and sent rivers of sweat flying through the air. The heat seemed to mean nothing to them. Their skins gleamed. Their eyes were bright as new coins. They made rhythmic grunting noises, oom oom oom, and the whole city seemed to shake beneath their tread.

To Little Father it looked more like the death dance than the dance of life. There was the frenzied stomp of mourning about it. But he was no expert on these things. The people had all sorts of beliefs that were mysteries to him, and which he hoped would melt away like snowflakes during his coming reign. Did they still put pressure on Allah to bring the rains by staking small children out in the blazing sun for days at a time outside the tombs of saints? Did they still practice alchemy on one another, turning wrapping paper into banknotes by means of spells? Did they continue to fret about vampires and djinn? It was all very embarrassing. Songhay was a modern state; and yet there was all this medieval nonsense still going on. Very likely the old Emir had liked it that way. But soon things would change.

The close formation of the dancers opened abruptly, and to his horror Little Father saw a group of foreigners standing in a little knot at the far side of the marketplace. He had only a glimpse of them; then the dance closed again and the foreigners were blocked from view. He touched Ali Pasha's arm.

"Did you see them?"

"Oh, yes. Yes!"

"Who are they, do you think?"

The vizier stared off intently toward the other side of the marketplace, as though his eyes were capable of seeing through the knot of dancers.

"Embassy people, Little Father. Some Mexicans, I believe, and perhaps the Turks. And those fair-haired people must be the English."

Here to gape at the quaint tribal dances, enjoying the fine barbaric show in the extravagant alien heat.

"You said they were coming by barge. How'd they get here so fast?"

Ali Pasha shook his head.

"They must have taken the motorboat instead, I suppose."

"I can't receive them here, like this. I never would have come here if I had known that they'd be here."

"Of course not, Little Father."

"You should have told me!"

"I had no way of knowing," said Ali Pasha, and for once he sounded sincere, even distressed. "There will be punishments for this. But come, Little Father. Come: to your palace. As you say, they ought not find you here this way, without a retinue, without your regalia. This evening you can receive them properly."

Very likely the newly arrived diplomats at the upper end of the marketplace had no idea that they had been for a few moments in the presence of the heir to the throne, the future Emir of Songhay, one of the six or seven most powerful men in Africa. If they had noticed anyone at all across the way, they would simply have seen a slender, supple, just-barely-still-youngish man with Moorish features, wearing a simple white robe and a flat red skullcap, standing beside a tall, powerfully built black man clad in an ornately brocaded robe of purple and yellow. The black man might have seemed more important to them in the Timbuctoo scheme of things than the Moorish-looking one, though they would have been wrong about that.

But probably they hadn't been looking toward Little Father and Ali Pasha at all. Their attention was on the dancers. That was why they had halted here, en route from the river landing to their various embassies.

"How tireless they are!" Prince Itzcoatl said. The Mexican envoy, King Moctezuma's brother. "Why don't their bones melt in this heat?" He was a compact copper-colored man decked out grandly in an Aztec feather cape, golden anklets and wristlets, a gold headband studded with brilliant feathers, golden ear-plugs and nose-plugs. "You'd think they were glad their king is dying, seeing them jump around like that."

"Perhaps they are," observed the Turk, Ismet Akif.

He laughed in a mild, sad way. Everything about him seemed to be like that, mild and sad: his droopy-lidded melancholic eyes, his fleshy downcurved lips, his sloping shoulders, even the curiously stodgy and inappropriate European-style clothes that he had chosen to wear in this impossible climate, the dark heavy woolen suit, the narrow gray necktie. But wide cheekbones and a broad, authoritative forehead indicated his true strength to those with the ability to see such things. He too was of royal blood, Sultan Osman's third son. There was something about him that managed to be taut and slack both at once, no easy task. His posture, his expression, the tone of his voice, all conveyed the anomalous sense of self that came from being the official delegate of a vast empire which—as all the world knew—had passed the peak of its greatness some time back and was launched on a long irreversible decline. To the diminutive Englishman at his side he said, "How does it seem to you, Sir Anthony? Are they grieving or celebrating?"

Everyone in the group understood the great cost of the compliment Ismet Akif was paying by amiably addressing his question to the English ambassador, just as if they were equals. It was high courtesy: it was grace in defeat.

Turkey still ruled a domain spanning thousands of miles. England was an insignificant island kingdom. Worse yet, England had been a Turkish province from medieval times onward, until only sixty years before. The exasperated English, weary of hundreds of years of speaking Turkish and bowing to Mecca, finally had chased out their Ottoman masters in the first year of what by English reckoning was the twentieth century, thus becoming the first of all the European peoples to regain their independence. There were no Spaniards here today, no Italians, no Portuguese, and no reason why there should be, for their countries all still were Turkish provinces. Perhaps envoys from those lands would show up later to pay homage to the dead Emir, if only to make some pathetic display of tattered sovereignty; but it would not matter to anyone else, one way or the other. The English, though, were beginning once again to make their way in the world, a little tentatively but nevertheless visibly. And so Ismet Akif had had to accommodate himself to the presence of an English diplomat on the slow journey upriver from the coast to the Songhay capital, and everyone agreed he had managed it very well.

Sir Anthony said, "Both celebrating *and* grieving, I'd imagine." He was a precise, fastidious little man with icy blue eyes, an angular bony face, a tight cap of red curls beginning to shade now into gray. "The king is dead, long live the king—that sort of thing."

"*Almost* dead," Prince Itzcoatl reminded him.

"Quite. Terribly awkward, our getting here before the fact. Or *are* we here before the fact?" Sir Anthony glanced toward his young charge-d'affaires. "Have you heard anything, Michael? Is the old Emir still alive, do you know?"

Michael was long-legged, earnest, milky-skinned, very fair. In the merciless Timbuctoo sunlight his golden hair seemed almost white.

The first blush of what was likely to be a very bad sunburn was spreading over his cheeks and forehead. He was twenty-four and this was his first notable diplomatic journey.

He indicated the flagpole at the eastern end of the plaza, where the black and red Songhay flag hung like a dead thing high overhead.

"They'd have lowered the flag if he'd died, Sir Anthony."

"Quite. Quite. They do that sort of thing here, do they?"

"I'd rather expect so, sir."

"And then what? The whole town plunged into mourning? Drums, chanting? The new Emir paraded in the streets? Everyone would head for the mosques, I suppose." Sir Anthony glanced at Ismet Akif. "We would too, eh? Well, I could stand to go into a mosque one more time, I suppose."

After the Conquest, when London had become New Istanbul, the worship of Allah had been imposed by law. Westminster Abbey had been turned into a mosque, and the high pashas of the occupation forces were buried in it alongside the Plantagenet kings. Later the Turks had built the great golden-domed Mosque of Ali on the Strand, opposite the Grand Palace of Sultan Mahmud. To this day perhaps half the English still embraced Islam, out of force of habit if nothing else, and Turkish was still heard in the streets nearly as much as English. The conquerors had had five hundred years to put their mark on England, and that could not be undone overnight. But Christianity was fashionable again among the English well-to-do, and had never really been relinquished by the poor, who had kept their underground chapels through the worst of the Islamic persecutions. And it was obligatory for the members of the governing class.

"It would have been better for us all," said Ismet Akif gravely, "if we had not had to set out so early that we would arrive here before the Emir's death. But of course the distances are so great, and travel is so very slow—"

"And the situation so explosive," Prince Itzcoatl said.

Unexpectedly Ismet Akif's bright-eyed daughter Selima, who was soft-spoken and delicate-looking and was not thought to be particularly forward, said, "Are you talking about the possibility that King Suleiyman of Mali might send an invasion force into Songhay when the old man finally dies?"

Everyone swung about to look at her. Someone gasped and someone else choked back shocked laughter. She was extremely young and of course she was female, but even so the remark was exceedingly tactless, exceedingly embarrassing. The girl had not come to Songhay in any official capacity, merely as her father's traveling companion, for he was a widower. The whole trip was purely an adventure for her. All the same, a diplomat's child should have had more sense. Ismet Akif turned his eyes inward and looked as though he would like to sink into the earth. But Selima's dark eyes glittered with something very much like mischief. She seemed to be enjoying herself. She stood her ground.

"No," she said. "We can't pretend it isn't likely. There's Mali, right next door, controlling the coast. It stands to reason that they'd like to have the inland territory too, and take total control of West African trade. King Suleiyman could argue that Songhay would be better off as part of Mali than it is this way, a landlocked country."

"My dear—"

"And the prince," she went on imperturbably, "is supposed to be just an idler, isn't he, a silly dissolute playboy who's spent so many years waiting around to become Emir that he's gone completely to ruin. Letting him take the throne would be a mistake for everybody. So this is the best possible time for Mali to move in and consolidate the two countries. You all see that. That's why we're here, aren't we, to stare the Malians down and keep them from trying it? Because they'd be too strong for the other powers' comfort if they got together with the Songhayans. And it's all too likely to happen. After all, Mali and Songhay have been consolidated before."

"Hundreds of years ago," said Michael gently. He gave her a great soft blue-eyed stare of admiration and despair. "The principle that the separation of Mali and Songhay is desirable and necessary has been understood internationally since—"

"Please," Ismet Akif said. "This is an unfortunate discussion. My dear, we ought not indulge in such speculations in a place of this sort, or anywhere else, let me say. Perhaps it's time to continue on to our lodgings, do you not all agree?"

"A good idea. The dancing is becoming a little repetitious," Prince Itzcoatl said.

"And the heat—" Sir Anthony said. "This unthinkable diabolical heat—"

They looked at each other. They shook their heads, and exchanged small smiles.

Prince Itzcoatl said quietly to Sir Anthony, "An unfortunate discussion, yes."

"Very unfortunate."

Then they all moved on, in groups of two and three, their porters trailing a short distance behind bowed under the great mounds of luggage. Michael stood for a moment or two peering after the retreating form of Selima Akif in an agony of longing and chagrin. Her movements seemed magical. They were as subtle as Oriental music: an exquisite semitonal slither, an enchanting harmonious twang.

The love he felt for her had surprised and mortified him when it had first blossomed on the riverboat as it came interminably up the Niger from the coast, and here in his first hour in Timbuctoo he felt it almost as a crucifixion. There was no worse damage he could do to himself than to fall in love with a Turk. For an Englishman it was virtual treason. His diplomatic career would be ruined before it had barely begun. He would be laughed out of court. He might just as well convert to Islam, paint his face brown, and undertake the pilgrimage to Mecca. And live thereafter as an anchorite in some desert cave, imploring the favor of the Prophet.

"Michael?" Sir Anthony called. "Is anything wrong?"

"Coming, sir. Coming!"

The reception hall was long and dark and cavernous, lit only by wax tapers that emitted a smoky amber light and a peculiar odor, something like that of leaves decomposing on a forest floor. Along the walls were bowers of interwoven ostrich and peacock plumes, and great elephant tusks set on brass pedestals rose from the earthen floor like obelisks at seemingly random intervals. Songhayans who might have been servants or just as easily high officials of the court moved among the visiting diplomats bearing trays of cool lime-flavored drinks, musty wine, and little delicacies fashioned from a bittersweet red nut.

The prince, in whose name the invitations had gone forth, was nowhere in sight so far as any of the foreigners could tell. The apparent host of the reception was a burly jet-black man of regal bearing clad in a splendid tawny robe that might actually have been made of woven lionskins. He had introduced himself as Ali Pasha, vizier to the prince. The prince, he explained, was at his father's bedside, but would be there shortly. The prince was deeply devoted to his father, said Ali Pasha; he visited the failing Emir constantly.

"I saw that man in the marketplace this afternoon," Selima said. "He was wearing a purple and yellow robe then. Down at the far side, beyond the dancers, for just a moment. He was looking at us. I thought he was magnificent, somebody of great importance. And he is."

A little indignantly Michael said, "These blacks all look alike to me. How can you be sure that's the one you saw?"

"Because I'm sure. Do all Turks look alike to you too?"

"I didn't mean—"

"All English look alike to us, you know. We can just about distinguish between the red-haired ones and the yellow-haired ones. And that's as far as it goes."

"You aren't serious, Selima."

"No. No, I'm not. I actually can tell one of you from another most of the time. At least I can tell the handsome ones from the ugly ones."

Michael flushed violently, so that his already sunburned face turned flaming scarlet and emanated great waves of heat. Everyone had been telling him how handsome he was since his boyhood. It was as if there was nothing to him at all except regularly formed features and pale flawless skin and long athletic limbs. The notion made him profoundly uncomfortable.

She laughed. "You should cover your face when you're out in the sun. You're starting to get cooked. Does it hurt very much?"

"Not at all. Can I get you a drink?"

"You know that alcohol is forbidden to—"

"The other kind, I mean. The green soda. It's very good, actually. Boy! Boy!"

"I'd rather have the nut thing," she said. She stretched forth one hand—her hand was very small, and the fingers were pale and perfect—and made the tiniest of languid gestures. Two of the black men with trays came toward her at once, and, laughing prettily, she scooped a couple of the nut-cakes from the nearer of the trays. She handed one to Michael, who fumbled it and let it fall. Calmly she gave him the other. He looked at it as though she had handed him an asp.

"Are you afraid I've arranged to have you poisoned?" she asked. "Go on. Eat it! It's good! Oh, you're so absurd, Michael! But I do like you."

"We aren't supposed to like each other, you know," he said bleakly.

"I know that. We're enemies, aren't we?"

"Not any more, actually. Not officially."

"Yes, I know. The Empire recognized English independence a good many years ago."

The way she said it, it was like a slap. Michael's reddened cheeks blazed fiercely.

In anguish he crammed the nut-cake into his mouth with both hands.

She went on, "I can remember the time when I was a girl and King Richard came to Istanbul to sign the treaty with the Sultan. There was a parade."

"Yes. Yes. A great occasion."

"But there's still bad blood between the Empire and England. We haven't forgiven you for some of the things you did to our people in your country in Sultan Abdul's time, when we were evacuating."

"*You* haven't forgiven *us*—?"

"When you burned the bazaar. When you bombed that mosque. The broken shopwindows. We were going away voluntarily, you know. You were much more violent toward us than you had any right to be."

"You speak very directly, don't you?"

"There were atrocities. I studied them in school."

"And when you people conquered us in 1490? Were you gentle then?" For a moment Michael's eyes were hot with fury, the easily triggered anger of the good Englishman for the bestial Turk. Appalled, he tried to stem the rising surge of patriotic fervor before it ruined everything. He signalled frantically to one of the tray-wielders, as though another round of nut-cakes might serve to get the conversation into a less disagreeable track. "But never mind all that, Selima. We mustn't be quarreling over ancient history like this." Somehow he mastered himself, swallowing, breathing deeply, managing an earnest smile. "You say you like me."

"Yes. And you like me. I can tell."

"Is that all right?"

"Of course it is, silly. Although I shouldn't allow it. We don't even think of you English as completely civilized." Her eyes glowed. He began to tremble, and tried to conceal it from her. She was playing with him, he knew, playing a game whose rules she herself had defined and would not share with him. "Are you a Christian?" she asked.

"You know I am."

"Yes, you must be. You used the Christian date for the year of the conquest of England. But your ancestors were Moslem, right?"

"Outwardly, during the time of the occupation. Most of us were. But for all those centuries we secretly continued to maintain our faith in—" She was definitely going to get him going again. Already his head was beginning to pound. Her beauty was unnerving enough; but this roguishness was more than he could take. He wondered how old she was. Eighteen? Nineteen? No more than that, surely. Very likely she had a fiancee back in Istanbul, some swarthy mustachioed fez-wearing Ottoman princeling, with whom she indulged in unimaginable Oriental perversions and to whom she confessed every little flirtation she undertook while traveling with her father. It was humiliating to think of becoming an item of gossip in some perfumed boudoir on the banks of the Bosporus. A sigh escaped him. She gave him a startled look, as though he had mooed at her. Perhaps he had. Desperately he sought for something, anything, that would rescue him from this increasingly tortured moment of impossible intimacy; and, looking across the room, he was astounded to find his eyes suddenly locked on those of the heir apparent to the throne of Songhay. "Ah, there he is," Michael said in vast relief. "The prince has arrived."

"Which one? Where?"

"The slender man. The red velvet tunic."

"Oh. Oh, yes. *Him.* I saw him in the marketplace too, with Ali Pasha. Now I understand. They came to check us out before we knew who they were." Selima smiled disingenuously. "He's very attractive, isn't he? Rather like an Arab, I'd say. And not nearly as dissolute-looking as I was led to expect. Is it all right if I go over and say hello to him? Or should I wait for a proper diplomatic introduction? I'll ask my father, I think. Do you see him? Oh, yes, there he is over there, talking to Prince Itzcoatl—" She began to move away without a backward look.

Michael felt a sword probing in his vitals.

"Boy!" he called, and one of the blacks turned to him with a somber grin. "Some of that wine, if you please!"

On the far side of the room Little Father smiled and signalled for a drink also—not the miserable palm wine, which he abhorred and which as a good Moslem he should abjure anyway, but the clear fiery brandy that the caravans brought him from Tunis, and which to an outsider's eyes would appear to be mere water. His personal cupbearer, who served no one else in the room, poured until he nodded, and slipped back into the shadows to await the prince's next call.

In the first moments of his presence at the reception Little Father had taken in the entire scene, sorting and analyzing and comprehending.

The Turkish ambassador's daughter was even more beautiful than Ali Pasha had led him to think, and there was an agreeable slyness about her that Little Father was able to detect even at a distance. Lust awoke in him at once and he allowed himself a little smile as he savored its familiar throbbing along the insides of his thighs. The Turkish girl was very fine. The tall fair-haired young man, probably some sort of subsidiary English official, was obviously and stupidly in love with her. He should be advised to keep out of the sun. The Aztec prince, all done up in feathers and gold, was arrogant and brutal and smart, as Aztecs usually were. The Turk, the girl's father, looked soft and effete and decadent, which he probably found to be a useful pose. The older Englishman, the little one with the red hair who most likely was the official envoy, seemed tough and dangerous. And over there was another one who hadn't been at the marketplace to see the dancing, the Russian, no doubt, a big man, strong and haughty, flat face and flat sea-green eyes and a dense little black beard through which a glint of gold teeth occasionally showed. He too seemed dangerous, physically dangerous, a man who might pick things up and smash them for amusement, but in him all the danger was on the outside, and with the little Englishman it was the other way around. Little Father wondered how much trouble these people would manage to create for him before the funeral was over and done with. It was every nation's ambition to create trouble in the empires of Africa, after all: there was too much cheap labor here, too much in the way of raw materials, for the pale jealous folk of the overseas lands to ignore, and they were forever dreaming dreams of conquest.

But no one had ever managed it. Africa had kept itself independent of the great overseas powers. The Pasha of Egypt still held his place by the Nile, in the far south the Mambo of Zimbabwe maintained his domain amidst enough gold to make even an Aztec feel envy, and the Bey of Marrakesh was unchallenged in the north. And the strong western empires flourished as ever, Ghana, Mali, Kongo, Songhay—no, no, Africa had never let itself be eaten by Turks or Russians or even the Moors, though they had all given it a good try. Nor would it ever. Still, as he wandered among these outlanders Little Father felt contempt for him and his people drifting through the air about him like smoke. He wished that he could have made a properly royal entrance, coming upon the foreigners in style, with drums and trumpets and bugles. Preceded as he entered by musicians carrying gold and silver guitars, and followed by a hundred armed slaves. But those were royal prerogatives, and he was not yet Emir. Besides, this was a solemn time in Songhay, and such pomp was unbefitting. And the foreigners would very likely look upon it as the vulgarity of a barbarian, anyway, or the quaint grandiosity of a primitive.

Little Father downed his brandy in three quick gulps and held out the cup for more. It was beginning to restore his spirit. He felt a sense of deep well-being, of ease and assurance.

But just then came a stir and a hubbub at the north door of the reception hall. In amazement and fury he saw Serene Glory entering, Big Father's main wife, surrounded by her full retinue. Her hair was done up in the elaborate great curving horns of the scorpion style, and she wore astonishing festoons of jewelry, necklaces of gold and amber, bracelets of silver and ebony and beads, rings of stone, earrings of shining ivory.

To Ali Pasha the prince said, hissing, "What's *she* doing here?"

"You invited her yourself, Little Father."

Little Father stared into his cup.

"I did?"

"There is no question of that, sir."

"Yes. Yes, I did." Little Father shook his head. "I must have been drunk. What was I thinking of?" Big Father's main wife was young and beautiful, younger, indeed, than Little Father himself; and she was an immense annoyance. Big Father had had six wives in his time, or possibly seven—Little Father was not sure, and he had never dared to ask— of whom all of the earliest ones were now dead, including Little Father's own mother. Of the three that remained, one was an elderly woman who lived in retirement in Gao, and one was a mere child, the old man's final toy; and then there was this one, this witch, this vampire, who placed no bounds on her ambitions. Only six months before, when Big Father had still been more or less healthy, Serene Glory had dared to offer herself to Little Father as they returned together from the Great Mosque. Of course he desired her. Who would not? But the idea was monstrous. Little Father would no more lay a hand on one of Big Father's wives than he would lie down with a crocodile. Clearly this woman, suspecting that the father was approaching his end, had had some dream of beguiling the son. That would not happen. Once Big Father was safely interred in the royal cemetery Serene Glory would go into chaste retirement, however beautiful she might be.

"Get her out of here, fast!" Little Father whispered.

"But she has every right—she is the wife of the Emir—"

"Then keep her away from me, at least. If she comes within five feet of me tonight, you'll be tending camels tomorrow, do you hear? Within *ten* feet. See to it."

"She will come nowhere near you, Little Father."

There was an odd look on Ali Pasha's face.

"Why are you smiling?" Little Father asked.

"Smiling? I am not smiling, Little Father."

"No. No, of course not."

Little Father made a gesture of dismissal and walked toward the platform of audience. A reception line began to form. The Russian was the first to present his greetings to the prince, and then the Aztec, and then the Englishman. There were ceremonial exchanges of gifts. At last it was the turn of the Turk. He had brought a splendid set of ornate daggers, inlaid with jewels. Little Father received them politely and, as he had with the other ambassadors, he bestowed an elaborately carved segment of ivory tusk upon Ismet Akif. The girl stood shyly to one side.

"May I present also my daughter Selima," said Ismet Akif.

She was well trained. She made a quick little ceremonial bow, and as she straightened her eyes met Little Father's, only for a moment, and it was enough. Warmth traveled just beneath his skin nearly the entire length of his body, a signal he knew well. He smiled at her. The smile was a communicative one, and was understood and reciprocated. Even in that busy room those smiles had the force of thunderclaps. Everyone had been watching. Quickly Little Father's gaze traversed the reception hall, and in a fraction of an instant he took in the sudden flicker of rage on the face of Serene Glory, the sudden knowing look on Ali Pasha's, the sudden anguished comprehension on that of the tall young Englishman. Only Ismet Akif remained impassive; and yet Little Father had little doubt that he too was in on the transaction. In the wars of love there are rarely any secrets amongst those on the field of combat.

Every day there was dancing in the marketplace. Some days the dancers kept their heads motionless and put everything else into motion; other days they let their heads oscillate like independent creatures, while scarcely moving a limb. There were days of shouting dances and days of silent dances. Sometimes brilliant robes were worn and sometimes the dancers were all but naked.

In the beginning the foreign ambassadors went regularly to watch the show. But as time went on, the Emir continued not to die, and the intensity of the heat grew and grew, going beyond the uncomfortable into the implausible and then beyond that to the unimaginable, they tended to stay within the relative coolness of their own compounds despite the temptations of the daily show in the plaza. New ambassadors arrived daily, from the Maori Confederation, from China, from Peru finally, from lesser lands like Korea and Ind and the Teutonic States, and for a time the newcomers went to see the dancing with the same eagerness as their predecessors. Then they too stopped attending.

The Emir's longevity was becoming an embarrassment. Weeks were going by and the daily bulletins were a monotonous succession of medical ups and downs, with no clear pattern. The special ambassadors, unexpectedly snared in an ungratifying city at a disagreeable time of year, could not leave, but were beginning to find it an agony to stay on. It was evident to everyone now that the news of Big Father's imminent demise had gone forth to the world in a vastly overanticipatory way.

"If only the old bastard would simply get up and step out on his balcony and tell us he's healthy again, and let us all go home," Sir Anthony said. "Or succumb at last, one or the other. But this suspension, this indefiniteness—"

"Perhaps the prince will grow weary of the waiting and have him smothered in a pillow," Prince Itzcoatl suggested.

The Englishman shook his head. "He'd have done that ten years ago, if he had it in him at all. The time's long past for him to murder his father."

They were on the covered terrace of the Mexican embassy. In the dreadful heat-stricken silence of the day the foreign dignitaries, as they awaited the intolerably deferred news of the Emir's death, moved in formal rotation from one embassy to another, making ceremonial calls in accordance with strict rules of seniority and precedence.

"His Excellency the Grand Duke Alexander Petrovitch," the Aztec major domo announced.

The foreign embassies were all in the same quarter of New Timbuctoo, along the grand boulevard known as The Street of All Nations. In the old days the foreigners had lived in the center of the Old

Town, in fine houses in the best native style, palaces of stone and brick covered with mauve or orange clay. But Big Father had persuaded them one by one to move to the New City. It was undignified and uncomfortable, he insisted, for the representatives of the great overseas powers to live in mud houses with earthen floors.

Having all the foreigners' dwellings lined up in a row along a single street made it much simpler to keep watch over them, and, in case international difficulties should arise, it would be ever so much more easy to round them all up at once under the guise of "protecting" them. But Big Father had not taken into account that it was also very much easier for the foreigners to mingle with each other, which was not necessarily a good idea. It facilitated conspiracy as well as surveillance.

"We are discussing our impatience," Prince Itzcoatl told the Russian, who was the cousin of the Czar. "Sir Anthony is weary of Timbuctoo."

"Nor am I the only one," said the Englishman. "Did you hear that Maori ranting and raving yesterday at the Peruvian party? But what can we do? What can we do?"

"We could to Egypt go while we wait, perhaps," said the Grand Duke. "The Pyramids, the Sphinx, the temples of Karkak!"

"Karnak," Sir Anthony said. "But what if the old bugger dies while we're gone? We'd never get back in time for the funeral. What a black eye for us!"

"And how troublesome for our plans," said the Aztec.

"Mansa Suleiyman would never forgive us," said Sir Anthony.

"Mansa Suleiyman! Mansa Suleiyman!" Alexander Petrovich spat. "Let the black brigand do his own dirty work, then. Brothers, let us go to Egypt. If the Emir dies while we are away, will not the prince be removed whether or not we happen to be in attendance at the funeral?"

"Should we be speaking of this here?" Prince Itzcoatl asked, plucking in displeasure at his earplugs.

"Why not? There is no danger. These people are like children. They would never suspect—"

"Even so—"

But the Russian would not be deterred. Bull-like, he said, "It will all go well whether we are here or not. Believe me. It is all arranged, I remind you. So let us go to Egypt, then, before we bake to death. Before we choke on the sand that blows through these miserable streets."

"Egypt's not a great deal cooler than Songhay right now," Prince Itzcoatl pointed out. "And sand is not unknown there either."

The Grand Duke's massive shoulders moved in a ponderous shrugging gesture.

"To the south, then, to the Great Waterfalls. It is winter in that part of Africa, such winter as they have. Or to the Islands of the Canaries. Anywhere, anywhere at all, to escape from this Timbuctoo. I fry here. I sizzle here. I remind you that I am Russian, my friends. This is no climate for Russians."

Sir Anthony stared suspiciously into the sea-green eyes. "Are you the weak link in our little affair, my dear Duke Alexander? Have we made a mistake by asking you to join us?"

"Does it seem so to you? Am I untrustworthy, do you think?"

"The Emir could die at any moment. Probably will. Despite what's been happening, or not happening, it's clear that he can't last very much longer. The removal of the prince on the day of the funeral, as you have just observed, has been arranged. But how can we dare risk being elsewhere on that day? How can we even *think* of such a thing?" Sir Anthony's lean face grew florid; his tight mat of graying red hair began to rise and crackle with inner electricity; his chilly blue eyes became utterly arctic. "It is *essential* that in the moment of chaos that follows, the great-power triumvirate we represent—the troika, as you say—be on hand here to invite King Suleiyman of Mali to take charge of the country. I repeat, your excellency: *essential*. The time factor is critical. If we are off on holiday in Egypt, or anywhere else—if we are so much as a day too late getting back here—"

Prince Itzcoatl said, "I think the Grand Duke understands that point, Sir Anthony."

"Ah, but does he? Does he?"

"I think so." The Aztec drew in his breath sharply and let his gleaming obsidian eyes meet those of the Russian. "Certainly he sees that we're all in it too deep to back out, and that therefore he has to abide by the plan as drawn, however inconvenient he may find it personally."

The Grand Duke, sounding a little nettled, said, "We are traveling too swiftly here, I think. I tell you, I hate this filthy place, I hate its impossible heat, I hate its blowing sand, I hate its undying Emir, I hate its slippery lecherous prince. I hate the smell of the air, even. It is the smell of camel shit, the smell of old mud. But I am your partner in this undertaking to the end. I will not fail you, believe me." His great shoulders stirred like boulders rumbling down a slope. "The consolidation of Mali and Songhay would be displeasing to the Sultan, and therefore it is pleasing to the Czar. I will assist you in making it happen, knowing that such a consolidation has value for your own nations as well, which also is pleasing to my royal cousin. By the Russian Empire from the plan there will be no withdrawal. Of such a possibility let there be no more talk."

"Of holidays in Egypt let there be no more talk either," said Prince Itzcoatl. "Agreed? None of us likes being here, Duke Alexander. But here we have to stay, like it or not, until everything is brought to completion."

"Agreed. Agreed." The Russian snapped his fingers. "I did not come here to bicker. I have hospitality for you, waiting outside. Will you share vodka with me?" An attache of the Russian Embassy entered, bearing a crystal beaker in a bowl of ice. "This arrived today, by the riverboat, and I have brought it to offer to my beloved friends of England and Mexico. Unfortunately of caviar there is none, though there should be. This heat! This heat! Caviar, in this heat—impossible!" The Grand Duke laughed. "To our great countries! To international amity! To a swift and peaceful end to the Emir's terrible sufferings! To your healths, gentlemen! To your healths!"

"To Mansa Suleiyman, King of Mali and Songhay," Prince Itzcoatl said.

"Mansa Suleiyman, yes."

"Mansa Suleiyman!"

"What splendid stuff," said Sir Anthony. He held forth his glass, and the Russian attache filled it yet again. "There are other and perhaps more deserving monarchs to toast. To His Majesty King Richard the Fifth!"

"King Richard, yes!"

"And His Imperial Majesty Vladimir the Ninth!"

"Czar Vladimir! Czar Vladimir!"

"Let us not overlook His Highness Moctezuma the Twelfth!"

"King Moctezuma! King Moctezuma!"

"Shall we drink to cooler weather and happier days, gentlemen?"

"Cooler weather! Happier days!—And the Emir of Songhay, may he soon rest in peace at last!"

"And to his eldest son, the prince of the realm. May he also soon be at rest," said Prince Itzcoatl.

Selima said, "I hear you have vampires here, and djinn. I want to know all about them."

Little Father was aghast. She would say anything, anything at all.

"Who's been feeding you nonsense like that? There aren't any vampires. There aren't any djinn either. Those things are purely mythical."

"There's a tree south of the city where vampires hold meetings at midnight to choose their victims. Isn't that so? The tree is half white and half red. When you first become a vampire you have to bring one of your male cousins to the meeting for the others to feast on."

"Some of the common people may believe such stuff. But do you think I do? Do you think we're all a bunch of ignorant savages here, girl?"

"There's a charm that can be worn to keep vampires from creeping into your bedroom at night and sucking your blood. I want you to get me one."

"I tell you, there aren't any vamp—"

"Or there's a special prayer you can say. And while you say it you spit in four directions, and that traps the vampire in your house so he can be arrested. Tell me what it is. And the charm for making the vampire give back the blood he's drunk. I want to know that too."

They were on the private upstairs porch of Little Father's palace. The night was bright with moonlight, and the air was as hot as wet velvet. Selima was wearing a long silken robe, very sheer. He could see the shadow of her breasts through it when she turned at an angle to the moon.

"Are you always like this?" he asked, beginning to feel a little irritable. "Or are you just trying to torment me?"

"What's the point of traveling if you don't bother to learn anything about local customs?"

"You do think we're savages."

"Maybe I do. Africa is the dark continent. Black skins, black souls."

"My skin isn't black. It's practically as light as yours. But even if it were—"

"You're black inside. Your blood is African blood, and Africa is the strangest place in the world. The fierce animals you have, gorillas and hippos running around everywhere, giraffes, tigers—the masks, the nightmare carvings—the witchcraft, the drums, the chanting of the high priests—"

"Please," Little Father said. "You're starting to drive me crazy. I'm not responsible for what goes on in the jungles of the tropics. This is Songhay. Do we seem uncivilized to you? We were a great empire when you Ottomans were still herding goats on the steppes. The only giraffe you'll see in this city is the stuffed one in my father's throne room. There aren't any gorillas in Songhay, and tigers come from Asia, and if you see a hippo running, here or anywhere, please tell the newspaper right away." Then he began to laugh. "Look, Selima, this is a modern country. We have motorcars here. We have a stock exchange. There's a famous university in Timbuctoo, six hundred years old. I don't bow down to tribal idols. We are an Islamic people, you know."

It was lunacy to have let her force him onto the defensive like this. But she wouldn't stop her attack.

"Djinn are Islamic. The Koran talks about them. The Arabs believe in djinn."

Little Father struggled for patience. "Perhaps they did five hundred years ago, but what's that to us? In any case we aren't Arabs."

"But there are djinn here, plenty of them. My head porter told me. A djinni will appear as a small black spot on the ground and will grow until he's as big as a house. He might change into a sheep or a dog or a cat, and then he'll disappear. The porter said that one time he was at the edge of town in Kabara, and he was surrounded by giants in white turbans that made a weird sucking noise at him."

"What is this man's name? He has no right filling your head with this trash. I'll have him fed to the lions."

"Really?" Her eyes were sparkling. "Would you? What lions? Where?"

"My father keeps them as pets, in a pit. No one is looking after them these days. They must be getting very hungry."

"Oh, you *are* a savage! You are!"

Little Father grinned lopsidedly. He was regaining some of the advantage, he felt. "Lions need to be fed now and then. There's nothing savage about that. *Not* feeding them, that would be savage."

"But to feed a servant to them—?"

"If he speaks idiotic nonsense to a visitor, yes. Especially when the visitor is an impressionable young girl."

Her eyes flashed quick lightning, sudden pique. "You think I'm impressionable? You think I'm silly?"

"I think you are young."

"And I think you're a savage underneath it all. Even savages can start a stock exchange. But they're still savages."

"Very well," Little Father said, putting an ominous throb into his tone. "I admit it. I am the child of darkness. I am the pagan prince." He pointed to the moon, full and swollen, hanging just above them like a plummeting polished shield. "You think that is a dead planet up there? It is alive, it is a land of djinn. And it must be nourished. So when it is full like this, the king of this land must appear beneath its face and make offerings of energy to it."

"Energy?"

"Sexual energy," he said portentously. "Atop the great phallic altar, beneath which we keep the dried umbilicus of each of our dead kings. First there is a procession, the phallic figures carried through the streets. And then—"

"The sacrifice of a virgin?" Selima asked.

"What's wrong with you? We are good Moslems here. We don't countenance murder."

"But you countenance phallic rites at the full moon?"

He couldn't tell whether she was taking him seriously or not.

"We maintain certain pre-Islamic customs," he said. "It is folly to cut oneself off from one's origins."

"Absolutely. Tell me what you do on the night the moon is full."

"First, the king coats his entire body in rancid butter—"

"I don't think I like that!"

"Then the chosen bride of the moon is led forth—"

"The fair-skinned bride."

"Fair-skinned?" he said. She saw it was a game, he realized. She was getting into it. "Why fair-skinned?"

"Because she'd be more like the moon than a black woman would. Her energy would rise into the sky more easily. So each month a white woman is stolen and brought to the king to take part in the rite."

Little Father gave her a curious stare. "What a ferocious child you are!"

"I'm not a child. You do prefer white women, don't you? One thing you regret is that I'm not white enough for you."

"You seem very white to me," said Little Father. She was at the edge of the porch now, looking outward over the sleeping city. Idly he watched her shoulderblades moving beneath her sheer gown. Then suddenly the garment began to slide downward, and he realized she had unfastened it at the throat and cast it off. She had worn nothing underneath it. Her waist was very narrow, her hips broad, her buttocks smooth and full, with a pair of deep dimples at the place where they curved outward from her back. His lips were beginning to feel very dry, and he licked them thoughtfully.

She said, "What you really want is an Englishwoman, with skin like milk, and pink nipples, and golden hair down below."

Damn Ali Pasha! Was he out of his mind, telling such stuff to her? He'd go to the lions first thing tomorrow!

Amazed, he cried, "What are you talking about? What sort of madness is this?"

"That is what you want, isn't it? A nice juicy golden-haired one. All of you Africans secretly want one. Some of you not so secretly. I know all about it."

No, it was inconceivable. Ali Pasha was tricky, but he wasn't insane. This was mere coincidence.

"Have you ever had an Englishwoman, prince? A true pink-and-gold one?"

Little father let out a sigh of relief. It was only another of her games, then. The girl was all mischief, and it came bubbling out randomly, spontaneously. Truly, she would say anything to anyone. Anything.

"Once," he said, a little vindictively. "She was writing a book on the African empires and she came here to do some research at our university. Our simple barbaric university. One night she interviewed me, on this very porch, a night almost as warm as this one. Her name was—ah—Elizabeth. Elizabeth, yes." Little Father's gaze continued to rest on Selima's bare back. She seemed much more frail above the waist than below. Below the waist she was solid, splendidly fleshly, a commanding woman, no girl at all. Languidly he said, "Skin like milk, indeed. And rosy nipples. I had never even imagined that nipples could be like that. And her hair—"

Selina turned to face him. "My nipples are dark."

"Yes, of course. You're a Turk. But Elizabeth—"

"I don't want to hear any more about Elizabeth. Kiss me."

Her nipples *were* dark, yes, and very small, almost like a boy's, tiny dusky targets on the roundness of her breasts. Her thighs were surprisingly full. She looked far more voluptuous naked than when she was clothed. He hadn't expected that. The heavy thatch at the base of her belly was jet black.

He said, "We don't care for kissing in Songhay. It's one of our quaint tribal taboos. The mouth is for eating, not for making love."

"Every part of the body is for making love. Kiss me."

"You Europeans!"

"I'm not European. I'm a Turk. You do it in some peculiar way here, don't you? Side by side. Back to back."

"No," he said. "Not back to back. Never like that, not even when we feel like reverting to tribal barbarism."

Her perfume drifted toward him, falling over him like a veil. Little Father went to her and she rose up out of the night to him, and they laughed. He kissed her. It was a lie, the thing he had told her, that Songhayans did not like to kiss. Songhayans liked to do everything: at least this Songhayan did. She slipped downward to the swirl of silken pillows on the floor, and he joined her there and covered her body with his own. As he embraced her he felt the moonlight on his back like the touch of a goddess' fingertips, cool, delicate, terrifying.

On the horizon a sharp dawn-line of pale lavender appeared, cutting between the curving grayness above and the flat grayness below. It was like a preliminary announcement by the oboes or the French horns, soon to be transformed into the full overwhelming trumpetblast of morning. Michael, who had been wandering through Old Timbuctoo all night, stared eastward uneasily as if he expected the sky to burst into flame when the sun came into view.

Sleep had been impossible. Only his face and hands were actually sunburned, but his whole body throbbed with discomfort, as though the African sun had reached him even through his clothing. He felt the glow of it behind his knees, in the small of his back, on the soles of his feet.

Nor was there any way to escape the heat, even when the terrible glaring sun had left the sky. The nights were as warm as the days. The motionless air lay on you like burning fur. When you drew a breath you could trace its path all the way down, past your nostrils, past your throat, a trickle of molten lead descending the forking paths into your lungs and spreading out to weigh upon every individual air-sac inside you. Now and then came a breeze, but it only made things worse: it gave you no more comfort than a shower of hot ashes might have afforded. So Michael had risen after a few hours of tossing and turning and gone out unnoticed to wander under the weird and cheerless brilliance of the overhanging moon, down from the posh Embassy district into the Old Town somehow, and then from street to street, from quarter to quarter, no destination in mind, no purpose, seeking only to obliterate the gloom and misery of the night.

He was lost, of course—the Old Town was complex enough to nego-tiate in daylight, impossible in the dark—but that didn't matter. He was somewhere on the western side of town, that was all he knew. The moon was long gone from the sky, as if it had been devoured, though he had not noticed it setting. Before him the ancient metropolis of mud walls and low square flat-roofed buildings lay humped in the thinning darkness, a gigantic weary beast slowly beginning to stir. The thing was to keep on walking, through the night and into the dawn, distract-ing himself from the physical discomfort and the other, deeper agony that had wrapped itself like some voracious starfish around his soul.

By the faint light he saw that he had reached a sort of large pond. Its water looked to be a flat metallic green. Around its perimeter crouched a shadowy horde of water-carriers, crouching to scoop the green water into goatskin bags, spooning it in with gourds. Then they straightened, with the full bags—they must have weighed a hundred pounds—bal-anced on their heads, and went jogging off into the dawn to deliver their merchandise at the homes of the wealthy. Little ragged girls were there too, seven or eight years old, filling jugs and tins to bring to their mothers. Some of them waded right into the pool to get what they wanted. A glowering black man in the uniform of the Emirate sat to one side, jotting down notations on a sheet of yellow paper. So this was probably the Old Town's municipal reservoir. Michael shuddered and turned away, back into the city proper. Into the labyrinth once more.

A gray, sandy light was in the sky now. It showed him narrow dusty thoroughfares, blind walls, curving alleyways leading into dark cul-de-sacs. Entire rows of houses seemed to be crumbling away, though they were obviously still inhabited. Under foot everything was sand, mak-ing a treacherous footing. In places the entrances to buildings were half choked by the drifts. Camels, donkeys, horses wandered about on their own. The city's mixed population—veiled Tuaregs, black Sudanese, aloof and lofty Moors, heavy-bearded Syrian traders, the whole West African racial goulash—was coming forth into the day. Who were all these people? Tailors, moneylenders, scribes, camel-breeders, masons, bakers, charm-sellers, weavers, bakers—necromancers, sages, war-locks, perhaps a few vampires on their way home from their night's toil—Michael looked around, bewildered, trapped within his skull by the barriers of language and his own disordered mental state. He felt as though he were moving about under the surface of the sea, in a medium where he did not belong and could neither breathe nor think.

"Selima?" he said suddenly, blinking in astonishment.

His voice was voiceless. His lips moved, but no sound had come forth.

Apparition? Hallucination? No, no, she was really there. Selima glowed just across the way like a second sun suddenly rising over the city.

Michael shrank back against an immense buttress of mud brick. She had stepped out of a doorway in a smooth gray wall that surrounded what appeared to be one of the palaces of the nobility. The building, partly visible above the wall, was coated in orange clay and had elaborate Moorish windows of dark wood. He trembled. The girl wore only a flimsy white gown, so thin that he could make out the dark-tipped spheres of her breasts moving beneath it, and the dark triangle at her thighs. He wanted to cry. Had she no shame? No. No. She was indifferent to the display, and to everything around her; she would have walked completely naked through this little plaza just as casually as she strode through in this one thin garment.

"Selima, where have you spent this night? Whose palace is this?"

His words were air. No one heard them. She moved serenely onward. A motorcar appeared from somewhere, one of the five or six that Michael had seen so far in this city. A black plume of smoke rose from the vent of its coal-burning engine, and its two huge rear wheels slipped and slid about on the sandy track. Selima jumped up onto the open seat behind the driver, and with great booming exhalations the vehicle made its way through an arched passageway and disappeared into the maze of the town.

An embassy car, no doubt. Waiting here for her all night?

His soul ached. He had never felt so young, so foolish, so vulnerable, so wounded.

"Effendi?" a voice asked. "You wish a camel, effendi?"

"Thank you, no."

"Nice hotel? Bath? Woman to massage you? Boy to massage you?"

"Please. No."

"Some charms, maybe? Good grigri. Souvenir of Timbuctoo."

Michael groaned. He turned away and looked back at the house of infamy from which Selima had emerged.

"That building—what is it?"

"That? Is palace of Little Father. And look, look there, effendi— Little Father himself coming out for a walk."

The prince himself, yes. Of course. Who else would she have spent the night with, here in the Old Town? Michael was engulfed by loathing and despair. Instantly a swarm of eager citizens had surrounded the prince, clustering about him to beg favors the moment he showed himself. But he seemed to move through them with the sort of divine indifference that Selima, in her all-but-nakedness, had displayed. He appeared to be enclosed in an impenetrable bubble of self-concern. He was frowning, he looked troubled, not at all like a man who had just known the favors of the most desirable woman in five hundred miles. His lean sharp-angled face, which had been so animated at the official reception, now had a curiously stunned, immobile look about it, as though he had been struck on the head from behind a short while before and the impact was gradually sinking in.

Michael flattened himself against the buttress. He could not bear the thought of being seen by the prince now, here, as if he had been haunting the palace all night, spying on Selima. He put his arm across his face in a frantic attempt to hide himself, he whose western clothes and long legs and white skin made him stand out like a meteor. But the prince wasn't coming toward him. Nodding in an abstracted way, he turned quickly, passed through the throng of chattering petitioners as if they were ghosts, disappeared in a flurry of white fabric.

Michael looked about for his sudden friend, the man who had wanted to sell him camels, massages, souvenirs. What he wanted now was a guide to get him out of the Old Town and back to the residence of the English ambassador. But the man was gone.

"Pardon me—" Michael said to someone who looked almost like the first one. Then he realized that he had spoken in English. Useless. He tried in Turkish and in Arabic. A few people stared at him. They seemed to be laughing. He felt transparent to them. They could see his sorrow, his heartache, his anguish, as easily as his sunburn.

Like the good young diplomat he was, he had learned a little Songhay too, the indigenous language. "Town talk," they called it.

But the few words he had seemed all to have fled. He stood alone and helpless in the plaza, scuffing angrily at the sand, as the sun broke above the mud rooftops like the sword of an avenging angel and the full blast of morning struck him. Michael felt blisters starting to rise on his cheeks. Agitated flies began to buzz around his eyes. A camel, passing by just then, dropped half a dozen hot green turds right at his feet. He snatched one out of the sand and hurled it with all his strength at the bland blank mud-colored wall of Little Father's palace.

❋

Big Father was sitting up on his divan. His silken blankets were knotted around his waist in chaotic strands, and his bare torso rose above the chaos, gleaming as though it had been oiled. His arms were like sticks and his skin was three shades paler than it once had been and cascades of loose flesh hung like wattles from his neck, but there was the brilliance of black diamonds in his glittering little eyes.

"Not dead yet, you see? You see?" His voice was a cracked wailing screech, but the old authoritative thunder was still somewhere behind it. "Back from the edge of the grave, boy! Allah walks with me yet!"

Little Father was numb with chagrin. All the joy of his night with Selima had vanished in a moment when word had arrived of his father's miraculous recovery. He had just been getting accustomed to the idea that he soon would be king, too. His first misgivings about the work involved in it had begun to ebb; he rather liked the idea of ruling, now. The crown was descending on him like a splendid gift. And here was Big Father sitting up, grinning, waving his arms around in manic glee. Taking back his gift. Deciding to live after all.

What about the funeral plans? What about the special ambassadors who had traveled so far, in such discomfort, to pay homage to the late venerable Emir of Songhay and strike their various deals with his successor?

Big Father had had his head freshly shaved and his beard had been trimmed. He looked like a gnome, ablaze with demonic energies. Off in the corner of the porch, next to the potted trees, the three marabouts stood in a circle, making sacred gestures at each other with lunatic vigor, each seeking to demonstrate superior fervor.

Hoarsely Little Father said, "Your majesty, the news astonishes and delights me. When the messenger came, telling of your miraculous recovery, I leaped from my bed and gave thanks to the All-Merciful in a voice so loud you must have heard it here."

"Was there a woman with you, boy?"

"Father—"

"I hope you bathed before you came here. You come forth without bathing after you've lain with a woman and the djinn will make you die an awful death, do you realize that?"

"Father, I wouldn't think of—"

"Frothing at the mouth, falling down in the street, that's what'll happen to you. Who was she? Some nobleman's wife as usual, I suppose. Well, never mind. As long as she wasn't mine. Come closer to me, boy."

"Father, you shouldn't tire yourself by talking so much."

"Closer!"

A wizened claw reached for him. Little Father approached and the claw seized him. There was frightening strength in the old man still.

Big Father said, "I'll be up and around in two days. I want the Great Mosque made ready for the ceremony of thanksgiving. And I'll sacrifice to all the prophets and saints." A fit of coughing overcame him for a space, and he pounded his fist furiously against the side of the divan. When he spoke again, his voice seemed weaker, but still determined. "There was a vampire upon me, boy! Each night she came in here and drank from me."

"She?"

"With dark hair and pale foreign skin, and eyes that eat you alive. Every night. Stood above me, and laughed, and took my blood. But she's gone now. These three have imprisoned her and carried her off to the Eleventh Hell." He gestured toward the marabouts. "My saints. My heroes. I want them rewarded beyond all reckoning."

"As you say, father, so will I do."

The old man nodded. "You were getting my funeral ready, weren't you?"

"The prognosis was very dark. Certain preparations seemed advisable when we heard—"

"Cancel them!"

"Of course." Then, uncertainly: "Father, special envoys have come from many lands. The Czar's cousin is here, and the brother of Moctezuma, and a son of the late Sultan, and also—"

"I'll hold an audience for them all," said Big Father in great satisfaction. "They'll have gifts beyond anything they can imagine. Instead of a funeral, boy, we'll have a jubilee! A celebration of life. Moctezuma's brother, you say? And who did the Inca send?" Big Father laughed raucously. "All of them clustering around to see me put away underground!" He jabbed a finger against Little Father's breast. It felt like a spear of bone. "And in Mali they're dancing in the streets, aren't they? Can't contain themselves for glee. But they'll dance a different dance now." Big Father's eyes grew somber. "You know, boy, when I really do die, whenever that is, they'll try to take you out too, and Mali will invade us. Guard yourself. Guard the nation. Those bastards on the coast hunger to control our caravan routes. They're probably already scheming now with the foreigners to swallow us the instant I'm gone, but you mustn't allow them to—ah—ah—"

"Father?"

Abruptly the Emir's shriveled face crumpled in a frenzy of coughing. He hammered against his thighs with clenched fists. An attendant came running, bearing a beaker of water, and Big Father drank until he had drained it all. Then he tossed the beaker aside as though it were nothing. He was shivering. He looked glassyeyed and confused. His shoulders slumped, his whole posture slackened. Perhaps his "recovery" had been merely the sudden final upsurge of a dying fire.

"You should rest, majesty," said a new voice from the doorway to the porch. It was Serene Glory's ringing contralto. "You overtax yourself, I think, in the first hours of this miracle."

Big Father's main wife had arrived, entourage and all. In the warmth of the morning she had outfitted herself in a startling robe of purple satin, over which she wore the finest jewels of the kingdom. Little Father remembered that his own mother had worn some of those necklaces and bracelets.

He was unmoved by Serene Glory's beauty, impressive though it was. How could Serene Glory matter to him with the memory, scarcely two hours old, of Selima's full breasts and agile thighs still glistening in his mind? But he could not fail to detect Serene Glory's anger. It surrounded her like a radiant aura. Tension sparkled in her kohl-bedecked eyes.

Perhaps she was still smoldering over Little Father's deft rejection of her advances as they were riding side by side back from the Great Mosque that day six months earlier. Or perhaps it was Big Father's unexpected return from the brink that annoyed her. Anyone with half a mind realized that Serene Glory dreamed of putting her own insipid brother on the throne in Little Father's place the moment the old Emir was gone, and thus maintaining and even extending her position at the summit of power. Quite likely she, like Little Father, had by now grown accustomed to the idea of Big Father's death and was having difficulty accepting the news that it would be somewhat postponed.

To Little Father she said, "Our prayers have been answered, all glory to Allah! But you mustn't put a strain on the Emir's energies in this time of recovery. Perhaps you ought to go."

"I was summoned, lady."

"Of course. Quite rightly. And now you should go to the mosque and give thanks for what has been granted us all."

Her gaze was imperious and unanswerable. In one sentence Serene Glory had demoted him from imminent king to wastrel prince once again. He admired her gall. She was three years younger than Little Father, and here she was ordering him out of the royal presence as though he were a child. But of course she had had practice at ordering people around: her father was one of the greatest landlords of the eastern province. She had moved amidst power all her life, albeit power of a provincial sort. Little Father wondered how many noblemen of that province had spent time between the legs of Serene Glory before she had ascended to her present high position.

He said, "If my royal father grants me leave to go—"

The Emir was coughing again. He looked terrible.

Serene Glory went to him and bent close over him, so the old man could smell the fragrance rising from her breasts, and instantly Big Father relaxed. The coughing ceased and he sat up again, almost as vigorous as before. Little Father admired that maneuver too. Serene Glory was a worthy adversary. Probably her people were already spreading the word in the city that it was the power of her love for the Emir, and not the prayers of the three saints, that had brought him back from the edge of death.

"How cool it is in here," Big Father said. "The wind is rising. Will it rain today? The rains are due, aren't they? Let me see the sky. What color is the sky?" He looked upward in an odd straining way, as though the sky had risen to such a height that it could no longer be seen.

"Father," Little Father said softly.

The old man glared. "You heard her, didn't you? To the mosque! To the mosque and give thanks! Do you want Allah to think you're an ingrate, boy?" He started coughing once again. Once again he began visibly to descend the curve of his precarious vitality. His withered cheeks began to grow mottled. There was a feeling of impending death in the air.

Servants and ministers and the three marabouts gathered by his side, alarmed.

"Big Father! Big Father!"

And then once more he was all right again, just as abruptly. He gestured fiercely, an unmistakable dismissal. The woman in purple gave Little Father a dark grin of triumph. Little Father nodded to her gallantly: this round was hers. He knelt at the Emir's side, kissed his royal ring. It slipped about loosely on his shrunken finger. Little Father, thinking of nothing but the pressure of Selima's dark, hard little nipples against the palms of his hands two hours before, made the prostration of filial devotion to his father and, with ferocious irony, to his stepmother, and backed quickly away from the royal presence.

❁

Michael said, distraught, "I couldn't sleep, sir. I went out for a walk."

"And you walked *the whole night long*?" Sir Anthony asked, in a voice like a flail.

"I didn't really notice the time. I just kept walking, and by and by the sun came up and I realized that the night was gone."

"It's your mind that's gone, I think." Sir Anthony, crooking his neck upward to Michael's much greater height, gave him a whipcrack glare. "What kind of calf are you, anyway? Haven't you any sense at all?"

"Sir Anthony, I don't underst—"

"Are you in *love*? With the Turkish girl?"

Michael clapped his hand over his mouth in dismay.

"You know about that?" he said lamely, after a moment.

"One doesn't have to be a mind-reader to see it, lad. Every camel in Timbuctoo knows it. The pathetic look on your face whenever she comes within fifty feet of you—the clownish way you shuffle your feet around, and hang your head—those occasional little groans of deepest melancholy—" The envoy glowered. He made no attempt to hide his anger, or his contempt. "By heaven, I'd like to hang your head, and all the rest of you as well. Have you no sense? Have you no sense whatsoever?"

Everything was lost, so what did anything matter? Defiantly Michael said, "Have you never fallen unexpectedly in love, Sir Anthony?"

"With a *Turk*?"

"Unexpectedly, I said. These things don't necessarily happen with one's political convenience in mind."

"And she reciprocates your love, I suppose? That's why you were out walking like a moon-calf in this miserable parched mudhole of a city all night long?"

"She spent the night with the crown prince," Michael blurted in misery.

"Ah. Ah, now it comes out!" Sir Anthony was silent for a while. Then he glanced up sharply, his eyes bright with skepticism. "But how do you know that?"

"I saw her leaving his palace at dawn, sir."

"Spying on her, were you?"

"I just happened to be there. I didn't even know it was his palace, until I asked. He came out himself a few minutes later, and went quickly off somewhere. He looked very troubled."

"He should have looked troubled. He'd just found out that he might not get to be king as quickly as he'd like to be."

"I don't understand, please, sir."

"There's word going around town this morning that the Emir has recovered. And had sent for his son to let him know that he wasn't quite as moribund as was generally believed."

Michael recoiled in surprise.

"Recovered? Is it true?"

Sir Anthony offered him a benign, patronizing smile.

"So they say. But the Emir's doctors assure us that it's nothing more than a brief rally in an inevitable descent. The old wolf will be dead within the week. Still, it's rather a setback for Little Father's immediate plans. The news of the Emir's unanticipated awakening from his coma must rather have spoiled his morning for him."

"Good," said Michael vindictively.

Sir Anthony laughed.

"You hate him, do you?"

"I despise him. I loathe him. I have nothing but the greatest detestation for him. He's a cynical amoral voluptuary and nothing more. He doesn't deserve to be a king."

"Well, if it's any comfort to you, lad, he's not going to live long enough to become one."

"What?"

"His untimely demise has been arranged. His stepmother is going to poison him at the funeral of the old Emir, if the old Emir ever has the good grace to finish dying."

"What? What?"

Sir Anthony smiled.

"This is quite confidential, you understand. Perhaps I shouldn't be entrusting you with it just yet. But you'd have needed to find out sooner or later. We've organized a little coup d'etat."

"What? What? What?" said Michael helplessly.

"Her Highness the Lady Serene Glory would like to put her brother on the throne instead of the prince. The brother is worthless, of course. So is the prince, of course, but at least he does happen to be the rightful heir. We don't want to see either of them have it, actually. What we'd prefer is to have the Mansa of Mali declare that the unstable conditions in Songhay following the death of the old Emir have created a danger to the security of all of West Africa that can be put to rest only by an amalgamation of the kingdoms of Mali and Songhay under a single ruler. Who would be, of course, the Mansa of Mali, precisely as your young lady so baldly suggested the other day. And that is what we intend to achieve. The Grand Duke and Prince Itzcoatl and I. As representatives of the powers whom we serve."

Michael stared. He rubbed his cheeks as if to assure himself that this was no dream. He found himself unable to utter a sound.

Sir Anthony went on, clearly and calmly.

"And so Serene Glory gives Little Father the deadly cup, and then the Mansa's troops cross the border, and we, on behalf of our governments, immediately recognize the new combined government. Which makes everyone happy except, I suppose, the Sultan, who has such good trade relationships with Songhay and is on such poor terms with the Mansa of Mali. But we hardly shed tears for the Sultan's distress, do we, boy? Do we? The distress of the Turks is no concern of ours. Quite the contrary, in fact, is that not so?" Sir Anthony clapped his hand to Michael's shoulder. It was an obvious strain for him, reaching so high. The fingers clamping into Michael's tender sunburned skin were agony. "So let's see no more mooning over this alluring Ottoman goddess of yours, eh, lad? It's inappropriate for a lovely blond English boy like yourself to be lusting after a Turk, as you know very well. She's nothing but a little slut, however she may seem to your infatuated eyes. And you needn't take the trouble to expend any energy loathing the prince, either. His days are numbered. He won't survive his evil old father by so much as a week. It's all arranged."

Michael's jaw gaped. A glazed look of disbelief appeared in his eyes. His face was burning fiercely, not from the sunburn now, but from the intensity of his confusion.

"But sir—sir—"

"Get yourself some sleep, boy."

"*Sir!*"

"Shocked, are you? Well, you shouldn't be. There's nothing shocking about assassinating an inconvenient king. What's shocking to me is a grown man with pure English blood in his veins spending the night creeping pitifully around after his dissolute little Turkish inamorata as she makes her way to the bed of her African lover. And then telling me how heartsore and miserable he is. Get yourself some sleep, boy. Get yourself some sleep!"

In the midst of the uncertainty over the Emir's impending death the semi-annual salt caravan from the north arrived in Timbuctoo. It was a great, if somewhat unexpected, spectacle, and all the foreign ambassadors, restless and by now passionately in need of diversion, turned out despite the heat to watch its entry into the city.

There was tremendous clamor. The heavy metal-studded gates of the city were thrown open and the armed escort entered first, a platoon of magnificent black warriors armed both with rifles and with scimitars. Trumpets brayed, drums pounded. A band of fierce-looking hawk-nosed fiery-eyed country chieftains in flamboyant robes came next, marching in phalanx like conquerors. And then came the salt-laden camels, an endless stream of them, a tawny river, strutting absurdly along in grotesque self-important grandeur with their heads held high and their sleepy eyes indifferent to the throngs of excited spectators. Strapped to each camel's back were two or three huge flat slabs of salt, looking much like broad blocks of marble.

"There are said to be seven hundred of the beasts," murmured the Chinese ambassador, Li Hsiao-ssu.

"One thousand eight hundred," said the Grand Duke Alexander sternly. He glowered at Li Hsiao-ssu, a small, fastidious-looking man with drooping mustachios and gleaming porcelain skin, who seemed a mere doll beside the bulky Russian. There was little love lost between the Grand Duke and the Chinese envoy. Evidently the Grand Duke thought it was presumptuous that China, as a client state of the Russian Empire, as a mere vassal, in truth, had sent an ambassador at all. "One thousand eight hundred. That is the number I was told, and it is reliable. I assure you that it is reliable."

The Chinese shrugged. "Seven hundred, three thousand, what difference is there? Either way, that's too many camels to have in one place at one time."

"Yes, what ugly things they are!" said the Peruvian, Manco Roca. "Such stupid faces, such an ungainly stride! Perhaps we should do these Africans a favor and let them have a few herds of llamas."

Coolly Prince Itzcoatl said, "Your llamas, brother, are no more fit for the deserts of this continent than these camels would be in the passes of the Andes. Let them keep their beasts, and be thankful that you have handsomer ones for your own use."

"Such stupid faces," the Peruvian said once more.

Timbuctoo was the center of distribution for salt throughout the whole of West Africa. The salt mines were hundreds of miles away, in the center of the Sahara. Twice a year the desert traders made the twelve-day journey to the capital, where they exchanged their salt for the dried fish, grain, rice, and other produce that came up the Niger from the agricultural districts to the south and east. The arrival of the caravan was the occasion for feasting and revelry, a time of wild big-city gaiety for the visitors from such remote and placid rural outposts.

But the Emir of Songhai was dying. This was no time for a festival. The appearance of the caravan at such a moment was evidently a great embarrassment to the city officials, a mark of bad management as well as bad taste.

"They could have sent messengers upcountry to turn them back," Michael said. "Why didn't they, I wonder?"

"Blacks," said Manco Roca morosely. "What can you expect from blacks."

"Yes, of course," Sir Anthony said, giving the Peruvian a disdainful look. "We understand that they aren't Incas. Yet despite that shortcoming they've somehow managed to keep control of most of this enormous continent for thousands of years."

"But their colossal administrative incompetence, my dear Sir Anthony—as we see here, letting a circus like this one come into town while their king lies dying—"

"Perhaps it's deliberate," Ismet Akif suggested. "A much needed distraction. The city is tense. The Emir's been too long about his dying; it's driving everyone crazy. So they decided to let the caravan come marching in."

"I think not," said Li Hsiao-ssu. "Do you see those municipal officials there? I detect signs of deep humiliation on their faces."

"And who would be able to detect such things more acutely than you?" asked the Grand Duke.

The Chinese envoy stared at the Russian as though unsure whether he was being praised or mocked. For a moment his elegant face was dusky with blood. The other diplomats gathered close, making ready to defuse the situation. Politeness was ever a necessity in such a group.

Then the envoy from the Teutonic States said, "Is that not the prince arriving now?"

"Where?" Michael demanded in a tight-strung voice. "Where is he?"

Sir Anthony's hand shot out to seize Michael's wrist. He squeezed it unsparingly.

In a low tone he said, "You will cause no difficulties, young sir. Remember that you are English. Your breeding must rule your passions."

Michael, glaring toward Little Father as the prince approached the city gate, sullenly pulled his arm free of Sir Anthony's grasp and amazed himself by uttering a strange low growling sound, like that of a cat announcing a challenge. Unfamiliar hormones flooded the channels of his body. He could feel the individual bones of his cheeks and forehead moving apart from one another, he was aware of the tensing and coiling of muscles great and small. He wondered if he was losing his mind. Then the moment passed and he let out his breath in a long dismal exhalation.

Little Father wore flowing green pantaloons, a striped robe wide enough to cover his arms, and an intricately deployed white turban with brilliant feathers of some exotic sort jutting from it.

An entourage of eight or ten men surrounded him, carrying iron-shafted lances. The prince strode forward so briskly that his bodyguard was hard pressed to keep up with him.

Michael, watching Selima out of the corner of his eye, murmured to Sir Anthony, "I'm terribly sorry, sir. But if he so much as glances at her you'll have to restrain me."

"If you so much as flicker a nostril I'll have you billeted in our Siberian consulate for the rest of your career," Sir Anthony replied, barely moving his lips as he spoke.

But Little Father had no time to flirt with Selima now. He barely acknowledged the presence of the ambassadors at all. A stiff formal nod, and then he moved on, into the midst of the group of caravan leaders. They clustered about him like a convocation of eagles. Among those sun-crisped swarthy upright chieftains the prince seemed soft, frail, overly citified, a dabbler confronting serious men.

Some ritual of greeting seemed to be going on. Little Father touched his forehead, extended his open palm, closed his hand with a snap, presented his palm again with a flourish. The desert men responded with equally stylized maneuvers.

When Little Father spoke, it was in Songhay, a sharp outpouring of liquid incomprehensibilities.

"What was that? What was that?" asked the ambassadors of one another. Turkish was the international language of diplomacy, even in Africa; the native tongues of the dark continent were mysteries to outsiders.

Sir Anthony, though, said softly, "He's angry. He says the city's closed on account of the Emir's illness and the caravan was supposed to have waited at Kabara for further instructions. They seem surprised. Someone must have missed a signal."

"You speak Songhay, sir?" Michael asked.

"I was posted in Mali for seven years," Sir Anthony muttered. "It was before you were born, boy."

"So I was right," cried Manco Roca. "The caravan should never have been allowed to enter the city at all. Incompetence! Incompetence!"

"Is he telling them to leave?" Ismet Akif wanted to know.

"I can't tell. They're all talking at once. I think they're saying that their camels need fodder. And he's telling them that there's no merchandise for them to buy, that the goods from upriver were held back because of the Emir's illness."

"What an awful jumble," Selima said.

It was the first thing she had said all morning. Michael, who had been trying to pay no attention to her, looked toward her now in agitation. She was dressed chastely enough, in a red blouse and flaring black skirt, but in his inflamed mind she stood revealed suddenly nude, with the marks of Little Father's caresses flaring like stigmata on her breasts and thighs. Michael sucked in his breath and held himself stiffly erect, trembling like a drawn bowstring. A sound midway between a sigh and a groan escaped him. Sir Anthony kicked his ankle sharply.

Some sort of negotiation appeared to be going on. Little Father gesticulated rapidly, grinned, did the open-close-open gesture with his hand again, tapped his chest and his forehead and his left elbow. The apparent leader of the traders matched him, gesture for gesture. Postures began to change. The tensions were easing.

Evidently the caravan would be admitted to the city.

Little Father was smiling, after a fashion. His forehead glistened with sweat; he seemed to have come through a difficult moment well, but he looked tired.

The trumpets sounded again. The camel-drovers regained the attention of their indifferent beasts and nudged them forward.

There was new commotion from the other side of the plaza.

"What's this, now?" Prince Itzcoatl said.

A runner clad only in a loincloth appeared, coming from the direction of the city center, clutching a scroll. He was moving fast, loping in a strange lurching way. In the stupefying heat he seemed to be in peril of imminent collapse. But he staggered up to Little Father and put the scroll in his hand.

Little Father unrolled it quickly and scanned it. He nodded somberly and turned to his vizier, who stood just to his left. They spoke briefly in low whispers. Sir Anthony, straining, was unable to make out a word.

A single chopping gesture from Little Father was enough to halt the resumption of the caravan's advance into the city. The prince beckoned the leaders of the traders to his side and conferred with them a moment or two, this time without ceremonial gesticulations. The desert men exchanged glances with one another. Then they barked rough commands. The whole vast caravan began to reverse itself.

Little Father's motorcar was waiting a hundred paces away. He went to it now, and it headed cityward, emitting belching bursts of black smoke and loud intermittent thunderclaps of inadequate combustion.

The prince's entourage, left behind in the suddenness, milled about aimlessly. The vizier, making shooing gestures, ordered them in some annoyance to follow their master on foot toward town. He himself held his place, watching the departure of the caravaneers.

"Ali Pasha!" Sir Anthony called. "Can you tell us what's happened? Is there bad news?"

The vizier turned. He seemed radiant with self-importance.

"The Emir has taken a turn for the worse. They think he'll be with Allah within the hour."

"But he was supposed to be recovering," Michael protested.

Indifferently, Ali Pasha said, "That was earlier. This is now." The vizier seemed not to be deeply moved by the news. If anything his smugness seemed to have been enhanced by it. Perhaps it was something he had been very eager to hear. "The caravan must camp outside the city walls until after the funeral. There is nothing more to be seen here today. You should all go back to your residences."

The ambassadors began to look around for their drivers.

Michael, who had come out here with Sir Anthony in the embassy motorcar, was disconcerted to discover that the envoy had already vanished, slipping away in the uproar without waiting for him. Well, it wasn't an impossible walk back to town. He had walked five times as far in his night of no sleep.

"Michael?"

Selima was calling to him. He looked toward her, appalled.

"Walk with me," she said. "I have a parasol. You can't let yourself get any more sun on your face."

"That's very kind of you," he said mechanically, while lunatic jealousy and anger roiled him within. Searing contemptuous epithets came to his lips and died there, unspoken. To him she was ineluctably soiled by the presumed embraces of that night of shame. How could she have done it? The prince had wiggled his finger at her, and she had run to him without a moment's hesitation. Once more unwanted images surged through his mind: Selima and the prince entwined on a leopardskin rug; the prince mounting Selima in some unthinkable bestial African position of love; Selima, giggling girlishly, instructing the prince afterward in the no doubt equally depraved sexual customs of the land of the Sultan. Michael understood that he was being foolish; that Selima was free to do as she pleased in this loathsome land; that he himself had never staked any claim on her attention more significant than a few callow lovesick stares, so why should she have felt any compunctions about amusing herself with the prince if the prince offered amusement? "Very kind," he said. She handed the parasol up to him and he took it from her with a rigid nerveless hand. They began to walk side by side in the direction of town, close together under the narrow, precisely defined shadow of the parasol beneath the unsparing eye of the noonday sun.

She said, "Poor Michael. I've upset you terribly, haven't I?"

"Upset me? How have you possibly upset me?"

"You know."

"No. No, really."

His legs were leaden. The sun was hammering the top of his brain through the parasol, through his wide-brimmed topee, through his skull itself. He could not imagine how he would find the strength to walk all the way back to town with her.

"I've been very mischievous," she said.

"Have you?"

He wished he were a million miles away.

"By visiting the prince in his palace that night."

"Please, Selima."

"I saw you, you know. Early in the morning, when I was leaving. You ducked out of sight, but not quite fast enough."

"Selima—"

"I couldn't help myself. Going there, I mean. I wanted to see what his palace looked like. I wanted to get to know him a little better. He's very nice, you know. No, nice isn't quite the word. He's shrewd, and part of being shrewd is knowing how to seem nice. I don't really think he's nice at all. He's quite sophisticated—quite subtle."

She was flaying him, inch by inch. Another word out of her and he'd drop the parasol and run.

"The thing is, Michael, he enjoys pretending to be some sort of a primitive, a barbarian, a jungle prince. But it's only a pretense. And why shouldn't it be? These are ancient kingdoms here in Africa. This isn't any jungle land with tigers sleeping behind every palm tree. They've got laws and culture, they've got courts, they have a university. And they've had centuries to develop a real aristocracy. They're just as complicated and cunning as we are. Maybe more so. I was glad to get to know the man behind the facade, a little. He was fascinating, in his way, but—" She smiled brightly. "But I have to tell you, Michael: he's not my type at all."

That startled him, and awakened sudden new hope. Perhaps he never actually touched her, Michael told himself. Perhaps they had simply talked all night. Played little sly verbal games of oneupmanship, teasing each other, vying with each other to be sly and cruel and playful. Showing each other how complicated and cunning they could really be. Demonstrating the virtues of hundreds of years of aristocratic inbreeding. Perhaps they were too well bred to think of doing anything so commonplace as—as—

"What *is* your type, then?" he asked, willy-nilly.

"I prefer men who are a little shy. Men who can sometimes be foolish, even." There was unanticipated softness in her voice, conveying a sincerity that Michael prayed was real. "I hate the kind who are always calculating, calculating, calculating. There's something very appealing to me about English men, I have to tell you, precisely because they *don't* seem so dark and devious inside—not that I've met very many of them before this trip, you understand, but—oh, Michael, Michael, you're terribly angry with me, I know, but you shouldn't be! What happened between me and the prince was nothing. Nothing! And now that he'll be preoccupied with the funeral, perhaps there'll be a chance for you and me to get to know each other a little better—to slip off, for a day, let's say, while all the others are busy with the pomp and circumstance—"

She gave him a melting look. He thought for one astounded moment that she actually might mean what she was telling him.

"They're going to assassinate him," he suddenly heard his own voice saying, "right at the funeral."

"What?"

"It's all set up." The words came rolling from him spontaneously, unstoppably, like the flow of a river. "His stepmother, the old king's young wife—she's going to slip him a cup of poisoned wine, or something, during one of the funeral rituals. What she wants is to make her stupid brother king in the prince's place, and rule the country as the power behind the throne."

Selima made a little gasping sound and stepped away from him, out from under the shelter of the parasol. She stood staring at him as though he had been transformed in the last moment or two into a hippopotamus, or a rock, or a tree.

It took her a little while to find her voice.

"Are you serious? How do you know?"

"Sir Anthony told me."

"Sir Anthony?"

"He's behind it. He and the Russian and Prince Itzcoatl. Once the prince is out of the way, they're going to invite the King of Mali to step in and take over."

Her gaze grew very hard. Her silence was inscrutable, painfully so.

Then, totally regaining her composure with what must have been an extraordinary act of inner discipline, she said, "I think this is all very unlikely."

She might have been responding to a statement that snow would soon begin falling in the streets of Timbuctoo.

"You think so?"

"Why should Sir Anthony support this assassination? England has nothing to gain from destabilizing West Africa. England is a minor power still struggling to establish its plausibility in the world as an independent state. Why should it risk angering a powerful African empire like Songhay by meddling in its internal affairs?"

Michael let the slight to his country pass unchallenged, possibly because it seemed less like a slight to him than a statement of the mere reality. He searched instead for some reason of state that would make what he had asserted seem sensible.

After a moment he said, "Mali and Songhay together would be far more powerful than either one alone. If England plays an instrumental role in delivering the throne of Songhay up to Mali, England will surely be given a preferential role by the Mansa of Songhay in future West African trade."

Selima nodded. "Perhaps."

"And the Russians—you know how they feel about the Ottoman Empire. Your people are closely allied with Songhay and don't get along well with Mali. A coup d'etat here would virtually eliminate Turkey as a commercial force in West Africa."

"Very likely."

She was so cool, so terribly calm.

"As for the Aztec role in this—" Michael shook his head. "God knows. But the Mexicans are always scheming around in things. Maybe they see some way of hurting Peru. There's a lot of sea trade, you know, between Mali and Peru—it's an amazingly short hop across the ocean from West Africa to Peru's eastern provinces in Brazil—and the Mexicans may believe they could divert some of that trade to themselves by winning the Mansa's favor by helping him gain possession of—"

He faltered to a halt. Something was happening. Her expression was starting to change, her facade of detached skepticism was visibly collapsing, slowly but irreversibly, like a brick wall undermined by a great earthquake.

"Yes. Yes, I see. There are substantial reasons for such a scheme. And so they will kill the prince," Selima said.

"Have him killed, rather."

"It's the same thing! The very same thing!"

Her eyes began to glisten. She drew even further back from him and turned her head away, and he realized that she was trying to conceal tears from him. But she couldn't hide the sobs that racked her.

He suspected that she was one who cried very rarely, if at all. Seeing her weep now in this uncontrollable way plunged him into an abyss of dejection.

She was making no attempt to hide her love of the prince from him. That was the only explanation for these tears.

"Selima—please, Selima—"

He felt useless.

He realized, also, that he had destroyed himself.

He had committed this monstrous breach of security, he saw now, purely in the hope of insinuating himself into her confidence, to bind her to him in a union that proceeded from shared possession of an immense secret. He had taken her words at face value when she had told him that the prince was nothing to her.

That had been a serious error. He had thought he was making a declaration of love; but all he had done was to reveal a state secret to England's ancient enemy.

He waited, feeling huge and clumsy and impossibly naive.

Then, abruptly, her sobbing stopped and she looked toward him, a little puffy-eyed now, but otherwise as inscrutable as before.

"I'm not going to say anything about this to anyone."

"What?"

"Not to him, not to my father, not to anyone."

He was mystified. As usual.

"But—Selima—"

"I told you. The prince is nothing to me. And this is only a crazy rumor. How do I know it's true? How do *you* know it's true?"

"Sir Anthony—"

"Sir Anthony! Sir Anthony! For all I know, he's floated this whole thing simply to ensnare my father in some enormous embarrassment. I tell my father there's going to be an assassination and my father tells the prince, as he'd feel obliged to do. And then the prince arrests and expels the ambassadors of England and Russia and Mexico? But where's the proof? There isn't any. It's all a Turkish invention, they say. A scandal. My father is sent home in disgrace. His career is shattered. Songhay breaks off diplomatic relations with the Empire. No, no, don't you see, I can't say a thing."

"But the prince—"

"His stepmother hates him. If he's idiotic enough to let her hand him a cup of something without having it tested, he deserves to be poisoned. What is that to me? He's only a savage. Hold the parasol closer, Michael, and let's get back to town. Oh, this heat! This unending heat! Do you think it'll ever rain here?" Her face now showed no sign of tears at all. Wearily Michael lowered the parasol. Selima utterly baffled him. She was an exhausting person. His head was aching. For a shilling he'd be glad to resign his post and take up sheep farming somewhere in the north of England. It was getting very obvious to him and probably to everyone else that he had no serious future in the diplomatic corps.

✺

Little Father, emerging from the tunnel that led from the Emir's palace to his own, found Ali Pasha waiting in the little colonnaded gallery known as the Promenade of Askia Mohammed. The prince was surprised to see a string charm of braided black, red, and yellow cords dangling around the vizier's neck. Ali Pasha had never been one for wearing grigri before; but no doubt the imminent death of the Emir was unsettling everyone, even a piece of tough leather like Ali Pasha.

The vizier offered a grand salaam. "Your royal father, may Allah embrace him, sir—"

"My royal father is still breathing, thank you. It looks now as if he'll last until morning." Little Father glanced around, a little wildly, peering into the courtyard of his palace. "Somehow we've left too much for the last minute. The lady Serene Glory is arranging for the washing of the body. It's too late to do anything about that, but we can supply the graveclothes, at least. Get the very finest white silks; the royal burial shroud should be something out of the Thousand and One Nights; and I want rubies in the turban. Actual rubies, no damned imitations. And after that I want you to set up the procession to the Great Mosque—I'll be one of the pallbearers, of course, and we'll ask the Mansa of Mali to be another—he's arrived by now, hasn't he?—and let's have the King of Benin as the third one, and for the fourth, well, either the Asante of Ghana or the Grand Fon of Dahomey, whichever one shows up here first. The important thing is that all four of the pallbearers should be kings, because Serene Glory wants to push her brother forward to be one, and I can't allow that. She won't be able to argue precedence for him if the pallbearers are all kings, when all he is is a provincial cadi. Behind the bier we'll have the overseas ambassadors marching five abreast—put the Turk and the Russian in the front row, the Maori too, and the Aztec and the Inca on the outside edges to keep them as far apart as we can, and the order of importance after that is up to you, only be sure that little countries like England and the Teutonic States don't wind up too close to the major powers, and that the various vassal nations like China and Korea and Ind are in the back. Now, as far as the decorations on the barge that'll be taking my father downriver to the burial place at Gao—"

"Little Father," the Vizier said, as the prince paused for breath, "the Turkish woman is waiting upstairs."

Little Father gave him a startled look.

"I don't remember asking her to come here."

"She didn't say you had. But she asked for an urgent audience, and I thought—" Ali Pasha favored Little Father with an obscenely knowing smile. "It seemed reasonable to admit her."

"She knows that my father is dying, and that I'm tremendously busy?"

"I told her what was taking place, majesty," said Ali Pasha unctuously.

"Don't call me 'majesty' yet!"

"A thousand pardons, Little Father. But she is aware of the nature of the crisis, no question of that. Nevertheless, she insisted on—"

"Oh, damn. Damn! But I suppose I can give her two or three minutes. Stop smiling like that, damn you! I'll feed you to the lions if you don't! What do you think I am, a mountain of lechery? This is a busy moment. When I say two or three minutes, two or three minutes is what I mean."

Selima was pacing about on the porch where she and Little Father had spent their night of love. No filmy robes today, no seductively visible breasts bobbing about beneath, this time. She was dressed simply, in European clothes. She seemed all business.

"The Emir is in his last hours," Little Father said. "The whole funeral has to be arranged very quickly."

"I won't take up much of your time, then." Her tone was cool. There was a distinct edge on it. Perhaps he had been too brusque with her. That night on the porch *had* been a wonderful one, after all. She said, "I just have one question. Is there some sort of ritual at a royal funeral where you're given a cup of wine to drink?"

"You know that the Koran doesn't permit the drinking of—"

"Yes, yes, I know that. A cup of *something*, then."

Little Father studied her carefully. "This is anthropological research? The sort of thing the golden-haired woman from England came here to do? Why does this matter to you, Selima?"

"Never mind that. It matters."

He sighed. She *seemed* so gentle and retiring, until she opened her mouth.

"There's a cup ceremony, yes. It isn't wine or anything else alcoholic. It's an aromatic potion, brewed from various spices and honeys and such, very disagreeably sweet, my father once told me. Drinking it symbolizes the passage of royal power from one generation to the next."

"And who is supposed to hand you the cup?"

"May I ask why at this particularly hectic time you need to know these details?"

"Please," she said.

There was an odd urgency in her voice.

"The former queen, the mother of the heir of the throne, is the one who hands the new Emir the cup."

"But your mother is dead. Therefore your stepmother Serene Glory will hand it to you."

"That's correct." Little Father glanced at his watch. "Selima, you don't seem to understand. I need to finish working out the funeral arrangements and then get back to my father's bedside before he dies. If you don't mind—"

"There's going to be poison in the cup."

"This is no time for romantic fantasies."

"It isn't a fantasy. She's going to slip you a cup of poison, and you won't be able to tell that the poison is there because what you drink is so heavily spiced anyway. And when you keel over in the mosque her brother's going to leap forward in the moment of general shock and tell everyone that he's in charge."

The day had been one long disorderly swirl. But suddenly now the world stood still, as though there had been an unscheduled eclipse of the sun. For a moment he had difficulty simply seeing her.

"What are you saying, Selima?"

"Do you want me to repeat it all, or is that just something you're saying as a manner of speaking because you're so astonished?"

He could see and think again. He examined her closely. She was unreadable, as she usually was. Now that the first shock of her bland statement was past, this all was starting to seem to him like fantastic nonsense; and yet, and yet, it certainly wasn't beyond Serene Glory's capabilities to have hatched such a scheme.

How, though, could the Turkish girl possibly know anything about it? How did she even know about the ritual of the cup?

"If we were in bed together right now," he said, "and you were in my arms and right on the edge of the big moment, and I stopped moving and asked you right then and there what proof you had of this story, I'd probably believe whatever you told me. I think people tend to be honest at such moments. Even you would speak the truth. But we have no time for that now. The kingship will change hands in a few hours, and I'm exceedingly busy. I need you to cast away all of your fondness for manipulative amusements and give me straight answers."

Her dark eyes flared. "I should simply have let them poison you."

"Do you mean that?"

"What you just said was insufferable."

"If I was too blunt, I ask you to forgive me. I'm under great strain today and if what you've told me is any sort of joke, I don't need it. If this isn't a joke, you damned well can't withhold any of the details."

"I've given you the details."

"Not all. Who'd you hear all this from?"

She sighed and placed one wrist across the other.

"Michael. The tall Englishman."

"That adolescent?"

"He's a little on the innocent side, especially for a diplomat, yes. But I don't think he's as big a fool as he's been letting himself appear lately. He heard it from Sir Anthony."

"So this is an English plot?"

"English and Russian and Mexican."

"All three." Little Father digested that. "What's the purpose of assassinating me?"

"To make Serene Glory's brother Emir of Songhay."

"And serve as their puppet, I suppose?"

Selima shook her head. "Serene Glory and her brother are only the ignorant instruments of their real plan. They'll simply be brushed aside when the time comes. What the plotters are really intending to do, in the confusion following your death, is ask the Mansa of Mali to seize control of Songhay. They'll put the support of their countries behind him."

"Ah," Little Father said. And after a moment, again, "Ah."

"Mali-Songhay would favor the Czar instead of the Sultan. So the Russians like the idea. What injures the Sultan is good for the English. So they're in on it. As for the Aztecs—"

Little Father shrugged and gestured to her to stop. Already he could taste the poison in his gut, burning through his flesh. Already he could see the green-clad troops of Mali parading in the streets of Timbuctoo and Gao, where kings of Mali had been hailed as supreme monarchs once before, hundreds of years ago.

"Look at me," he said. "You swear that you're practicing no deception, Selima?"

"I swear it by—by the things we said to each other the night we lay together."

He considered that. Had she fallen in love with him in the midst of all her game-playing? So it might seem. Could he trust what she was saying, therefore? He believed he could. Indeed the oath she had just proposed might have more plausibility than any sort of oath she might have sworn on a Koran.

"Come here," he said.

She approached him. Little Father swept her up against him, holding her tightly, and ran his hands down her back to her buttocks. She pressed her hips forward. He covered her mouth with his and jammed down hard, not a subtle kiss but one that would put to rest forever, if that were needed, the bit of fake anthropology he had given to her earlier, about the supposed distaste of Songhayans for the act of kissing. After a time he released her. Her eyes were a little glazed, her breasts were rising and falling swiftly.

He said, "I'm grateful for what you've told me. I'll take the appropriate steps, and thank you."

"I had to let you know. I was going just to sit back and let whatever happened happen. But then I saw I couldn't conceal such a thing from you."

"Of course not, Selima."

Her look was a soft and eager one. She was ready to run off to the bedchamber with him, or so it seemed. But not now, not on this day of all days. That would be a singularly bad idea.

"On the other hand," he said, "if it turns out that there's no truth to any of this, that it's all some private amusement of your own or some intricate deception being practiced on me by the Sultan for who knows what unfathomable reason, you can be quite certain that I'll avenge myself in a remarkably vindictive way once the excitements of the funeral and the coronation are over."

The softness vanished at once. The hatred that came into her eyes was extraordinary.

"You black bastard," she said.

"Only partly black. There is much Moorish blood in the veins of the nobility of Songhay." He met her seething gaze with tranquility. "In the old days we believed in absorbing those who attempt to conquer us.

These days we still do, something that the Mansa of Mali ought to keep in mind. He's got a fine harem, I understand."

"Did you *have* to throw cold water on me like that? Everything I told you was the truth."

"I hope and believe it is. I think there was love between us that night on the porch, and I wouldn't like to think that you'd betray someone you love. The question, I suppose, is whether the Englishman was telling *you* the truth. Which still remains to be seen." He took her hand and kissed it lightly, in the European manner. "As I said before, I'm very grateful, Selima. And hope to continue to be. If I may, now—"

She gave him one final glare and took her leave of him. Little Father walked quickly to the edge of the porch, spun about, walked quickly back. For an instant or two he stood in the doorway like his own statue. But his mind was in motion, and moving very swiftly.

He peered down the stairs to the courtyard below.

"Ali Pasha!"

The vizier came running.

"What the woman wanted to tell me," Little Father said, "is that there is a plot against my life."

The look that appeared on the vizier's face was one of total shock and indignation.

"You believe her?"

"Unfortunately I think I do."

Ali Pasha began to quiver with wrath. His broad glossy cheeks grew congested, his eyes bulged. Little Father thought the man was in danger of exploding.

"Who are the plotters, Little Father? I'll have them rounded up within the hour."

"The Russian ambassador, apparently. The Aztec one. And the little Englishman, Sir Anthony."

"To the lions with them! They'll be in the pit before night comes!"

Little Father managed an approximation of a smile.

"Surely you recall the concept of diplomatic immunity, Ali Pasha?"

"But—a conspiracy against your majesty's life—!"

"Not yet my majesty, Ali Pasha."

"Your pardon." Ali Pasha struggled with confusion. "You must take steps to protect yourself, Little Father. Did she tell you what the plan is supposed to be?"

Little Father nodded. "When Serene Glory hands me the coronation cup at the funeral service, there will be poison in the drink."

"Poison!"

"Yes. I fall down dead. Serene Glory turns to her miserable brother and offers him the crown on the spot. But no, the three ambassadors have other ideas. They'll ask Mansa Suleiyman to proclaim himself king, in the name of the general safety. In that moment Songhay will come under the rule of Mali."

"Never! To the lions with Mansa Suleiyman too, majesty!"

"No one goes to the lions, Ali Pasha. And stop calling me majesty. We'll deal with this in a calm and civilized way, is that understood?"

"I am completely at your command, sir. As always."

Little Father nodded. He felt his strength rising, moment by moment. His mind was wondrously clear. He asked himself if that was what it felt like to be a king. Though he had spent so much time being a prince, he had in fact given too little thought to what the actual sensations and processes of being a king might be, he realized now. His royal father had held the kingdom entirely in his own hands throughout all his long reign. But something must be changing now.

He went unhurriedly to the edge of the porch, and stared out into the distance. To his surprise, there was a dark orange cloud on the horizon, sharply defined against the sky.

"Look there, Ali Pasha. The rains are coming!"

"The first cloud, yes. There it is!" And he began to finger the woven charm that hung about his neck.

It was always startling when the annual change came, after so many months of unbroken hot dry weather. Even after a lifetime of watching the shift occur, no one in Songhay was unmoved by the approach of the first cloud, for it was a powerful omen of transition and culmination, removing a great element of uncertainty and fear from the minds of the citizens; for until the change finally arrived, there was always the chance that it might never come, that this time the summer would last forever and the parched world would burn to a crisp.

Little Father said, "I should go to my father without any further delay. Certainly this means that his hour has come."

"Yes. Yes."

The orange cloud was sweeping toward the city with amazing rapidity. In another few minutes all Timbuctoo would be enveloped in blackness as a whirling veil of fine sand whipped down over it. Little

Father felt the air grow moist. There would be a brief spell of intolerable humidity, now, so heavy that breathing itself would be a vast effort. And then, abruptly, the temperature would drop, the chill rain would descend, rivers would run in the sandy streets, the marketplace would become a lake.

He raced indoors, with Ali Pasha following along helterskelter behind him.

"The plotters, sir—" the vizier gasped.

Little Father smiled. "I'll invite Serene Glory to share the cup with me. We'll see what she does then. Just be ready to act when I give the orders."

There was darkness at every window. The sandstorm was at hand. Trillions of tiny particles beat insistently at every surface, setting up a steady drumming that grew and grew and grew in intensity. The air had turned sticky, almost viscous: it was hard work to force oneself forward through it.

Gasping for breath, Little Father moved as quickly as he was able down the subterranean passageway that linked his palace with the much greater one that shortly would be his.

The ministers and functionaries of the royal court were wailing and weeping. The Grand Vizier of the realm, waiting formally at the head of the Stairs of Allah, glared at Little Father as though he were the Angel of Death himself.

"There is not much more time, Little Father."

"So I understand."

He rushed out onto his father's porch. There had been no opportunity to bring the Emir indoors. The old man lay amidst his dazzling blankets with his eyes open and one hand upraised. He was in the correct position in which a Moslem should pass from this world to the next, his head to the south, his face turned toward the east. The sky was black with sand, and it came cascading down with unremitting force. The three saintly marabouts who had attended Big Father throughout his final illness stood above him, shielding the Emir from the shower of tiny abrasive particles with an improvised canopy, an outstretched bolt of satin.

"Father! Father!"

The Emir tried to sit up. He looked a thousand years old.

His eyes glittered like lightning-bolts, and he said something, three or four congested syllables. Little Father was unable to understand a thing. The old man was already speaking the language of the dead.

There was a clap of thunder. The Emir fell back against his pillows. The sky opened and the first rain of the year came down in implacable torrents, in such abundance as had not been seen in a thousand years.

In the three days since the old Emir's death Little Father had lived through this scene three thousand times in his imagination. But now it was actually occurring. They were in the Great Mosque; the mourners, great and simple, were clustered elbow to elbow; the corpse of Big Father, embalmed so that it could endure the slow journey downriver to the royal burial grounds, lay in splendor atop its magnificent bier. Any ordinary citizen of Songhay would have gone from his deathbed to his grave in two hours, or less; but kings were exempt from the ordinary customs.

They were done at last with the chanting of the prayer for the dead. Now they were doing the prayer for the welfare of the kingdom. Little Father held his body rigid, barely troubling to breathe. He saw before him the grand nobles of the realm, the kings of the adjacent countries, the envoys of the overseas lands, all staring, all maintaining a mien of the deepest solemnity, even those who could not comprehend a word of what was being said.

And here was Serene Glory, now, coming forth bearing the cup that would make him Emir of Songhay, Great Imam, master of the nation, successor to all the great lords who had led the empire in grandeur for a thousand years.

She looked magnificent, truly queenly, more beautiful in her simple funeral robe and unadorned hair than she could ever have looked in all her finery. The cup, a stark bowl of lustrous chalcedony, so translucent that the dark liquor that would make him king was plainly visible through its thin walls, was resting lightly on her upturned palms.

He searched her for a sign of tremor and saw none. She was utterly calm. He felt a disturbing moment of doubt.

She handed him the cup, and spoke the words of succession, clearly, unhesitatingly, omitting not the smallest syllable. She was in full control of herself.

When he lifted the cup to his lips, though, he heard the sharp unmistakable sound of her suddenly indrawn breath, and all hesitation went from him.

"Mother," he said.

The unexpected word reverberated through the whitewashed alcoves of the Great Mosque. They must all be looking at him in bewilderment.

"Mother, in this solemn moment of the passing of the kingship, I beg you share my ascension with me. Drink with me, mother. Drink. Drink."

He held the untouched cup out toward the woman who had just handed it to him.

Her eyes were bright with horror.

"Drink with me, mother," he said again.

"No—no—"

She backed a step or two away from him, making sounds like gravel in her throat.

"Mother—lady, dear lady—"

He held the cup out, insistently. He moved closer to her. She seemed frozen. The truth was emblazoned on her face. Rage rose like a fountain in him, and for an instant he thought he was going to hurl the drink in her face; but then he regained his poise. Her hand was pressed against her lips in terror. She moved back, back, back.

And then she was running toward the door of the mosque; and abruptly the Grand Duke Alexander Petrovich, his face erupting with red blotches of panic, was running also, and also Prince Itzcoatl of Mexico.

"No! Fools!" a voice cried out, and the echoes hammered at the ancient walls.

Little Father looked toward the foreign ambassadors. Sir Anthony stood out as though in a spotlight, his cheeks blazing, his eyes popping, his fingers exploring his lips as though he could not believe they had actually uttered that outcry.

There was complete confusion in the mosque. Everyone was rushing about, everyone was bellowing. But Little Father was quite calm. Carefully he set the cup down, untouched, at his feet. Ali Pasha came to his side at once.

"Round them up quickly," he told the vizier. "The three ambassadors are persona non grata. They're to leave Songhay by the next riverboat. Escort Mansa Suleiyman back to the Embassy of Mali and put armed guards around the building—for purely protective purposes, of course. And also the embassies of Ghana, Dahomey, Benin, and the rest, for good measure—and as window-dressing."

"It will be done, majesty."

"Very good." He indicated the chalcedony cup. "As for this stuff, give it to a dog to drink, and let's see what happens."

Ali Pasha nodded and touched his forehead.

"And the lady Serene Glory, and her brother?"

"Take them into custody. If the dog dies, throw them both to the lions."

"Your majesty—!"

"To the lions, Ali Pasha."

"But you said—"

"To the lions, Ali Pasha."

"I hear and obey, majesty."

"You'd better." Little Father grinned. He was Little Father no longer, he realized. "I like the way you say it: *Majesty.* You put just the right amount of awe into it."

"Yes, majesty. Is there anything else, majesty?"

"I want an escort too, to take me to my palace. Say, fifty men. No, make it a hundred. Just in case there are any surprises waiting for us outside."

"To your old palace, majesty?"

The question caught him unprepared. "No," he said after a moment's reflection. "Of course not. To my new palace. To the palace of the Emir."

Selima came hesitantly forward into the throne room, which was one of the largest, most forbidding rooms she had ever entered. Not even the Sultan's treasurehouse at the Topkapi Palace had any chamber to match this one for sheer dismal mustiness, for clutter, or for the eerie hodgepodge of its contents. She found the new Emir standing beneath a stuffed giraffe, examining an ivory globe twice the size of a man's head that was mounted on an intricately carved spiral pedestal.

"You sent for me, your highness?"

"Yes. Yes, I did. It's all calm outside there, now, I take it?"

"Very calm. *Very* calm."

"Good. And the weather's still cool?"

"Quite cool, your majesty."

"But not raining again yet?"

"No, not raining."

"Good." Idly he fondled the globe. "The whole world is here, do you know that? Right under my hand. Here's Africa, here's Europe, here's

Russia. This is the Empire, here." He brushed his hand across the globe from Istanbul to Madrid. "There's still plenty of it, eh?" He spun the ivory sphere easily on its pedestal. "And this, the New World. Such emptiness there. The Incas down here in the southern continent, the Aztecs here in the middle, and a lot of nothing up here in the north. I once asked my father, do you know, if I could pay a visit to those empty lands. So cool there, I hear. So green, and almost empty. Just the red-skinned people, and not very many of them. Are they really red, do you think? I've never seen one." He looked closely at her. "Have you ever thought of leaving Turkey, I wonder, and taking up a new life for yourself in those wild lands across the ocean?"

"Never, your majesty."

She was trembling a little.

"You should think of it. We all should. Our countries are all too old. The land is tired. The air is tired. The rivers move slowly. We should go somewhere where things are fresh." She made no reply. After a moment's silence he said, "Do you love that tall gawky pink-faced Englishman, Selima?"

"Love?"

"Love, yes. Do you have any kind of fondness for him? Do you care for him at all? If love is too strong a word for you, would you say at least that you enjoy his company, that you see a certain charm in him, that— well, surely you understand what I'm saying."

She seemed flustered. "I'm not sure that I do."

"It appears to me that you feel attracted to him. God knows he feels attracted to you. He can't go back to England, you realize. He's compromised himself fifty different ways. Even after we patch up this conspiracy thing, and we certainly will, one way or another, the fact still remains that he's guilty of treason. He has to go somewhere. He can't stay here—the heat will kill him fast, if his own foolishness doesn't. Are you starting to get my drift, Selima?"

Her eyes rose to meet his. Some of her old self-assurance was returning to them now.

"I think I am. And I think that I like it."

"Very good," he said. "I'll give him to you, then. For a toy, if you like." He clapped his hands. A functionary poked his head into the room.

"Send in the Englishman."

Michael entered. He walked with the precarious stride of someone who has been decapitated but thinks there might be some chance of keeping his head on his shoulders if only he moves carefully enough. The only traces of sunburn that remained now were great peeling patches on his cheeks and forehead.

He looked toward the new Emir and murmured a barely audible courtly greeting. He seemed to have trouble looking in Selima's direction.

"Sir?" Michael asked finally.

The Emir smiled warmly. "Has Sir Anthony left yet?"

"This morning, sir. I didn't speak with him."

"No. No, I imagine you wouldn't care to. It's a mess, isn't it, Michael? You can't really go home."

"I understand that, sir."

"But obviously you can't stay here. This is no climate for the likes of you."

"I suppose not, sir."

The Emir nodded. He reached about behind him and lifted a book from a stand. "During my years as prince I had plenty of leisure to read. This is one of my favorites. Do you happen to know which book it is?"

"No, sir."

"The collected plays of one of your great English writers, as a matter of fact. The greatest, so I'm told. Shakespeare's his name. You know his work, do you?"

Michael blinked. "Of course, sir. Everyone knows—"

"Good. And you know his play *Alexius and Khurrem*, naturally?"

"Yes, sir."

The Emir turned to Selima. "And do you?"

"Well—"

"It's quite relevant to the case, I assure you. It takes place in Istanbul, not long after the Ottoman Conquest. Khurrem is a beautiful young woman from one of the high Turkish families. Alexius is an exiled Byzantine prince who has slipped back into the capital to try to rescue some of his family's treasures from the grasp of the detested conqueror. He disguises himself as a Turk and meets Khurrem at a banquet, and of course they fall in love. It's an impossible romance— a Turk and a Greek." He opened the book. "Let me read a little. It's amazing that an Englishman could write such eloquent Turkish poetry, isn't it?"

> *From forth the fatal loins of these two foes*
> *A pair of star-cross'd lovers take their life;*

Whose misadventur'd piteous overthrows
Do with their death bury their parents' strife—

The Emir glanced up. "'Star-cross'd lovers.' That's what you are, you know." He laughed. "It all ends terribly for poor Khurrem and Alexius, but that's because they were such hasty children. With better planning they could have slipped away to the countryside and lived to a ripe old age, but Shakespeare tangles them up in a scheme of sleeping potions and crossed messages and they both die at the end, even though well-intentioned friends were trying to help them. But of course that's drama for you. It's a lovely play. I hope to be able to see it performed some day."

He put the book aside. They both were staring at him.

To Michael he said, "I've arranged for you to defect to Turkey. Ismet Akif will give you a writ of political asylum. What happens between you and Selima is of course entirely up to you and Selima, but in the name of Allah I implore you not to make as much of a shambles of it as Khurrem and Alexius did. Istanbul's not such a bad place to live, you know. No, don't look at me like that! If she can put up with a ninny like you, you can manage to get over your prejudices against Turks. You asked for all this, you know. You didn't *have* to fall in love with her."

"Sir, I—I—"

Michael's voice trailed away.

The Emir said, "Take him out of here, will you, Selima?"

"Come," she told the gawking Englishman. "We need to talk, I think."

"I—I—"

The Emir gestured impatiently. Selima's hand was on Michael's wrist, now. She tugged, and he followed. The Emir looked after them until they had gone down the stairs.

Then he clapped his hands.

"Ali Pasha!"

The vizier appeared so quickly that there could be no doubt he had been lurking just beyond the ornate doorway.

"Majesty?"

"We have to clear this place out a little," the Emir said. "This crocodile—this absurd giraffe—find an appropriate charity and donate them, fast. And these hippo skulls, too. And this, and this, and this—"

"At once, majesty. A clean sweep."

"A clean sweep, yes."

A cool wind was blowing through the palace now, after the rains. He felt young, strong, vigorous. Life was just beginning, finally. Later in the day he would visit the lions at their pit.

A TIP ON A TURTLE

Amazing Stories, *the first all-science-fiction magazine ever published, constantly kept reinventing itself in its long history, which covered the years from 1926 to 1995. Its first editor, Hugo Gernsback, wanted to educate people to the wonders of science and technology through the medium of science fiction, and the stories he published were often fattened with lengthy passages of lecture and festooned with footnotes. Then it passed into the hands of the Ziff-Davis pulp-magazine chain, which turned it into a slam-bang action magazine for boys. After fifteen years of that, it evolved into an elegant slick-paper magazine that published thoughtful stories by the likes of Ray Bradbury and Theodore Sturgeon and Robert A. Heinlein, and (when that policy failed to bring in the desired dollars) it reverted to formula fiction once again, about 1955. That was the year I came on the scene as a professional s-f writer, and in youthful glee I filled the pages of* Amazing *with pulpy epics with titles like "Guardian of the Crystal Gate" and "The Monster Died at Dawn."*

Later editors made periodic attempts at upgrading the quality of Amazing's *fiction—notably Cele Goldsmith in 1964 and George Scithers in 1982. I upgraded right with them, and my stories appeared regularly in* Amazing *across the decades. Indeed, Scithers commissioned a story from me, for a higher price than the magazine had been wont to pay, for his first issue. When yet another ambitious new editor, Kim Mohan, took over the once-again-moribund* Amazing Stories *in 1990 and turned it into a gloriously printed large-sized magazine with dazzling interior illustrations in four colors, he too invited me to contribute a short story for the first of the* renovated issues. I had just finished "A Tip on a Turtle" the day he asked, and had sent it off to Playboy, where I was a regular contributor. My old friend Alice Turner, Playboy's acute and demanding fiction editor, had reservations, however, about my use of a female protagonist, Playboy being, after all, a men's magazine; she thought the story would be more at home in Cosmopolitan or one of its competitors. But when Mohan told me he would pay Playboy/Cosmopolitan-level rates for a new short story from me for Amazing, I obligingly diverted the piece in his direction, and he ran it in his May, 1991 issue. Playboy, though, is a mass-circulation publication read mainly by people who would never go near a science-fiction magazine, and so the tone of this one, with its mainstream-reader orientation, is as far removed from "The Monster Died at Dawn" and my other early Amazing contributions as it is possible to be.

The sun was going down in the usual spectacular Caribbean way, disappearing in a welter of purple and red and yellow streaks that lay across the wide sky beyond the hotel's manicured golf course like a magnificent bruise. It was time to head for the turtle pool for the pre-dinner races. They held the races three times a day now, once after lunch, once before dinner, once after dinner. Originally the races had been nothing more than a casual diversion, but by now they had become a major item of entertainment for the guests and a significant profit center for the hotel.

As Denise took her place along the blazing bougainvillea hedge that flanked the racing pool a quiet deep voice just back of her left ear said, "You might try Number Four in the first race."

It was the man she had noticed at the beach that afternoon, the tall tanned one with the powerful shoulders and the tiny bald spot. She had been watching him snorkeling along the reef, nothing visible above the surface of the water but his bald spot and the blue strap of his goggles and the black stalk of the snorkel. When he came to shore he walked right past her, seemingly lost in some deep reverie; but for a moment, just for a moment, their eyes had met in a startling way. Then he had gone on, without a word or even a smile. Denise was left with the feeling that there was something tragic about him, something desperate, something haunted. That had caught her attention. Was he down here by himself? So it appeared. She too was vacationing alone. Her marriage had broken up during Christmas, as marriages so often did, and everyone had said she ought to get away for some midwinter sunshine. And, they hadn't needed to add, for some postmarital diversion. She had been here three days so far and there had been plenty of sunshine but none of the other thing, not for lack of interest but simply because after five years of marriage she was out of practice at being seduced, or shy, or simply uneasy. She had been noticed, though. And had done some noticing.

She looked over her shoulder at him and said, "Are you telling me that the race is fixed?"

"Oh, no. Not at all."

"I thought you might have gotten some special word from one of the hotel's boys."

"No," he said. He was very tall, perhaps too tall for her, with thick, glossy black hair and dark, hooded eyes. Despite the little bald spot he was probably forty at most. He was certainly attractive enough, almost movie-star handsome, and yet she found herself thinking unexpectedly that there was something oddly asexual about him. "I just have a good feeling about Number Four, that's all. When I have a feeling of that sort it often works out very well." A musical voice. Was that a faint accent? Or just an affectation?

He was looking at her in a curiously expectant way.

She knew the scenario. He had made the approach; now she should hand him ten Jamaican dollars and ask him to go over to the tote counter and bet them on Number Four for her; when he returned with her ticket they would introduce themselves; after the race, win or lose, they'd have a daiquiri or two together on the patio overlooking the pool, maybe come back to try their luck on the final race, then dinner on the romantic outdoor terrace and a starlight stroll under the palisade of towering palms that lined the beachfront promenade, and eventually they'd get around to settling the big question: his cottage or hers? But even as she ran through it all in her mind she knew she didn't want any of it to happen. That lost, haunted look of his, which had seemed so wonderfully appealing for that one instant on the beach, now struck her as simply silly, melodramatic, overdone. Most likely it was nothing more than his modus operandi: women had been falling for that look of masterfully contained agony at least since Lord Byron's time, probably longer. But not me, Denise told herself.

She gave him a this-leads-nowhere smile and said, "I dropped a fortune on these damned turtles last night, I'm afraid. I decided I was going to be just a spectator this evening."

"Yes," he said. "Of course."

It wasn't true. She had won twenty Jamaican dollars the night before and had been looking forward to more good luck now. Gambling of any sort had never interested her until this trip, but there had been a peculiar sort of pleasure last night in watching the big turtles gliding toward the finish line, especially when her choices finished first in three of the seven races. Well, she had committed herself to the sidelines for this evening by her little lie, and so be it. Tomorrow was another day.

The tall man smiled and shrugged and bowed and went away. A few moments later Denise saw him talking to the leggy, freckled woman from Connecticut whose husband had died in some kind of boating accident the summer before. Then they were on their way over to the tote counter and he was buying tickets for them. Denise felt sudden sharp annoyance, a stabbing sense of opportunity lost.

"Place your bets, ladees gemmun, place your bets!" the master of ceremonies called.

Mr. Eubanks, the night manager—shining black face, gleaming white teeth, straw hat, red-and-white-striped shirt—sat behind the counter, busily ringing up the changing odds on a little laptop computer. A boy with a chalkboard posted them. Number Three was the favorite, three to two; Number Four was a definite long shot at nine to one. But then there was a little flurry of activity at the counter, and the odds on Four dropped abruptly to five to one. Denise heard people murmuring about that. And then the tote was closed and the turtles were brought forth.

Between races the turtles slept in a shallow, circular concrete-walled holding tank that was supplied with sea water by a conduit running up from the beach. They were big green ones, each with a conspicuous number painted on its upper shell in glowing crimson, and they were so hefty that the brawny hotel boys found it hard going to carry them the distance of twenty feet or so that separated the holding tank from the long, narrow pool where the races were held.

Now the boys stood in a row at the starting line, as though they themselves were going to race, while the glossy-eyed turtles that they were clutching to their chests made sleepy graceless swimming motions in the air with their rough leathery flippers and rolled their spotted green heads slowly from side to side in a sluggish show of annoyance. The master of ceremonies fired a starter's pistol and the boys tossed the turtles into the pool. Graceless no longer, the big turtles were swimming the moment they hit the water, making their way into the blue depths of the pool with serene, powerful strokes.

There were six lanes, separated by bright yellow ribbons, but of course the turtles had no special reason for remaining in them. They roamed about randomly, perhaps imagining that they had been returned to the open sea, while the guests of the hotel roared encouragement: "Come on, Five! Go for it, One! Move your green ass, Six!"

The first turtle to touch any part of the pool's far wall was the winner. Ordinarily it took four or five minutes for that to happen; as the turtles wandered, they sometimes approached the finish line but didn't necessarily choose to make contact with it, and wild screams would rise from the backers of this one or that as their turtle neared the wall, sniffed it, perhaps, and turned maddeningly away without making contact.

But this time one of the turtles was swimming steadily, almost purposefully, in a straight line from start to finish. Denise saw it moving along the floor of the pool like an Olympic competitor going for the gold. The brilliant crimson number on its back, though blurred and mottled by the water, was unmistakable.

"Four! Four! Four! Look at that bastard go!"

It was all over in moments. Four completed its traversal of the pool, lightly bumped its hooked snout against the far wall with almost contemptuous satisfaction, and swung around again on a return journey to the starting point, as if it had been ordered to swim laps. The other turtles were still moving about amiably in vague circles at mid-pool.

"Numbah Four," called the master of ceremonies. "Pays off at five to one for de lucky winnahs, yessah yessah!"

The hotel boys had their nets out, scooping up the heavy turtles for the next race. Denise looked across the way. The leggy young widow from Connecticut was jubilantly waving a handful of gaudy Jamaican ten-dollar bills in the face of the tall man with the tiny bald spot. She was flushed and radiant; but he looked down at her solemnly from his great height without much sign of excitement, as though the dramatic victory of Number Four had afforded him neither profit nor joy nor any surprise at all.

The short, stocky, balding Chevrolet dealer from Long Island, whose features and coloration looked to be pure Naples but whose name was like something out of *Brideshead Revisited*—Lionel Gregson? Anthony Jenkins?—something like that—materialized at Denise's side and said, "It don't matter which turtle you bet, really. The trick is to bet the boys who throw them."

His voice, too, had a hoarse Mediterranean fullness. Denise loved the idea that he had given himself such a fancy name.

"Do you really think so?"

"I know so. I been watching them three days, now. You see the boy in the middle? Hegbert, he's called. Smart as a whip, and damn strong. He reacts faster when the gun goes off. And he don't just throw his turtle quicker, he throws it harder. Look, can I get you a daiquiri? I don't like being the only one drinking." He grinned. Two gold teeth showed. "Jeffrey Thompkins, Oyster Bay. I had the privilege of talking with you a couple minutes two days ago on the beach."

"Of course. I remember. Denise Carpenter. I'm from Clifton, New Jersey, and yes, I'd love a daiquiri."

He snagged one from a passing tray. Denise thought his Hegbert theory was nonsense—the turtles usually swam in aimless circles for a while after they were thrown in, so why would the thrower's reaction time or strength of toss make any difference?—but Jeffrey Thompkins himself was so agreeably real, so cheerfully blatant, that she found herself liking him tremendously after her brush with the Byronic desperation of the tall man with the little bald spot. The phonied-up name was a nice capping touch, the one grotesque bit of fraudulence that made everything else about him seem more valid. Maybe he needed a name like that where he lived, or where he worked.

Now that she had accepted a drink from him, he moved a half step closer to her, taking on an almost proprietary air. He was about two inches shorter than she was.

"I see that Hegbert's got Number Three in the second race. You want I should buy you a ticket?"

The tall man was covertly watching her, frowning a little. Maybe he was bothered that she had let herself be captured by the burly little car dealer. She hoped so.

But she couldn't let Thompkins get a ticket for her after she had told the tall man she wasn't betting tonight. Not if the other one was watching. She'd have to stick with her original fib.

"Somehow I don't feel like playing the turtles tonight," she said. "But you go ahead, if you want."

"Place your bets, ladies gemmun, place your bets!"

Hegbert did indeed throw Number Three quickly and well, but it was Five that won the race, after some minutes of the customary random noodling around in the pool. Five paid off at three to one. A quick sidewise glance told Denise that the tall man and the leggy Connecticut widow had been winners again.

"Watch what that tall guy does in the next race," she heard someone say nearby. "That's what I'm going to do. He's a pro. He's got a sixth sense about these turtles. He just wins and wins and wins."

But watching what the tall man did in the next race was an option that turned out not to be available. He had disappeared from the pool area somewhere between the second and third races. And so, Denise noted with unexpectedly sharp displeasure, had the woman from Connecticut.

Thompkins, still following his Hegbert system, bet fifty on Number Six in the third race, cashed in at two to one, then dropped his new winnings and fifty more besides backing Number Four in the fourth. Then he invited Denise to have dinner with him on the terrace. What the hell, she thought. Last night she had had dinner alone: very snooty, she must have seemed. It hadn't been fun.

In the uneasy first moments at the table they talked about the tall man. Thompkins had noticed his success with the turtles also. "Strange guy," he said. "Gives me the creeps—something about the look in his eye. But you see how he makes out at the races?"

"He does very well."

"Well? He cleans up! Can't lose for winning."

"Some people have unusual luck, I suppose."

"This ain't luck. My guess is maybe he's got a fix in with the boys—like they tell him what turtle's got the mojo in the upcoming race. Some kind of high sign they give him when they're lining up for the throw-in."

"How? Turtles are turtles. They just swim around in circles until one of them happens to hit the far wall with his nose."

"No," said Thompkins. "I think he knows something. Or maybe not. But the guy's hot for sure. Tomorrow I'm going to bet the way he does, right down the line, race by race. There are other people here doing it already. That's why the odds go down on the turtle he bets, once they see which one he's backing. If the guy's hot, why not get in on his streak?"

He ordered a white Italian wine with the first course, which was grilled flying fish with brittle orange caviar globules on the side. "I got to confess," he said, grinning again, "Jeffrey Thompkin's not really my name. It's Taormina, Joey Taormina. But that's hard to pronounce out where I live, so I changed it."

"I did wonder. You look—is it Neapolitan?"

"Worse. Sicilian. Anybody you meet named Taormina, his family's originally Sicilian. Taormina's a city on the east coast of Sicily. Gorgeous place. I'd love to show you around it some day."

He was moving a little too fast, she thought. A lot too fast.

"I have a confession too," she said. "I'm not from Clifton any more. I moved back into the city a month ago after my marriage broke up."

"That's a damn shame." He might almost have meant it. "I'm divorced too. It practically killed my mother when I broke the news. Well, you get married too young, you get surprised later on." A quick grin: he wasn't all that saddened by what he had learned about her. "How about some red wine with the main course? They got a good Brunello here."

A little later he invited her, with surprising subtlety, to spend the night with him. As gently as she could she declined. "Well, tomorrow's another day," he said cheerfully. Denise found herself wishing he had looked a little wounded, just a little.

The daytime routine was simple. Sleep late, breakfast on the cottage porch looking out at the sea, then a long ambling walk down the beach, poking in tide pools and watching ghostly gray crabs scutter over the pink sand. Mid-morning, swim out to the reef with snorkel and fins, drift around for half an hour or so staring at the strangely contorted coral heads and the incredibly beautiful reef creatures. It was like another planet, out there on the reef. Gnarled coral rose from the sparkling white sandy ocean floor to form fantastic facades and spires through which a billion brilliant fishes, scarlet and green and turquoise and gold in every imaginable color combination, chased each other around. Every surface was plastered with pastel-hued sponges and algae. Platoons of tiny squids swam in solemn formation. Toothy, malevolent-looking eels peered out of dark caverns. An occasional chasm led through the coral wall to the deep sea beyond, where the water was turbulent instead of calm, a dark blue instead of translucent green, and the ocean floor fell away to invisible depths. But Denise never went to the far side. There was something ominous and threatening about the somber outer face of the reef, whereas here, within, everything was safe, quiet, lovely.

After the snorkeling came a shower, a little time spent reading on the porch, then the outdoor buffet lunch. Afterwards a nap, a stroll in the hotel's flamboyant garden, and by mid-afternoon down to the beach again, not for a swim this time, but just to bake in the blessed tropical sun. She'd worry about the possibility of skin damage some other time: right now what she needed was that warm caress, that torrid all-enfolding embrace. Two hours dozing in the sun, then back to the room, shower again, read, dress for dinner. And off to the turtle races. Denise never bothered with the ones after lunch—they were strictly for the real addicts—but she had gone every evening to the pre-dinner ones.

A calm, mindless schedule. Exactly the ticket, after the grim, exhausting domestic storms of October and November and the sudden final cataclysm of December. Even though in the end she had been the one who had forced the breakup, it had still come as a shock and a jolt: she too getting divorced, just another pathetic casualty of the marital wars, despite all the high hopes of the beginning, the grand plans she and Michael had liked to make, the glowing dreams. Everything dissolving now into property squabbles, bitter recriminations, horrifying legal fees. How sad: how boring, really. And how destructive to her peace of mind, her self-esteem, her sense of order, her this, her that, her everything. For which there was no cure, she knew, other than to lie here on this placid Caribbean beach under this perfect winter sky and let the healing slowly happen.

Jeffrey Thompkins had the tact—or the good strategic sense—to leave her alone during the day. She saw him in the water, not snorkeling around peering at the reef but simply chugging back and forth like a blocky little machine, head down, arms windmilling, swimming parallel to the hotel's enormous ocean frontage until he had reached the cape just to the north, then coming back the other way. He was a formidable swimmer with enough energy for six men.

Quite probably he was like that in bed, too, but Denise had decided somewhere between the white wine and the red at dinner last night that she didn't intend to find out. She liked him, yes. And she intended to have an adventure of some sort with *someone* while she was down here. But a Chevrolet dealer from Long Island? Shorter than she was, with thick hairy shoulders? Somehow she couldn't. She just couldn't, not her first fling after the separation. He seemed to sense it too, and didn't bother her at the beach, even had his lunch at the indoor dining room instead of the buffet terrace. But she suspected she'd encounter him again at evening turtle-race time.

Yes: there he was. Grinning hopefully at her from the far side of the turtle pool, but plainly waiting to pick up some sort of affirmative signal from her before coming toward her.

There was the tall dark-haired man with the tiny bald spot, too. Without the lady from Connecticut. Denise had seen him snorkeling on the reef that afternoon, alone, and here he was alone again, which meant, most likely, that last night had been Mme. Connecticut's final night at the hotel. Denise was startled to realize how much relief that conclusion afforded her.

Carefully not looking in Jeffrey Thompkins' direction, she went unhesitatingly toward the tall man.

He was wearing a dark cotton suit and, despite the warmth, a narrow black tie flecked with gold, and he looked very, very attractive. She couldn't understand how she had come to think of him as sexless the night before: some inexplicable flickering of her own troubled moods, no doubt. Certainly he didn't seem that way now. He smiled down at her. He seemed actually pleased to see her, though she sensed behind the smile a puzzling mixture of other emotions— aloofness, sadness, regret? That curious tragic air of his: not a pose, she began to think, but the external manifestation of some deep and genuine wound.

"I wish I had listened to you last night," she said. "You knew what you were talking about when you told me to bet Number Four."

He shrugged almost imperceptibly. "I didn't really think that you'd take my advice. But I thought I'd make the gesture all the same."

"That was very kind of you," she said, leaning inward and upward toward him. "I'm sorry I was so skeptical." She flashed her warmest smile. "I'm going to be very shameless. I want a second chance. If you've got any tips to offer on tonight's races, please tell me. I promise not to be such a skeptic this time."

"Number Five in this one," he replied at once. "Nicholas Holt, by the way."

"Denise Carpenter. From Clifton, New Jer—" She cut herself off, reddening. He hadn't told her where he was from. She wasn't from Clifton any longer anyway; and what difference did it make where she might live up north? This island resort was intended as a refuge from all that, a place outside time, outside familiar realities. "Shall we place our bets?" she said briskly.

Women didn't usually buy tickets themselves here. Men seemed to expect to do that for them. She handed him a fifty, making sure as she did so that her fingers were extended to let him see that she wore no wedding band. But Holt didn't make any attempt to look. His own fingers were just as bare.

She caught sight of Jeffrey Thompkins at a distance, frowning at her but not in any very troubled way; and she realized after a moment that he evidently was undisturbed by her defection to the tall man's side and simply wanted to know which turtle Holt was backing. She held up her hand, five fingers outspread. He nodded and went scurrying to the tote counter.

Number Five won easily. The payoff was at seven to three. Denise looked at Holt with amazement.

"How do you do it?" she asked.

"Concentration," he said. "Some people have the knack."

He seemed very distant, suddenly.

"Are you concentrating on the next race, now?"

"It'll be Number One," he told her, as though telling her that the weather tomorrow would be warm and fair.

Thompkins stared at her out of the crowd. Denise flashed one finger at him.

She felt suddenly ill at ease. Nicholas Holt's knack, or whatever it was, bothered her. He was too confident, too coolly certain of what was going to happen. There was something annoying and almost intimidating about such confidence. Although she had bet fifty Jamaican dollars on Number One, she found herself wishing perversely that the turtle would lose.

Number One it was, though, all the same. The payoff was trifling; it seemed as if almost everyone in the place had followed Holt's lead, and as a result the odds had been short ones. Since the races, as Denise was coming to see, were truly random—the turtles didn't give a damn and were about equal in speed—the only thing governing the patterns of oddsmaking was the way the guests happened to bet, and that depended entirely on whatever irrational set of theories the bettors had fastened on. But the theory Nicholas Holt was working from didn't appear to be irrational.

"And in the third race?" she said.

"I never bet more than the first two. It gets very dull for me after that. Shall we have dinner?"

He said it as if her acceptance were a foregone conclusion, which would have offended her, except that he was right.

The main course that night was island venison. "What would you say to a bottle of Merlot?" he asked.

"It's my favorite wine."

How did he do it? Was everything simply an open book to him?

He let her do most of the talking at dinner. She told him about the gallery where she worked, about her new little apartment in the city, about her marriage, about what had happened to her marriage. A couple of times she felt herself beginning to babble—the wine, she thought, it was the wine—and she reined herself in. But he showed no sign of disapproval, even when she realized she had been going on about Michael much too long. He listened gravely and quietly to everything she said, interjecting a bland comment now and then, essentially just a little prompt to urge her to continue: "Yes, I see," or "Of course," or "I quite understand." He told her practically nothing about himself, only that he lived in New York—where?—and that he did something on Wall Street—unspecified—and that he spent two weeks in the West Indies every February but had never been to Jamaica before. He volunteered no more than that: she had no idea where he had grown up— surely not in New York, from the way he spoke—or whether he had ever been married, or what his interests might be. But she thought it would be gauche to be too inquisitive, and probably unproductive. He was very well defended, polite and calm and remote, the most opaque man she had ever known. He played his part in the dinner conversation with the tranquil, self-possessed air of someone who was following a very familiar script.

After dinner they danced, and it was the same thing there: he anticipated her every move, smoothly sweeping her around the open-air dance floor in a way that soon had everyone watching them. Denise was a good dancer, skilled at the tricky art of leading a man who thought he was leading her; but with Nicholas Holt the feedback was so complex that she had no idea who was leading whom. They danced as though they were one entity, moving with a single accord: the way people dance who have been dancing together for years. She had never known a man who danced like that.

On one swing around the floor she had a quick glimpse of Jeffrey Thompkins, dancing with a robust redhaired woman half a head taller than he was. Thompkins was pushing her about with skill and determination but no grace at all, somewhat in the style of a rhinoceros who has had a thousand hours of instruction at Arthur Murray. As he went thundering past he looked back at Denise and smiled an intricate smile that said a dozen different things. It acknowledged the fact that he was clumsy and his partner was coarse, that Holt was elegant and Denise was beautiful, that men like Holt always were able to take women like Denise away from men like Thompkins. But also the smile seemed to be telling her that Thompkins didn't mind at all, that he accepted what had happened as the natural order of things, had in fact expected it with much the same sort of assurance as Holt had expected Number Five to win tonight's first race. Denise realized that she had felt some guilt about sidestepping Thompkins and offering herself to Holt and that his smile just now had canceled it out; and then she wondered why she had felt the guilt in the first place. She owed nothing to Thompkins, after all. He was simply a stranger who had asked her to dinner last night. They were all strangers down here: nobody owed anything to anyone.

"My cottage is just beyond that little clump of bamboo," Holt said, after they had had the obligatory beachfront stroll on the palm promenade. He said it as if they had already agreed to spend the night there. She offered no objections. This was what she had come here for, wasn't it? Sunlight and warmth and tropical breezes and this.

As he had on the dance floor, so too in bed was he able to anticipate everything she wanted. She had barely thought of something but he was doing it; sometimes he did it even before she knew she wanted him to. It was so long since she had made love with anyone but Michael that Denise wasn't sure who the last one before him had been; but she knew she had never been to bed with anyone like this. She moved here, he was on his way there already. She did this, he did it too. That and that. Her hand, his hand. Her lips, his lips. It was all extremely weird: very thrilling and yet oddly hollow, like making love to your own reflection.

He must be able to read minds, she thought suddenly, as they lay side by side, resting for a while.

An eerie notion. It made her feel nakeder than naked: bare right down to her soul, utterly vulnerable, defenseless.

But the power to read minds, she realized after a moment, wouldn't allow him to do that trick with the turtle races. That was prediction, not mind-reading. It was second sight.

Can he see into the future? Five minutes, ten minutes, half a day ahead? She thought back. He always seemed so unsurprised at everything. When she had told him she didn't intend to do any betting, that first night, he had simply said, "Of course." When his turtle had won the race he had shown no flicker of excitement or pleasure. When she had apologized tonight for not having acted on his tip, he had told her blandly that he hadn't expected her to. The choice of wine—the dinner conversation—the dancing—the lovemaking—Could he see everything that was about to happen? *Everything?*

On Wall Street, too? Then he must be worth a fortune.

But why did he always look so sad, then? His eyes so bleak and haunted, those little lines of grimness about his lips?

This is all crazy, Denise told herself. Nobody can see the future. The future isn't a place you can look into, the way you can open a door and look into a room. The future doesn't exist until it's become the present.

She turned to him. But he was already opening his arms to her, bringing his head down to graze his lips across her breasts.

She left his cottage long before dawn, not because she really wanted to but because she was unwilling to have the maids and gardeners see her go traipsing back to her place in the morning still wearing her evening clothes, and hung the DO NOT DISTURB sign on her door.

When she woke, the sun was blazing down through the bamboo slats of the cottage porch. She had slept through breakfast and lunch. Her throat felt raspy and there was the sensation of recent lovemaking between her legs, so that she automatically looked around for Michael and was surprised to find herself alone in the big bed; and then she remembered, first that she and Michael were all finished, then that she was here by herself, then that she had spent the night with Nicholas Holt.

Who can see the future. She laughed at her own silliness.

She didn't feel ready to face the outside world, and called room service to bring her tea and a tray of fruit. They sent her mango, jackfruit, three tiny reddish bananas, and a slab of papaya. Later she suited up and went down to the beach. She didn't see Holt anywhere around, neither out by the reef as he usually was in the afternoon, nor on the soft pink sand. A familiar stocky form was churning up the water with cannonball force, doing his laps, down to the cape and back, again, again, again. Thompkins. After a time he came stumping ashore. Not at all coy now, playing no strategic games, he went straight over to her.

"I see that your friend Mr. Holt's in trouble with the hotel," he said, sounding happy about it.

"He is? How so?"

"You weren't at the turtle races after lunch, were you?"

"I never go to the afternoon ones."

"That's right, you don't. Well, I was there. Holt won the first two races, the way he always does. Everybody bet the way he did. The odds were microscopic, naturally. But everybody won. And then two of the hotel managers—you know, Eubanks, the night man who has that enormous grin all the time, and the other one with the big yellow birthmark on his forehead?—came over to him and said, 'Mr. Holt, sah, we would prefer dat you forego the pleasure of the turtle racing from this point onward.'" The Chevrolet dealer's imitation of the Jamaican accent was surprisingly accurate. "'We recognize dat you must be an authority on turtle habits, sah,' they said. 'Your insight we find to be exceedingly uncanny. And derefore it strikes us dat it is quite unsporting for you to compete. Quite, sah!'"

"And what did he say?"

"That he doesn't know a goddamned thing about turtles, that he's simply on a roll, that it's not his fault if the other guests are betting the same way he is. They asked him again not to play the turtles—'We implore you, sah, you are causing great losses for dis establishment'—and he kept saying he was a registered guest and entitled to all the privileges of a guest. So they canceled the races."

"Canceled them?"

"They must have been losing a fucking fortune this week on those races, if you'll excuse the French. You can't run parimutuels where everybody bets the same nag and that nag always wins, you know? Wipes you out after a while. So they didn't have races this afternoon and there won't be any tonight unless he agrees not to play." Thompkins smirked. "The guests are pretty pissed off, I got to tell you. The management is trying to talk him into changing hotels, that's what someone just said. But he won't do it. So no turtles. You ask me, I still think he's been fixing it somehow with the hotel boys, and the hotel must think so too, but they don't dare say it. Man with a winning streak like that, there's just no accounting for it any other way, is there?"

"No," Denise said. "No accounting for it at all."

It was cocktail time before she found him: the hour when the guests gathered on the garden patio where the turtle races were held to have a daiquiri or two before the tote counter opened for business. Denise drifted down there automatically, despite what Thompkins had told her about the cancelation of the races. Most of the other guests had done the same. She saw Holt's lanky figure looming up out of a group of them. They had surrounded him, they were gesturing and waving their daiquiris around as they talked.

It was easy enough to guess that they were trying to talk him into refraining from playing the turtles so that they could have their daily amusement back.

When she came closer she saw the message chalked across the tote board in an ornate Jamaican hand, all curlicues and flourishes:

TECHNICAL PROBLEM
NO RACES TODAY
YOUR KIND INDULGENCE IS ASKED

"Nicholas?" she called, as though they had a prearranged date.

He smiled at her gratefully. "Excuse me," he said in his genteel way to the cluster around him, and moved smoothly through them to her side. "How lovely you look tonight, Denise."

"I've heard that the hotel's putting pressure on you about the races."

"Yes. Yes." He seemed to be speaking to her from another galaxy. "So they are. They're quite upset, matter of fact. But if there's going to be racing, I have a right to play. If they choose to cancel, that's their business."

In a low voice she said, "You aren't involved in any sort of collusion with the hotel boys, are you?"

"You asked me that before. You know that that isn't possible."

"Then how are you always able to tell which turtle's going to win?"

"I know," he said sadly. "I simply do."

"You always know what's about to happen, don't you? Always."

"Would you like a daiquiri, Denise?"

"Answer me. Please."

"I have a knack, yes."

"It's more than a knack."

"A gift, then. A special—something."

"A something, yes." They were walking as they talked; already they were past the bougainvillea hedge, heading down the steps toward the beachfront promenade, leaving the angry guests and the racing pool and the turtle tank behind.

"A very reliable something," she said.

"Yes. I suppose it is."

"You said that you knew, the first night when you offered me that tip, that I wasn't going to take you up on it. Why did you offer it to me, then?"

"I told you. It seemed like a friendly gesture."

"We weren't friends then. We'd hardly spoken. Why'd you bother?"

"Just because."

"Because you wanted to test your special something?" she asked him. "Because you wanted to see whether it was working right?"

He stared at her intently. He looked almost frightened, she thought. She had broken through.

"Perhaps I did," he said.

"Yes. You check up on it now and then, don't you? You try something that you know won't pan out, like tipping a strange woman to the outcome of the turtle race even though your gift tells you that she won't bet your tip. Just to see whether your guess was on the mark. But what would you have done if I *had* put a bet down that night, Nicholas?"

"You wouldn't have."

"You were certain of that."

"Virtually certain, yes. But you're right: I test it now and then, just to see."

"And it always turns out the way you expect?"

"Essentially, yes."

"You're scary, Nicholas. How long have you been able to do stuff like this?"

"Does that matter?" he asked. "Does it really?"

He asked her to have dinner with him again, but there was something perfunctory about the invitation, as though he were offering it only because the hour was getting toward dinnertime and they happened to be standing next to each other just then. She accepted quickly, perhaps too quickly. But the dining terrace was practically empty when they reached it—they were very early, on account of the cancelation of the races—and the meal was a stiff, uncomfortable affair. He was so obviously bothered by her persistent inquiries about his baffling skill, his special something, that she quickly backed off, but that left little to talk about except the unchanging perfect weather, the beauty of the hotel grounds, the rumors of racial tension elsewhere on the island. He toyed with his food and ate very little. They ordered no wine. It was like sitting across the table from a stranger who was dining with her purely by chance. And yet less than twenty-four hours before she had spent a night in this man's bed.

She didn't understand him at all. He was alien and mysterious and a little frightening. But somehow, strangely, that made him all the more desirable.

As they were sipping their coffee she looked straight at him and sent him a message with her mind:

Ask me to come dancing with you, next. And then let's go to your cottage again, you bastard.

But instead he said abruptly, "Would you excuse me, Denise?"

She was nonplussed. "Why—yes—if—"

He looked at his watch. "I've rented a glass-bottomed boat for eight o'clock. To have a look at the night life out on the reef."

The night was when the reef came alive. The little coral creatures awoke and unfolded their brilliant little tentacles; phosphorescent organisms began to glow; octopuses and eels came out of their dark crannies to forage for their meals; sharks and rays and other big predators set forth on the hunt. You could take a boat out there that was equipped with bottom-mounted arc lights and watch the show, but very few of the hotel guests actually did. The waters that were so crystalline and inviting by day looked ominous and menacing in the dark, with sinister coral humps rising like black ogres' heads above the lapping wavelets. She had never even thought of going.

But now she heard herself saying, in a desperate attempt at salvaging something out of the evening, "Can I go with you?"

"I'm sorry. No."

"I'm really eager to see what the reef looks like at—"

"No," he said, quietly but with real finality. "It's something I'd rather do by myself, if you don't mind. Or even if you do mind, I have to tell you. Is that all right, Denise?"

"Will I see you afterward?" she asked, wishing instantly that she hadn't. But he had already risen and given her a gentlemanly little smile of farewell and was striding down the terrace toward the steps that led to the beachfront promenade.

She stared after him, astounded by the swiftness of his disappearance, the unexpectedness of it.

She sat almost without moving, contemplating her bewildering abandonment. Five minutes went by, maybe ten. The waiter unobtrusively brought her another coffee. She held the cup in her hand without drinking from it.

Jeffrey Thompkins materialized from somewhere, hideously cheerful. "If you're free," he said, "how about an after-dinner liqueur?" He was wearing a white dinner jacket, very natty, and sharply pressed black trousers. But his round neckless head and the blaze of sunburn across his bare scalp spoiled the elegant effect. "A Strega, a Galliano, a nice cognac, maybe?" He pronounced it coneyac.

"Something weird's going on," she said.

"Oh?"

"He went out on the reef in one of those boats, by himself. Holt. Just got up and walked away from the table, said he'd rented a boat for eight o'clock. Poof. Gone."

"I'm heartbroken to hear it."

"No, be serious. He was acting really strange. I asked to go with him, and he said no, I absolutely couldn't. He sounded almost like some sort of a machine. You could hear the gears clicking."

Thompkins said, all flippancy gone from his voice now, "You think he's going to do something to himself out there?"

"No. Not him. That's one thing I'm sure of."

"Then what?"

"I don't know."

"A guy like that, all keyed up all the time and never letting on a thing to anybody—" Thompkins looked at her closely. "You know him better than I do. You don't have any idea what he might be up to?"

"Maybe he just wants to see the reef. I don't know. But he seemed so peculiar when he left—so rigid, so *focused*—"

"Come on," Thompkins said. "Let's get one of those boats and go out there ourselves."

"But he said he wanted to go alone."

"Screw what he said. He don't own the reef. We can go for an expedition too, if we want to."

✺

It took a few minutes to arrange things. "You want a guided tour, sah?" the boy down at the dock asked, but Thompkins said no, and helped Denise into the boat as easily as though she were made of feathers. The boy shook his head. "Nobody want a guide tonight. You be careful out there, stay dis side the reef, you hear me, sah?"

Thompkins switched on the lights and took the oars. With quick, powerful strokes he moved away from the dock. Denise looked down. There was nothing visible below but the bright white sand of the shallows, a few long-spined black sea urchins, some starfish. As they approached the reef, a hundred yards or so off shore, the density of marine life increased: schools of brilliant fishes whirled and dived, a somber armada of squids came squirting past.

There was no sign of Holt. "We ought to be able to see his lights," Denise said. "Where can he have gone?"

Thompkins had the boat butting up against the flat side of the reef now. He stood up carefully and stared into the night.

"The crazy son of a bitch," he muttered. "He's gone outside the reef! Look, there he is."

He pointed. Denise, half rising, saw nothing at first; and then there was the reflected glow of the other boat's lights, on the far side of the massive stony clutter and intricacy that was the reef. Holt had found one of the passageways through and was coasting along the reef's outer face, where the deep-water hunters came up at night, the marlins and swordfish and sharks.

"What the hell does he think he's doing?" Thompkins asked. "Don't he know it's dangerous out there?"

"I don't think that worries him," said Denise.

"So you do think he's going to do something to himself."

"Just the opposite. He knows that he'll be all right out there, or he wouldn't be there. He wouldn't have gone if he saw any real risk in it."

"Unless risk is what he's looking for."

"He doesn't live in a world of risk," she said. "He's got a kind of sixth sense. He always knows what's going to happen next."

"Huh?"

Words came pouring out of her. "He sees the future," she said fiercely, not caring how wild it sounded. "It's like an open book to him. How do you think he does that trick with the turtles?"

"Huh?" Thompkins said again. "The future?" He peered at her, shaking his head slowly.

Then he swung sharply around as if in response to some unexpected sound from the sea. He shaded his forehead with his hand, the way he might have done if he were peering into bright sunlight. After a moment he pointed into the darkness beyond the reef and said in a slow awed tone, "What the fuck! Excuse me. But Jesus, will you look at that?"

She stared past him, toward the suddenly foaming sea.

Something was happening on the reef's outer face. Denise saw it unfolding as if in slow motion. The ocean swelling angrily, rising, climbing high. The single great wave barrelling in as though it had traveled all the way from Alaska for this one purpose. The boat tilting up on end, the man flying upward and outward, soaring gracefully into the air, traveling along a smooth curve like an expert diver and plummeting down into the black depths just beside the reef's outer face. And then the last curling upswing of the wave, the heavy crash as it struck the coral wall.

In here, sheltered by the reef, they felt only a mild swaying, and then everything was still again.

Thompkins clapped his hand over his mouth. His eyes were bulging. "Jesus," he said after a moment. "Jesus! How the fuck am I going to get out there?" He turned toward Denise. "Can you row this thing back to shore by yourself?"

"I suppose so."

"Good. Take it in and tell the boat boy what happened. I'm going after your friend."

He stripped with astonishing speed, the dinner jacket, the sharply creased pants, the shirt and tie, the black patent leather shoes. Denise saw him for a moment outlined against the stars, the fleshy burly body hidden only by absurd bikini pants in flamboyant scarlet silk. Then he was over the side, swimming with all his strength, heading for one of the openings in the reef that gave access to the outer face.

❋

She was waiting among the crowd on the shore when Thompkins brought the body in, carrying it like a broken doll. He had been much too late, of course. One quick glance told her that Holt must have been tossed against the reef again and again, smashed, cut to ribbons by the sharp coral, partly devoured, even, by the creatures of the night. Thompkins laid him down on the beach. One of the hotel boys put a beach blanket over him; another gave Thompkins a robe. He was scratched and bloody himself, shivering, grim-faced, breathing in windy gusts. Denise went to him. The others backed away, stepping back fifteen or twenty feet, leaving them alone, strangely exposed, beside the blanketed body.

"Looks like you were wrong," Thompkins said. "About that sixth sense of his. Or else it wasn't working so good tonight."

"No," she said. For the past five minutes she had been struggling to put together the pattern of what had happened, and it seemed to her now that it was beginning to come clear. "It was working fine. He knew that this would happen."

"What?"

"He knew. Like I said before, he knew everything ahead of time. Everything. Even this. But he went along with it anyway."

"But if he knew everything, then why—why—" Thompkins shook his head. "I don't get it."

Denise shuddered in the warm night breeze. "No, you don't. You can't. Neither can I."

"Miss Carpentah?" a high, strained voice called. "Mistah Thompkins?"

It was the night manager, Mr. Eubanks of the dazzling grin, belatedly making his way down from the hotel. He wasn't grinning now. He looked stricken, panicky, strangely pasty-faced. He came to a halt next to them, knelt, picked up one corner of the beach blanket, stared at the body beneath it as though it were some bizarre monster that had washed ashore. A guest had died on his watch, and it was going to cost him, he was sure of that, and his fear showed in his eyes.

Thompkins, paying no attention to the Jamaican, said angrily to Denise, "If he knew what was going to happen, if he could see the fucking future, why in the name of Christ didn't he simply not take the boat out, then? Or if he did, why fool around outside the reef where it's so dangerous? For that matter why didn't he just stay the hell away from Jamaica in the first place?"

"That's what I mean when I tell you that we can't understand," she said. "He didn't think the way we do. He wasn't like us. Not at all. Not in the slightest."

"Mistah Tompkins—Miss Carpentah—if you would do me de courtesy of speaking with me for a time—of letting me have de details of dis awful tragedy—"

Thompkins brushed Eubanks away as if he were a gnat.

"I don't know what the fuck you're saying," he told Denise.

Eubanks said, exasperated, "If de lady and gemmun will give me deir kind attention, *please*—"

He looked imploringly toward Denise. She shook him off. She was still groping, still reaching for the answer.

Then, for an instant, just for an instant, everything that was going on seemed terribly familiar to her. As if it had all happened before. The warm, breezy night air. The blanket on the beach. The round, jowly, baffled face of Jeffrey Thompkins hovering in front of hers. Mr. Eubanks, pale with dismay. An odd little moment of deja vu. It appeared to go on and on. Now Eubanks will lose his cool and try to take me by the arm, she thought; now I will pull back and slip on the sand; now Jeffrey will catch me and steady me. Yes. Yes. And here it comes. "Please, you may not ignore me dis way! You must tell me what has befallen dis unfortunate gemmun!" That was Eubanks, eyes popping, forehead shiny with sweat. Making a pouncing movement toward her, grabbing for her wrist. She backed hastily away from him. Her legs felt suddenly wobbly. She started to sway and slip, and looked toward Thompkins. But he was already coming forward, reaching out toward her to take hold of her before she fell. Weird, she thought. Weird.

Then the weirdness passed, and everything was normal again, and she knew the answer.

That was how it had been for him, she thought in wonder. Every hour, every day, his whole goddamned life.

"He came to this place and he did what he did," she said to Thompkins, "because he knew that there wasn't any choice for him. Once he had seen it in his mind it was certain to happen. So he just came down here and played things through to the end."

"Even though he'd *die?*" Thompkins asked. He looked at Denise stolidly, uncomprehendingly.

"If you lived your whole life as if it had already happened, without surprise, without excitement, without the slightest unpredictable event, not once, not ever, would you give a damn whether you lived or died? Would you? He knew he'd die here, yes. So he came here to die, and that's the whole story. And now he has."

"Jesus," Thompkins said. "The poor son of a bitch!"

"You understand now? What it must have been like for him?"

"Yeah," he said, his arm still tight around her as though he didn't ever mean to let go. "Yeah. The poor son of a bitch."

"I got to tell you," said Mr. Eubanks, "dis discourtesy is completely improper. A mahn have died here tragically tonight, and you be de only witnesses, and I ask you to tell me what befell, and you—"

Denise closed her eyes a moment. Then she looked at Eubanks.

"What's there to say, Mr. Eubanks? He took his boat into a dangerous place and it was struck by a sudden wave and overturned. An accident. A terrible accident. What else is there to say?" She began to shiver. Thompkins held her. In a low voice she said to him, "I want to go back to my cottage."

"Right," he said. "Sure. You wanted a statement, Mr. Eubanks? There's your statement. Okay? Okay?"

He held her close against him and slowly they started up the ramp toward the hotel together.